THE
HEARSE
YOU CAME IN ON

THE
HEARSE
YOU CAME IN ON

•

TIM COCKEY

HYPERION

New York

During the writing of this book, the author painstakingly deleted from his memory all details of any person he has ever seen or met, anywhere, anytime. Any resemblance to any persons walking the earth, not walking the earth, or lying really, really still is purely coincidental.

Library of Congress Cataloging-in-Publication Data

Cockey, Tim.
    The hearse you came in on / by Tim Cockey. — 1st ed.
        p.   cm.
    ISBN 0-7868-6570-9
    I. Title.
    PS3553.O277H43   1999
    813'.54—dc21   99-22210
                                                                              CIP

FIRST EDITION

Design by Abby Kagan

10   9   8   7   6   5   4   3   2   1

IN MEMORY OF

TEDDY HARTMAN

who would have
laughed the loudest.

ACKNOWLEDGMENTS

I don't know if some of the people whose names follow qualify as immensely patient, bullheaded or delusional for the certainty they had that this book would eventually be written and published. All I can say is that it feels great to prove them right (such a smart bunch), and I want to thank them for the numerous enthusiasms and encouragements that they have tossed at me over the years: Jim McGreevey; Ted Manekin & Lisa Hayes; Aimee-Sawyer Philpott, who would be singing these acknowledgments if this were a movie and not a book; Kate (Crazy Woman) Horsley, who can't spell my name but who otherwise writes cyclones; Michele Kragalott, Kathleen Kelly, Joanne Bennett (thanks for buying hardback, Jo), Rick Pantaleoni, Evelyn Rossetti, Clay Squire, Stephen Dixon, Gram Slaton, Paul Bennett, Caroline Davis Chapin, Steve Blizzard, Rick & Helen Feete; Judy Scheel and Howard Kogan, for helping me locate my missing pen; Annette Kramer, Melissa Proctor Carroll, Peter Close, Linda Russell Selway, Rennie Higson, Espen & Patty Brooks; Francine Jones, G2 Toth, Lynn Holst, Regina Porter, Kate Clark, Monica Goldstein; forty-four cheers and counting to my ever-loving Ma and her ever-loving Powell; to Idaho's finest, Jim Cockey, and his finest, Bernie Cockey; Charlie Cockey of San Francisco's Fantasy, Etc. (official nepotistic plug); Chris & Alice Cockey, John, Gloria, Suzie and Ellie Merryman; Mama Grace and all them Hartmans; thanks to Jennifer Barth, my incisive and insightful word surgeon at Hyperion; special thanks to Marie Edwards, who stood at the rail cheering this one on; to literary midwife extraordinaire, Alice Peck (thank you, Alice); to my agent, the cool, calm killer herself, Victoria Sanders; and finally, last but first, the one and ornery Wendy Barrie-Wilson, who has enough faith, heart and tenacious belief within her to start a whole new religion . . . thank you, masked man.

I was going along just fine, solemnly chaperoning the dead into their graves and pretty much otherwise minding my own business, when the woman calling herself Carolyn James stuck her halfway-pretty face into my life and scattered all hell to the wind.

Of course that's the way life works, isn't it. They say something as simple as a well-placed sneeze by the right person at just the right moment can change the course of history. I can believe that. Life is funny that way. My ex-wife is a born-again Buddhist (among several other provocative things), and she likens the course of life to one long stumbling forward. The quality of the life, Julia says, is a matter of how adroitly you negotiate the ten thousand obstacles that come into your path as you stumble along. At the end of life, of course . . . you *will* finally fall down. Can't avoid it. The final stumble. Now I don't happen to think that this is necessarily certified Buddhist rhetoric, but why split hairs. It gets the point across.

And *my* point is simply that I was stumbling along just fine in my little old life when with no warning whatsoever an obstacle in a tennis dress and a baggy sweater stepped in front of me and put my adroitness to the test. It might not have been the sneeze that changed the world, but it sure as hell pitched me forward, I can tell you that.

I'm thirty-four years old and six foot three. That's way too young to fall down. And way too far to drop.

. . .

On this particular day of my stumbling forward—it was a Wednesday, it was May—Aunt Billie and I were holding a wake in Parlor One. The funeral home that I operate with my aunt is located in a section of Baltimore known as Fells Point. It's an area where I spent most of my so-called formative years, a largely working-class neighborhood that hugs a jagged corner of the Baltimore harbor just a mile or so east of the downtown. Our establishment is several blocks in from the harbor itself, down past the string of small shops and bars that line the waterfront there. As somebody is always bringing up the irony of our being just a stone's throw from a bar called The Dead End Saloon—which is the last bar on the stretch—I'll bring it up now. No, we're not affiliated. We were here first. My ugly Uncle Stu started the business soon after World War II, where he saw considerable action, including the god-awful Normandy invasion. Although one might conjecture that the idea of becoming a mortician was some sort of cathartic response to the horrific sight of so many bodies lying about, the truth is considerably less psychological. According to family legend, ugly Uncle Stu's decision came after he was handed the bill for his father's funeral. Whether as a hedge against having to pay through the nose for his own eventual interment or just as a nifty new way to turn a buck, family legend vacillates. Despite the fact that my aunt and uncle were childless, they named their establishment Sewell & Sons Family Funeral Home. This was Billie's idea. She was the one who injected into the business the much needed "warm and fuzzy" that my uncle sorely lacked.

We're a remarkably nondescript establishment on a remarkably nondescript block of largely—yes—nondescript flagstone row houses. You could be leaning up against the wall of Sewell & Sons smoking a cigarette and not even realize that you're standing in front of a funeral home. We're a modest operation, with two parlors and two full-time employees, myself and Aunt Billie. We're both certified morticians, which means we're licensed to do all the things with the bodies that most people don't want to hear about. Billie is a refugee from Old South aristocracy, and she maintains that strata's peculiar relationship with death, which I feel is generally more congenial and accommodating than you find elsewhere. And as Billie had a fair hand in raising me, a good share of her influence has seeped into me. It's this convivial relationship with death, I think, that sets Sewell & Sons apart from the competition. This, plus Billie's standing offer of brandy to our guests.

Our dead guest of honor this particular day was a retired firefighter from Towson, which is just north of the city. He had died of natural causes—if a heart attack is a natural cause—and his widow had informed Aunt Billie that he would be drawing a modest-sized crowd. There's a hard plastic curtain on runners that divides the two parlors. On those occasions when we expect an overflow crowd, we pull the curtain open to create one large room. The wake for my parents for example. *That* had been a big turnout. A standing-room-only affair. This one wasn't.

Aunt Billie was handling the fireman's funeral. We trade off. I was sitting in my office just off the front lobby, feet up on my desk, reading the obituaries (kidding). Actually, I was reading a copy of the Thornton Wilder play *Our Town* and for reasons that I'll explain later, I was in a cranky mood. And a restless one. I had probably picked the play up and set it down and sighed and then picked it back up again (down again, sigh again) about a dozen times already before I finally just tossed the damn thing aside and decided to check out the action in Parlor One.

The joint was jumping. Seniors and semi-seniors (what Billie and I call "Aarpies") were milling about the room, clustering here and there, speaking in low voices, cupping one another's hands and very studiously avoiding the guest of honor—Mr. Weatherby—who was off at the far end of the room laid out in his coffin (the Embassy model; very popular), as dead as dead could be. My cranky countenance wouldn't do here so I re-set my face and moved solicitously about the room. I think I've mentioned already that I'm a handsome fellow. If not, I'm mentioning it now. Black hair. Blue eyes. Pretty good skin. Dynamite chin. I've been told that I look like one of those TV doctors who are constantly mixing it up with his attractive patients. It's a fantastic face for this profession. Puts people at ease. If I had a nickel for every "you don't look like an undertaker" I've heard I'd tell Donald Trump he can stop shining my shoes now and get back to whatever he was up to before I hired him.

I worked the room, squeezed a few hands and was assured each time that the retired firefighter had been "a good man." That's pretty standard. It's only the occasional live wire who sidles up to tell you that the recently deceased was a no-good son of a bitch.

I spotted Billie off in a corner with Mrs. Weatherby, her blue hands oyster-shelled over the widow's paw, her Helen Hayes smile roaring full blast. As I headed over to offer my condolences to Mrs. Weatherby, Billie looked up and saw me coming. She gave me her Boris Karloff face—which is Billie's signal to me that I'm scowling too much—then jerked her head in the direction of the coffin. There, partially obscured by a huge horseshoe of gladiolus (compliments of Weatherby's old fire station), stood a woman. Not an Aarpy, but a woman in her early thirties. She was tall, about five nine or ten. She was dressed in an oversized navy blue sweater and a short short short white pleated skirt from which a very nice pair of matching legs extended several miles down into a plain white pair of tennis shoes. Women's size eight, I'd say. White anklets with rabbit tails completed the portrait. De rigueur garb for a wake, no question about it. Her hair—coal black with a touch of cranberry—fell in unbrushed waves to her shoulders and at the moment was obscuring her face. One hand was resting lightly on the foot of the coffin. The other hand was rising up toward the hidden face as a shudder suddenly went through her shoulders . . . and she sneezed.

Allergies, she would tell me later. To flowers and to death.

I stumbled forward.

She looked up as I approached. No. That's not quite right. What she did was she flicked her head, like someone who has just heard a gun go off, and she nailed me with a pair of hot hazel eyes. I nearly tripped on a piece of air. The look that she was giving me was somewhere between that of the deer in the crosshairs and the one holding the rifle. She had a somewhat heart shaped face, a pointed chin, a smallish red mouth and a terrifically sexy Roman nose. The eyes were deeply set, large and currently mistrusting. Because I'm tall and she was tall I took a nanosecond to imagine the two of us happily married and raising a batch of tall mistrusting children together. Then I held out my hand and introduced myself.

"Hello, I'm Hitchcock Sewell."

She inspected my face for a second and then gave me her hand. The one from the coffin, not the one she had just sneezed into.

"That's a funny name," she said.

Which of course I've heard a thousand times before.

Color flashed across her cheeks like lightning just below the surface and she wavered slightly, holding on to my hand a fraction too long, to steady herself. The mother of my future tall mistrusting children had been drinking. She let go of my hand and looked down at Mr. Weatherby.

"Did you know him well?" I asked.

The woman shook her head.

"I've never seen him before in my life," she announced. There was a touch of defiance in her tone, as well as in the way she squared off in front of me. Her eyes flittered around the room. "Is that his wife?"

Aunt Billie was still jawing with Mrs. Weatherby over by the plastic curtain. They had been joined by an animated ostrich with Coke-bottle glasses who was apparently taking her tongue out for a walk.

"Yes. That's her."

"I have to say something."

"It's not necessary."

"Of course it's necessary. I can't just wander in and wander out like I own the place. It's a funeral."

"Actually, it's a wake."

"You know what I mean." She looked over toward the door. "Can you get me out of here?"

"Sure."

She took a steadying step forward. At least that was the idea. Her shoulder grazed the horseshoe bouquet and we both snatched at it to keep it from toppling. I reached for her elbow. Instinctively, she drew back.

"I'm not a little old lady."

"But you *are* a little unsteady." She tried to glare at me, but apparently her fire was going out.

She sounded defeated. "I haven't had a good day."

"If it means anything," I said diplomatically, "I haven't either. What say we scram." I held out my arm. I'm a sucker for cheap theatrics sometimes, I readily admit it. She hesitated. "It's an arm," I pointed out. "It won't bite."

The interloper flashed me a peeved look and slid her arm through mine. We stepped away from the coffin, long tall me in my dark suit, long tall she in her short short skirt. Several centuries of heads turned in our direction as we crossed the room. As Mrs. Weatherby looked up, the woman on my arm hissed at me. "What do I say?"

"Tell her he was a good man. That seems to be the consensus."

"Seriously."

"He was a fireman. Tell her that he rescued your cat from a tree a long time ago and that you've never forgotten him."

"Could we maybe find something a little cornier?"

As we approached, the ostrich was going on about some sort of carpeting trauma she had recently experienced. I could see that Billie was grateful for my arrival. I silenced the ostrich with the sheer force of my interruption.

"Mrs. Weatherby, I'm Hitchcock Sewell, Billie's nephew. I'm terribly sorry for your loss." I swung my mystery guest into place. "This is—"

"Carolyn James." Her expression softened beautifully as she took hold of the widow's hand. "I'm so sorry. Your husband was . . . you don't know me. He . . . I . . . I had a cat."

I came to the rescue.

"Your husband rescued Miss James's cat some years ago," I explained. "From a tree. The cat was pregnant. Miss James was so grateful to your husband that she named one of the kittens Weatherby. In his honor." The woman at my side stiffened as I plunged forward. "Miss James happened to see the notice in the paper this afternoon right after a set of tennis—as you can see—and she just had to rush over here and pay her respects."

The widow muttered something in response. I missed it altogether. She had not let go of Carolyn James's hand.

Aunt Billie chimed in. "That was very thoughtful of you, Miss James."

Billie flashed me a get-her-the-hell-out-of-here look. I drew Carolyn James back from the gals and steered her toward the door.

"What the hell was all that about the pregnant cat?" she hissed.

I was nodding solemnly at a ghostly couple who were just coming into the room. "It'll give her something to tell around the bridge table."

Out in the lobby I asked Carolyn James if she wanted to sign the guest book. We keep one on a gold-plated stand in case people want to comment on what a rousing good time they had. She declined.

"I think I'll just disappear quietly," she said, turning away from me and stepping over to the door. I trailed her. We reached for the doorknob simultaneously. I got there first, and held on to it.

"Do you think, just possibly, that maybe you owe me an explanation?" I said. "I mean, before you 'disappear quietly' maybe you'd like to tell me why you wandered in here in the first place? We don't get many drop-ins."

"I'd rather not," she said. But when I refused to release the doorknob she relented. She squared off in front of me.

"I apologize for crashing your party, Mr. Sewell."

"Accepted."

"It won't happen again."

I gave a little shrug. "You're always welcome."

Her eyes narrowed and she checked me out closely, one eye at a time.

"It was impulsive, my coming in here. Okay? I stopped in to see . . . to see about arranging a funeral."

"That's it? Then why all the fuss? Look, my office is right here. Why don't we—"

"I changed my mind." She gave her head a little flip and glared hotly at me. "Can I go now?"

"I hope you haven't changed your mind because of that cat nonsense just now. My aunt can handle the arrangements if that would make you feel better. I wouldn't take it personally. In fact—"

"There's not going to be a funeral," she snapped. I could see faint yellow starbursts pulsing in her eyes. She cocked a challenging eyebrow at me. "Have you got that?"

"Squared away, ma'am." As I pulled the door open for her, I asked, "When you were thinking of burying someone, may I ask who exactly you had in mind?"

The lava shifted in her eyes. She sighed.

"Yes," she said. "Me."

CHAPTER 2

My parents were local television personalities in Baltimore back in the old mom-and-pop days of Charm City, before its several heralded face-lifts and makeovers. My father worked up on Television Hill, in the studios of WBAL, overlooking the gray rock valley of Hampden, the old mill town, on the banks of the rarely mighty Jones Falls River. He was something of a utility man back then, reading the news, doing commercials for local merchants, introducing the late night movie on Friday nights and—in a rotating assortment of silly hats—the kiddy cartoons on Saturday mornings. Those were the days when local TV was still making it up as it went along, "giving radio a face" is how I once heard it put. My father's face was friendly and unremarkable. He used to brag that he was as ubiquitous as a church key. A funny brag, if you think about it.

My mother on the other hand was an exotic import from New York City, a stalled actress in the off-off scene who came down to Baltimore to essay the role of Mary Pickersgill in a fifteen-minute film that the Smithsonian Institution was putting together to accompany its display of Mrs. Pickersgill's oversized flag—the original Star-Spangled Banner—that had flapped in the wind over Fort McHenry during the otherwise nearly forgotten War of 1812. I wouldn't be so crass as to accuse my own darling mother of compromising her virtue to get the part, but the fact remains that a first-generation Italian American with shiny black hair, olive skin, a slight accent and hips like a Vespa motor scooter wouldn't exactly be the logical first choice to portray the vaguely spinsterish and patently Waspy Ms. Pickersgill. At any rate, "somehow" she got the part and she took the train down from New York for the shoot. My dad was tapped to be Francis Scott Key, local boy and scribe of the national anthem. I don't believe that the historical Pickersgill and Key ever actually met, despite their significant relationships to Old Glory. But the make-believes certainly did, forging an alternate history with their clandestine coupling on the second floor of the Flag House down on East Pratt Street after the film crew had wrapped for the day. For a five-dollar entrance fee you can still visit the Star-Spangled Banner Flag House and see for yourself the actual room where my parents bumped and giggled in the off-hours to conceive their dear little pumpkin. When I was a teenager the Flag House was a must-go whenever I started courting a new flame. I never quite presumed I would be so lucky as to star in an actual reenactment of my parent's infamous tryst . . . but it gave me an easy opening to drop the subject of sex into the conversation. Which, on balance, rarely hurts.

You can also see where the lady made the flag.

My parents fell instantly in love, and so the discovery that my mother was pregnant with me apparently did not introduce panic. The acting scene in New York had been a constant sputter anyway, so my mother was easily convinced to move down to Baltimore and set up shop here. They married, and some months after my birth my mother began doing odd jobs at the TV station, voiceovers and the like. The station added a Bowling for Dollars show on Friday nights from seven to seven-thirty and tapped my father to host it. He convinced the station to let him bring my mother into the picture to help him in his little chats with the contestants. The pair of them were so charming and silly that soon those chats were taking up nearly as much time as the breathtaking bowling. I made my television debut, in fact, on that show. I was not quite a year old and I brought a whiff of scandal to the program as I nestled in my beautiful mother's arms unbuttoning the top three buttons of her blouse while she and my father yak yak yakked with some kid from Dundalk who was looking to make a few bucks knocking down pins.

Eventually the bowling show died—and my parents popped up with a little talk show of their own, one of the first of the now-glutted genre. Cross-dressing in-laws and mothers who sleep with their daughters' boyfriends were keeping a lower profile back in those days. My parents interviewed players for the Colts and the Orioles, common folk who did interesting things, local chefs, high school coaches, you name it. It didn't really matter who they talked to or what they talked about, so long as everybody had a chummy time. I popped up occasionally on this show as well, telegenic pip that I was. God help me, I even sat there on the set once in a straw boater and a seersucker suit while my parents chatted with Bing Crosby himself, who was in town to perform at the Painters Mill Music Fair. Bing could barely take his nasty eyes off my mother. All those old Hollywood heyday types are as horny as goats; they're constantly trolling for it. Bing was sent packing as quickly as possible and my father personally apologized to me for making me wear that getup.

Most of my looks come from my mother, the dark hair, the blue eyes. Though the pirate's smile . . . that's compliments of my dad.

As for the wary eye I cast upon the world, you can chalk that up to the indiscriminate Fates that would take such a wonderful pair of people as my parents and send their car hurtling into the path of a beer truck on their way to, of all places, the hospital. My mother was pregnant with my little sister. When her labor pains had begun in earnest, I was dropped off with my ugly Uncle Stu and Aunt Billie, at the funeral home. The driver of the beer truck said it happened in an instant. They swerved. It was over. Ugly Uncle Stu took the phone call. His end of the conversation was minimal, and when he set the phone back down on the receiver all he said was "They're all dead" and then he dropped into a chair and began to sob. The only time I ever saw him cry. I stayed in the room and watched him for several minutes, then went upstairs and kicked a hole in the wall.

As I think I've mentioned, the turnout for their funeral was huge. The mayor himself showed. Even with the plastic curtain drawn back between Parlors One and Two, the crowd spilled into the entrance hall and out onto the street. I was a handsome devil in my little dark suit. Twelve years old. People touched me lightly as if I were a saint. I remember thinking that there were enough flowers to clog a sewer system and that if Bing Crosby dared to show his face I'd make him eat every single one of them. I also remember thinking, later that night as I stared out the window of my new bedroom, that if nothing else I sure as hell had just gotten over and done with what would certainly be the very worst day of my life. There couldn't be any doubt about that. Nothing but blue skies from then on.

At his funeral the next day, Mr. Weatherby didn't give us any trouble. None of his pallbearers were too tall or too short—which sometimes results in a weight distribution crisis—and none of his mourners flew into show-stopping paroxysms of grief. The widow sobbed politely and was gently tended to by her chums. The weather cooperated. Barometer held steady. Temperatures ran a comfortable seventy-three. We were coming off a mild winter, so the spring bloomings had come early; the burgeoning buds by the cemetery's front gate provided an appropriately poignant counterpoint to the frank task of planting the depleted Mr. Weatherby deep deep below the topsoil. The canopy over the grave site itself carved a brilliant white triangle against the blue sky and offered a cooling shade to the half-dozen plastic folding chairs beneath it. Mr. Weatherby's casket (the Embassy model; have I mentioned that?) really showed its stuff there out under the sun. Mahogany is a beautiful wood even in its natural state. Lacquer it up and it practically hums.

Though this was Aunt Billie's funeral, she had been hit with a nasty cold, so I had taken it. I was standing silently off to the side, hands cupped at my crotch, my eye on the bagpiper who was planted some twenty feet off, getting ready to squeeze his cow bladder. Despite the kilts and feathers and all the rest of it, our bagpiper is no more Scottish than the ayatollah. He is an Italian electrician named Tony Marino. Tony's sad tale runs as follows: A Highlands lassie on a church choir trip to Rome stole and then broke his teenage heart outside the Colosseum (". . . the ruins, the ruins . . .") and Tony subsequently took up the bagpipes so as to further torment his forlorn soul. He even traveled to Scotland the following year on an odyssey to track down his lost lassie love, failing to locate her but fully saturating himself in all things Scottish. To this day he starts his morning with kippers and a shot of Macallans. To his credit, Tony Marino is a dynamite bagpiper. Although it is mostly "Amazing Grace" and "Danny Boy" that the bereaved tend to request, Tony includes Verdi and

Puccini in his repertoire. He can also bleat out an "Ave Maria" that'll do you in.

The Widow Weatherby had chosen "Amazing Grace." At my discreet signal Tony puffed up his bag and launched into the dirge. How sweet the sound. When Tony finished his tune, he lowered his pipes and wiped an authentic tear from his eye. Love is a needle in your neck sometimes, I swear. The priest scattered his final words over Mr. Weatherby and the deed was done. The widow stood a moment at the coffin, looking like she had just remembered the name of some restaurant that her husband had asked her about last week and that she would now have to simply hold on to forever. She placed a veined hand on the casket and muttered something that I missed altogether, then blended back in with the flock making their way across the graves to their cars. Tony, five foot two and as swarthy as a Sicilian boot, stood erect and stock-still as the mourners passed.

I lagged behind. My job was done. I don't usually attend the post-funeral bash. It's my task—or Billie's—to get the deceased safely to this point, hovering six feet above their final earthly stop. Then I sign off and pass things along to the cemetery folk. And so it was this time. Four guys you wouldn't let near your front door emerged from behind the trees and continued an argument they had been having about Cal Ripken's back pains as they played out the canvas straps holding the coffin aloft. Before the box sank below the surface one of the lugs snatched the flower arrangement off and tossed it aside. They take them home to the missus.

"Hey, Kid, you gonna help?"

This was the captain of the crew, a cigar-chomping bulldog with ears the size of Chincoteague oysters. He loved calling me "Kid." I loved calling him "Pops." So much love.

"Not today, Pops. I've got a hangnail."

Pops thought that was the funniest thing he had ever heard. He shoved the lug next to him. "Did you hear what the kid said? He said he's got a hangnail!" The guy curled his lip. You could see he thought it was a riot.

I left them. At the road Tony was packing his bagpipes into the trunk of his car. I declined the offer of a ride. I wanted to walk. I had a few things I wanted to think about.

I swung by my place—which is four doors down from the funeral home—and took my hound dog Alcatraz out for a walk and a pee. He was ever so grateful. He left his love letters all up and down the block, then I took him over to Aunt Billie's for cocktails. Alcatraz had soup. He loves soup.

"Who was that girl?" Billie asked me. "You know who I mean. The crasher."

I told her I didn't know. "She said she wanted to arrange her own funeral."

Billie was at the lowboy, making old-fashioneds. A post-mortem favorite. She muddled the fruit with a little silver hammer.

"Isn't she a little young for that?"

"I'd say so."

Billie brought me my drink and she took hers over to her favorite chair. She slipped off her shoes after she sat down, and Alcatraz immediately trotted over and dropped to the floor in front of her. Billie rested her feet gently on his soft wrinkles.

"Did she leave a deposit?" Billie asked.

"It didn't get that far," I said, raising my glass. "She changed her mind."

Billie smiled, bringing her glass to her lips. "Oh, she decided to live. That's nice."

CHAPTER 3

I think I mentioned that on the day that Carolyn James walked into and out of my life, I was in a cranky mood. Saying "yes" when I really mean "no" does that to me. Gets me cranky. And damn my soul to the eternal hell it deserves, that is what I had just recently done, agreeing to slap on a gray mustache and a folksy sort of fedora to play the part of the Stage Manager for an upcoming Gypsy Players production of *Norman Rockwell's Fever Dream*, more popularly known as *Our Town*. Gil Vance, the visionary behind this inspired choice, stressed my height and my solid good looks (that's a quote) in his campaign to nudge me out of yet another of my amateur retirements from the nonprofessional stage. He also invoked the local notoriety of my late parents. Gil is also never too shameless to swaddle his cudgel with my parents' former celebrity when he is hammering away at my ego. And of course ego is exactly the place at which you hammer away when you're trying to convince someone to get up on the stage.

"Hitch, you have no idea how many lesser talents are after me to get this role. The role of the Stage Manager demands someone of your stature, somebody who can fulfill the sacred contract between the actors and the audience. I can't have just any old ham up there, Hitch, I need you. You were born for this role. It's in your blood."

"No" is one of the easiest words to form in your mouth; you hardly have to move a muscle. But for reasons only the Laughing Gods know, I had ended up moving too many muscles in my chat with Gil over at Jimmy's Coffee Shop, and my dozen refusals had culminated in a commitment to do the damn show. All my hopes that my last Gypsy fiasco—the big dopey Swede in *Anna Christie*—might have been my swan song were obliterated.

Good lord. The Stage Manager. Not even the gently wooden Dr. Gibbs. No. *The Stage Manager*. The ringmaster. All those lines. All that corn.

I'm several generations removed from the days when college kids took to the craze of seeing how many of them they could stuff inside a telephone booth or a VW Bug, but thanks to the postage-stamp-sized stage of the Gypsy Players Theater and the brilliant decision to mount a play requiring several dozen warm bodies, I got a whiff of the old claustrophobic pastime at the first rehearsal of *Our Town*. Gil Vance herded his cast up onto the little Gypsy stage then sat back in the fifth row and instructed us "to mill."

We "milled." We also bumped and scuffed and knocked elbows and kicked toes. It didn't feel a thing like a town; it felt like a holding tank. As we stumbled about onstage, I suddenly found myself face-to-face with Julia Finney, my extremely gorgeous semi-nymphomaniac quasi-Buddhist and eternally charming ex-wife. Go figure.

"Well if it isn't Hitchcock Sewell."

"Hello there, Julia. What brings you to our town?"

"Very funny, Hitch. I see Gil roped you into this circus, too. What did he do, play on your vanity?"

"Basically."

"Me too," she sighed. "I'm a fucking pushover, I swear. Don't we have better things to do with our time?"

"You'd think so, but here we are."

Julia shook her head. "You I understand. You're around dead people all day. What's my excuse?"

I thought about that one. "You thrive on complications? The bigger the mess the happier you are."

She squinted at me. "Wait a minute. Wasn't I married to you or something?" Before I could parry, she said, "Let's talk later. I've got to mill."

She slithered off toward the far corner of the stage—all of some fifteen feet away—then turned and cocked an eyebrow and playfully stuck her tongue out at me. Gil finally clapped his hands together. Like a sea lion.

"Very good, people. V-e-r-y good. Could you take a seat please. I want to go over with you my concept of what we'll be doing in this production."

The citizens of Grover's Corners gathered round. I'd say that maybe half of them actually listened to Gil in earnest. The other fifty percent had been through all this before and we took the time to catch up on our daydreaming. Gil's "concept" probably had some interesting angles, but it didn't really matter. They'd never make it to the stage. The Gypsy Players have a long tradition of panic. Costumes rip, tempers flare, scenery wobbles, the lighting board burns up, rehearsals bog down over minutiae, the flu du jour sweeps through the cast just before opening . . . In all my experience with this outfit, there has never been time for "concept." Learn the lines, say them in order, pray for a moment or two of panache. That's the concept. Whatever daring conceits Gil Vance cooks up in the privacy of his own head simply drains through the floorboards. I'm sure it frustrates the hell out of him—if he even notices—but that's show biz.

So I tuned out while Gil explained exactly how this production would ultimately never be. He kept referring to "our stage manager" and sweeping his hand in my direction, a dozen or so dutiful heads swinging with him each time. As the ringleader of this circus, I would be playing a pivotal role in bringing the concept to life. I guess I should have been listening, but I just couldn't. I had other things on my mind. The closest I could come to paying attention to what was going on around me was to imagine the funeral scene at the end of the play. Natch. But in my version, seated there in the cemetery among the dedicated Gypsy Players, playing dead, wasn't sweet Emily Gibbs. It was Carolyn James.

Bury me.

Julia wasn't paying attention either. She sat on the edge of the stage fiddling with her long black braid. When our eyes met she held the braid up for me to see. A hangman's knot. And for the second time in twenty minutes, she cocked an eyebrow at me.

Oh. I see. It's going to be like that.

Julia's studio is on the second floor of an old fire station which had—irony of ironies—been gutted by a fire years back while its crew was off battling a blaze several blocks away. A new firehouse had been built elsewhere, the old one left vacant for a number of years until Julia's number hit and she started getting big bags of money for her paintings. That's when she took up work and residence on the second floor of the old fire station and opened up her gallery down below. The old fireman's pole had remained in place, both a decorative touch as well as a nifty way to sweep down and check on the customers.

In the rear of the studio was Julia's kitchenette and behind three antique screens, her bedroom, consisting of a bed and a bathrobe. A sculptor friend had designed the bed. Its headboard was a tangle of black steel in the shape of a spiderweb.

My fingers were still laced in it when Julia came in from the kitchenette with a tray. She was wearing the room's other accoutrement—the bathrobe—along with the devil's grin that was all too easy for me to translate. *Gotcha.*

Julia folded onto the bed and set the tray on my stomach.

"Remind me again why we divorced?" she said.

"We didn't get along? We fought?"

"I miss our fights."

"I don't."

She sighed. "There it is then. We don't see eye to eye."

There were two tiny cups and a brass coffeepot on the tray. Julia poured out two thimbles of mud, took one up and sipped on it. She gave me a rabbit's wince. "But we schtupped well together. That's important."

I agreed with her. I untangled my fingers from the headboard and scooted up. She lifted the tray from my tummy and set it on the bed. "You schtup well with everyone," I reminded her. "That was one of the reasons we fought."

"You are such a prude, Hitch." Julia's black braid was snaked around her neck where it disappeared into the cleavage of her robe. "Promiscuity is the last great weapon against the increasing sterility of our culture," she declared.

"You're telling me that you screw for the betterment of mankind?"

"Absolutely." Devil's grin. "Don't you feel better?"

I had to admit that I did. Julia's cobweb bed had a way of inspiring its inhabitants to behave as if they were suddenly endowed with several extra sets of limbs. The hour just passed had been so filled with arms and legs moving in so many directions it might have seemed that the entire cast of *Our Town* had been involved in the bacchanalia.

Why Julia and I had decided to get married in the first place was a mystery. Why mess up a good thing? The divorce—a mere year and a half later—made so much more sense to us both that we had consummated it right here on this very playing field. Since then I had only occasionally found myself drawn back to the web. Sex with Julia was a difficult habit to break. Especially since I was the only one of us trying to break it.

I sipped my mud. Julia sat cross-legged in front of me—I wished that damn braid would get out of her cleavage—and told me about a man she was seeing.

"I don't want to tell you his name. You'd yell at me."

"I know him?"

She shrugged. "Not directly, no. But I'm sure you know who he is and you wouldn't approve."

"That's nice of you to care."

"Oh I do care, Hitch. You're a good judge of character, and I know you'd judge him harshly. He's the total opposite of me. But he's great in the sack."

"Then he's not your total opposite."

"That's sweet. Thank you." Julia finally pulled her braid free from the robe and sat stroking it like a cat. "So tell me about *your* love life. Have you scored any beautiful widows?"

"I don't fraternize with the clientele."

"But, Hitch, they're so vulnerable."

"You are a perverse piece of work, Julia."

"I'm an artist. I live to explore."

And to prove her point she slipped the robe off her shoulders, swept the tray onto the floor and launched an expedition that began at my thighs and swiftly branched out in all directions. We ended up in a happy heap down at the foot of the bed, Julia purring like a panther.

"That was nice." She checked her watch. "I've got to get going."

She took a quick shower. While we were getting dressed I told her about Carolyn James. She was intrigued.

"Did she say why she wanted you to bury her?"

"She didn't explain a thing. She just said it then left."

"I see."

"She'd been drinking," I added.

"Hmmmm, that's either celebrating or commiserating."

"I'm leaning toward the latter. She seemed a trifle lost."

"So you had a sad drunk girl on your hands." Julia yanked her belt tight. She had slipped into slacks and a plain white shirt. She ran a lipstick over her lips. "And you say she was attractive?"

"She grew on me very quickly."

Julia turned toward me, smacking her lipsticked lips. "Good color?"

"Dandy."

"So Hitch, aren't you curious?" she asked.

"Yes I'm curious. But there's nothing I can do about it."

"Well you know her name. Why don't you try to track her down?"

"How? And even if I could locate her, then what? Tell her I've got a nice little plot all laid out for her?"

"You can be such a dud sometimes. This is a real-life bona fide mystery woman. I'd root like a pig until I found her."

"You can be so elegant sometimes."

She laughed. "Fuck that shit. Now come on. I've got to scoot. I'll see you in rehearsal."

I groaned. She followed me out to the studio. The place was a mess of canvases. Abstracts, mainly. Stuff you learned in kindergarten. Julia made a good living. She had been discovered a number of years ago by a social hotshot on the board of the Walters Art Gallery. They had a brief affair. The guy talked Julia up to his crowd and her sales and commissions took off. She was hanging all over town now. She was also, for some reason, a very big deal in Scandanavia. They loved her over there. A certified "darling."

Julia kicked loose the wooden slats around the fireman's pole. "By the way, who are you in the play?" I asked as I took hold of the pole. "Mrs. Gibbs?" She rolled her eyes.

"I'm Emily. Teen teen soda pop queen." She gave me a challenging look. "Go ahead. Say it."

"Well, no offense of course. But aren't you a little old and worn out and gone to seed to play Emily?"

She laughed. "I sure am. And you're a bit of a wet clueless pup to be the sagely old stage manager, ain't cha? It's all a part of Gil's concept. Or weren't you listening?"

"No. I was flirting with my ex-wife."

She grinned at that. "The Stage Manager and little Emily humping it up. Now *that's* a concept."

"This production is doomed," I said.

She waved her hand in the air. "Of course it is, they always are. That's the fun of it. Another Gypsy Players tragedy. Now scoot."

She goosed me and gave me a peck on the cheek. I hugged the pole and stepped into the void. I landed in the gallery. There were no customers, only Chinese Sue behind the cash register leafing languidly through a magazine. Chinese Sue isn't really Chinese. She's from Dundalk, which is about as blue-collar as you get in Baltimore. But she wears velvet jackets and cuts her hair in bangs and stares at you as if she hasn't a clue what you just said, and that furthermore, she doesn't care. I've no explanation for her. That's what people call her. And she runs Julia's gallery. Anyway, when I came down the pole, she didn't even look up.

As it turned out, I didn't have to root like a pig to locate Carolyn James. She was waiting for me when I got back to work. Aunt Billie handed me the paperwork the moment I walked in the door.

"Suicide," she said. "Asphyxiation. It just breaks my heart."

I hurried down to the basement, where we prep our customers. A waifish redhead was stretched out in front of me, a slightly agonized look forever etched into her freckled face. She was about five four, and skinny. The skin around her left eye was discolored, almost green. She had recently suffered a black eye.

I had never seen her before in my life.

CHAPTER 4

The details on the dead woman were few. She had lived in an apartment in Charles Village, over near Johns Hopkins University and had been found in a garage in the alley behind her building, in the front seat of a Honda Civic that was idling very high, filling the garage with its deadly exhaust. There was no doubt that the death was intentional; several towels had been stuffed along the bottom of the garage door. If that weren't convincing enough, then the rippled plastic tubing that ran from the exhaust to the crack in the driver's-side window was pretty persuasive. It came from a vacuum cleaner that the police found while inspecting Carolyn James's apartment. It's doubtful that she was just clearing the air. As far as the police were concerned, the case was shut before it even had a chance to open.

As far as *they* were concerned.

Carolyn James, aged twenty-seven, had been employed as a caterer's assistant. The head of the catering company said that she was a diligent, responsible worker who did as she was told, no more, no less. She had been employed for about a year, her first job since moving to Baltimore from somewhere out west. She had no family that anyone could find, and was single, though apparently there was a man in her life. The exact nature of the relationship was a little fuzzy. The head caterer described the fellow to me as "a cocky bastard son of a bitch Grade-A prick." If this caterer cooks like he swears, I want some.

"He's a good-looking guy. A real Joe Stud type," he said to me. "Which was why I could never quite figure the two of them out. Carolyn was a nice kid and all, but she wasn't exactly Sophia Loren."

It seemed to me that he was setting the bar kind of high, but I remained silent.

"I wouldn't exactly describe her as homely, but she didn't really have a lot of personality. She was shy, basically. And this guy of hers . . . well, he came on strong. It never made much sense to me."

My little chat with the head of the catering company took place in Parlor Two, where we had laid out the unfortunate caterer's assistant for her viewing. Billie had a wake going over in Parlor One, for a beloved old high school teacher. Popular enough in fact to have almost warranted pulling open the plastic curtain, had we not been conducting a double-header. As for Carolyn James, she pulled a miserably small crowd. Aside from the head of the catering company and a few of her co-workers, there was the man who had discovered her in the exhaust-filled garage, a butcher from the Eddie's Supermarket where she had done her shopping and her across-the-hall neighbor, an elderly cuss named Mr. Castlebaum. This left only two people conspicuous by their absence. One was the cocky bastard son of a bitch Grade-A prick. The other was the woman who had borrowed Carolyn James's name long enough to tell me—in her own peculiar way—that the not-terribly-popular caterer's assistant would soon be Parlor Two's unhappy guest of honor.

This was Baltimore, not Denmark. But something here still stank.

The buzz coming from Parlor One made it sound like bingo night at the local fire hall compared to what we had going in Two. We had us a small somber wake for a friendless young lady who had decided to click off the program early. The whole thing got me sad and it got me angry. Aunt Billie could see it in my face later when she pulled herself away from her Mardi Gras and found me sitting in my office with my chin on my fists.

"Bad one?" she asked.

"A low show."

"Oh, that's too bad. And such a young girl. Maybe it'll pick up tomorrow at the funeral. You know how that can sometimes happen."

I looked over at her standing there at the door. Betty Crocker's sweet old mother.

"Your teacher went well?"

"Lovely," she said. "They laughed, they cried."

I do love my little auntie.

The fake Carolyn James did not show at the funeral the next day. I didn't really expect that she would. Whatever bizarre reason the woman had for impersonating the caterer's assistant and putting in an early request for burial would have to remain a mystery. I sifted and resifted my ten minutes with her but came up with nothing. She was, as Julia had said, a Mystery Woman. Bona fide Sister Cipher. A Face Without a Name.

Lady X.

I did however have the pleasure of meeting the son of a bitch bastard Grade-A prick. I knew his name already from the paperwork that Billie had handed me when I had come back from my tryst with my ex-wife. His name was Guy Fellows. I kid you not. Some parents simply have no regard. Mr. Fellows had apparently handled the funeral arrangements in record time, over the phone. He bought Carolyn James the least expensive coffin the law would allow (the Pauper's Pillbox, we call it in the trade), and he had left it to Billie to suggest the cemetery and to arrange for the plot. His attentiveness was touching, to say the least.

Guy Fellows showed up at the cemetery wearing khaki slacks, a navy blue sport coat and a faded maroon club tie. He was—as advertised—a good-looking fellow. Tanned and trim, his hand-combed sandy hair featured a jaunty cowlick in the front which lent an unmistakable devil-may-care sexiness to his surfer-boy looks. And as with a certain breed of pretty boys, this guy wore his arrogance on his sleeve. He arrived at the grave site with his hands in his pockets, like he was posing for a fashion shoot. I watched him closely as he looked down at the coffin. It wasn't sadness in those sharp blue eyes. It was irritation. If Carolyn James's suicide ruffled him at all, it was largely because the funeral was interrupting his busy busy day. Even his one show of tenderness went sour. After staring at the coffin for some ten seconds he reached out and placed a hand on it. He drummed his fingers a few times then withdrew the hand, bumping the flower arrangement and knocking it down into the grave. "Shit," he muttered, and then stepped back under the canopy. Lovely bloke all around.

The service was brief. Like Carolyn James's life. When it was over, Guy Fellows turned and walked away. The priest looked a little lost, having no one to console. I shook his hand. He shook his head.

"We could have phoned this one in, couldn't we've? That was the saddest funeral I've done all year, Hitch. What? Did she have the plague?"

But before I could answer we were interrupted by a ruckus over by the cars. Guy Fellows and Carolyn James's across-the-hall neighbor, the elderly Mr. Castlebaum, were engaged in a shouting match. I hurried over.

Castlebaum: *You're a bum!*

Fellows: *Shut up!*

Castlebaum: *I won't shut up! You're a bum! You killed that girl!*

Fellows: *You don't know what you're talking about, old man.*

Castlebaum: *I heard the way you treated her! You think these aren't ears?*

Fellows: *Why don't you mind your own goddamn business?*

Castlebaum: *Don't you "goddamn" me in a cemetery, you Nazi!*

Fellows: *Fuck off!*

That's when Mr. Castlebaum went for him. The old guy went for the face. His hand whipped across Guy Fellows's cheek and left a pair of claw marks. The younger man responded instantly, growling "You little *bastard!*" as he jabbed a rabbit punch to the old man's jaw. The little old knight went down.

"Hey!" I rushed in. I looked around for Sam. He's our hearse driver. Big as a wall. Nice kid. He's also a bouncer at several clubs around town. But he was nowhere to be seen.

Fellows was quick. The instant I registered on his screen he wheeled around and sent out another piston jab, catching me on the side of my nose. The jolt shot right to my toes. In an instant I could taste blood. Then he hit me again, this one missing my face and landing instead on my windpipe. It literally took my breath away. Guy Fellows was in a boxer's crouch now, but he didn't go for a third hit. Mr. Castlebaum was on his fanny, shaking off the sucker punch. I saw Fellows's eyes flick back in the old guy's direction and I tried to warn him off, but my throat was still collapsed. All I managed was a hiss. Then I measured my height advantage over the Grade-A prick and shoved him as hard as I could. He slammed against the side of the hearse. When he tried to straighten back up I shoved him again, harder. To be honest, I was beginning to enjoy this. I had his reach measured now and I knew he couldn't get to my face. He whipped my arms away from him.

"Hey, buddy, get out of my face!" he snapped. "Why don't you mind your own business!"

I shoved him again. I croaked, "This *is* my business. I'm in charge of this funeral."

The guy sneered. But he remained leaning back against the hearse. "Nice job, buddy."

I rubbed my sleeve along my face and got a nice blood streak for my efforts. My nose was pulsing. Mr. Castlebaum was slowly getting to his feet. I turned to him.

"Are you okay?"

Guy Fellows answered first. "He's fine. I barely touched him."

"Is beating up on old men one of your hobbies?" I asked.

"Hey, buddy, what I do is my own business."

I was getting a little tired of being called buddy. "Why don't you apologize."

"He came after me first," Fellows snapped.

"Okay, okay. Hold on," I said. "Look, tensions can run high at funerals. I'm sure Mr. Castlebaum didn't mean anything—"

"Like hell I didn't! I meant every word. This guy is a punk!"

Fellows slapped a hand down on top of the hearse. "Hey, old man, want a ride?"

Ding! Round two. The old man dove at the young man and they started to mix it up again. This time I squeezed in between the two, wedging Mr. Castlebaum aside and taking hold of Guy Fellows's sporty lapels. Enough was enough was enough. I jerked our faces so close together we could have kissed. We played a quick game of eye chicken.

"Can we stop this now?"

"Let me go," he hissed.

"Not until you show a little more respect."

"What are you, an Eagle Scout?"

I thought I had a good hold of the guy's jacket so I rattled him hard. But he slipped right out of my hands and went slamming against the hearse again, this time giving the top of the door a good rap with his head. It sounded like an ax blow to a log. He came up in a fury.

"Goddamn it!" He leaped at me, kicking and scratching. No more boxer stuff. I caught a few fingernails to the cheek. Finally Sam appeared. He hurried over, still pulling up his fly. Sam is basically a square human being, half fat, half muscle. He's a good kid, although I've told him more than once about peeing in the cemetery when he's on the job. He's got a bladder the size of a shot glass. Sam removed Guy Fellows from me. Simple as that. Fellows shook himself free and took a few steps away, holding up his hands as if to show he was unarmed. "Okay, okay, that's it, I'm fine. I'm cool."

"Are you all right, Mr. Sewell?" Sam asked me.

"I'm fine, Sam. Thank you." I signaled Sam to escort Mr. Castlebaum to his car. The old man went without a fight. Well, without further fight. Guy Fellows was settling down. He straightened his collar and tie and finger-combed his raffish mop. A long slow grin grew on his face as he looked back up at me.

"I got you good, didn't I?" He reached into his jacket pocket and handed me a handkerchief. The corner of it went swiftly red as I dabbed it at my nose.

"You sucker punched me."

Fellows laughed. "Then I guess that makes you the sucker." He put his fingers to his cheek to see if the old guy had drawn any blood. "Crazy old coot."

"He doesn't seem to like you."

Fellows shrugged. "He's one of those busybody neighbors. Thinks he's everyone's father. He's upset about . . . you know."

"Aren't you?"

He looked past me toward the grave. "Well sure. Sure I'm upset. I mean, what the hell? Who knew the damn girl was going to go and kill herself?"

It was a rhetorical question. But it just so happened that I had an answer. Or part of an answer. I started to ask him if he knew anything about the dark-haired woman with legs to her ears, but something called back the question. Instead I asked him if he knew the deceased well. It was a throwaway question.

"We were friends."

"And you have no idea why she killed herself?"

He shrugged. "I guess she was unhappy."

"When I'm unhappy I watch a Marx Brothers movie or I go out and drink too much," I said. "I don't go napping in a garage with the engine on."

His eyes narrowed. "Maybe she didn't like the Marx Brothers."

Smart aleck. I didn't like him. He was a slime. A good-looking slime, a handsome clotheshorse slime, but still a slime. He didn't give a tinker's ass about his dead "friend," that was clear. I wondered why he even showed up for her funeral, let alone paid for it. Assuming his check was good. I thought again about asking him about the fake Carolyn James, but something again held me back. For some reason I didn't want to imagine that she had anything whatsoever to do with this guy, even though I had a strong and uneasy suspicion that she did. Very much did. And in the next twenty seconds, my suspicions were pretty much confirmed.

"So do you really run this place?" Guy Fellows asked.

"I run the funeral home."

He looked me up and down.

"You don't look like an undertaker."

"So I've been told. So what about you? Do you look like what you do?"

"What do I look like I do?"

It was a straight line that ran all the way to the coast, but I ignored it and shrugged. "Surprise me."

"I'm a tennis pro," he said. "I give lessons. Baltimore Country Club. Do you play?"

"I've been known to knock the ball over the fence a few times."

He appraised me. "You've got a good physique for tennis. You've got long arms. Good range. If you're quick, that's it."

I am quick. But I wasn't at that moment. At that moment I was seeing a pair of tennis shoes and a short white pleated skirt and a pair of long legs slicing back and forth across a clay court while this weasel peppered the ball left and right without even breaking a sweat. I was seeing Lady X toweling off after her lesson, having a few drinks with James Dean here in the clubhouse, then driving down to my funeral home to mess with my head.

Guy Fellows was saying something to me.

"Is there much money in it?"

"In what?"

He held out his arms and pivoted left and right, taking in the cemetery.

"Oh. That. Yes," I said. "The funeral biz. It's steady. How about the tennis gig?"

He bobbed his head. "It's a living."

He dropped to a boxer's stance and threw a fake punch my way, missing by a mile.

"No hard feelings, huh?" He reached out and gave me a slap on the arm. "See you around the cemetery."

He laughed and then walked off. Who could have known how nearly right he was.

CHAPTER 5

I took my mystery to the Screaming Oyster Saloon. The S.O.S. is a dockside joint, a ramshackle old building that looks as if it might at any minute lean too far and slip right into the oily harbor. There's a vaguely nautical motif about the place, mainly the sort of flotsam you'd expect to find washed up on the beach in the weeks after a ship has broken apart out on the rocks. Netting, some wooden casks, thick rope knotted into monkey's fists . . . junk basically, touched with brine. Dominant in the sunless room is a weathered dinghy that hangs above the bar, a receptacle of years and years of bottles and cans sent there by the deft hook shots of the drinkers at the bar. It's not uncommon as the night moves along at the Oyster for these hook shots to lose some of their deftness. Bottles and cans bounce off the side of the dinghy and come right back down, sometimes landing harmlessly, sometimes shattering on impact, occasionally cracking open an unsuspecting forehead. Drink at the Oyster long enough and you learn where to stand. That's the theory anyway.

The Oyster is a mom-and-pop place in the truest sense. The mom and pop who run it are Frank and Sally Finney. They're Julia's parents, my former in-laws. If you've read your Mother Goose then you are already familiar with Frank and Sally. They appear in those pages under the name of Mr. and Mrs. Jack Sprat. Sally is as big as a piano, a large round woman with a big round red face, short arms and large meaty hands. Sally's voice is as big as her body, something which comes in handy when running a bar like this. I've seen her break up a fight that was clear across the room just by bellowing at the participants to take the damn thing outside.

Frank, on the other hand, is a tall crooked stick with an Adam's apple that rivals his nose, and a basset hound face that promises the end of life as we know it at any minute now. Every mug he lands on the bar lands there with the heavy thud of finality. If you're in a good mood and you don't want to be, Frank's your man. He doesn't even have to speak, he'll simply open up his bleak vortex for you and down you go.

One other feature of the S.O.S. worth mentioning. There is a black door at the far end of the bar that costs Frank and Sally a biannual payoff to the city building inspectors to keep it operational instead of nailed shut. The little fee is well worth it, though, on those occasions where a friendly neighborhood bar brawl threatens to get out of hand, when Sally is sometimes able to herd her unsuspecting pugilists through the black door and right into the harbor outside. It's a great show, and Sally will usually spot the bar a free round of drafts after the show, laughing like a witch in the wind as she pulls back on her sticks. If you can take her at her word—which I think I do—nobody has drowned yet. In the harbor, that is.

It being early afternoon, the Oyster was pretty sparsely inhabited. Frank was working the bar alone, so the general atmosphere was subdued. Nearly dead, in fact. Tony Marino was on his usual stool at the end of the bar stirring his Scotch with his pinky. Another Oyster regular, Edie Velvet, was parked midway down the bar, gazing up at the television in the corner. Barely taller than her barstool and very nearly its weight, Edie predated even Frank and Sally Finney at the Oyster. Her father, a third-rate jockey named Bud Velvet, owned the place back before Frank and Sally, a hedge against his consistently poor showings at Pimlico. When he sold the place to the Finneys, his daughter apparently came with the deal. I liked old Edie a lot. If you could get past the mass of wrinkles and the ill-fitting clothes, there were remarkably soft and friendly eyes in there. A downright elegant nature. As I entered the bar, Edie raised her glass an extra inch in the air by way of greeting and soundlessly said my name before returning her gaze to the TV.

A soap opera was on. The volume was off. Ken and Barbie knockoffs were snarling at each other up on the screen. I slid onto a stool and asked

Frank to draw me a Guinness. I glanced back up at the television and the pretty couple were already kissing. Man, they move fast on TV.

"Who'd you bury today, Hitchcock?" Tony asked. He stopped taking his drink's temperature and puckered a sip. "I saw you leaving for the cemetery. Didn't seem like much of a crowd."

"It was only about a half dozen. A young woman."

"A woman?" He shook his head sadly. "They didn't want the pipes, huh?"

"They barely wanted the casket. This was a real nobody, Tony. No friends. No family."

Tony grimaced. "God, that's terrible."

I glanced back up at the television. The Barbie girl was crying now and her boyfriend was looking very uneasy. Frank dropped a coaster in front of me.

"Thank you, Frank," I said. A low rumble sounded from somewhere in the back of the barkeep's throat. "Did Julia tell you that we're going to be in another play together over at the Gypsy?" I said with excessive cheer, just for counterpoint. "They're doing *Our Town*."

Frank clawed the towel off his shoulder and swatted it at a fly on the bar.

"Whore."

Uh-oh, he was in *that* mood. It was a lost battle, but I gave it a volley anyway.

"You shouldn't judge her so harshly, Frank. Julia's a free spirit. It takes all kinds to make a world."

Frank was unimpressed with my defense of his daughter, as I knew he would be. I guess it's hard for some fathers to watch their daughter develop into comely devils.

"Who is she seeing now?" Tony asked. Frank turned to him and counted off silently on his long bony fingers—one, two, three, four—then he looked over at me with his watery eyes. He *was* interested in the answer.

"Actually, I don't know," I said. "She told me that she's seeing a real nice fellow, but wouldn't tell me his name."

"You should have held on to that woman, Hitchcock," Tony said.

"Try holding on to the tail of a tornado," I said. It's possible that Edie smiled at this, though her large glass was obscuring her face. Frank set my Guinness in front of me. I took a sip. It was warm and perfect. God love the Irish.

Silence fell over the bar, except for the TV set. The guy up there was slamming the door behind him. The girl took a quivering close-up as the screen went blank. A commercial for Jell-O came on. Edie skidded her glass across the bar for a refill.

I switched to bourbon after my second Guinness and found myself once more thinking about the woman I had just buried. She was out there this very minute, already being forgotten by the handful of people who had bothered showing up to pay her their last respects. Normally I would be detaching at this point, throwing the ropes onto the deck and letting the little craft drift off and away. But it wasn't happening. The fake Carolyn James—Lady X—had slipped one of those ropes around my ankle, and I was being pulled into the drink. I looked up at the mirror behind the bar and imagined that I saw her there. I imagined her sliding onto the stool next to mine, gesturing toward my drink, telling Frank she'd have what I was having. I imagined her turning towards me on her stool, lifting the glass to her lips, shooting me again with her eyes. *Well . . . ?*

I ordered another bourbon from Frank and glared straight ahead at the mirror. I was aware by then that the bourbon was doing a lot of the thinking for me. Of course that was the whole idea.

The next day, nursing a hard-cotton head from the previous day's meditations at the Oyster, I drove my Chevy Nothing over to Carolyn James's apartment building. She had lived in a section of the city known as Charles Village, so named for Charles Carroll of Carrollton, a wealthy Baltimore landowner and New World aristocrat and one of the signers of the Declaration of Independence. Carolyn James had lived on Calvert Street (Lord Calvert, a buddy of Chuck's), midway between Hopkins University and the now vacant Memorial Stadium. Mr. Castlebaum buzzed me in.

"So, an undertaker who makes house calls. Should I be concerned?"

Cute. "Yes. I thought I'd swing by and measure you."

He invited me into his apartment and offered me a cup of tea. "It's just tea," he told me as I eyeballed his ancient furniture. "None of this fancy crap. It's just tea."

I chose a buxom armchair. "Just tea is just fine," I assured him.

As Mr. Castlebaum puttered about in the kitchen, he called out to me in the living room.

"So let me guess. You want to know more about my neighbor. You're upset that such a young woman would take her own life like that and it's been bothering you ever since the funeral. It just doesn't make sense. Am I right so far?"

Basically he was and I told him so. I spotted a large black cat with army green eyes staring at me from a nearby windowsill. It didn't seem to particularly care for me. A second cat came into view on the couch. And then two more over by the radiator. The room began to purr ominously. Mr. Castlebaum was moving about in the kitchen getting the tea paraphernalia together.

"So you can't get her out of your mind and now you think you're falling in love with her. You are becoming obsessed. Am I still right?"

I respected his imagination but I thought I had better cut him off there.

"Actually, Mr. Castlebaum, I was sort of curious to learn more about the relationship with Guy Fellows."

I could hear the disappointment in his voice. "Oh. The bum."

"Yes. The bum."

Mr. Castlebaum poked his head in from the kitchen.

"Sugar? Lemon? I take a little rum and honey with my tea when I get a cold. You feeling sick?"

"Sugar's fine," I said. "And milk." The black cat shifted, eyeing me suspiciously. I was invading his dairy cache.

Mr. Castlebaum came back into the room with a tray which he set down atop a pile of old *Look* magazines on the coffee table.

The tea was sour.

"He's a bad man," Mr. Castlebaum said, settling onto his couch. "I heard him a lot, you know. Yelling. He was bad to her. He came and he went at all hours of the day and night. He slammed the doors, he didn't care that there are other people living in the building. And he hit her."

"He hit her?"

"That's what I said. I would see her sometimes in the hallway or out walking on the street. And I could see the bruises. And sometimes she was wearing sunglasses on the days when there was no sun. You tell me what that means. I'll tell you it doesn't mean she was a movie star. It means that her eyes are black. You saw him. You saw how he behaved at her funeral. He hit me."

"He hit me too."

The arms went into the air. "He hits everyone. He thinks he is Joe Louis. He's a bully, that's all. He's a Nazi. And he killed her."

"And you got the definite impression that this dark-haired woman visiting was hiding from Guy Fellows."

"I tell you what I saw. Am I a mind reader?"

I was thinking he was an exhausting old man who ought to let some fresh air into his apartment. He slapped his hands down on his bony knees. End of story. It wasn't much. I thanked him for the tea and for his time. He waved his arms impatiently in the air.

"Forget the tea. It was lousy."

At the door, he hesitated. "There is one more thing I can tell you. When the young woman dies. She is found in her car in the garage. The police come by and they ask me who is the landlord so that they can inform him. Well, I am the landlord. I own this palace. Since before you were born. I get the key and I let them into the apartment. It was a mess. But I don't mean she is a messy person, this poor dead girl. I mean a tornado has come through, Drawers are hanging open. Pillows and clothes are on the floor. Books. Plates. A lamp is broken. It is a mess."

"Like someone was looking for something? That kind of a mess?"

He nodded. "It could be."

"Are her belongings still in there?" I asked.

"No. The bum came by the next day and threw most of it in boxes and told me to call the Goodwill truck. I told him to call the damn Goodwill truck himself, what do I look like? The place is for rent right now. Do you know anyone?"

I was staring at the stairwell, at the darkened corner where the fake Carolyn James had hidden from Guy Fellows. What exactly was the connection between the two women? According to Mr. Castlebaum, Guy Fellows had total access to this apartment, coming and going at will, and slapping poor Carolyn James around in the bargain. What would have happened if he had spotted the fake Carolyn James lurking there in the stairway?

Mr. Castlebaum seemed to be waiting for an answer to his question. My head was shaking absently.

"No . . . I don't know anybody."

I took the Jones Falls Expressway north to the Falls Road exit, then north again, a right on Seminary Road, and then left on something or other, then northeast, south, west and north again . . . a curvy country road that took me eventually to the manicured acres of the Baltimore Country Club. I pulled into the large lot next to the club's mighty Georgian mansion, slipping my Chevy Nothing in amongst the BMW 750s and the Mercedes SLs. It was a lovely spring day. The country club's gardeners had done a good job. Jonquils and tulips and columbine bloomed everywhere amidst large sculpted ponds of myrtle, which is a ground-hugging ivy that looks as soft as hair.

I spotted a miniature tractor with a small wiry fellow behind the wheel. He had a baseball cap pushed back on his head and he was giving marching orders to a pair of slouching guys in matching green overalls who were standing there holding rakes. As I headed over, the guys with rakes dispersed. Boss man remained in his saddle. The little white oval on his overalls told me that his name was Rudy. The baseball cap suggested that he favored Pepsi, though he was clearly of a different generation. His boots were the color of meatloaf.

I gave him an *Our Town* greeting.

"Howdy."

I got one back. "Howdy."

"Rudy is it?" I swung out my hand. Why I was acting so folksy I'm not sure, but I felt like an idiot. Rudy's hand felt like finely ground glass in a baseball mitt.

"What can I do ya fer?" he chirped. I was pretty sure he was making fun of me.

"My name is Hitchcock Sewell."

"That's quite a name."

"It's a family name."

"I imagine so."

"People call me Hitch."

"That would've been my guess." His eyes were twinkling. "People call me Rudy."

"So the sign says."

"What can I do ya fer, Hitch," he said again. This time he cracked an obvious smile.

"I'm looking for Guy Fellows. I understand he's the tennis pro here."

Rudy nodded. "You looking to take lessons?"

"Well, no. I just wanted to talk to him."

Rudy looked me up and down. "Are you married?"

"Excuse me?"

"Are you married? Hitched. Hooked up. Got yourself a steady gal? Spoken for? Engaged?"

I cocked my head at the elfin man. "Are you asking me for a date, Rudy?"

Rudy laughed at that. "Afraid I'm spoken for. No, it's just, well, you're not looking to take lessons and you're not here to tell Fellows to steer clear of any lady friend of yours. That just about makes you an oddball." He put a finger to the brim of his cap and nudged it further back on his head.

"Is he here?"

Rudy glanced over his shoulder at the tennis courts. They had a green mesh netting running along the fences. I could only make out flashes of white to go along with the irregular *boink* of a ball.

"Funny thing is, he isn't. His first lesson is at ten o'clock and it's already past one, but he hasn't showed up." The little guy chuckled. "Some of these ladies haven't been stood up since they were twelve. You want to see some real fireworks, come around when they catch up to him."

Just then a red BMW pulled up in the parking lot and a Grace Kelly look-alike got out. She was well-tailored and posture-perfect in that look-don't-touch kind of way. The air parted for her as she made her way on clicking high heels along the walkway to the mansion. Rudy and I suspended all conversation as she moved by, which is what men generally do when a stunning woman passes within, say, a quarter mile of us. The fake Grace Kelly stepped coolly through the large oak door of the club's mansion as if it weren't even there.

"There's one," Rudy muttered.

"One what?"

"A former student of your tennis pro." Rudy gave me a big old-fashioned wink. "They were pretty dedicated doubles players for a while there, if you hear me."

I heard him. "Popular guy, huh?"

"Fellows? Well he's not my type."

"Rudy, you wouldn't know anything about his girlfriend, would you?"

"You want to narrow that down for me a little?"

"Do you know if he has a girlfriend? I mean, a steady one?"

"Well if he does he's smart enough not to bring her around here."

"I guess that makes sense."

Rudy and I chatted a bit more. I complimented him on the landscaping. He told me that he had a crew of four men plus himself. He told me about the recent major re-landscaping project. He told me about his useless son-in-law, whom he had hired to help out and then fired for hot-rodding in the golf carts. He showed me a photograph of his granddaughter—the only good thing his useless son-in-law had ever produced—who, I was to understand, might be an actual genius in the field of mathematics. She was being tested for it later this month. He told me about a hurricane and a problem with the wiring in the house that he and his wife—another photo—owned down in Bethany Beach. Rudy was a sweet fellow but he was blind to body language. I was holding a forty-five degree angle toward the parking lot for what felt like ten years until I finally just had to insert a handshake into the middle of it all and thank him for his time. I left the wiry Scheherazade perched atop his miniature tractor and headed back to the parking lot.

A police car pulled in just as I was about to get into my car. A uniformed cop was behind the wheel. His passenger got out. No uniform. He wore a dull tweed jacket over a white shirt and a snot green tie. He was very short—in the Napoleonic range—and stocky. A wrestler's physique. He had small ears, a pink face and yellow hair that was either cut in a horrendous style or was one of the world's worst ever toupees. He gave me the look that a lot of short men give me, the one that says "I could knock you over, big guy, if I felt like it." I resisted the urge to pat him on the head and waited until he had slammed his door closed before getting into my car and firing her up. A cloud of blue exhaust belched onto his knees as he crossed behind me. I caught his sneer in the rearview mirror. The uniformed cop was picking his teeth and staring straight ahead, but I was pretty sure I saw him chuckling.

As I pulled away, I saw that the keeper of the yellow hair was approaching Rudy. I watched as Rudy tilted back his hat and rubbed his overused jaw.

What can I do ya fer?

Two hours later Billie called me out of a wake in Parlor Two. She was frowning.

"There's a man here to see you."

It was the guy with the yellow hair. He was standing at the front door. He made no sign of recognition, so I didn't either.

"Are you Hitchcock Sewell?"

"Yes."

"I'm Detective John Kruk." He flashed a badge. "I'd like to talk with you."

"About what?"

"I'd like to talk with you."

"You said that. I'm in the middle of a wake."

"This is important."

People were still arriving. I saw several of them eyeing the police car, which was parked out in the street, angled behind the hearse as if it had pulled the wagon over for speeding.

"Can it wait?" I asked.

"Not really."

"Well, could you at least move the car?" He was tapping a pencil impatiently against his notebook and didn't answer. "I have bereaved people here," I explained. "A police car can be unsettling."

"That's funny. I always thought that police cars made people feel safe."

"Not at funerals."

He aimed his pencil at me. "You mean wake."

I wasn't in the mood. "Can you just tell me what this is about?"

"That was you out at the country club this afternoon, wasn't it."

"Yes, it was. What did you do, follow me here?"

"Have you been out there to the club before today, Mr. Sewell?"

"The country club? Oh. Sure. I'm a big deal up there."

"Are you being sarcastic, Mr. Sewell?"

Before I could reply (sarcastically, I'd bet on it), Aunt Billie came up behind me.

"Hello. Is there a problem?"

"No problem," I said.

"You two should get out of the doorway," Billie said.

"I'm trying to get him to move the car."

Kruk broke in. "Forget the car. The car isn't what's important here, Mr. Sewell."

I snapped. "Then *move* the damn thing. We've got a dead person in there, Detective, and that's the important thing here. People are here to pay their respects. Don't they give you sensitivity training where you work?"

Aunt Billie took in a sharp breath. She hates it when I get belligerent.

Kruk hooked his thumbs into his belt and rocked back on his heels. Classic ham.

"Well you know something, Mr. Sewell. We've got a dead body too. Except nobody's come by to pay ours any respects. Ours has a knife in its gut."

Aunt Billie gasped.

"What dead body," I said. "What are you talking about?"

Kruk kept up with the pencil-tapping. I wondered if it was supposed to unnerve me. "If the sight of a police car out front here has you so upset, maybe you should just come on down with me to the station, Mr. Sewell, where it's an everyday occurrence."

I asked again. "Who's dead?"

The detective glanced down at his notebook. "A man by the name of Fellows."

"Guy Fellows? The tennis pro?"

"You know him?"

"You know I know him. At least, I know who he is. That's why you're here?"

Kruk rocked back on his heels again. "That's right." He consulted his notebook again. "I understand you and Mr. Fellows had a fight. Just yesterday I believe."

"You've done your homework."

"He hit you."

"So?"

"So sometimes that pisses people off. It would piss me off." He turned to Billie. "Excuse me, ma'am."

"It did piss me off." I said. "But are you suggesting that I stabbed him because of it? I don't usually go around stabbing people who piss me off."

He looked at me sharply. "Don't *usually*?"

"That was a little joke, Detective."

"So you think this is funny? You think a man found dead with a knife in his gut is a funny joke?"

"Not to him it's not."

"And not to me either." Kruk flipped his notebook shut. "Okay, that's it. We'll do this downtown. I don't want to disturb these people any more than I already have. Why don't you get in the big bad car, Mr. Sewell."

I looked at him like he was crazy. "You're kidding, right?"

"Now!"

Aunt Billie made a shooing gesture.

"Just go, Hitchcock. The officer won't take no for an answer. Isn't that right?"

"Detective," Kruk grunted.

Billie rolled her eyes.

In twenty minutes, I was in the hot seat at district police headquarters. The place wasn't quite how it always appears on television, though it looked like they were making every effort. There were no tube-topped hookers, no wild-haired guy proclaiming his innocence to the ceiling, no just-found runaway boy on a bench getting a life lesson from Detective Sensitive. However, there did seem to be a phone ringing endlessly somewhere off in the background. And the coffee was downright toxic.

Joe Friday beat me with a rubber hose until I cracked and told him where the loot was stashed. Then we moved on to the matter of Guy Fellows.

I was assured that I was not a suspect. Then I was asked several dozen questions about my dustup with the dead tennis stud, all of which made me *feel* like a suspect. Apparently, Mr. Castlebaum had already been grilled. He was the one who gave me up.

"Who hit who first?" Kruk asked me.

"Him. And it's whom."

"What's whom?"

"Never mind," I said. "Anyway, I didn't hit him. I shoved him."

"Why?"

"Because he hit me."

"And why did he hit you?"

"Because I was breaking up his fight with Mr. Castlebaum."

"We have Mr. Castlebaum's statement."

"Then you know all this already."

The interview was taking place in Kruk's office. The detective was somewhat dwarfed behind his large gray desk. I was in the only chair in the room other than Kruk's, a small wobbly wood thing which I dwarfed. Detective Kruk and I really should have traded places. The dirt-stained windows behind the detective deflected any hope that the incoming sunshine would cheer up the place. The office smelled vaguely of a gas leak. Summing up, the place fit Kruk like a perfectly ill-fitting suit.

"Mr. Castlebaum says that you hit Mr. Fellows."

"Mr. Castlebaum is wrong."

"Are you saying he's lying?"

"I'm saying he got it wrong. He was on the ground after all."

"And why is that again?"

"Because Guy Fellows had just hit him."

"That was before or after you hit him?"

"I didn't hit anybody. I shoved him." I was getting tempted to show the little detective how I did it. Kruk glanced at his damned notebook. I was beginning to guess it was all tic-tac-toe. Or girlie doodles.

"Mr. Castlebaum didn't say anything about any shoving."

I sighed. "I can't help that. I shoved. I'm saying it now. Write it down in your notebook. Suspect shoved dead man. Dead man was still alive at the time."

"You're not a suspect, Mr. Sewell."

"So you've said."

"At least not a very good one."

I threw up my hands. "I'm sorry, Detective. I'll try to do better next time."

Kruk actually showed the beginnings of a grin. He leaned back in his squeaky chair and crossed his short arms on his chest. "Why were you at the country club today?"

"Is that a crime?"

"I didn't say it was. I'm just curious about the chain of events that has you in a fight with Guy Fellows yesterday and then off asking a lot of questions about him today when somewhere in between those two days someone is twisting a knife into his gut." Kruk spread his hands. "You can see why I might be curious?"

Of course I could. But I didn't think that he would find any of my explanations satisfying. The conveniently absent Mystery Woman. It would sound like a rotten lie told by a rotten liar.

"I didn't kill Guy Fellows," I said. Might as well get it on the record.

Detective Kruk laced his fingers together and cracked his knuckles. He was apparently a bottomless storehouse of stock gestures. I shook my head slowly. What in the goddamn hell was I doing here?

"Kruk. What is that? Finnish?"

"Dutch." He leaned forward on his desk. "Do you have any ideas who would want to kill Guy Fellows?"

"Like I told you . . . ten times. I never set eyes on him until yesterday at the funeral."

"Look. If you have any information that is pertinent to this case, you are bound by law to tell me, Mr. Sewell. Do you?"

"No," I lied.

"Then that'll be all for now." He picked up some papers that were on his desk.

"That's it? Are you going to ask me to stay close to the city for the next several days?"

"Were you planning on taking a trip?"

"No. But I just figured—"

I was interrupted by Kruk's phone.

"Yeah . . . Uh-huh . . . Okay. I'll send him over." He hung up the phone. "Well, you seem to be a popular fellow Mr. Sewell. Before you go, Detective Zabriskie wants to see you."

"Who's Detective Zabriskie?"

Kruk gave me his poker face. "Detective Zabriskie is the person who wants to see you. Take a left out the door here, end of the hall, last door on the right."

As I reached the door of his office, Kruk said, "Oh . . . and I'd like you to stick close to the city for the next several days." I stopped and turned around. Kruk was fiddling with the papers. He looked up at me. I guess that thing he was doing with his mouth was a grin.

Such a card. I left him to masticate on our interview and followed his directions to the office at the end of the hall. I stepped inside. For a moment I thought that it was empty. There was no one behind the desk. Suddenly the door was swinging closed behind me. I turned to see a familiar pair of hazel eyes and a small mouth, all linked up to a nice long pair of legs.

"Mr. Sewell. I'm Detective Kate Zabriskie. It's nice to see you again."

Lady X motioned for me to take a seat.

"I think we need to talk."

CHAPTER 8

Detective Kate Zabriskie stared at me as she spoke on the phone. It had buzzed the moment I took a seat. Her end of the conversation was minimal and terse. Mainly she bobbed her head. "No . . . uh huh . . . right." All the time she held me in the tractor beam of her eyes, as if I might flee the moment she glanced away.

Fat chance.

The conversation ended and she put the phone back down on the cradle.

"How are you Mr. Sewell?" she asked.

"Oh, let's see, I'm fine. You?"

She leaned back in her chair and crossed her arms. "I guess that depends."

"On what?"

"On you."

The great and powerful me. I leaned forward and rested my arms on Detective Zabriskie's desk. I motioned the woman forward as if I had a secret I was sharing and didn't want anyone else to overhear. She leaned in. I hissed.

"What the *fuck* is going on here?"

It startled her. But she recovered instantly. "Fair question. Let me see if I can answer you." She leaned back in her chair again and took a moment to sort her thoughts. "For starters, I'm not Carolyn James. I gather you picked up on that."

"A little dead bird told me."

"I'm very sorry about that. That was stupid of me. It was reckless. I was . . . a little rattled that day."

"Impersonating a soon-to-be suicide can shake a person up. Or at least so I'm told. I've never done it."

"You're angry with me."

Well where should we deliver the new car, Johnny? "Yeah, I think you could say I'm a little out of sorts, Miss—" I double-checked the nameplate on her desk. "Miss Zabriskie. Or if I turn this around will it say something else?"

"No. That's it. Kate Zabriskie. I'll show you my driver's license if you'd like."

"I'll believe you," I said. "Again."

She made a tent of her fingers and brought it to her lips. She was staring hard again. Right through me. More accurately, she was staring at me the way a person does at a half-finished puzzle. It was disconcerting, to say the least.

"Would you mind not staring at me that way?" I asked.

She blinked, snapping out of it. "I'm sorry. I was . . . I was just thinking."

"Well how about just talking? I mean, I hate to say that I think you owe me an explanation, but etc., etc., you owe me an explanation."

"You're right. I do."

"So what's this all about? Why did you tell me that you were Carolyn James? Why did you ask about funeral arrangements? How did you know that she was going to kill herself? What exactly is—"

I cut myself off. I've heard that intelligence can be measured by the time required for synaptic sparks to flare between two seemingly random thoughts. I suddenly felt very synaptically challenged.

"Carolyn James didn't kill herself," I said. "Did she?"

"Why do you say that?"

"Because you *knew* she was going to be dead. Unless you run a damned good psychic hotline in your spare time the only way you could know something like that is by knowing that she was going to be killed."

"Are you suggesting that I killed Carolyn?"

I didn't much care for the poker face that came with that question. But it was the right question.

"I don't know what I'm suggesting," I said cautiously. "But you might be on to something."

Detective Zabriskie lowered her finger tent. Her face softened. So did her voice.

"I was trying to save Carolyn James, Mr. Sewell."

"From killing herself?"

"From being killed."

"Somebody wanted to kill her?"

She nodded. When she spoke, there was no mistaking the sadness in her voice. "They didn't get their chance. Carolyn took care of the problem for them."

The detective redirected her gaze to a water spot up on the ceiling vaguely in the shape of South America. Outside the window directly behind Kate Zabriskie's head a flashing neon sign with burlesque letters reading: "She Feels Guilty" was being hoisted into view. I blinked and it was gone.

I cut into her reverie. "Are you going to explain any of this to me?"

"It's complicated," she said.

I laughed out loud at that. I couldn't help it. Detective Zabriskie went cold on me.

"I said it was complicated, I didn't say it was funny."

"I know it's not funny. Two people I never knew are dead and Napoleon down the hall there has dragged me down here so that he can stick a few pins into me. So I know it's not really funny. That weird stunt you pulled on me, that wasn't funny. But now you're saying it's complicated. *That's* worth a definite chuckle. It had sure as hell *better* be complicated, Detective. What I'd like is for you to uncomplicate it for me."

"Wouldn't you rather just drop it?"

"What do you mean, 'drop it'? You mean, drop it drop it?"

"I mean forget about it. Let it go. Chalk it up as a peculiar week. A *funny* week if you prefer. I'm suggesting that you just file this away as someone else's business, Mr. Sewell, and go on about your life."

I shook my head slowly. "Can't do that, Detective."

"You should."

"Let's say I'm uncommonly curious."

"Let's say you're unwisely curious."

"Okay, doc, let's say that. That's fine. But unwise or not, I'm still curious. And you still owe me an explanation."

"I am trying to keep you from getting involved in something unpleasant," she said tersely.

"Then you should have thought of that before you sashayed into my place of business under the assumed name of a soon-to-be-dead person and asked me to bury you."

"I know I should have, damn it. I was having a *bad day*. Do you know what that is?"

"I think I've read about them."

She slammed her hands down on her desk. "Why are you being so sarcastic?"

"Why are you being so secretive?"

"I'm a cop! It's part of my job!"

"I thought your job was to serve and protect."

The next thing I knew, the woman was on her feet. She snatched up a staple gun from her desk and threw it against the wall. Her face was flashing crimson. A light on her telephone lit up and she picked up the receiver. "No. No problem. Thanks." She slammed the phone down and glared over at me. I kept my trap shut. After all, somewhere in this office this woman had a gun. Kate Zabriskie waited a good ten seconds, maybe more then she measured out her words.

"It *is* my job, Mr. Sewell. That's exactly what it is. And I did a rotten job of protecting Carolyn James, okay? And I don't feel very good about it. Okay? In fact, I feel horrible about it. So now I am trying to protect you and you're not letting me."

"I'm not in any danger."

"That's true. You're not. So how about we keep it that way? How about you let me serve and protect?"

We squared off for another ten seconds of silence. She spoke first.

"Are you going to back out of this, Mr. Sewell?"

"No."

She let out a most unhappy sigh. "Then we need to talk."

I spread my hands. "Voilà."

"Not here. I would prefer that we take our conversation out of this building. Can you meet me . . ." She consulted a desk calendar. "Tomorrow night? Say, six?"

"Six."

"How about we meet at the Museum of Art? Behind Hopkins. They stay open late on Mondays."

"This is to be a cultural date?"

She looked at me coolly. "This is not to be any sort of a date, Mr. Sewell. You're insisting on an explanation. That's what you'll get. Do you know the Cone Collection?"

I nodded.

"Why don't you meet me there. By the big Matisse. The big blue one."

"The big blue Matisse. Six o'clock."

As I got up from my chair a thought occurred to me. "Does Detective Kruk know about your coming to the funeral home?"

Her face was expressionless. "Let's talk about this later."

I headed for the door. She stopped me with a question.

"Did you tell him?"

I stopped and turned back around. "I didn't know it was you. Remember?"

She had once more made a tent of her fingers. "But did you mention anything about a woman posing as Carolyn James?"

I pulled open the door.

"Let's talk about this later."

"Hitch!"

I hadn't even reached the sidewalk. I turned at the sound of my name. A man in a snappy trench coat, open and flapping, was bounding down the steps toward me. Big smile on his face. It was Joel Hutchinson.

We pounded each other's shoulders and swapped a hearty handshake, then each took a step back to assess the ravages of the years.

"You look like hell!"

"You look worse!"

We pounded each other's shoulders again.

"What brings you here," Hutch asked. "Are you finally fessing up to the bull in the bowling alley?"

"Hey, that was you. I only helped you squeeze him into the service elevator, if you recall. Thank you, Mr. Broken Toe."

"I deny everything!"

"Christ, Hutch, you never denied *anything*."

"Well I've changed all that, buddy boy. Now I deny everything. I'm in politics."

I gave him another punch on the shoulder. We men love this sort of pummeling. "Aw, that's a tough break, Hutch. Is there anything I can do to help you out?"

"Very funny, Sewell. Very funny. So how the hell are you doing? I hear you're burying dead people now?"

"They're the best kind, ha-ha."

"And you got married, right? An artist or some such?"

"Extended road test," I said. "We called it quits after a year. How about you? Does the woman exist who can break the back of the mighty Joel Hutchinson?"

"You'll never guess, but she does."

"You're kidding."

"Nope. Her name is Christy. She's got me beaten down, Hitch, and I love it. A mortgage, a couple of cars, two point five children and a golden retriever named Max. It's Have a Nice Day Sweetie and Honey I'm Home. Leave it to goddamn Beaver."

"We're living in an age of miracles, Hutch. That's what I've been hearing."

He laughed. "It must be."

We continued sparring in this fashion awhile longer. I knew Joel Hutchinson from college, Frostburg State, a small gray institution of higher education and advanced beer swilling tucked away in the mountains of western Maryland. Every college has its wild man and Hutch had been ours. Hutch was always up for anything. And he was also brilliant, so his escapades rarely hurt his academic standing. Hutch was one of those guys that you figured would end up either dead, in prison, or conducting the business of his vast empire from a beach somewhere on his very own island. I was a little disappointed to hear that he was now a political flack.

Hutch told me that he was the campaign manager for Alan Stuart, who was Baltimore's police commissioner. The current governor of Maryland was fading into the political sunset, and I had heard rumors that the city's top cop had been considering a run. Hutch confirmed it.

"Alan's announcing tomorrow for the governor's race."

Alan Stuart was a no-nonsense hard-nosed type, a solid law-and-order man. That's about all I knew. Now I knew that Joel Hutchinson was going to be coordinating his campaign for governor. He'd either win by a land-slide or explode in a scandal. Hutch was no middle-grounder, and my bet was that his candidate wasn't either.

"Look," Hutch said, "we'll have to get together sometime. Though to be honest, I don't know when. This campaign will be sucking me under, I'm sure."

"Maybe I'll come in and lick some envelopes for you," I said.

Hutch laughed. "I might take you up on that." He double-pumped my arm. "By the way. What are you doing here anyway?"

"Oh. Nothing." I told him in briefest form that I had recently had some contact with a fellow who had been found murdered in his home this morning. You know, that sort of thing. Hutch nodded thoughtfully.

"That wouldn't be Guy Fellows, would it?"

"Well, yes. It would be him exactly. How did you know that?"

"Just a guess. I was inside just now and I caught some of the talk. It's my job to be nosy. Tennis guy right? Mr. Joe Stud?"

"That's the one."

"And so what's your connection again?"

"None really. I mean, I didn't know him. He showed for a funeral yesterday. We had a little argument. The guy was a hothead. Anyway, the police wanted to hear my version of it. Fellows wasn't talking. Obviously."

Hutch completely missed my joke. He pulled an electronic thingy from his coat pocket and flipped it open. I prepared to be beamed up, but it didn't happen. "Look, Hitch. Are you free tomorrow? I'd really love to catch up." He poked a few tiny keys and pursed his lips as he scanned his thingy. "How about ten-thirty?"

I had no thingy to consult so I rubbed my chin. "Fine."

"You're free?"

"If no one dies, yes."

He gave me a queer look, then got it. "I get it. You're a regular Bob

Hope. So look, do you know Sammy's? Little coffee shop, just north of the courthouse?"

"I'm sure I can find it."

"Meet me there at ten-thirty. We can catch up some more. Then I'll take you to a bona fide political rally. Do you think you can stand the excitement?"

"I'll get to bed early."

Hutch slammed me on the shoulder. "Tomorrow then."

"Tomorrow." I slammed him back.

Hutch headed off down the sidewalk. As he moved, he pulled a little black phone from his pocket and flipped it open. Hutch was all up-to-date, that's for sure. He was well into a conversation by the time he had crossed the street and vanished around the corner.

So I had two appointments for tomorrow. Sammy's and the big blue Matisse.

I wondered for a moment if I should pop back into the police station and ask Detective Kruk if they had chosen a funeral home to handle the arrangements for Guy Fellows. But I decided that might look to be in poor taste.

CHAPTER 9

Trouble was brewing in *Our Town*. It was coming in the form of a triangle, that most time-honored chestnut of romantic bliss and woe. In this case, however, the thing was twisting into something more closely resembling a rhombus.

It should come as no surprise that my ex-wife was in the middle of it. Young Michael Goldfarb, the nice Jewish boy who was playing George Gibbs, was smitten. Michael had been in several Gypsy productions already. Anyone familiar with Michael's earnest but hopelessly wooden acting style could have spotted the depth of his infatuation immediately upon observing his first read-through of the play's soda fountain scene. The soda fountain scene is the falling-in-love scene and Michael Goldfarb aced it. Or at least he oozed it. Julia sat center stage in Pocahontas braids, her elbows on a sawhorse representing the soda fountain counter, sucking air through a straw while Michael Goldfarb melted all over her. Julia had steadfastly refused to make eye contact with the smitten boy, which only served to stoke his fires. The more disinterestedly Julia cast her black eyes where Michael wasn't looking, the more eagerly he had bobbed and weaved in his attempts to trap her gaze. The result was a very peculiar dance between the two, effusive versus elusive. It absolutely shot the scene all to hell. It's not supposed to be about lust. But of course our Zen director did nothing about it. And why should he? He was in love as well. Not with Julia, but with Julia's erstwhile Romeo.

"He's marvelous, isn't he?" Gil whispered breathlessly from his director's station in the ninth row. "Have you ever seen someone emote so?"

The answer was yes, and he was sitting in the director's station in the ninth row in near ecstasy.

To complete our unhappy rhombus, it was becoming apparent that Libby Maslin, the medical transcriptionist who was playing the part of George Gibbs's mother had also crossed the line and was panting over the young man who was portraying her son. Ah, theater. Where hormones come to play.

"What has he got that I ain't got," I asked Julia during a break in rehearsal. Her answer was extraordinarily direct.

"His virginity."

"*What?* How do you know that?"

Julia leveled me with a look. "Trust me on this. I know them when I see them."

"Well, he's certainly eager to lose it."

She sighed. "I know. He is."

"Jules, you look sad. I would have thought you go for this sort of thing. In fact I *know* you go for this sort of thing."

"I just can't right now, Hitch." She was clearly frustrated. "I know it sounds ass-backwards, but I just don't have the energy or the time to sit up on the pedestal while Michael Goldfarb adores the living hell out of me. Do you have any idea how much whimpering at my feet that poor boy would subject himself to if I took his silly cherry? Flowers and phone calls and bad poems and sweet little gestures every five minutes."

"I never did any of that."

"No. You're a much more practical romantic."

"If that makes any sense."

"It doesn't. But that's what you are. Or at least you were. I think there might be a new you emerging. I haven't decided."

Libby Maslin was crossing the stage just then holding a paper cup in each hand. She found Gil and Michael seated on the lip of the stage, discussing Michael's subtext no doubt. Libby stood there like a faithful hound until Michael finally noticed her. She handed him one of the paper cups. Gil gave her a look like a sour prune.

"I'm staying out of all that," Julia said. "I'm too old for it. Frankly, I wish I had said no to Gil in the first place."

"We're ego gluttons, Julia. Admit it."

"I know. But I can't understand why sex doesn't take care of that."

"It's too private. Too one-on-one. You need the adoring crowd. Speaking of which."

Michael Goldfarb had left his little confab with Gil Vance and was approaching us. He stopped in front of Julia. He said nothing. He just stood there looking at her. If I say it was creepy, I'm saying the truth. Julia turned to me and made a shoulder-shrugging face. She looked preposterously sexy in those double braids.

"I could lead this one over a cliff." To Michael she said, smiling brightly, "Michael? Hello, dear. Would you like to follow me over a cliff?"

He didn't say no, he didn't say yes. Out from behind his back came a box of chocolates.

"They're kosher," he said.

Julia's eyebrows ascended. "Meaning?"

"They've been blessed by a rabbi."

Julia opened the box and held it out to me. "Do you want one, Hitch? They've been blessed by a rabbi."

I picked a chocolate out of the box and turned it around in my hands. Somewhere out there a rabbi actually blesses boxes of chocolates. It's almost too much. What a big beautiful world. Sometimes.

I rolled out of bed, walked Alcatraz around and around the block, then headed downtown.

Sammy's Coffee Shop on Calvert Street couldn't give a damn for the late twentieth century. It especially couldn't give a damn for its industrial solvents and cleaning products, the ones which might have managed to eat through the decades of ground-in grit and soot sealed into its linoleum floors and tiny tabletops in a permanent dead-dishwater patina. Apparently Sammy also keeps his wait staff sealed in a time vault. Beehives in hair nets, eyeglasses on chains and faces like those repellent little troll dolls that were once so inexplicably popular. Sammy himself mans the counter, a disagreeable old guy dragged along by a toothpick. The younger version of his face, seemingly sucking the same toothpick, can be seen in the several hundred black-and-white photographs tacked up all around the place, posing with the various celebrities and politicos and mobsters who have dallied with acid indigestion at Sammy's over the years.

Hutch pointed out Police Commissioner Alan Stuart's photograph. It was hung on one of the side walls.

"When he wins the election, Sammy will move it nearer to the cash register. That's your prime real estate."

"Right up there next to Cher," I said. "That would be peachy."

We were seated at one of the tiny tables. I had gone to put a matchbook under one of the short legs to keep the table from wobbling and had found another matchbook there already. The Pep Boys. Manny, Moe and Jack. All your automotive accessory needs. My dad had voiced a few of their commercials way back when. Our waitress came over to take our orders. Late breakfast for each. She fetched a coffeepot that had been sitting on the burner since the Hoover administration and filled us up. I took a sip and asked Hutch how he was so sure his man was going to take the election.

"He's it," Hutch said. "There is no other choice. Look who the Democrats are putting up. Spencer Davis?"

"Didn't he once have a blues band?"

"*That* Spencer Davis would be a better choice. At least he could keep them grooving. Nah, this guy is a noodle. He's the district attorney. He's got a little Kennedy complex."

"You mean members of his family keep dying tragically in between sex scandals?"

Hutch laughed. "Not quite. But he comes from money like that. He spends all his energies propping up the poor. Thinks he's the next Bobby. Sounds swell, I know. But we're not electing a social worker, we're electing a governor. Davis thinks on a single track. Flip the power from the haves to the have-lesses as often as you can and you've reset the balance. That's his whole agenda. That's not justice, it's payback politics. It's two wrongs make a right. But they don't. We learned that in kindergarten. Everything you need to know, right? Spencer Davis is a good-looking rich boy, everybody's chum. He thinks that the noblest form of political behavior is slumming. I'm sorry, but in politics especially I just don't buy the do-gooder act. He's pretending he's something he's not. Dress it up any way you like, but I still call that dishonest."

It was quite a nice speech, except that it didn't say anything about why Alan Stuart's shit didn't stink.

"And your man?" I asked. "He invented sliced bread?"

"My man invented the means of protecting it, which is ultimately just as important. Look, Alan Stuart is a tough, edgy son of a bitch, you're not going to hear me pretend otherwise. He can turn on the charm when he wants to, just like Spencer Davis, but he rarely feels the need to. Alan likes to mix it up with people. He's a head-knocker. Unlike Davis, you can never be sure which heads he's going to be knocking together from one day to the next. That's what makes him so effective. He's multidimensional. He just wants to solve problems, period. He doesn't want to be your friend, he just wants to solve the problem. You've seen what he has done as police commissioner. He gets his man. It's pretty basic. And he instills that ethic in his soldiers. People are wary of Alan. They know that they'd better play it straight around him because he's always carrying his big club. Spencer Davis is a dinner guest. Alan Stuart killed the steer. That's the difference."

Our food arrived. My two little eggs and two sausages looked sort of paltry against Police Commissioner Stuart's fabled steer. But then I wasn't running for governor. Hutch was emptying a bottle of ketchup onto his home fries. Without looking up he changed the subject.

"So now what's all this about you and this Guy Fellows character again?"

I took a bite of sausage. Burned the tip of my tongue.

"It's nothing. Like I said. He got a little unruly at his friend's funeral and I got in the way of his fist."

"He hit you?"

"I got him under control."

"And then you went off the next day and whacked him, huh?"

"That's the whole story."

"But seriously, the police don't think you had anything to do with it, do they?"

"They're just doing their job. Asked me a hundred questions. Actually, the same dozen questions a hundred times."

"Whose funeral was it?"

"A lady friend of his. Apparently he had a lot of lady friends."

"Is that so?"

"So I gathered."

"Gathered? From who?" Hutch hadn't touched his food, simply made a bloody mess out of his home fries. His fork was dangling from his clenched hands like a pendulum.

"A gardener at the country club, since you ask. But since you ask, why are you asking? I mean, why are you so interested in this, Hutch?"

Hutch shrugged, then stabbed his home fries again. "I don't know. Just curious about you fighting with someone you've supposedly never met."

"*Supposedly?* You don't believe me?"

"I believe you. I'm sorry. Bad choice of words. I guess I'm jumpy. Big day. Let's drop it."

The waitress brought us our check. Hutch reached across the table to stop me from going for my money. "Expenses," he said, reaching for his wallet.

"I don't know, Hutch. Wouldn't that suggest a tacit approval of your candidate on my part?"

"If I could buy a vote for two eggs and a coffee, I'd bring this baby in w-a-y under budget."

"I also had two sausages," I reminded him.

He grinned. "Pork. The politician's lollipop."

Hutch and I left the coffee shop to head over to City Hall Plaza. At the corner a bum was leaning against a lamppost. I didn't know they still did that. I gave him a dollar.

"Why do you do that?" Hutch asked as we jaywalked across the street. "Don't you believe in evolution?"

"Sure. We're all descended from the flounder, but what does that have to do with anything?"

"I mean survival of the fittest. Rising to the challenges. Not feeding off of others who have done it."

"Hutch, I gave a bum a buck. It doesn't hurt me, it might help him. If Darwin were down on his luck I'd toss him a George too. The guy looked hungry."

"You think he's going to spend your dollar on a sandwich?"

"It's his dollar now. I'm not going to tell him how to spend it. What am I, the State Department?"

"I just get tired of those people."

We had reached the other side of the street. In front of us was City Hall Plaza. And we were not alone. News vans were illegally parked at odd angles, their dish antennas popping from the roofs like . . . well, like dish antennas. A crowd of several hundred was either gathered or milling, depending on your spin. It was the lunch hour. The weather was perfect, a deep blue sky overhead, a half dozen perfect clouds, shirtsleeve temperature. A balmy breeze was circulating through the crowd like a congenial warm-up act.

Hutch led me around the periphery of the plaza, over to the steps of City Hall. This was where the speech would take place. The camera crews and the reporters were already in place, given special vantage by an arrangement of blue police barricades. I stood at the edge of the barricade while Hutch wandered off, chatting up the media folk and handing out what I assumed were copies of the upcoming speech. I watched as Hutch shot the breeze for a few minutes with a small, attractive woman. It was one of our newer TV news reporters, Mimi Wigg. Ms. Wigg came over from Cleveland about a year ago, and I understand Cleveland was still pissed about it. As I heard it, Mimi Wigg was being groomed to share the anchor desk with Jeff Simons, and very possibly take it over after Simons retired. Simons was our venerable and far-and-away most popular TV news anchor. He'd been reading news off the TelePrompTer to the citizens of Baltimore for nearly twenty years. He was only in his late fifties, but he had apparently been suffering some health problems in recent months. Also, there was the issue of Simons's recent face-lift (undertaken over the protest of station management), which in conjunction with his trademark cowlick had suddenly—literally overnight—given him the appearance of a ventriloquist's dummy. The public's discomfort was showing in the ratings, which had been flaking away ever since Simons's varnished new face made its appearance. Mimi Wigg, on the other hand, was younger by thirty years and her skin was still supple. Small looking on television, in person she was downright puny. Her shoulders were about the width you'd pull your dental floss. Her hair—which looked to be the heaviest part of her body—was a sort of cranberry-blackberry concoction. I really don't mean any disrespect, but the woman had a noticeably large head as compared to the birdbone frame on which it was anchored. Maybe that's what made her so perfect for TV news. Her huge fake smile was one of her other big assets. She was thrashing Hutch with it mercilessly as he happily kissed up to her over by her news van.

Hutch finally finished his sweatless little chore and came back over to me. He handed me a copy of the speech.

"You seem to have a good rapport with the press," I noted.

"Pretty good, yeah, for the most part. We feed each other. Or off each other, if you're cynical. But I'll tell you, it's all pretty thin. Today's friend is tomorrow's shithead. If they catch even a whiff of something that doesn't smell quite right, they're on the air with it in a heartbeat holding their noses and saying 'P-U, something *stinks.*' "

I noted that some people would call that reporting. Hutch shrugged the point away.

"The concept of objectivity is a farce."

"That's a pretty hard view," I said.

"I don't have any illusions, Hitch. Only saints and martyrs are truly objective. Take a look at our press corps over there. Do you see any saints or martyrs?"

No, I most certainly did not. I saw big guys shouldering cameras like they were bazookas and crackly crisp reporters preening in preparation for their stand-up. Mimi Wigg was on her tiptoes, looking into her news van's door mirror and poking her fingernails into her hair as if it were a balloon she was attempting to puncture.

"We're in the same dance," Hutch went on. "It's just a matter of who thinks they're leading."

Mimi Wigg came down off her toes. Turning in the direction of her cameraman, she threw her head back and ran her small hands down along the back of her skirt, over her cute little rear end.

"That one definitely thinks she's leading," Hutch remarked. He glanced down at the speech in his hands. "Look, I have to go hit a few points with Alan. You can stick around, right?"

"Sure."

"Great. I'll find you."

He took off. In another few minutes, several dozen uniformed policemen and policewomen moved up into position halfway up the steps of City Hall. They formed a solid blue line on either side of a podium and stood there erect, staring off at the horizon. Two dozen police officers. Earning time and a half for the special duty. Add that to the eggs and sausage and already the Stuart campaign seemed a little fiscally flabby. And the guy hadn't even announced yet.

Then Alan Stuart appeared at the podium and announced. I had seen him before on television, at the hospital bedsides of wounded cops or bathed in minicam lights at the scene of a shooting. Unlike many people you see from television, he actually looked larger in person, though this might have partially had to do with the placement of the podium, several steps higher than the phalanx of police officers. In any case, the man knew how to fill a suit. And he knew how to deliver a speech. He sounded very little like a seasoned politician and very much like a slightly pissed off citizen. However, he wasn't taking the populist route. Spencer Davis had already carved out that niche. Alan Stuart came across as a solid powerful man who had grown weary of waiting for others to do the right thing.

Every good political speech includes a catchy little refrain that the candidate can come back to over and over. He (or she) needs a place where he (or she) can hammer his (or her) fists into the air and against the podium. Alan Stuart's chant was eloquent and blunt. "Enough already!" I could already see the bumper stickers. I mean, I could *literally* see them. Several of Hutch's minions were scurrying about the crowd handing out red, white and blue bumper strikers that read just that. "Enough Already/Stuart for Governor." The candidate stood on the steps of City Hall, flanked by that impressive display of law and order, and offered himself up to get the goddamn job done. "Enough already!" he bellowed. After a few rounds he was receiving affirmative responses back from some in the crowd (though they could have been plants). It was the perfect chant. The sound bite was in the can. Hutch could be proud.

Politically speaking, I'm either jaded or apathetic, if there's even a difference anymore. About halfway through the speech, *I* had had enough already. This guy was solid and square-jawed handsome, manly enough to feel comfortable using a pair of half-glasses to read his speech. Alan Stuart was well on his way to becoming William Holden. Except that something about him irritated me (William Holden never irritated me, except in *Sabrina*). Maybe it had something to do with Hutch and the hard slant he seemed to take about the common folk and the little people and all that. Yes. I decided that was it. Both Hutch and his candidate delivered their message with crystal clarity. The message was that their moral bulldozer was already idling off to the side and it was only a matter of fitting on their hard hats and climbing up behind the wheel. *You Have Been Warned.*

I folded Alan Stuart's speech into a paper airplane and launched it into the cheering crowd.

Goddamn it, it flew beautifully. I believed I was looking at the next governor.

CHAPTER 10

I was late in meeting Detective Kate Zabriskie by the big blue Matisse. An emergency had come up at the office. Actually, not an emergency. A dead guy. Kind of embarrassing, really. One of those situations involving ropes and plastic bags and having sex all by yourself that is supposed to generate a simply incredible feeling. Maybe it did, but in this case it also generated a fatal oxygen loss, so on balance how good could it really have been? Anyway, I had to handle the preliminaries with the guy's parents (you can imagine how comfortable *that* was) and so I was running a little late.

Kate was sitting on an oversized ottoman in the center of the gallery browsing though the museum's pamphlet about the Cone sisters. She looked up as I approached. She looked disappointed.

"I was hoping you wouldn't show."

"That's novel. A gal who wants to be stood up. You could be drummed out of the sisterhood if this gets out."

"I was hoping you had changed your mind, that's all."

"Changed it for what?" I quipped.

Kate Zabriskie showed me a half-inch space between her thumb and finger. "That's how much patience I have for your wisecracks right now."

She stood up and waggled the pamphlet at me. "Do you know about these women? They're fascinating."

"The Cone girls? Yes, I know all about them. My ex-wife is a painter. She forced me to kneel at the altar of the Cones. A regular pair of fairy godmothers."

I took the pamphlet from her and glanced at it. There was Etta Cone seated atop an elephant, looking ridiculous.

"There's something about a woman in a pith helmet, isn't there?"

The former Lady X pointed at the huge Matisse. "What do you think of that?"

It was a huge canvas, about a fifteen-foot square, ninety percent of it simply plain flat blue. A pair of black lines snaked vertically down the middle, managing to give the unmistakable impression of a woman in a gleeful dance twirl. Something most nearly resembling a fried egg appeared to be standing in for a flower. I told the lady that I was duly impressed.

"I used to come here a lot as a kid," Kate said wistfully, still staring up at the canvas. "I grew up in Hampden, so it wasn't much of a walk. You know Hampden, don't you? It's a world away from the place."

Small square houses, plaster elves out front, Bud in the fridge, Grandma smoking cigarettes at the backyard picnic table. Sure, I knew Hampden.

"Hampden's okay," I said. "Unless you're a snob. You're not a snob, are you, Detective?"

"You can call me Kate. And no, I'm not a snob. I've got nowhere to stand to be a snob from. I'm a first-generation Polish Jew from a rock-solid working-class neighborhood. I've got a name that people either misspell or laugh at, or both. My father was a world-class drunk and my mother was a world-class victim. I work at a job where half my time is spent with criminals, lowlifes and lawyers, if you can tell the difference. Now if you can figure out where I might manage to shove all that aside and find the nerve to be a snob I'll give you five bucks and a blow job." She added swiftly, "That's a cop phrase, Mr. Sewell. Don't get any ideas."

My grin, I'm sure, was practically cracking my face. "Oh now you're going to *have* to call me Hitch."

Kate leveled me with those hot hazel eyes. "Look, I didn't come here to talk about me."

I stepped up to her and brushed a nonexistent piece of lint off her shoulder.

"Lady, I beg to differ."

We left the big blue Matisse and made our way slowly though the rest of the Cone sisters' modernist acquisitions: Gauguin's *Woman With A Mango*, Degas's bronze ballerina, Picasso's various crooked people . . . The Monday night crowd was fairly sparse. A few students from the Maryland Institute of Art sat cross-legged on the floor in front of Monet's nearsighted studies of cathedrals, sketching in their notebooks; couples walked slowly around the galleries, muttering softly to each other; there was a colorless man in a gray suit who appeared to have gotten glued to the floor in front of one of Gauguin's Tahiti paintings. The rooms were climate controlled, completely without shadows and hermetically quiet. The security guards rocked on their heels and stared off into the middle distance.

Kate and I floated from room to room, stopping randomly in front of the various paintings. Kate L-shaped her arms to rest her chin in the cup of her hand as she studied the works. I like this stuff too, but I was more interested in taking a half step back so that I could spy on the former fake Carolyn James from Hampden by way of Kraków. My pretty detective was definitely in her civvies tonight. She was wearing a sage green houndstooth suit, tailored to a T, a jaunty little sort of Edwardian flair to the jacket. Her blouse was cream-colored, with little soft buttons the shape of televisions, and she was wearing heels, albeit half heels. Not the sort of getup for chasing robbers. With a blush that wouldn't quite go away and all sorts of interesting things happening around the eyes, it was evident that Kate Zabriskie had fancied some brushwork of her own before coming out to play.

"Are you going somewhere later?" I asked her after we had been soaking up a field of lilies for several minutes. She turned her head and gave me one of those looks that you can't really read. The secret look of women.

"Why do you ask?"

"You look too good to be wasting it on a bunch of paintings or on me, for that matter."

"Well thank you for that." Since she was pre-blushed, I couldn't tell if my compliment had drawn forth any additional color. She added, "In fact I am going somewhere later. I have an obligation."

"God I hope it's not a date. Not if you're using a word like that."

"It's not a date, believe me. It's a fund-raiser. My boss is running for governor. Tonight is his first big bash. All the troops are expected to show. They want a high body count. So to speak."

"Alan Stuart, right? How about that. I was on hand this afternoon when he made his big announcement."

"You were? At City Hall?"

"Yes ma'am." I waggled a finger in her face. "Enough already."

Kate rolled her eyes. "You can say that again."

We moved on. Eventually we were passing the same paintings and busts and sculptures a second and third time. The glued-down man was gone now. So were the Art Institute Rembrandts. Kate and I found ourselves in front of a Cézanne, a gauzy, almost pallid rendering of a Tuscan village wrapped atop a hillside. Some slender pines in the foreground. A hazy tanned sky. Very nice. A place I wouldn't at all mind being. I pictured myself on the neighboring hillside, the one overlooking the scene. I was standing there along with . . . well sure, why not, with Kate Zabriskie. In our dusty paisan garb, gnats darting all around, the chittering of unseen crickets in the heat.

"I've been assigned to the Guy Fellows case."

I was jerked abruptly back to Baltimore. Kate was still looking straight ahead at the painting, though clearly she was not caught up in the crackling sizzle of Cézanne's sun.

"I don't know your profession. Is that good news or bad news?"

"To be honest, I'm not really sure yet. Kruk's been reassigned. He's not real happy about it."

"Why was he pulled off the case?"

Kate shrugged. "Every office has its politics. He was put on a different case. There's no shortage of murders, that's one thing. Still, it was a lousy thing to do. Reassigning always is."

"So now you're the big cheese, eh? They must have faith in you."

"What's that supposed to mean?"

"Just that . . . well, they figure you can solve it."

"Of course, they figure I can solve it. I wouldn't be on the force otherwise." She turned to face me. "Look, pulling Kruk for me doesn't mean they don't have faith in him. Like I said, it's office politics. John Kruk's damn good. He rubs people the wrong way sometimes, but these things aren't a personality contest."

"So am I still a suspect?"

"Frankly, you're a lousy suspect."

"This is what I've been hearing. Not that I mind one bit. So who is? A good suspect, I mean."

"I'd rather not discuss it any further right now."

"Fair enough."

Kate stepped over to a Picasso. "Let me ask you something. You were at City Hall today when Alan announced his candidacy. Did you just happen to be there?"

I told her about running into my old college chum out in front of the police station.

"So you know Joel Hutchinson?" she said.

"I could tell you stories."

"I'm sure you could. Come on. Let's go."

As we started to make our way toward the exit, I broached the subject that we had thus far avoided.

"Speaking of stories, I was under the impression that you were going to be telling me one tonight. About why you were posing as Carolyn James?"

"I know I was. It's just . . . well, I'm not sure exactly where to start."

"Dare I suggest, 'at the beginning'?"

Kate stopped suddenly. She turned and studied my face. Intently.

"That's what I'm beginning to think," she said finally.

Just as suddenly as she had stopped she turned and exited the gallery. I held back—I wanted to watch her legs go back and forth—then I followed.

I caught up to her at the top of the steps out in front of the museum. Halfway down the steps *The Thinker* was still thinking. The stone lions flanking the museum steps continued their silent roars. Over against the cool marble of Neptune, a homeless guy was already nestling in under his newspaper blanket, dreaming no doubt of fishes. The sun was just about down now—a Tang-colored sliver of sky all that remained. A rat ran across the street on its way to Wyman Park as the streetlights flickered on. Monday night in Charm City.

Kate took hold of my arm. "Let's go."

The Peabody Conservatory Library is a jaw-dropping piece of work, a cozy rectangular room that soars up and up and up, wrapped with spectacular wrought-iron walkways at each flight. Narrow aisles lead off each walkway back into the stacks of books. At the dizzying top of it all is the stained glass ceiling, an octagonal moonglow of oyster white glass with chips of dazzling green and blue and blood red all held apiece with hard black spiderings of solder. With a couple of drinks and a squint up at those curlicued railings you can pretty easily call forth an entire New Orleans neighborhood drifting out from the stacks, women in their bandannas and loose cotton dresses resting their arms on the black railings, calling across the square to each other or pointing down at some silly chicanery in the courtyard down below, a pig chasing a dog, or a cop chasing a cat, or maybe just the warm sun slowly chasing shadows out of their corners. I don't know a damn thing about music—and the Peabody Conservatory is a place where they crank out musicians for a living—so I have no idea what kinds of books are up there in the endless stacks. But it's a hell of a room, and it adds more than a little touch of class to whatever function the Peabody trustees happened to rent it out for. It's no cheesy hotel ballroom, that's for sure.

It's where Joel Hutchinson had chosen to throw Alan Stuart's kickoff party.

"None of that populist crap here, eh, Hitch?"

Hutch and I were standing just inside the entrance. The place was abuzz with Alan Stuart's faithful: men and women in their elegant skins. Everyone was smiling and chatting away, being led around the room by their napkin-wrapped drink glasses. Among the glitterati, I recognized Harlan Stillman, senior senator from the Eastern Shore. Senator Stillman was a slow-talking, quick-thinking devil of a politician who had been in the state senate now for something like a hundred and fifty years, give or take a few. Most definitely old-style. A student of cornpone. Still, Senator Stillman was a shrewd and powerful player. His influence was as deep as the proverbial hills. The kind of politician who can get dead men to vote. If Alan Stuart had Harlan Stillman on his side, Spencer Davis had better just get a copy of his résumé on over to Kinko's. The election was over.

I watched as the grand old man slowly loaded his tobacco pipe and got it going. We're a No Smoking Please world these days, but no one was about to tell that to Harlan Stillman. The blonde hourglass attached to his arm was either his date or his granddaughter. I wouldn't have dared to bet which. I complimented Hutch on the little quartet parked off in the corner that was providing the soiree with a classy little soundtrack. "They come with the space," Hutch said. "It's Peabody's little way to plug what they do."

Hutch hadn't been as surprised to see me as I would have thought. With no particular fanfare, he gave my hand a few pumps when I walked into the room.

"Good to see you again, Hitch. You looking for some more free sausage?"

I gave him a ha-ha. But he was already focusing on the lovely woman standing next to me.

"Hello, Kate."

"How are you doing, Joel?"

"I don't get paid to complain. How about you?"

"Besides having my arm twisted to come here? I'm fine."

"You should look at it as a perk," Hutch said.

Kate turned to me. "This is a perk."

"I don't know perks," I remarked. "I'll get a discount on my coffin when the time comes. That's about it."

Hutch grinned at Kate. "There you go. Now isn't this little perk looking better already?"

"Yes, Joel, your party is better than a funeral," Kate said flatly. "I won't argue with you."

Hutch was enjoying this. "Go ahead, Kate, argue with me. It's what you do best. Well, I mean, it's one of what you do best."

"Fuck you, Joel."

And with that, Kate stormed off. That's when Hutch had said, "None of that populist crap here, eh, Hitch?"

My gaze followed Kate. She was aiming straight for the bar. I said to Hutch, "So I take it you two have met."

Hutch laughed as he rolled his eyes. "Kate Zabriskie hates my guts."

"That was kind of my impression."

"It goes way back."

"Gut hating usually does."

"Kate's got a big chip on her shoulder." Hutch waved across the room at someone, I couldn't tell who. "I don't know if you follow the news much, but she got her fifteen minutes about five, six months ago."

I shook my head. Knew nothing about it.

"The short version is, she got some headlines. Hero cop. That sort of thing. She didn't handle it well. Understandable reasons. But that's her business. Anyway, since signing on with Alan I've been trying to get her to go along with a couple of spots. TV. Maybe print. She'd be a real asset."

"Is that right?"

"Sure. Women look up to her. And men want to fuck her."

"I'm glad to see you're choosing your words so carefully."

"Hey, don't get sore, Hitch. You know what I mean."

"You just said what you mean."

"That I did. The thing is, I could do a lot with this hero cop business. It's a good angle. But Kate won't have any of it."

"Maybe she doesn't support Stuart."

"Bullshit. She *adores* Alan Stuart. She's just got her nose out of joint on this thing." He broke off to shake someone's hand, then he went on. "It all became moot anyway. Alan pulled me back. She's a detective now, he reminded me, not a street cop. Her face shouldn't be plastered everywhere, yah, yah, yah."

"That sounds reasonable."

"It is, sure. I didn't argue. But still . . . I'm definitely not on that lady's Christmas list."

"She's Jewish."

"Whatever. You know what I mean. There's bad chemistry there."

"Sad tale."

Hutch pumped another well-heeled paw, steered it off toward the bar, then he turned back to me with a quizzical look on his face.

"So, just what are you doing here with Kate Zabriskie anyway?"

I gave him my best ear-to-ear. "I look up to her."

Hutch snickered. "Yeah. Right."

I spotted Alan Stuart off on the far side of the room. He was working his crowd, listening intently one instant, exploding with a powerful laugh the next. I scanned unsuccesfully for a glimpse of Kate.

I asked Hutch, "Was that guy ever a street cop? I mean, do they really come up through the ranks like that? Somehow I can't picture him in a blue suit swinging a billy."

"Oh absolutely. Alan Stuart was a flatfoot. Started out on the street. Clubbed his way to the top. You're looking at a hardworking self-made man there. And don't think the governorship of Maryland is the end of it. From Annapolis you can practically see the damn White House. It's just over the river. The times are very favorable for a guy like Alan Stuart. This governorship could be just the thing to line him up for the big one."

"Hutch, I don't want to be the wet rag, but isn't your Baltimore city police chief hyperventilating a little here? I mean, the guy just announced yesterday for governor and you're already picking out new drapes for the Oval Office."

"Hitch. Answer me this. Who did Nixon tap to be his veep? A no-name governor from, gee, was it Maryland?"

"You're referring to the guy who failed to pay his taxes and was drummed out of office in disgrace?"

"Alan pays his taxes. I checked." Hutch slapped me on the shoulder. "Look, I have to go and kiss some fanny. The bar's over there. Top-shelf only. Enjoy yourself. I'll catch up with you later. I'm glad you could make it."

He pumped my hand again and then waded off into the crowd. I spotted Jeff Simons, standing next to a bust of Mozart, a semicircle of admirers fanned out in front of him. It's true, he wasn't looking his usual TV-glow self. His trademark cowlick was performing superbly and he was sporting his perpetual tan, but his eyes carried a sort of watery look, certainly not the crystal-clear sparkle of trust and mirth that had kept him at Baltimore's bosom for nearly two decades. I had met the man a number of times. His mother and my aunt are old friends and ruthless cribbage players. The two meet once a week to race each other around the table. Billie and I play, too. That's usually how we decide who takes on the next funeral.

I finally spotted Kate, coming back my way. I met her halfway. She handed me a glass.

"Do you like bourbon?"

"That's damned good detective work. How'd you guess?"

"I didn't, really. It's what I like. I'm drinking vicariously."

Kate was holding a flute, popping with amber bubbles.

"Champagne?" I asked,

"Ginger ale."

She caught me not asking the question that was floating before us. She clinked her glass to mine. "It's one of my rules. No drinking in public places."

"That would make you the exact opposite of a social drinker," I observed.

She took a sip of her ginger ale, keeping her eyes on me. "That would be absolutely correct." The message was clearer than her ginger ale. Subject closed.

We mingled. Kate didn't really seem to know too many of the guests either, except for a few of her colleagues. She caught a couple of "Welcome backs" from her brethren. "I've been on a leave of absence," she explained. She didn't elaborate. I looked up at one point and spotted Detective Kruk, standing near one of the stacks. He was gazing down at the gathering, an unlit cigarette in his mouth. From where I stood it looked as if he had maybe ironed his wrinkles. But apparently there was nothing to be done about that hair. He might have been looking down at Kate and me. I couldn't tell.

Kate was speaking.

"Did Joel explain to you why I was so friendly to him just now?"

"What? Oh. Um . . . no. Well. He told me you wouldn't cooperate with the Stuart for Governor campaign."

We had wandered over by the quartet. I had no idea in hell what they were playing. I just knew that I couldn't tap my toe to it.

"He told you *that*?"

"Yes. Why? Isn't it true?"

"Sure, it's true. But that's not why we don't get along." She took a sip of her ginger ale. "Joel Hutchinson is jealous, pure and simple. Alan . . . Alan took me under his wing, I guess you could say. The phrase you hear is, 'I came up fast.' It's a long story. Bottom line is your college buddy is a control freak. He wants Alan all to himself and for some reason I threaten him."

She took another sip. "Plus he made a pass at me and I told him to buzz off."

"Hutch made a pass at you?"

"Several. Men don't always bounce back so well after they've gotten rejected. Have you noticed?"

"Who says I've ever been rejected?"

"Who says I was saying you had? I only asked if you had noticed."

She gave me one of those looks. Challenging. At least that's what the bourbon in me was saying. But maybe it wasn't a challenging look at all. Maybe, I thought, it's a warning. Maybe she was warning me not to make a pass at her. What a shame. The prospect of completing a successful pass with this off-duty detective was striking me as a fantastic idea. Of course, I didn't even know if she was married, or maybe had a squeeze of her own already. No rings—I had checked earlier—but these days that doesn't always tell the whole story. Anyway, I passed on the pass.

"So, you're telling me that Hutch the family man is a farce."

"Ninety percent of family men are farces," Kate said flatly. "Men are genetically programmed to stray. And to cheat. And to lie. And to—"

"Whoa, whoa, this is my fellow ape you're smearing here. I'm bound by tribal law to defend my own."

"I wouldn't waste your breath."

"Damn it, Detective, you're not going to turn out to be one of those beautiful man-hating types, are you? It's gals like you who really ruin the party."

"No. It's men like Joel Hutchinson who ruin the party. I think the first deadly sin ought to be arrogance. You can trace all the others back to that."

"You didn't answer my question," I said. "Are you a beautiful man-hater?"

Her eyes narrowed with suspicion. But at the same time, crimson rose to her cheeks.

"Are you making a pass at me?"

"I'm just a horny arrogant ape. Programmed to lie, cheat, etc., etc."

"You didn't answer my question."

"And you didn't answer mine."

"It's a draw."

We clinked glasses. God, this was all getting too cute.

Two surprises awaited me at the party. Surprise number one appeared some half hour or so after this little buzza-buzza about the transgressions and transparencies of all men. I was three bourbons in and only a few frilly snacks down, so the evening had begun to take on a warm fuzzy glow. The women were all growing prettier and the men were all becoming much less handsome and charming than myself.

In walked a fellow about as handsome and charming as myself. I vaguely recognized him, the way you recognize a celebrity on the street simply as someone familiar, before actually making the ID. This guy was roughly my contemporary, maybe a few years younger. And about fifteen million dollars richer. He was a good-looking Joe with an easy smile. Of course, give me fifteen million dollars and I'll bet my smile will be easy too. He was as dashing in his tux as James Bond himself. I muttered to Kate, "Be careful, his bowtie is really a camera." She gave me a sideways look like I was crazy.

"Who is that," I asked.

She answered, "Peter Morgan."

Of course. Peter Morgan. Of the Baltimore County Morgans. The racehorse Morgans. The new opera house Morgans. The railroad money Morgans. This town has Morgans coming out of its ears. Granddaddy Morgan had been the last of the family to have had to actually roll up his sleeves and squeeze money out of sweat. He had made his bundle in the early part of the century working on the railroads all the livelong day, and his success had left most of the subsequent Morgans happily strumming on the old million-dollar banjo ever since. However, I did recall hearing or reading somewhere that this particular Morgan, this dapper devil who had just come into the room, was one of the ones who still kept a hands-on involvement with the family business. While most of us run our little train sets around the Christmas tree, Peter Morgan ran his around the whole country. At least a goodly portion of it. Interstate transport of goods. It can bring in a few extra bucks. All this and good looks too. Gee whiz. Peter Morgan was a pretty high-profile man-about-town. Known to be something of a lady-killer, his privileged arm was custom-built for wrapping around beautiful women.

And a particularly beautiful woman was wrapped around it this evening. Her dress was a form-fitting off-the-shoulder number that hugged her hourglass figure from her ample breasts to just below the knees, with a side split that offered a generous peekaboo of commendable thigh. The dress was an aquamarine color, with a print that featured large fishes and seahorses randomly aswim. Her hair was up in a bun and there was a silly tiara perched atop it, obviously glass and glue. Long shimmery earrings that must have set the gal back a good five and a half bucks dangled from her ears. And she was barefoot. I heard a guy make a crack about her as she and Peter Morgan swept into the room.

"Looks like Peter's got himself a free spirit weirdo."

I jabbed the guy gently in the ribs. "Careful there," I said. "That's my free spirit weirdo ex-wife you're talking about."

Julia had come to the ball.

The pair created a nice little stir. What percentage of the buzz came from the simple fact of Morgan being present and how much from the barefoot bohemian on his arm was difficult to tell. But the combination was killer. Money and art. There's something undeniably lusty about it.

Julia was just as surprised to see me there as I was to see her. She gave me the Mae West once-over.

"Nice suit."

"So this is the man you've told me so little about." She introduced me to Peter Morgan. "She's been keeping you a secret," I said to the millionaire.

Julia gave a fake blush. "Well, you know, I don't like to brag." She leaned in to me and stage whispered for all to hear, "He's loaded!"

I shook hands with the loaded man. Solid grip. He looked me dead in the eye. Seemed friendly enough. I didn't like him.

"Nice to meet you, Hitchcock."

"Please," I vamped, "call me Hitchcock."

"Hitch and I were married briefly," Julia offered. "It wreaked havoc on our friendship, so we hurried out of it." She cocked her head and gave me her Audrey Hepburn smile. Everything but the batting lashes.

"Thank you for sharing that lovely story." I introduced Julia and Peter Morgan to Kate.

"Like Zabriskie Point," Peter Morgan observed.

Julia fished. "And that would be . . . ?"

Morgan explained that it was a place in Death Valley. Julia's eyes flashed. She was clearly having fun. "Oh, are you one of the Death Valley Zabriskies?"

"Kraków," Kate said in perfect deadpan. "By way of Hampden." She turned to Morgan. "Blue blood. Blue collar. We're quite a diverse little crowd, aren't we?"

Morgan actually blushed at this. I guessed it was a little sore spot, his being filthy rich and socially superior. Who would have guessed?

"Where are your shoes, Julia?" I pointed at her toes. "You have no idea when they last cleaned this floor."

Morgan answered for her. "Hell, she wanted to wear flippers. I'm serious. To go with her dress. They're out in the car."

"You should see this car, Hitch," Julia said. "It's the size of a small country." She touched her fingers to her tiara. "You like?"

"Chintzy. Nice. You've got a whole Cinderella-at-the-ball motif going on here. Except you've lost both your slippers."

"Funny. Isn't this a great dress? I found it in that vintage flophouse on Aliceianna Street and I fell in great big love with it."

"I think it's pretty," Kate offered. Julia smiled at this.

"Thank you. Yours too."

"Mine's not supposed to be pretty," Kate said. "But thank you."

I didn't want to be left out of this, so I said to Morgan, "Hey, you look swell too."

Morgan gave me sort of a sideways snicker. He took hold of Julia's arm.

"It was nice to meet you both," he said. "We're going to circulate."

"Mill," Julia corrected, mugging a big face. She couldn't resist a thoroughly silly over-the-shoulder wave as Morgan tugged her away. A seahorse wiggled on my ex-wife's fanny as she sashayed off. Alan Stuart had spotted them and was making his way over.

"Would you mind if we left now?" Kate said. "I'm looking at those railings up there and beginning to imagine throwing people off of them." Kate gave me a terse look. "That's the sign of a girl no longer having a good time, don't you think?"

As we started for the door, surprise number two made her appearance. She came into the room and made her way directly over to Alan Stuart and was immediately drawn under his arm as he kissed the offered cheek. She was blonde, an extremely pretty blonde woman. Former debutante. Perfect teeth. Perfect poise.

"She looks familiar," I observed.

"That's Alan's wife. She's another Morgan," Kate said. "Amanda Morgan. Amanda Morgan Stuart. She's Peter Morgan's twin sister."

"Small world."

Amanda Stuart was performing with all of the grace and charm to be expected of her in her role as the wanna-be next first lady of the State of Maryland.

"She doesn't look like her brother," I remarked. "Except maybe in the teeth."

"Boy/girl twins aren't identical."

"She does look familiar though," I said for the second time. I was certain now that I had seen her before, but I just couldn't place it.

"Well, she looks a little like Grace Kelly, doesn't she? Maybe that's it."

Amanda Stuart was laughing at something that her husband had just said. Even across the room I could hear the laugh, like the tinkle of shattering crystal.

That was it exactly. Grace Kelly. Crossing in front of me and disappearing into the Baltimore Country Club's mansion. A cool sliver of ice on a warm day. One half of a recent doubles pair.

Not the half so recently stabbed to death.

Kate Zabriskie decided to become a cop on an evening in July when she was twelve years old. It was one of Baltimore's typically miserable Julys, a choking humidity, thick and doughy from the very moment you fall out of bed in the morning until you finally collapse back into it at night.

The houses in Hampden sit pretty close to one another, so it could have been any one of several neighbors who called the police to complain about the racket next door. Len Zabriskie's naturally short temper was popping off like Chinese firecrackers in the hopeless July heat. Kate would not be able to recall with any true accuracy what flashpoint events of that particular evening set her father off. Len Zabriskie was apparently a simple man, about as complex as a square box. There didn't require any intricate pathway from cause to effect. Born stupid and raised dull, he maintained a fairly primal approach to life and especially to life's obstacles and irritations. Translation: He beat the living crap out of his wife and daughter if they so much as sneezed funny.

Kate didn't entertain me with a wealth of details, so I won't either. When the police came into the little house this particular July evening—not their first visit—Kate's mother was unconscious on the floor, a tiny red river making its way from the nasty cut on her head to a newly forming pool on the carpet. Len Zabriskie was sitting on a chair in the little linoleum kitchen, crying his eyes out and refusing to give up to the police the dark-haired twelve-year-old daughter he was bear-hugging so hard she could barely breathe.

"That was his version of being tender," Kate said ruefully. "Hugging me so tight that he literally cracked one of my ribs. I heard it pop. So did he. It only made him squeeze me tighter."

Len Zabriskie had no intention of releasing his daughter as he sat there blubbering and babbling. Kate implored him to let her go, and she implored the two police officers to help her. But it was when they grabbed at the big man's arms that he had crushed his daughter tighter and cracked her tiny rib. So it was a standoff. The older of the two cops went back into the front room to tend to Kate's mother, and the younger cop pulled up a chair—setting it some five feet away from Len Zabriskie—and began to taunt him. In a calm, steady monotone the young police officer called Len Zabriskie every name in the book, as if he were reading from a list of one thousand insults. He held a steady cadence as he pounded away against the man's character, race, nationality, sexual proclivities, the whole seven, eight and nine yards. Whether it was in the relentless hammering itself or whether the young man finally hit upon a specific assault that inflamed Len Zabriskie to the erupting point, Kate honestly doesn't know. What she does know is that suddenly she was being dumped on the floor and her father was all over the young cop, one hand on his throat, the other slamming into his face. "Run!" the officer managed to gurgle, but Kate had remained right where she had been dropped, transfixed and horrified that the stranger coming in off the street had offered himself up as red meat to her rabid-dog father.

Len Zabriskie put a pretty good beating on the young policeman before the cop's partner came rushing in and handled the big man with his billy club. A little more bad dancing among the three of them and Len Zabriskie was finally facedown on the floor, his hands cuffed behind his back. The young cop's face was already swelling up. His mouth had filled with blood. With a magician's move, he reached into his mouth and came out with a large shiny tooth, which he held up for the startled Kate to see. "What do you think this will fetch from the tooth fairy?" he asked her, giving up a great big bloody smile. Kate sprang to her feet, leaped over her father lying there on the floor and, ignoring her own cracked rib, threw herself into a hug with the young hero.

And that's one of the ways that cops are born.

Kate told me her story at the Screaming Oyster. After leaving the Alan Stuart love fest at the Peabody Library, I had confronted her on the front steps.

"Something is not kosher in Pickleville. Are you going to explain what's been going on here or am I going to have to beat it out of you."

Bad choice of words, I know. But I didn't know it then. Kate had followed me in her car down to the Screaming Oyster.

"Are you okay driving?" she asked. "I'd hate to have to pull you over if you start weaving."

"Are you carrying handcuffs?"

"Drive," she said. "I'll follow."

I had originally suggested we go to a coffee shop, but Kate said no to that. "I'm a cop. It would be like going to the office." Good point.

The Oyster was awash with the regular crowd. Tony Marino was keeping his stool at the end of the bar from floating away. Edie Velvet was parked beneath the hanging dinghy. Sally and Frank were fricking and fracking behind the bar. The TV was on, the jukebox was playing, the pinball machine by the door was ringing and clicking like a spastic robot. Bookstore Bill and Al the video guy—two more S.O.S. regulars—were at their usual table, arguing as usual. The day these two stop disagreeing on everything is to be Earth's final day, I'm convinced. Having grabbed a beer and a lemonade, I had steered Kate over to a table in the rear of the bar. Once we sat down, the noise cloud remained just above our heads, allowing us to have our little chat without resorting to too much yelling.

Kate had to work at not letting her story catch in her throat. I suspected it wasn't a tale that she spun on a regular basis. Her voice was low and largely without inflection as she described the abrupt and violent ways of her father. When she got to the part about little Kate leaping over her father to hug her hero, the moment when she decided in that place beneath conscious knowing that she was going to do this same sort of work when she grew up, Kate leaned back in her chair and ran her hand through her hair. She stubbed out her umpteenth cigarette and pushed the overflowing glass ashtray away from her.

"I'm going to quit one day," she said.

"If you don't get them, they'll get you."

Kate frowned. "I'm not talking about smoking. I'm talking about quitting my job."

"Your job? You'd give up being a cop?"

"I've lost my edge. I became a cop because a cop rescued me from my father. It was such a . . . I don't know, such a noble thing to do. 'Don't hit her, hit me.' That's how he handled it. God, what a hero, you know what I mean? And I thought, this is what the world needs, more people like that. More people who will stick out their own necks for others. That's nuts, isn't it."

"What's nuts about it?"

"Wanting to be someone who volunteers to take somebody else's punches? You don't think that's a little misguided?"

"It's very Christ-like," I noted.

"I'm Jewish."

"So was he."

She pulled out another cigarette. "You want to hear some more stories?"

"Do you know any bedtime stories?"

She lit her cigarette and let the match drop to the floor. She blew her smoke just over my head. "Only if you want bad dreams."

When Kate Zabriskie met Charley Russell he was already a detective. Kate was still a uniformed police officer.

"I was a patrol car cop. A glorified traffic director. I handed out parking tickets and speeding tickets, I told the frat boys at Johns Hopkins to turn their stereos down. In between all that excitement I also handled my share of bad guys. Mainly muggers and petty thieves. The occasional murderer. I ordered men twice my size to put their hands on the hood and spread 'em." She paused and looked over at me. "No wisecracks?"

I shrugged. Too easy. She went on. She told me that she made her arrests, offered her testimony in court, helped to add a layer or two of scum to that which was already festering there behind bars.

She also got to realize her dream. She got to barge into houses and apartments in the greater Baltimore metropolitan area and play the hero for women and children whose husbands and daddies were beating up on them.

"It felt great at first," she told me. "All noble and righteous and powerful."

But as the domestic disturbance calls continued, became in fact all too frequent, Kate realized that for all of her intervening there was always going to be another brute across town somewhere harassing his supposed loved ones. She was a blue Band-Aid at best. She tried to remind herself that this was a job that she had to take one day at a time. "Step between just one ballistic jerk and his human punching bag and you've done a good thing. I knew that." She knew that the young cop who had poked his chair into her father's cage and drawn his wrath had done a good thing, a hell of a good thing. He might even have saved her life. And yet Kate found herself growing more and more despondent.

"I didn't want to be the cavalry anymore. Coming to the rescue was fine, but it was too little too late. Mop-up work. I would see the expressions on the faces of those women and children and it was always the same expression. It was gratitude, sure. But it was mainly this scared, shell-shocked look that said, 'Where the hell have you been all this time?' It was 'Thanks, but the damage has been done.' And I understood that. I'd cuff these bastards and I'd wish that somehow I could have done this earlier too, yesterday or a year ago, before the trouble even got started. Before the hitting. Or worse."

Kate finished off her lemonade and slid the glass angrily across the table. "We can't arrest men who badger or belittle their wives or their girlfriends. That's the problem. *That's* where I wanted to stop it. Not after the bruises started to rise. Somehow I'd like to have been able to spot the guys on the street right before they even met their future wives and girlfriends. I wanted to be able to stick my pistol into their face and tell them not to even think about it, buster. It's absurd, I know. But I got real tired of climbing in at the tail end of the problem. It wasn't enough for me.

"Then I met Charley and we started dating. He was a detective. He had started off as a patrolman, like me, then worked his way up. And I'd listen to what he was doing and it sounded a lot better than what I was doing. Detectives get to identify a problem and go after it closer to the source. They don't bust a kid for smoking dope on the corner. They seize shipments at the docks and drag off Mr. Big in cuffs. They get to come into the station and throw the big fish down onto the floor. The stuff you get trophies for. So I decided to become a detective. Of course, it had no real connection with any new ability to head off a wife beater at the pass, or a child abuser. But it just seemed more rewarding overall, trying to root out the nest itself, whatever it was, instead of just slamming the vipers with my club one at a time."

A few tables away, a couple of guys and a girl got up and started playing darts. Kids from the suburbs. Kate glanced over at them, then continued.

"I worked overtime. I stuck my nose into other people's investigations. I made myself available for stakeouts and as backup. In departmental lingo, I kissed the brass butt. That's how you climb the ladder. And making detective is definitely climbing a ladder."

So Kate climbed. She knew it would be a matter of years, but she was okay with that. She and Charley moved in together. "About this same time last year," she said. "May. We got married in late summer.

"We had to hold off on the honeymoon. Charley had just been assigned a case. An industrial waste dumping scam. Bogs for bucks, he called it. He figured it would take several months. But we made our plans. Mexico. It's cheap there and we just wanted to go to a beach someplace and flop down on the sand. We got brochures and looked at them a couple of times a week.

"It was about a month or so after we got married that Charley had to take the case undercover. He insisted on not giving me too many details about what he was up to. That's a smart professional choice when you've got two cops who are sharing the same home. The department encourages that sort of demarcation among its married couples. All I really knew was that basically Charley had to pose as a laborer. The work really knocked him out at first. He'd come home completely beat. He assured me that what he was doing wasn't dangerous. I knew better than to believe him. Still, he said he had complete control over the situation."

Kate's eyes were brimming with tears. They came on without warning. She seemed a little surprised herself, and bit down on her lip and looked away. I started to speak, but she held up her hand.

"I was called in for backup one night, over in Sparrows Point. It was a stakeout at a warehouse and it was going all wrong. Two detectives were pinned down. My partner and I hustled over there. You know my partner. Kruk."

"The golden-haired boy? You were partners?"

"Briefly. Anyway, it was all screwed up. One of the detectives—a guy named Connolly—had been hit in the leg. When Kruk and I got there, Connolly had just gotten outside the warehouse. He was okay. Kruk got to work putting a tourniquet on his leg. I drew my gun and went in. I found Lou, that's the other detective. Lou signaled me down. There was a guy up on a walkway, about thirty feet overhead. He had a barrel or something he was hiding behind. Lou couldn't get a clear shot on him. Basically it was a game of chicken."

The dart players started cheering on each shot. Kate locked onto the action as she continued. Her head didn't move, but her eyes followed each dart as it hit the cork target.

"All of a sudden, about twenty feet away from me, someone stepped out of the shadows."

"There were two men?"

"Yes. And this one had the drop on me. I saw his arm rising and I knew he had me. I swung around anyway. Suddenly I recognized his face. But before I could say anything . . . there was a shot. He dropped."

Over by the dartboard a chant had started up. It was the girl's turn. I leaned closer over the table so that I could hear the rest of Kate's story.

"I spun around to see where the hell the shot had come from. Just as I did, Lou was squeezing off a shot at the guy up on the walkway. It was perfect. Nailed him."

"Wait. I'm confused. This guy down on the ground, the one who was about to shoot you . . . who shot him?"

"Apparently the one on the walkway."

"But that doesn't make any sense. Weren't they in on this together?"

"That's what you'd figure, right? Though at the time I wasn't really thinking straight." Kate's eyes followed one of the darts as it zoomed though the air. It veered left of the bull's-eye, missed by a mile. "I was too busy screaming."

"Screaming?"

"The guy on the ground. I was screaming for him to move." Kate gave me a dark look over the table. "It was Charley. On undercover. It was my husband. I was screaming for him to move. So that he could show me that he wasn't dead."

A huge cheer went up from the dart players. *Bull's-eye.* The girl leaped up and down like a game show winner. Kate glared over at the high fives, then she looked back at me. All signs of life had gone out of her eyes.

"I was wasting my breath."

CHAPTER 13

One of our chief suppliers of coffins, based in Nebraska, was rolling out several new models. He had been trying to get me on the phone to make his pitch. I'll be the first to admit, I'm a hard sale. I'm no pine box purist, mind you, but I do happen to feel that if the basic realities of dying haven't changed much over the course of the history of mankind then the need to constantly upgrade the exigencies of burial is a little difficult to justify as being for anything other than a profit. The implication that we've been getting it wrong for over a thousand years now . . . well, that's something I just find difficult to swallow. Give me a sturdy box and a soft pillow and let's call it a deal.

I avoided the supplier's calls all day.

That night I made my pitch to Gil Vance for a lectern. The idea struck me as I crossed the square on my way to the Gypsy Playhouse.

"The audience is a voyeur, Gil, am I right? They're sitting out there, hidden in the dark, watching the goings on of this town, peeking in. Our town is in a goldfish bowl."

Gil's eyes went wide. Christ. He was seeing a literal goldfish bowl up onstage. I'd be giving my lines dressed in a Diver Dan getup.

"Okay. Gil, look. As it stands now you have the Stage Manager tramping around out there, unseen by the characters on the stage, but in full view and conversational mode with the members of the audience. But the Stage Manager literally moseying about on the fringes of the action like that . . . well, it sort of muddles things up, don't you think?"

Gil was taking this all in with some very serious head nods. Which meant he had no idea in hell what I was saying. "How does it muddle things up?" he asked.

"The Stage Narrator is . . . he's in the way," I declared. "He is standing in front of the action. Is he part of the play or is he part of the audience?"

"Both," said Gil.

"Muddle," said I.

"Hitch, why don't you tell me what you're saying," Gil suggested.

I threw myself at his feet. "Give me a lectern, Gil. We've got a nice one at the funeral home that I can appropriate if you need it. Plant me off to the side. Let me read my lines as if I am giving a lecture. Or a sermon. Or . . . or like an anthropologist. Giving a slide show! That's it. *That's* what I'm saying, Gil. The Stage Manager is an anthropologist. He is reading from his field notes, delivering a lecture about the feeding and mating habits of the New England WASP, circa blah blah blah. It makes perfect sense." I took a deep breath. "Give me a pith helmet."

"You want a lectern and a pith helmet?"

"Yes! And a pointer! Why not? Put me in a tweed jacket and a bow tie like Indiana Jones's daddy."

Gil was shaking his head. "Tweed jacket doesn't work with the pith helmet."

"Forget the pith helmet." I flipped the imaginary helmet out of the discussion with a flick of my wrist. "Professor Stage Manager. That's the thing. We'll stick me off in the corner, stage left—"

"I was thinking stage right—"

"Stage right is perfect! You've got the eye here, Gil. You're the director. Maybe you'll want to give me a pair of Teddy Roosevelt eyeglasses." I was piling it on now. "I can take them on and off. On when I'm reading—"

"Reading?"

"From my field notes."

"Right, right, the field notes."

Gil was staring out into the darkness. The gears were turning. Bow ties and wire-rimmed glasses and pointers were all crunching under the gears and coming back out the other side, unscathed. I sat silently as Gil reinvented the wheel.

He mused, "Maybe we can even save the pith helmet, Hitch. Maybe each time you take *off* your glasses to watch the action, you could put *on* the pith helmet. You're 'back out in the field' so to speak."

I would look like today's new idiot doing that, fumbling with glasses and pith helmets every twenty seconds. But what the hell did I care? I had scored my touchdown. I left Gil to savor his new vision and found Julia in the back row of the theater. She was as hungover as I was buoyant.

"I'm a free man," I announced as I slid into the seat next to her and threw my long legs over the seat in front, just as she was doing.

"Tell me you didn't quit. I'll murder you if you quit."

"I'm no quitter Mrs. Sewell-no-more. I'm still in. But I don't have to learn my lines. I'm going to read them, from a lectern."

"You are going to *read* your goddamn lines?"

"Yes ma'am. It's a concept."

"Well son of a bitch. I want a concept like that."

"Oh I don't know, Jules. I kind of like the one you're working on."

She eyed me suspiciously. "Which one would that be?"

"The debauched, promiscuous, hungover little Emily."

She placed her head in her hands. "Emily the town whore," she moaned.

"We could replace your milk shakes with Harvey Wallbangers."

"Misery loves company, Hitch. And you're too damned giddy for me this morning. Go away."

"I'm sorry, darling. I'll stop crowing. It's pretty unattractive, I know. So you drank too much free booze last night? Nice party, huh?"

"I can handle alcohol when I have a chance to sleep it off," Julia said. She pivoted her head tenderly in my direction and gave me the best she could do of a smile. "But I was up all night. How about you, loverboy? None other than the infamous Lady X, eh? And a cop no less. Did she bring her handcuffs?"

"Afraid not."

"That's too bad. Did she tell you why she pretends to be dead women? Is it just something that she does for kicks?"

"We didn't get that far."

"No offense, Romeo, but it sounds like you didn't get anywhere at all."

"You, on the other hand, seem pretty cuddly with your millionaire," I observed.

Julia ran a hand through her hair. "He wants me to marry him. He's completely nuts about me."

"Or maybe he's just completely nuts."

"You don't think I'd make a good wife?"

"It's the free spirit versus monogamy clash you've got to consider. Not to mention, whether or not you love him."

"I have a great capacity for love."

"Ergo the clash."

Gil was calling his actors to the stage. *Clap, clap, clap.* Julia meandered down to the lip of the stage. Michael Goldfarb found his way over and plopped down next to her. The Valkyrie and the puppy dog.

Gil addressed his troupe. "People. We're going to introduce a new concept to the production today. I want all of you—with the exception of Hitchcock—to start thinking of yourselves as participants in a live-action slide show. I want you to think of our set here as the projection screen, in . . . in an old boys' boarding school lecture hall." Man oh man, Gil moves fast. Julia looked back at me and silently mouthed, "What the fuck?" I'm sure that I looked like a tomato trying not to explode. I didn't dare laugh out loud.

Gil was beaming. "This will be good," he promised. "This will be very good." To his stage manager he hissed, "See if you can find me a pair of wire-rimmed glasses. Like Teddy Roosevelt wore."

CHAPTER 14

Hutch was right. Spencer Davis—the fellow running against Alan Stuart for governor—really does look like a Kennedy wanna-be. He has Kennedy teeth, a dazzling set of chompers that go off like a flashbulb when he smiles. It is a winning smile and it is attached to a face that pulses with sincerity and good intentions. Such a shame the guy is a politician. We'll never really know the truth.

I was watching District Attorney Spencer Davis up on the TV set in the ceiling corner above the Screaming Oyster's bar. The volume was off, so I couldn't hear the platitudes. The news was covering an appearance the candidate had made that afternoon at a shelter for minority homeless women with AIDS-infected children with learning disabilities brought on by toxic groundwater seepage into the plumbing of their methadone clinic whose subsequent closing had only added to the ranks of the jobless . . . or something. As I said, the volume was down, so the specifics were nebulous. But clearly Candidate Davis and his gigawatt smile thought that some things in this old world of ours needed improving. And he was probably right. Utopia is still right around the biggest damn corner you've ever seen.

Under the guise of "balanced reporting," the news then followed the Spencer Davis "story" with some footage from the previous evening's cocktail bash at the Peabody Conservatory Library. No crack babies here, ladies and gentlemen. I pointed up at the TV set.

"Hey, Sally, this is the thing I told you about. That thing. The political thing." My skills of articulation sometimes astound even me.

"Oooh, do you think my baby will be on TV?"

I noticed that Frank—who was close enough to have heard us—was pretending not to pay attention to the TV. But he was doing a lousy job.

"That's sweet, isn't it," Sally said to me softly. "The old bastard really does care. In his old bastard sort of way."

Julia didn't make the news. But Amanda Stuart did. The camera lingered on her ice-sculpture face for about ten seconds, which in TV time is an eternity. She was beaming her best vote-for-my-husband smile.

"Is that the wife?" Sally sniffed.

"That's her."

"Looks like someone."

"Grace Kelly," I said.

"Grace Kelly. Now there was one beautiful woman. If looks could kill." Sally moved along down the bar to wake up one of her customers.

The camera zoomed in just then on Amanda Stuart, who apparently noticed it for the first time. Her eyes flicked an infinitesimal dagger—just a filament of irritation—before Jeff Simons's plastic face suddenly reappeared on the screen, momentarily yakking into the wrong camera.

I had been drinking beer but now I switched to bourbon. The first one was good. The second one was better. The third one was jealous of the first two.

It can get complicated.

If looks could kill.

I dropped the words into my glass and stirred them in with my pinky.

Looks can kill.

People can kill.

People with looks can kill.

By God, Holmes himself would have been sorely pressed to keep one step ahead of such deductive brilliance. I hadn't allowed the thought to take form the night before. But it took form now. As the TV news flickered with the images of a Cal Ripken triple and a pissed-off visiting pitcher, the thought came into perfect focus.

Amanda Stuart killed Guy Fellows.

This qualified as a *"Wow."* Followed by a *"Shit!"*

Jesus, what is this world coming to? I poured yet another drink down my throat. Okay. Do your worst, truth serum. Show old Hitchcock the foggy light.

I can no longer remember how it came to be that I chose Frostburg State College as the place to sharpen my three R's. Maybe it's just that they were the first college to accept me and I wanted to show my appreciation. It was probably something like that.

As I mentioned earlier, Frostburg is where I met Joel Hutchinson. Hutch was a brilliant student as well as a glorious mischief maker. He was also what I came to think of as aggressively loyal. Once he had latched on to a person he polished them up like they were a neglected trophy he had just discovered up in the attic. Hutch seemed to operate at his highest pitch when he was encouraging others to go beyond their perceived limits. He was a boundary pusher. Other people's boundaries.

To be more precise, he was a charming bully.

My actual friendship with Hutch reached its peak the night we left that Brahma bull dropping its loads of steaming shit onto the varnished wood of the student union's fourth-floor bowling alley. As you can imagine, we felt unconquerable. It took real teamwork to get the bull out of its pasture, loaded into the van that Hutch had appropriated from the college's Sanitation Services Department, into the student union service elevator and onto the lanes at three in the morning. Why we bothered to do it is irrelevant. It was a moon shot; a mountain climb; do it because it is there. Briefly it made blood brothers of the two of us. Batman and Robin. Butch and Sundance. Humpty and Dumpty. Hitch and Hutch.

And then Hutch kidnapped Professor Smollett on my behalf, and that soured things between us.

Professor Alfred Smollett, in his early fifties, was considered something of a guru in the Frostburg sociology department. The reason for this is that some six or seven years earlier he had published a book that briefly caught the country's popular imagination. Entitled *She Sings, He Swings*, it made the argument for separate evolutionary paths for the human male and the human female, the core premise being that the female of the species has traveled further from her ape ancestors than we brutish males.

The book opens with a totally absurd chapter about body hair and takes off from there. As the underlying thesis of a purportedly scholarly rumination, it's pretty damned weird. But weird sells, and *She Sings, He Swings* swung onto the *New York Times* best-seller list. Professor Smollett hopped around the country on a promotional book tour, during which he apparently discovered the rock-star status that is sometimes awarded the published author. It certainly didn't hurt that his book was basically high praise to women and a man-slammer all at once. In other words, the guy got laid *a lot*. He came back from his tour, filed for divorce from his evolutionary-superior wife and got a pretty bad hair weave. The book slid off the best-seller list after a few more months, and Professor Alfred Smollett settled into a career of feeding from the female ranks of the freshman class, for whom *She Sings, He Swings* was, naturally, required reading for the Sociology 101 general requirement credit.

I had a beef with Professor Smollett. As an inferior ape myself, I considered it patently unfair that while I had to preen and prance and bring forth great gushes of charm and cajolings in order to get the occasional Frostburg coed to go to bed with me, Alfred Smollett and his rice-paddy hair weave could sit back in his dusty little office and pull off his celebrity Svengali game with much less effort and considerably better success overall. I'm not accusing all the Frostburg women of mindlessly goose-stepping into the creep's bed, mind you. But fledgling coeds are easy targets for creeps like Smollett. It was a game for him. Shooting fish in a barrel.

It especially irked me when he aimed his disgusting old pistol at Angela Poe. That was my beef. Angela Poe was the sweetest, shyest, doe-eyed girl/woman you could ever hope to have a silly crush on. She was in one of Smollett's classes with me. Sophomore year. I can't speak for fish or koalas or spider monkeys, but men fantasize. And it's not always just whips and chains. My classroom fantasies about Angela Poe were pure enough to stuff a cloud with. Angela Poe didn't even know how pretty she was, or how her quiet voice and her large dark eyes and her nervous smile made me want to set up police barricades around her desk so that I could warn everyone to just stay away, move on please, let this one pass through. Fantasies, like I say. We get them. Angela Poe was the perfect virgin and I wanted her to stay that way, haughty presumptive idiot that I was. The difference between me and Alfred Smollett was that he didn't want her to stay that way.

And she didn't. And that was my beef.

The day that I saw Angela Poe sitting in class with a faraway look of shock and shame on her pretty face, I knew that something terribly abrupt and life-altering had taken place. I suspected that I knew the source. When I saw the look that flickered between Angela Poe and the great professor as he strode into the room . . . I knew what had happened to her and with whom.

But that was a day for *me* to react, if I so chose. Not Hutch.

But it was Hutch, loyal Hutch, who got hold of the same van we had used to squire around the Brahma bull. It was Hutch who got Alfred Smollett from behind and taped a bandanna over his eyes and hustled him into the van. And it was Hutch who drove the randy professor around for hours, haranguing him on a bullhorn—compliments of the Athletic Department. "You fuck with *them*, I'll fuck with *you!*" The bullhorn—aided by a slight German accent—disguised his voice sufficiently. Alfred Smollett sat balled up in the rear of the van, helpless. Hutch never once mentioned Angela Poe by name, but Smollett must have gotten the point. Hutch spent several hours bouncing his amplified voice off the thin tin of the van, reviling Alfred Smollett up, down and through the middle for leading young innocents into his bed. He jerked the van wildly, sending his captive flopping helplessly from one side of the van to the other.

Hutch had me keeping tabs on a piece of paper. He wanted exactly one hundred "I'm sorrys" from Alfred Smollett before he would let him go. The first twenty or so were arrogant and contentious. But Hutch was good with that bullhorn. He got spooky. He got the good old professor pretty rattled. By the seventieth "I'm sorry," there were tears flowing from under the bandanna. By ninety he was all-out blubbering. By the time Smollett reached one hundred, I was practically sick to my stomach. Hutch pulled the van over in front of a sorority house and dumped the old goat onto the sidewalk. I watched him through the side mirror as we pulled away.

"You happy?" Hutch asked, beaming from ear to ear like the Cheshire cat. "He really pissed you off, didn't he? You feel better now? Huh?"

I sure as hell didn't. I felt sick to my stomach. That kind of loyalty I can do without.

Sally was waving something in front of my face. It was her hand.

"Earth to Hitchcock. Are you there?"

It took a few fat seconds for me to travel back from the Frostburg campus of yesteryear to the noisy world of today's Screaming Oyster. A few barstools down, Edie Velvet casually launched an empty beer bottle into the overhead dinghy. Another bottle leaped free from the boat and hit the floor with a *pop*, shattering green glass everywhere. The *pop* was what snapped me out of it.

"Sure, Sally, I'm here."

"Where the hell were you just now?"

"I was just thinking," I said.

Sally snorted. She reached under the bar and slammed a handful of darts onto the counter. "Go throw some darts, son. Shake it off. Do your heavy thinking elsewhere."

It was sound advice. I took up the darts and headed over to the dartboard. I was annoyed with myself for having dredged up the memory of Hutch and his oversized "favor" to me. I remembered how ashamed I had felt the next day to even glance at Angela Poe. And of course the Laughing Gods just can't resist the temptation to have their fun. It was that very next day that Angela Poe had approached me with some sort of question about an upcoming exam. It was a trumped-up question, simply an excuse to get me into a conversation. She liked me. And all I could do was mutter a half-assed answer to her question and walk away.

Thwack. Thwack. Thwack.

I threw some darts. No bull's-eyes. A biker type with an oversized mustache yelled over at me from his table.

"You stink, man!"

"I'm trying to miss the little spot in the middle," I answered back. "It's not so easy."

The guy tugged on one end of his mustache. "In that case, man, you're pretty good."

I wasn't completely obeying Sally's advice. I was still thinking. And I didn't much care for where it was taking me. The longer I considered the possibility that Amanda Stuart had murdered Guy Fellows, the more likely it seemed to me that Joel Hutchinson could not be out of the loop. If *I* knew . . . or at least had good cause to speculate, then there was no way in hell that Hutch hadn't scratched his chin about the same thing. This was the candidate's wife, after all. And Hutch was the candidate's puppet master.

But there was something even more unsettling than the thought that Amanda Stuart had blood on her hands or that perhaps Hutch had helped her to clean it off. I was still seeing young Hutch's smiling face as he hit the accelerator. *"You happy? Do you feel better now?"*

Mr. Fix-it. I didn't care one bit for that.

I flipped the dart into my opposite hand and chucked it. I didn't even look at the target. But the Laughing Gods were on duty. It was a perfect bull's-eye.

The grizzly guy was laughing so hard it turned into a coughing fit. But not before he had roared, "Oh, man, now you *really* stink!"

CHAPTER 15

Life goes on. Death too.

We buried the guy who had choked to death having altogether too much fun all by himself. Rather than the usual intonations of "He was such a good person," Parlor Two was filled with the dead guy's buddies snickering to each other, "What a jerk."

You really had to feel for his parents.

What a jerk.

After the burial, since I was in the neighborhood, I stopped by the grave of Carolyn James. Cheap Guy Fellows had arranged for the smallest of stones, the simple rectangle tucked into the earth. No headstone. The grass over the grave was still lime-colored. In about a week or two, three weeks at the tops, the grass would lose its new-sprung sheen and Pops and company would crisscross it with their mowers. At that point, the grave of Carolyn James would be just another among a thousand.

I went back to the grave site of the foolish sex addict. Pops and his boys were lowering the casket into Mother Earth. I intervened when one of them started to filch the casket's bouquet and took it over to the grave of Carolyn James and set it down on her little gravestone. Twenty-seven years old. What makes a person who has only lived twenty-seven years want to turn out the lights? How could the great dark void come to look like a viable alternative to life? Well, I'm no Philosopher King, so I knew about how far I would get trying to pluck answers to those kinds of questions out of the air. Sometimes it doesn't pay to generalize anyway. Carolyn James's reasons were specific to her. She had run out of options, or at least she had run out of the ability to recognize any options. And so she had hopped into her car, turned the key and hightailed it to nowhere. Final Destination.

I drove out to Loch Raven Reservoir, about a half hour's drive, parked at a turnoff by the woods, hiked a quarter of a mile in to the cliffs, stripped down to my boxers and dove in. In my mind's eye it was a perfect Tarzan dive, strong and straight and lithe. To the less biased I probably looked like a large frog being tossed off the cliff. I hit the water and found no alligators to wrestle, so I swam out to the middle of the reservoir and then back again. It took me about forty minutes round-trip. When I pulled myself up onto one of the large boulders at the edge of the water, I was exhausted and pleased. I stretched out on the boulder and let the clouds entertain me for a while. A hawk circled overhead. A chipmunk skittered nearby. The wind cooled me; the sun warmed me. I was nearing a Perfect Moment experience when a county cop in an electric-powered boat veered into my little cove and laid down the law about no swimming in the reservoir. He was nice enough about it. Young guy. Acne scars. I made my way back up the cliff, back to my car, and drove back into the city. As I got off the expressway a car in front of me was drifting into my lane. I leaned hard on the horn.

Welcome back, bubba.

Kate and I met at Haussner's Restaurant on Eastern Boulevard. Haussner's is a huge restaurant—two very large rooms—that manages nonetheless to force a sense of intimacy down your throat by filling every square corpuscle of wall space with paintings. Stacked as many as nine and ten high, Haussner's walls constitute a remarkable gallery of totally adequate canvases, paintings of forgotten royalty, gentry, both landed and debauched, wild-eyed rustics, pastoral glens, ships at sea and still lifes of all sorts, from fruit bowls to dead rabbits hanging by their bloody paws. The great charm of the place though, oddly enough, lies in its unstuffiness. The waiters and waitresses are about as pretentious as a beer bottle. Baltimore doesn't do pretentious anyway nearly so well as it does bonhomie, and Haussner's is a great example. Their menu is as extensive as their art collection; two entire pages of choices typewritten onto hard pink paper, no less than fifty dinners to choose from, all of them ample and purportedly scrumptious.

I got the finnan haddie. I always get the finnan haddie. It is located near the bottom of the right-hand page of the menu. My gaze just naturally dropped there the first time I ate here and so I ordered it and liked it and I've stuck with it ever since.

Kate ordered the red snapper.

"I've always wondered about the red snapper," I lied.

Kate seemed more relaxed than in any of our previous encounters. She pointed out a painting of a little boy with chalky white skin dressed in a *Pagliacci* outfit and dragging a small wooden boat on a string. What looked like a leather medicine ball sat off in the background, half obscured in shadow, next to a stuffed lion.

"Who would think to paint something like that? It's creepy." Her eyes left the painting and found mine. "Speaking of creepy. How did you get into the funeral business anyway?"

I had picked up the pepper shaker and rested it on the tines of my fork, which tilted the handle about forty-five degrees. If I had slammed down suddenly on the handle of my fork it would have launched the pepper shaker maybe as far as the next table, where an elderly couple sat sipping soup in silence. I didn't. I demilitarized the shaker. Kate was waiting for my answer. I wasn't in the mood to go into the business about my parents and the beer truck. It seemed that all Kate and I had talked about so far were those who were no longer with us. I wanted to leave my parents out of it.

"It's a family business," I said finally.

"Does it ever bother you? I mean, it must."

"Why should it? Undertakers are among the top three oldest professions, next to lawyers and prostitutes. And *we* don't have to hustle for business."

Kate laughed. I couldn't be certain, but I believed it was the first time I had seen her laugh. I mean truly laugh, without that caution of hers I had already come to recognize sliding instantly into place.

"You have a pretty laugh," I observed.

"Thank you." She added, "So do you in fact."

Pretty? Well. I've never heard that one.

"Tell me about your marriage," Kate said. "I'm sorry. That's abrupt. I mean, about . . ."

Suddenly she was blushing.

"What? My divorce?"

"Forget I said anything. Really. It's none of my business."

"I'll tell you what. You can ask me any questions you want, anything at all . . ."

Kate picked up on my tone. "But what?"

"But first you've got to get the elephant out of the room. I want to know about Carolyn James. I want to know why you were pretending to be her. I want to know why she killed herself. I want to know why you tried to arrange her funeral before she was even dead."

Kate gave me an unhappy look. "Will there be anything else, sir?"

"I'll think of something."

Kate fiddled with her silverware. "All right. To your first question . . . Carolyn was in fear for her life. She was scared to death. Literally, as it turned out."

"Who was she afraid of? Fellows?"

"She wasn't afraid that Guy would kill her, if that's what you mean. But he did hit her. He hit her a lot. He was very bad to her. And she was incapable of breaking free from him. It's . . . Unfortunately, that's often how it goes."

"But if she was afraid that someone was going to kill her and it wasn't Guy Fellows, then who?"

"The same people who killed Fellows."

"People?"

"Person. Whatever. Carolyn was in a panic. I could see that. God, she was all alone here. No family. No real friends. The only person who she really counted on was Guy and he was using her as his punching bag. Abuse is the damnedest thing. You'd think that more people could simply walk away from it. Say 'No, no more,' and just leave. But the victim mentality, it's insidious. And in Carolyn's situation, there was more."

"More? More what?"

"In addition to the abuse, Guy had involved her in . . . well, he had involved her in a situation that—I said this already—scared the hell out of her. I wanted to save her. Do you understand that? I wanted to save her."

I saw the woman across the table from me as a little girl, leaping over the body of her handcuffed father and into the arms of her rescuer, her hero cop.

"I understand."

Our salads had arrived. We didn't touch them.

"So why didn't you just get her away from Fellows?" I asked. "Get her out of town altogether."

Kate was shaking her head. "No good. Carolyn wasn't simply being paranoid about her life being in danger. She *was* in danger. And she would have been tracked down. When it came down to it, she couldn't really hide. That was the problem. There was no real way out."

It hit me just then. At least a part of it. "You wanted to fake a funeral. That's what you were after that day, wasn't it? You wanted to pretend that Carolyn James was dead so that not only could she disappear, but no one would go looking for her."

Kate picked up her fork and pointed it at me. "That is exactly the stupid idea that I had."

"I don't know, Kate. It sounds inspired."

"Could I have pulled it off?"

"I seriously doubt it."

"Then we're back to stupid."

She poked at her salad. Came up with a cherry tomato. "It was an impulsive thought, Hitch. When I came to your place I . . . I just needed to think. I was really not having such a great day myself. I was trying to sort out a lot of things. I ended up down in your neck of the woods and I happened to see people going into this funeral home. I got this crazy idea. What if people were to think that Carolyn had killed herself? It certainly wasn't beyond imagining. As we now know. And the next thing I knew I was standing behind a bunch of flowers staring down at a man in a coffin."

"Who wanted to kill her? Who did she need to run from? You're a cop. Why didn't she just ask you for help?"

"Carolyn didn't know I was a cop."

"Who did she think you were?"

Kate lowered her eyes. "She thought I was Guy Fellows's lover. Or I guess you ought to say, one of them."

"Were you?"

Our meals arrived just then. My finnan haddie came with a swirl of garlic mashed potatoes and a tiny gathering of broccoli and carrots. As always. Kate's red snapper looked delicious. It spanned the entire length of the plate, had been deboned and was opened up like an unzipped jacket. We each got a tiny plate stacked with lemon slices. We also each got an iced tea. Kate's fish came with a side of rice. At Haussner's they don't offer to pepper mill your food for you. They figure you're old enough to handle that yourself.

Kate looked across the table at me as the flavors rose into our faces.

"Yes," she said.

I remember chewing the finnan haddie. I just don't remember tasting it.

Kate refused to discuss Guy Fellows or Carolyn James anymore over dinner.

"Hitch, I need a break. Can we make this a real date?"

"You mean you want me to pay for everything and then kiss you good night at your door?"

"That's exactly what I mean. With lots of small talk in between. I know it's make-believe, but I am exhausted with reality. I just need a time-out."

"I'm probably not your best bet then," I warned her. "You've got me crawling with questions."

"I know. I understand. It's just . . . Hitch, I'm in some very hot water. There are some bad things taking place. I really don't want you to get involved."

"What kind of hot water?"

She made her appeal. "A regular little date? Please? Like two boring people with simple boring problems? Just this one night? I promise to ruin your life just as swiftly as I can later. But not tonight."

"Such an offer."

"You know what I mean. No cops and robbers. I guess I'm really not as cut out for this job as I thought I was. Or as I once was. I want a perfectly pedestrian evening. Will you be my dull guy?"

It was such an oddly appealing appeal.

"Okay, lady, you've got it. Just this once. As dull as they come. Now snap up your snapper, before it gets cold."

We ate our fish. We talked a bit more about some of the paintings. I told her about Julia's work and how she had become a darling in the local art scene, as well as a big hit in Scandinavia.

"That's peculiar," Kate observed.

I shrugged. "France has got Jerry Lewis. Scandinavia's taken on my ex-wife."

"She's very pretty," Kate said. "I'll bet there were more than a few sprained necks after that party the other night."

"Julia's okay," I agreed. "She's just not a horse you put a saddle on, that's all."

"So you don't think she'd marry Peter Morgan? If he asked, that is."

"Oh, he's already asked. And I don't know. Julia is a glutton for experiences. I'd imagine getting married to a multimillionaire could have its allure."

Kate made a face. "You mean there are women who marry men just for their money?"

"I know, you're shocked."

We rattled on this way for a while. Kate said she wanted boring. You can't get much more boring than chitchat about the ex, now can you?

We swapped innocuous tales of youth. I told Kate about my parents, about their salad days as local TV celebrities. She told me about summer vacations to western Maryland, camping at Deep Creek Lake. I told her about the time I got knocked out by a foul ball at a baseball game and how for the first several minutes after I came to I thought my name was Ralph.

Dessert was good. A choice of three thousand pies. I paid the bill. Kate said, "Thank you, Ralph." Our dull date was going just ducky.

We went to the Inner Harbor and rented a paddleboat, which is a molded plastic boat that among other things is not designed for the comfort of anyone who is six foot three. I listened to my knees as they moved up and down next to my ears. I felt like a gigantic grasshopper. The late summer sunset had finally concluded, but the glow from the shops and restaurants of the Harbor Place pavilions kept the night sky bleached with sufficient light that none of us out there in our paddleboats risked colliding with one another. After an hour of this, Captain Kate and I came ashore and strolled along the boat piers beneath Federal Hill and laughed at some of the names that people gave to their boats. Kate got a particular kick out of *E.S. Crow.* She asked me what I thought would be a good name for a boat if she owned it.

"That's easy," I said. *"Zabriskie Punt."*

We climbed Federal Hill and sat on the cannons that were aimed at the harbor. I told her about my having been conceived at the Flag House. I pointed across the harbor, to the east. "Just over there. Near the Shot Tower." I looked over at her. "Maybe I'll take you there sometime."

Kate slipped off her cannon and came over to mine. In the near darkness, her face was a pearl white heart, bordered by the swirls of her black hair.

"Thanks for the date, Hitch," she said softly.

"You're very welcome."

We kissed. A five-second kiss, that's all. I had to lean over from my cannon perch. Kate grazed my cheek with the back of her fingers.

"You'd probably be smart to forget all about me right now," she said in a near whisper. "I mean it."

"I know you do," I answered. "But I'm afraid I'm really, really stupid."

Someone somewhere far off let off a firecracker. Kate's face was still aimed up at me. "Well then kiss me again, stupid." Just like in the movies.

I did. This one lasted fifteen seconds. But only half as long as the next one, which brought me down off my cannon so that I could wrap my arms around her.

"I've never kissed a cop before," I confessed.

"I've never kissed an undertaker."

"A night of firsts," I observed.

Kate leaned forward and gave my earlobe a tiny nibble. Her whispered response was an observation that the night was still young.

"If we hurry, there'll be time for seconds."

Men's shirts were made for women. No two ways around it. It doesn't work the other way around. An otherwise naked man stepping into a bedroom wearing some lady's dress and carrying two mugs of coffee just doesn't play the same as a woman holding the two mugs, wearing an oversized men's button-up shirt (partially buttoned) and not a stitch of anything else. Call it a cliché of a man's fantasy if you want to, I don't really care. I'm human. Male human. And as I scooted up on the pillows to make way for Kate Zabriskie, I couldn't decide what to compliment her on first, the aroma of the coffee or the spectacular way she looked in my shirt. I opted to try for both.

"You look as good as that coffee smells."

"I'll bet you say that to all the women who bring coffee to your lazy ass in bed."

"I probably would, you're right. But with them I might just be trying to score points. With you I absolutely mean it. You look good enough to drink."

She handed me a mug. "Start with this."

We sipped. Kate brought her coffee mug up to her chin and let the steam rise up into her face. She smiled at me through the mist.

"You've got a sappy look on your face, Mr. Sewell."

"I'm a postcoital sentimentalist. I'm tempted to lock the doors and preserve this moment forever."

"Sweet thought. I could really wrap you around my finger, couldn't I?"

I reached out and tapped her on the calf. "I'd prefer these."

"Don't go getting the wrong impression of me, just because I kiss on the first date."

"It's not the kiss that's giving me this impression," I said.

"It's all your fault anyway," Kate said.

"How so?"

"The cannon. You sitting up on that cannon. Very provocative."

"Indeed."

Kate leaned over and set her coffee mug down on the floor. "Hmmm, that sappy sentimental look is gone already. Is that it for the postcoital whatever-it-was?"

"Sentimentalism."

"Is it over?"

"Yes. I feel a definite precoital rumbling coming on," I said.

"A rumbling?"

"Yes."

"Are you sure it's not your stomach? I could feed you."

I set my coffee mug down too. "I believe you could."

"Shall I tell you what's on the menu?"

"I believe I've already peeked."

"Okay then." Kate licked a fake pen and poised it above a fake order pad. "Fire away."

I woke back up in the late morning. A stray curlicue of Kate's hair was tickling my nose, and my right arm—trapped beneath her shoulders— was asleep and tingling. I had to go to the bathroom. Badly. I cautiously stretched my left leg, then had to freeze instantly as the calf threatened to cramp. My elbow itched. The trapped one. Kate was snoring ever so lightly. I was face-to-face with a tiny mole on the back of her neck that I hadn't noticed before. It looked like a ladybug. There was a small puckered scar on her left shoulder. I didn't much care for the wallpaper in her bedroom. I was starving now, for real. I spotted my shirt on the floor. A large coffee stain was settling into the fibers.

Perfect once can never be perfect again. Our evening's sex and our morning's banter were already being dipped in sepia. Ready soon for framing and remembering when. Right now, though, I had to pee.

I sneezed and my leg cramped.

"Ow!"

Kate jerked awake as I lunged to grab hold of my calf. My dead arm flopped aimlessly and thwacked her on the back.

"Hey! What are you doing!"

"Nothing."

"Jesus!"

If anyone happens to have a stopwatch handy I'd be curious to know how long it took for the old honeymoon to be over.

"I've got to pee," Kate and I announced at the exact same time. We locked eyes, waiting for the other to say, "You first." I finally said it.

"Thank you," Kate said. Though it wasn't much of a thank-you. She kicked over the other coffee mug on her way to the bathroom. "Ow!" She glared at me.

"What?" I said.

"Nothing." She limped off to the bathroom, giving my shirt a hard look as she passed it.

And people wonder why I live by myself.

The sky had disappeared as thick purple-gray clouds sank into place. A cool breeze lifted the white curtains of Kate's living room windows and held them there as a rumble sounded outside. This was followed immediately by an abrupt *crack* . . . and then the steady *shoosh* of rain began.

Kate and I were dressed. Separate showers and a sheepish late breakfast behind us, we were back on balance. I had offered to leave, but Kate was insistent.

"Please stay. We have to talk."

I phoned Aunt Billie to see if there were any dead people I had to deal with. Nope. I phoned Gil Vance and got his answering machine. A fake Bette Davis implied that Gil's current indisposition was the result of some sort of naughty distraction and asked the caller to please leave a message, "*after the god . . . damn . . . beep.*" I told Bette to tell Gil that I had been in a plane crash in the Andes mountains but that the donkeys were on the way and I should be back for tomorrow's rehearsal, but would miss today's.

"What was that about?" Kate asked.

"I'm in a community theater production of *Our Town*. I'm playing the Stage Manager. I just got out of having to memorize my lines, so they won't really need me much for rehearsals anyway."

"You're an actor? An actor and an undertaker?"

"I play the harmonica too. I'm a Renaissance man."

"I wouldn't go that far."

The rain continued to come down in sheets and buckets and cats and dogs. It was a real mess out there. Kate had turned on a single lamp, next to the couch. The room took on a buttery glow. All very comforting.

She tuned the radio to a classical station, but kept the volume down low. We could still hear the rain as well as the steady drip drip drip of the overflow from a clogged rainspout just above the window. I stretched out on the couch and was flipping through a magazine about tropical islands. Kate was fidgety. Finally, I lowered the magazine and asked her if she wanted to talk about last night. She threw me a warm smile.

"There's no need."

"Do you want to talk about when we got up?"

"There's definitely no need for that."

"Okay. Well, if you do want to talk about anything, you can reach me here in Tahiti."

I returned to my magazine. More blue water. More white sand. More ads for rum. A violin piece was playing on the radio. Urgent yet smooth. The rain continued. I turned a page.

"Hitch. I need to talk."

Kate had gotten to her feet. She stepped over to the window, looked out at the rain, then stepped right back to her chair and dropped into it. I eased over to a sitting position, tossing the magazine onto the coffee table.

"I need to tell you what's going on," Kate said. She fidgeted with a hangnail. "You want to know, right?"

"I have to know. I have one foot in and one foot out and I'm running out of feet."

Kate said nothing. And then, quietly, she started to cry. She didn't sob; tears simply started down her face. "I'm sorry," she said, holding her hand up to silence me. "Wait. Just hold on a minute." I did, and in another few seconds she was able to turn off the faucets. A low rumble of thunder sounded as Kate sniffed away the last of her tears.

"I'm supposed to feel better after that," she said.

"Do you?"

She stood up again. "No. I still feel like shit." But she sounded better. She stepped over to her bookcase. There were maybe a dozen or so VCR tapes lined up on one of the shelves. She pulled one down.

"Are you ready to get caught up in something very unpleasant and very dangerous?"

I got a glimpse of the title on the video box. "I think you're overestimating the power of *Pinocchio*," I said. "It gets pretty dicey in the whale sequence, but it all works out in the end."

"It's not *Pinocchio*," she said flatly. "I just keep it in the box."

She slid the tape into her VCR, picked up the remote and joined me on the couch.

"Okay. Sit back. But don't enjoy the show."

She hit the remote. The TV screen flickered a few times, then went to static. Kate hit the mute button.

"No audio?" I asked.

"There is. But I can't bear to listen."

The static disappeared abruptly. I was looking at a video image of a bedroom. It was clearly an amateur video. The date and time were burned into the lower left of the screen, the digital numbers clicking off second by second.

"It's a bed," I said.

"Yes."

"Very subtle. The way it's just sitting there."

"Shut up."

Movement. The camera suddenly moved, a jerky pan to the left. Two people were coming into the room, a man and a woman. The woman had her head down, an arm on the man's shoulder for support as she hopped on one foot, pulling the shoe off the other foot. The man was looking directly at the camera. He certainly seemed aware that it was there and that someone was recording the scene. He ran his fingers quickly through his boyish mop.

"Guy Fellows," I said. Kate made no response. She was concentrating on the TV screen. "Who's the woman?"

"Watch."

The camera panned shakily back to the original position, centering on the bed. I still couldn't make out the woman's face as she and Fellows reached the bed. His back was in the way. They kissed. The woman's arms came around, one arm across Fellows's back, the other at an angle, her fingers splaying out over the back of his head. Apparently he was unbuttoning his shirt, for suddenly he held it open and the woman helped to pull it off of him, never breaking the kiss. Then she dug her fingernails into his shoulder.

"God," Kate muttered in disgust.

The camera started to zoom in, until the back of Guy Fellows practically filled the screen.

"The cameraman stinks," I said.

"It's not a man," Kate said. "It's Carolyn James."

Guy Fellows's big head tilted to the right and he went in for a taste of the woman's neck. She had thrown back her head, as if to show him her throat. As it happened, it made for a pretty nifty first shot of her face. Ready for her close-up. Lips parted and eyes closed, she reacted to whatever it was that Fellows was doing to her neck—reacted warmly—and then she opened her eyes. She was looking in the direction of the camera.

"She doesn't know she's being filmed," I said.

Kate verified. "No, sir, she does not."

Kate stood up abruptly. "I'll be back in a minute. I really don't want to see this again. You can turn it off when you've seen enough. If you watch the whole thing, I'll understand. I did the first time. It's a very sexy train wreck."

She touched me lightly on the shoulder as she crossed in front of me and went into the bedroom. I settled in to watch the grim show. No surprises really. I'll simply tell you that the appetite for sex between the two folks on the video was very highly pitched. The camera was unable to capture all of it in precise detail as occasionally the contortions of limbs left nothing but a flank or a thigh centered on the screen. But in zooming back, the woman's face—more often than Guy's—came back into view and each time it held an expression that can best be described as one of exquisite pain. I was tempted to unmute the TV, but I pretty much knew what sort of noises I would hear, and I didn't want Kate, waiting it out in her bedroom, to hear them.

After about ten minutes, I hit the pause button. The image froze. The woman was on top of Guy. Her cello-shaped torso was centered on the screen.

"I've paused it!" I called out.

Kate appeared in the doorway.

"How much longer does it go on?" I asked.

"This episode? Maybe another five minutes."

"There are more?"

"Oh yes. There are a half dozen on that tape alone."

"You mean there's another tape?"

"Allegedly."

"Same stuff?"

"Same stuff."

"I don't know, that seems like overkill to me," I said.

"It seems like it to me, too." Kate paused. "Are you going to watch any more?"

"No. I think I've figured out the major themes. Boy meets girl. Screws her ten ways to Sunday. The end."

"Do you recognize 'the girl'?"

"Oh yes. I recognize her. She gets more close-ups than Dan Rather."

"That was the point, of course. She had to be recognizable."

I centered my thumb over the frame-by-frame button of the remote and began to punch it. Onscreen, the woman's torso hardly seemed to move at first. Only after about five clicks did it suddenly jerk a little and then move a tiny bit with each subsequent click of the frame. Her head had been tossing side to side before I paused the image. It continued now, in the halting fashion. I click-click-clicked until she came to the apex of her head toss. The hair was held motionless in midair, like Kate's curtains when the storm had begun. The profile was sharp: the small nose, the high cheeks, the subtle look of the fox in her heavy-lidded eyes. It occurred to me that the last time I had seen this face had also been on TV. It had tossed a peeved look at the camera. This time, though, there was nothing peevish about the expression on the face of the police commissioner's wife. Amanda Stuart was having her groove thing shaken by the Baltimore Country Club's tennis pro. He was apparently shaking it good and Mrs. Stuart was loving every second of it.

"Pretty, isn't she?" Kate said. "She looks sort of like Grace Kelly."

"Everyone says that. A little bigger in the hips, I think."

"I was talking about her face."

"I'm going to guess that this video was not made solely to reveal to the world Amanda Stuart's hubba-hubba hips."

Kate answered, "I think what she is doing with them is more the point. And with who."

"Whom."

"Oh, Hitch. What-fucking-ever."

Guy Fellows had been attempting to blackmail Alan Stuart. A dozen still shots taken from the video had appeared in the mail one morning several months ago at Alan Stuart's office. The images were slightly fuzzy, having lost a bit of their clarity in the transfer from video. But they were still sharp enough to guarantee the Alan Stuart for Governor campaign a lock on the love-a-good-sleazy-scandal vote, if little else. Fellows was demanding a modest one hundred thousand dollars, in return for which Alan Stuart would receive the entire videotaped escapades of his energetic wife. It was a one-shot deal. Money for tape. Or two tapes, according to Kate. The original, in Fellows's possession, and a copy as a security measure being kept by the reluctant cameraperson, Carolyn James. That was the tape that Kate had.

But Alan Stuart hadn't bought into it, not for a single sliver of a second. Big men squish small bugs. Not the other way around. Guy Fellows was good-looking and sexy. He apparently had a killer serve and an equally effective follow-through. But going up against the likes of Alan Stuart showed that despite all that, he was also just plain stupid. And the proof was in the proverbial pudding. Alan Stuart was still up and walking around and making plans to govern the State of Maryland. And for reasons that one would have to assume simply couldn't be unrelated to this blackmail attempt, Guy Fellows was rotting in the ground. This couldn't have been a part of his plan. Unless he was *really* stupid.

Kate had not been in on the game at the very beginning—she was just one of Alan Stuart's loyal soldiers—but she was able to reconstruct the basic sequence of things.

Alan Stuart was not going to squander any of his—or his campaign's—money on Guy Fellows. That was the first decision, and the easiest one to make. The likelihood of yet another duplicate tape having been made for the purposes of future extortion if, say, Stuart were to win the governor's race (or even later, should he set his sights higher) seemed almost a foregone conclusion. There was simply no way to guarantee that Guy Fellows wouldn't hold his dirty pictures of pretty Amanda over her husband's head from now until Doomsday (which keeps getting rescheduled, have you noticed?). And there was no way that someone like Alan Stuart would ever allow himself to be told when and how high to jump by the likes of a Guy Fellows. Not now. Not ever.

According to Kate, the entire affair of the videotape had been kept quiet, handled solely by Alan Stuart and Joel Hutchinson. My old buddy Hutch. Seems like he was just born for this kind of thing. I could easily picture him in Alan Stuart's office, tie loosened, sleeves rolled to the elbows, feet up on a low table, throwing out his speculative "*Well, what if this . . . maybe if we try that . . .*" as his candidate paced back and forth calmly plotting strategies one minute, hurling curses at his wife and Guy Fellows the next.

But would Hutch have said, *What if we just kill him?* That hyperbolic smile rose up again in my mind's eye. *Are you happy? Do you feel better now?*

Was Hutch *this* nuts?

Guy Fellows made no effort to conceal his identity in the photographs. And even if he had, a few sharp shakes and a slap would have gotten the name out of Amanda Stuart anyway. According to Kate, it was Hutch who had pointed this out and it was Hutch who came to the conclusion that Guy Fellows had a partner. The photographs that had landed on Alan Stuart's desk were clearly taken off of a videotape. What's more, the various angles and close-ups of the pictures made it clear that these images were not the job of a stationary camera hidden somewhere in the room. Someone had been at the controls of the video camera, seeing to it that Amanda Stuart's face got plenty of exposure. Along with the rest of her. And this—I can just see Hutch gravely stroking his chin over this one—*this* was a problem.

Guy Fellows was cleanly in their sights. What to do with him specifically would have to be worked out. What if, what if, what if . . .

But his partner. That was a problem.

"Joel began to refer to Guy's partner as 'Insurance,' " Kate said to me. "That's what he would say. 'We can't lay a finger on Guy Fellows until we've also fingered Insurance.' That's how he talked."

And that was the problem. The fact is, Guy Fellows hadn't even needed to use the U.S. Postal Service to deliver his dirty pictures. He could have waltzed into Alan Stuart's office in his birthday suit and slapped the nasty goods down on his desk. "My name is Guy Fellows. I'm here because your wife and I have been bopping like bunnies. Here are the pictures to prove it. I've got the home video version back at my place and it can be yours for just nineteen ninety-nine, plus ninety-nine thousand and change for shipping and handling. And by the way, if you touch so much as a single hair on my beautiful birthday suit my partner will be only too glad to give the eleven o'clock news something to drool over." He could have taken a handful of cigars from Alan Stuart's humidor (if one existed), lit one up and moonwalked a complete backwards circle around the room, shaking a hat in the air like Jimmy Durante.

Stupid men with balls. Sometimes a very frustrating combination.

The afternoon's rainstorm had finally ended, leaving behind a gray hollow sky and a peculiar stillness to the air. I think that Kate and I were beginning to suffer the first stages of cabin fever, having now been inside her apartment for some twenty hours straight. The end of the rainstorm brought with it a ball of clammy hot air. Apparently Kate didn't own an air conditioner and I couldn't see a fan anywhere. We were seated apart from each other as she told me her story. I was still on the couch. She sat across from me in a large chair, her legs pretzeled beneath her. She was chewing absently on a plastic straw as she spoke.

"I got a call from Alan some months ago, asking me to come in and see him. The call came from him directly, not from his secretary. We met at the end of the workday. At the end of *his* workday, I should say. Police shifts don't really line up with the nine-to-fivers. Alan offered me a drink. And I knew right there that something was wrong."

"Because cops don't drink while on duty?" I'd seen my *Dragnet*. I know this stuff.

She shook her head. "Because I had developed a not-so-great relationship with alcohol over the past couple of months, and Alan knew that."

"Oh."

"He knew it full well. So when he offered me a drink, my radar went up immediately. Alan is a smart man. Think what you want about his character or his politics, but you've got to hand it to him for his smarts. He knew that I'd smell danger and that I'd automatically start to protect myself. He knew that."

"Wait. I don't understand all this. Was he being a good guy or a bad guy? I'm confused."

"Bad. Count on it."

"So then why do something, offer you a drink, if he knew it would put you on guard?"

"That's Alan's way of pretending to level the playing field. It's a mind game. Alan enjoys putting all the pieces on the table. Exposing his tactics. He'll come right out and say, "Okay, now I'm going to find a way to make you walk off the edge of that cliff over there, you think I'm not?' "

"He sounds like a mean bastard."

"That's the only kind I know."

Kate uncoiled from the chair and went over to the window.

"Alan put me on alert immediately. What he wanted was my full attention. He wanted me to know that this was serious business he was calling me into his office to discuss. And he wanted me to be vulnerable. That was really the bottom line."

"You declined the drink."

"I said to him, 'You *know* I wouldn't like a drink.' He gave me his best smile and said, 'Yes, I know.' It was cat and mouse. He was just setting up the game and letting me know which parts we were playing.

"Alan said that he wanted me to take a temporary leave of absence from the force. This wasn't my first. I took one after my husband died. In fact I had only been back a little over a month."

"Why did he want you to take another leave?"

"He showed me the photographs. He was very simple about it. Not at all emotional. His wife looking like a goddamn porn star and he simply sits there at his desk and watches me flip through the pictures. Politicians can stop their own hearts from beating. I mean that literally, I really do. Anyway, he told me the name of the man in the photographs. Guy Fellows. He said, 'I believe you have already met my lovely wife.' He told me that Guy Fellows taught tennis at the country club and that his wife had been taking lessons and that—obviously—the two had gotten involved sexually. He said that Guy Fellows was attempting to blackmail him, that there was an entire video collection out there. What he needed was my help. There was a partner. The person who had taken the actual video. Until they knew the partner's identity they could not make a move on Guy."

" 'Make a move.' Do you think that meant kill him?"

Kate pursed her lips. "I don't think so. Or I certainly didn't think so at the time, anyway. The police commissioner is not going to call one of his grunts into the office and discuss plans to murder someone. He didn't say what he meant. He probably didn't even know yet himself. He just knew that he had to have the other person in hand before he could make any moves."

"So your job was to locate the partner."

"Yes."

"But why the leave of absence? He was giving you a job assignment, right?"

"There is undercover and there is undercover. Alan couldn't have any paperwork on this. An official assignment would have meant a file. Reports. Those photographs would have had to go into the file. The basic facts of the top cop's wife boffing the tennis pro would have had to go into that file. Even under normal circumstances, this would have been a little rough for Mr. Stuart. In light of a gubernatorial campaign, it was a nonissue. There would be no files. There would be nothing to leak to the press, or to the other campaign. It was all to be handled off the books. The only way I could do that was to take a leave of absence.

"And so I did. I did my boss's bidding. I went out and got myself a nice little country club wardrobe. Behind the scenes, Alan quietly made the arrangements with the club. I have no idea what he told them. But voilà. Instant member. No background checks of my Mayflower ancestry. Nothing. Katie Zabriskie from Thirty-eighth Street in Hampden, member in good standing of the Baltimore Country Club. Wouldn't my father have gotten a roar out of that! I almost wished he were still alive, just to see it."

I noted the "almost" of that last statement. I think she noted me noting it. We didn't mention it. She went on.

"The rest is pretty simple and, frankly, none of your business. I did my job. I infiltrated. I contacted my target. This is the lingo we use. I have to say, the contact part was pretty damned easy. Guy was an outrageous flirt. He was running a real number at that club, I can tell you."

"So then Amanda Stuart wasn't his only, uh, extracurricular student?"

"Hitch, you're such a pilgrim. No, she wasn't. He was on the make with any number of women there. Some of them weren't married, so you have to pretty much dismiss them. Or at least downgrade them."

"What do you mean?"

"As suspects."

"Suspects?"

"Murder. Hitch, are you forgetting that we're talking about a man who has been murdered?"

Holy moly, and I used to think I was a smart little pumpkin. It had never even occurred to me that there might be someone out there completely unrelated to Alan and Amanda Stuart who might have held a murderous grudge against Guy Fellows. Other lovers. Other pissed-off hubbies.

Kate continued. "He was sleeping with a number of other women. He might have been blackmailing any one of them as well. Who knows? That's a part of what I had to investigate. What did you think, my entire task was to go to bed with this guy and squeeze the name of his partner in crime out of him? I don't mean to sound offended, Hitch, but I'm offended. I'm a detective."

I muttered an apology. Though I wasn't exactly certain what I was apologizing for.

"Let me just get this all clear," I said. "Alan Stuart, your boss, very possibly the next governor of this state, calls you into his office and tells you that some huckster tennis pro is screwing his wife and is threatening to go public with dirty videos and that he—Stuart—wants you to go out there and slither in between the guy and his sheets as part of your *job*? That's in your job description? Fetch coffee, seduce suspects?"

"I don't fetch coffee," Kate said flatly.

"I'm sorry, but am I misguided here in thinking that something about all of this maybe, just maybe, puts Alan Stuart in a somewhat unfavorable light?"

"Did you hear me say I was happy about it?"

"I'm just—"

"I wasn't then and I'm not now. And I'd appreciate your not sitting there on my couch taking cheap shots at me."

"I'm sorry, Kate. I don't mean to be doing that. I just don't see where this guy gets the authority to tell you to go to bed with a blackmailer."

Kate took a deep breath and stared out the window. I had looked out of it earlier. There is nothing to see. A street. Cars driving by. Rows of brownstones across the street.

Kate turned back to look at me. Her anger was gone. She looked pale and uncertain.

"He doesn't have the authority, Hitch. There are strict departmental regulations about that sort of thing."

"Then how—" I cut myself off. She was going to tell me. I didn't need to badger.

"It wasn't an official investigation," she said slowly. "It was strictly off the books. There were no regulations to follow. I had to be as free as I needed to be to get as close to Guy Fellows as I needed."

She came away from the window.

"It wasn't an official investigation," she said again. "There is no paperwork. Alan called me into his office and then into his confidence. He asked me to go after Guy Fellows and to root out everything that I could." She sighed. "He asked me to do it as a personal favor to him."

"Kate . . ." I hesitated, seeing the forlorn look that had come over her face. "Oh, Kate, isn't that an awfully large favor?"

She sighed. "Yes it is."

"Could you have just said no?"

She lowered her head. I could barely hear her answer. "I owed him."

I stood up from the couch—finally—and went over to her. I touched her on the arm and she looked up into my face. God, she looked exhausted.

"You *owed* him? You owed him what? You owed him a favor? Kate, how big a favor can you owe a person?"

She searched my face, but it was clear she wasn't finding what she needed there. She stepped past me and disappeared into the kitchen. I heard a cabinet door being shut. She reappeared, holding a bottle of Wild Turkey and two glasses.

"Would you do the honors?"

I didn't move. "What are you doing?" I asked.

"I'm asking you to pour me a drink. I'm in my own home, for Christ's sake."

"Are you sure?"

"Hitch, I'm not sure of anything, okay? That's the whole problem. But maybe if I can get everything out on the table I can start to sort it out better. I'm sorry . . . I'm sorry if this stuff helps me do it, but right now it does. So do you want to lecture me or be my friend?"

I didn't really think that the two choices she offered me were the only ones that should be available. She didn't wait for me to answer.

"Never mind. I can pour." She sat down on the couch and poured two inches into one of the glasses. She looked up at me. "For God's sake, don't make me drink alone. Please."

I motioned for her to pour out a second glass. She did. I picked it up. She picked up hers as well and held it just beneath her chin. She had trouble getting her words out.

"The reason . . . the favor that I owed Alan. The . . . reason he could feel so confident in calling me in and asking me to . . . to do his dirty work for him . . ." She took a tiny sip.

"I lied to you, Hitch. I lied to you the other night, about my husband."

"The shoot-out?"

"That part was true. The shoot-out was true. The bungled stakeout. All that was all true. It just happened a little differently from how I told you. The guy up on the walkway? The one who I said shot Charley?"

I nodded.

"He didn't shoot Charley. He shot me. He shot me in the shoulder. That was the scar you were so polite not to ask me about last night."

It was this morning, but I didn't quibble.

"Okay," I said. "So he shot you. And your . . . whoever he was, the other cop—"

"Lou. Lou Bowman."

"Bowman. He shot the guy up on the walkway. Was that part true?"

"That part was true."

"So what am I missing, Kate?"

"You're missing Charley. That's what you're missing. You're missing my husband who is lying on the ground bleeding to death."

"But you've just said that the guy on the walkway didn't shoot him."

Kate held up her glass, out at arm's length. "You see how steady that is? Do you see how the glass isn't shaking? We're trained to be steady like that. Hours and hours at the firing range so that if and when the time comes, we'll come up with our guns as steady as I'm holding this glass. And pow, pow, pow."

She was absolutely right. The glass was as steady as could be. She finished off her drink, then set the glass back onto the table.

"The guy up on the walkway didn't kill my husband," Kate said. "He didn't shoot Charley." She whispered. "I did."

In a movement so swift I barely saw it, Kate snatched up her glass and aimed it at me like a pistol.

"Pow."

CHAPTER 18

God, what a sad mess. I don't mean my apartment, I mean Kate Zabriskie and the numerous tangles that were doing their number on her. My apartment *was* a mess, though as usual I pinned the blame on Alcatraz, lovably clumsy Clydesdale that he is. I actually need a bigger place or a smaller dog. But I'm happy with both of what I've got, so I manage.

After Kate's shocker, she had asked me to leave. When I asked if she was going to be all right she had said "No. But I'll be worse if you're here trying to be nice to me. It's a mess, Hitch. You don't even know the half of it."

She had gone to a nice old rolltop desk and pulled a thick envelope from one of the drawers and handed it to me.

"Is this the half of it?" I had asked.

"I can't talk about this anymore today. Tonight. Whatever. I'm exhausted. Read these. It's mainly fiction, but you'll get some idea of . . . well, just read it."

The envelope was filled with newspaper clippings. I spread them out on my bed and sat Buddha-style on a pillow as I went over them. They were all from the previous fall. I sorted them by date. I tried to keep in mind what Kate had told me: mainly fiction.

TWO KILLED IN WAREHOUSE SHOOTING
Police Trap Turns Deadly

UNDERCOVER COP KILLED IN CROSSFIRE
Police Investigating Possible Ambush

POLICE WIFE SHOT HUSBAND'S KILLER
Detective Took Out Husband's Killer
Seconds After Fatal Shot

BITTER JUSTICE FOR WIDOW
Commissioner Stuart Calls Officer Zabriskie
a Hero; Funeral Set for Tomorrow

HERO WIDOW BIDS FAREWELL TO HERO HUSBAND
Huge Turnout for Det. Chas. Russell;
Katherine Zabriskie Cleared in Killing
of Husband's Murderer

A thin red line was ripping the horizon by the time I finished going over all of the clippings. The men of the purple dawn had already come by and rattled the neighborhood's trash cans into their truck. The seagulls were awake, sending their laughter through the sky. All across Baltimore, razors and toasters were doing their thing.

Kate told me that she had shot and killed her own husband. By mistake of course. Crossed wires and botched communications and who knows what else had landed Charley Russell on the wrong side of a police stakeout, and even more cruelly, his nearly new wife on the other side, pistol at the ready, steady as a mountain—per police training—squeezing off a single shot in the second before recognizing her target as her own beloved husband. She told me this much, and this much only: "I saw a man coming up with a gun and I shot him. He dropped immediately. A second later I took a bullet in the shoulder from the guy up on the walkway. Lou—he was the detective there with me—Lou nailed him. And that was the end of the truth."

The clippings included a standard police academy mug shot of Katherine Zabriskie, a remarkably bland photograph in my view, just another earnest smiling face under a slightly too-large police hat. There was a picture of her husband as well. He was a solidly handsome guy with a tidy little policeman's mustache. Two kids in love. It was a heartbreaker.

It finally dawned on me that I really needed to get some sleep. I flipped off the light, only to find that it had ceased doing any good about an hour ago. Day had dawned. I put a pillow over my head and suffocated myself to sleep.

CHAPTER 19

I had a funeral slotted for the morning. The Webster funeral. Though when I got to my office, the paperwork on my desk said it was the Weber funeral. It was a typo. God, I hoped the gravestone was right. There's nothing you can do with a misspelled headstone that reads "Weber" except to keep it to the side and wait to see if anyone named Weber kicks and drops. Though it dawned on me that I could call up a guy I used to know named Weber and see if he had any interest. We used to be good friends, but we had a falling out some years back over something small and petty. I don't suppose a phone call from me offering him a misspelled gravestone with his name on it would do much to thaw the ice between us.

Moot point anyway. When I got to the cemetery the gravestone read "Webster," not "Weber." The funeral went off without a hitch. Or with just one, if you're referring to me. I shook a half-dozen Webster hands and lent my hanky to the widow. As we were leaving the cemetery I saw one of the guests, a stocky balding guy with a thick Norse-looking beard pull out a tobacco pipe from his coat pocket, load it and stoke it. After a few puffs he tapped his pipe against the coffin then put it back in his pocket. A little ashes-to-ashes thing. You'd be surprised how many people have their little personal rituals. This guy wandered back over to his wife, who poked him lovingly in the gut. They headed off to their car with their arms around each other.

After I got back from the funeral I went out to the end of the pier that runs past the Screaming Oyster Saloon and gazed out over the harbor. I've been doing this ever since I was a kid. It's not really much of a view, but for some reason it has always worked for me as the place to do my hard thinking. The busy world of commerce was well under way. Across the harbor, a long, low-riding barge pulled slowly away from the Bethlehem Steel plant, where turn-of-the-century chimney stacks were belching steam out into the sky. My mother used to try to convince me that this is where clouds were made. *You see, Hitchcock? You see? There they are! Look. Brand-new!* Just beyond the Beth Steel plant is the Domino sugar sign, a huge rectangle of steel and pink neon. And beyond that, the big spindly cargo cranes over at Sparrows Point. Somewhere back there, Kate Zabriskie had shot her husband.

I had gone out to the pier in the hopes of sorting through the tangle of all the dead people who seemed to be piling up around Kate Zabriskie. The fictions chronicled in the newspaper clippings had actually revealed an awful lot, even as they obscured an awful lot. For one thing, Alan Stuart was a master manipulator, even by highly successful politician standards. The puppeteering he had apparently performed around the death of Kate's detective husband was no lightweight tug of the string. He did no less then reassign the responsibility for the death of Charley Russell from one person to another. I'm not privy to all that would be required to hush up the tragedy of one cop accidentally shooting another cop, but I have to imagine that Alan Stuart worked his strings pretty deftly and pretty damned swiftly to pull it off. Aside from the issue of the coroner's report, which certainly would have distinguished the type of bullet that brought down Detective Russell, there was the business of the other cops on the scene. Surely they knew what went down. Their stories all had to be made to square with the brand-new truth. How had Alan Stuart managed to get all of these puppets so perfectly lined up?

A tugboat gave off three sharp blasts.

No. I was asking the wrong question. "How" is a matter of logistics. Gargantuan logistics in this case, but apparently doable. The newspaper fiction proved that much.

The real question was "Why?" Why would Alan Stuart clamber through these kinds of hoops? I made an invisible disk of the word "chivalry" and flung it out at the water. It sank immediately. No way. Kate Zabriskie was a beat cop. The commissioner of the city's police force is not going to risk his entire career in order to buoy a beat cop, I don't care how dishy her legs are.

That's when I left the pier and got into my car and drove straight down to police headquarters.

Kate wasn't in. But Detective John Kruk was. He saw me standing at the front desk and he motioned for me to step into his office.

"Take a seat, Mr. Sewell." I did. He got right to the point. "Mr. Sewell, would you mind telling me again where you were last Saturday night?"

"God, are we back to that?"

"You're answering my question with a question. I don't like that."

"You don't?" I couldn't resist. The detective waited. His expression was telling me that he had all day to wait. I continued. "I just want to get this straight. I'm not considered a suspect in this murder, but you would like to hear my alibi anyway, is that it?"

"I would."

"And if I don't have one?"

"You're asking questions again."

I shook my fist melodramatically in the air. "Well I'm sorry, Detective. But I want some answers, damn it!"

Way back in the prehistoric past of the clan of Kruk, a tiny smile was perhaps once cracked. If so, the perpetrator was immediately bludgeoned to death and the errant gene forever snuffed out.

The detective leaned forward and laced his fingers together on top of his desk.

"I'm going to be straight with you, Mr. Sewell. The murder of a hot-head tennis pro is not the sort of crime that keeps me awake at night. I didn't know him, and from the sound of things, I wouldn't have liked him. It's a little like your job. You don't have to care one way or the other about the people you're putting into the ground, do you. You just do it. It's what you're trained to do, it's what you're paid to do."

A fine little speech. But what the hell was he getting at?

"I'm sure you know, I'm not even working this case anymore," Kruk continued. "It's been handed to Detective Zabriskie."

"She told me."

Kruk unlaced his fingers and sat back in his chair. "I saw the two of you at the fund-raiser the other night. That's not real professional of her, seeing you socially. Suspect or not. Not while this case is still open. Detective Zabriskie knows that."

"Then shouldn't you be having this little chat with Detective Zabriskie?"

"I should and I will. But she hasn't reported in for work today. You wouldn't by any chance have any idea why, would you?"

I pictured the pretty detective at home crying her eyes out into her pillow. *Pow.*

"Nope."

"Well, I happened to see you out there in the office wandering around looking kind of lost, so I thought I'd call you in for a little chat."

"That was so kind of you," I said, smiling broadly enough to show I didn't mean it.

He spread his hands beatifically. "I'm a public servant, Mr. Sewell."

"Look, Detective, am I at all out of line in asking you if my social life, or for that matter, Detective Zabriskie's, is actually any of your business? I seem to be missing something here."

"You're not missing anything, Mr. Sewell. You're right. It's not technically any of my business. It's not my case and I'm not Detective Zabriskie's baby-sitter."

"Nor mine."

"Or yours. That's right. Why don't you just put it down as my good deed for the day, okay?" He paused. No public servant crap this time. Kruk drilled me with his small eyes. "Things are going to be getting a little messy around here, Mr. Sewell. I'm only trying to keep the bit players out of the picture. For their own sake as well as mine. Now why don't you show me you know how to take a hint."

I had a feeling that whatever "mess" he was referring to, he wasn't going to share it with me. A hubbub sounded just then from the open area outside Kruk's office. Kruk was looking past me to see what it was.

"Can I go now?" I asked.

He waved his hand in the air. "Go."

I got out of the chair and stepped to the door. The hubbub was coming from across the main room. It looked to me like some sort of reunion. A stocky guy in civilian clothes was surrounded by cops, who were slapping his back and punching his arm and all that other sort of camaraderie pummeling that goes on. The guy didn't look exactly comfortable with it all either. He had a hard smile tacked on his face. He was a beefy man. Square head. Small black eyes. Black hair in tight curls, receding to the top of his broad forehead. He looked like Tony Bennett, but Tony Bennett on mean pills.

It sounded like the cops were chanting "You! You! You!" But then I realized that they were chanting the guy's name: "Lou! Lou! Lou!"

Kruk stepped up next to me and watched the little scene with fairly undisguised distaste.

"Who's Mr. Popular?" I asked.

"Lou Bowman," Kruk said, almost as if to himself. "What the hell do you know. Lottery goddamn Lou."

"Lottery Lou? That wouldn't by any chance be someone who hands out winning tickets, would it?" The way everyone was kissing up to the guy it certainly seemed like that was the case.

Kruk grunted. "Fat chance. Bowman used to work here. He was a detective. He played the lottery every week. Never missed a week."

"So what happened? Did he hit the jackpot?"

Kruk crossed his arms on his chest, one hand sliding up to cup his chin. His eyes narrowed as he watched the activity across the room.

"Better. Go figure this. He never hits. Not even a four match. Then one day, a wealthy aunt dies. Leaves Lou the whole damn farm. Suddenly a cop's salary is chump change."

"He quit?"

Kruk was tugging on a nonexistent goatee. "Didn't even give us time to kiss his lucky ass good-bye. Moved up to Maine."

"What's in Maine?" I asked.

Kruk let out a soft snort. "It's not here." He turned and went back into his office. Apparently Kruk wasn't the backslapping type. I looked back over at the scene. Lottery Lou didn't look like the type either. He looked like a bulldog that was being forced to stand there and be fussed over by a group of poodle lovers.

As I turned to leave I caught sight of someone else who was also observing the little reunion. He was standing half hidden in the far doorway to my left, practically in the stairwell. He was unnoticed at first by the back-slapping men across the room. I'm positive. Had they seen him, they would have reacted. Even at this distance, the cold anger in the man's eyes was palpable. It was Police Commissioner Stuart. As I watched, though, I became aware that one of the men—Lou Bowman himself—had picked up on his former boss's presence across the room. I saw the stocky ex-cop toss a very unloving glance of his own over toward the door-way. When I looked back, Stuart was gone. I caught just a glimpse of the shadow of his broad shoulders disappearing down the stairs.

Before I left the station I wrote a short note to Kate on the back of a Wanted poster that I found floating near the top of a trash can. I guess they got the guy. Or stopped caring. I folded up the note and begged an envelope off the front desk cop and wrote on it: "Kate Zabriskie/Personal".

"Can you see that Detective Zabriskie get this?" I asked the desk cop.

He looked at the envelope. "It's personal?"

"So it says."

"I'll see that she gets it."

"Thank you."

"Don't mention it."

"Too late for that."

I left. I guess the note wasn't really all that personal. It read: "Call me. H."

There was a note on my windshield when I got to my car. Gosh, every-one was passing notes today. Mine was from the City of Baltimore. They didn't like where I had chosen to park my car. For eighty-five dollars, though, they'd be happy to forget all about it.

I got into my car and tried to peel out. Chevy Nothings don't peel out. I ran two red lights and took a left turn from the right lane. Might as well get my money's worth.

CHAPTER 20

Gil Vance was insisting that I attend a rehearsal, so I did. My pith helmet and Teddy Roosevelt glasses were waiting for me, as was a wooden lectern that the prop mistress had dug up. Our gold-plated number at the funeral home had been deemed too ornate. Betty the prop mistress also handed me a large felt caterpillar.

"What's this?" I asked.

"That's your mustache."

"I'm supposed to *wear* this?"

"Here's your spirit gum," Betty said, ignoring my objections. Prop mistresses have to do this. Three-quarters of their time is spent ignoring rude objections from thespian snobs.

"I can't wear this. I'll look ridiculous," I sputtered. Betty gave me her "get real" look. I was already holding a pith helmet and a pair of Teddy Roosevelt eyeglasses. Heaven forbid I suddenly look ridiculous adding one more prop to the mix. I held the thing to my lip. It smelled like dust and it itched like crazy.

"Looks great," Betty said, not even bothering to sound like she meant it. She moved off to disappoint someone else. I pinched a little spirit gum onto the scratchy felt thing and attached it to the crotch of a plaster knock-off of the Venus de Milo, that was on a nearby shelf. It looked better on her, I'm sure.

Gil had gotten a message from Chinese Sue that Julia wouldn't be making the rehearsal, so there went my playmate for the evening. Gil said that he would read Julia's lines. We were slotted to go over the soda fountain scene tonight. Michael Goldfarb and Gil Vance were going to sit at the sawhorse soda counter and make gaga eyes at each other while sipping from a large glass of fake malted milk. Libby Maslin had volunteered to stand in for the part of Emily, but Gil had nixed the idea. "You're the boy's mother. We can't go mixing him up that way." Oh, I see . . . not *that* way.

As the rehearsal got under way, Betty the prop mistress resurfaced. She was holding what looked like a licorice black shoelace in her hand. It was another mustache, a black waxed number. Snidely Whiplash. I liked it.

Gil wasn't so sure. "It makes you look like a villain."

"Gil, I think the folksy nice-guy Stage Manager thing has been done to death. There's a darkness to this play. Can't we think something along the lines of . . . say, *Cabaret*? 'Good evening madams and monsieurs. *Willkommen* to our town. Vatch your steps, pleeze.' "

Gil was fiddling absently with his malted-milk straw. He squinted into the footlights, attempting to conjure up the vision.

"*Willkommen*," he said, tentatively first, and then a second time with zest. "*Willkommen!* I'm seeing it. Yes! We can try that out." Then he frowned. "But what about the pith helmet? Are you still an anthropologist?"

God help me, I wasn't about to lose my lectern.

"Absolutely. This is just a facet of the Stage Manager. The guy needs a facet, let's face it."

"So we keep the pith helmet and the wire-rimmed glasses and we add the diabolical mustache. Is that it?"

"You've got a hell of a show here, Gil," I said, donning the helmet and giving it a jaunty tap on the top.

Gil turned to Michael. "What do you think, Michael?"

I thought the young man's answer displayed an impressive sense of timing.

"Well .`. . you know . . . I was going to talk to you about my yarmulke."

Gil blinked. "What about it?"

"I want to wear it during the show."

Gil was no dummy. He couldn't very well give me the wax mustache and not let Michael Goldfarb have his yarmulke. "Of course. Of course you can wear it." Libby Maslin had just stepped onto the stage. She planted her feet firmly and addressed Gil with uncommon passion.

"If he wears one, I wear one."

"But . . . but, Libby, you're not even Jewish," Gil said weakly.

"Doesn't matter. He's my son. How would it look?"

How it would look is ridiculous. Women don't even wear yarmulkes. Even I knew that. So did Michael Goldfarb, but he was keeping his mouth shut. Gil looked as if he was about to get sick. He shaded his eyes and called out into the dark, "Betty! Please locate two yarmulkes."

"I have one," Michael said dryly. "And I can get one for Miss Maslin."

Libby Maslin looked as if she was about to take the boy into her spinster breast.

"Call me Libby."

This damned rehearsal hadn't even begun and the thing was slipping out of Gil's trembling hands. I couldn't wait to tell Julia. I wondered where she was.

The message on my phone machine said, "I'm here." This was followed by a familiar set of sounds, voices, tinny music, some clicks and clacks, a familiar female laugh . . .

I found Kate sitting at the bar talking to Sally.

"I hope you two are talking about me," I said, sliding onto a barstool.

Sally answered, "You would be . . . ?"

Kate was drinking cranberry juice. I pointed at her glass. "I'll have one of those."

Kate reached out and touched Sally on the arm. "What does he usually have?"

"Turkey."

"Give him that."

Sally gave me my drink. Kate and I retreated to a table in the back.

As soon as we sat down, Kate spoke up. "One thing, Hitch. Please don't patronize me. About the liquor. I've got a little thing with liquor right now. You don't. I appreciate it, but it's the wrong way to be nice."

I tapped my whiskey glass against her cranberry glass. "Deal."

Kate asked me if I had read the clippings that she had given me. Hero Widow Kills Husband's Killer. I told her that I had.

"What did you think of all that?" she asked.

I wasn't sure where to start. "I think something very bizarre went down, but I don't know what. All I kept thinking was, why would Alan Stuart do all that. It was him, right? Who got that story going?"

Kate nodded. "It was him all right. He was already there at the hospital when they brought Charley in. Charley was . . . he was announced dead on arrival."

"Kate, I'm so sorry."

"I appreciate that, but look. I can't go back to the 'sorry' place. I really can't." She gave a big sigh. "Alan requisitioned an office at the hospital. He took me in there. You can imagine, I was in shock. Nothing was real. I knew that Charley was dead. I knew that I had killed him. But I wasn't feeling it. That's pretty standard."

"Shock."

"Exactly." She took a sip of her cranberry juice. "Alan did a very mean thing then. The first of many, as it turned out. He badgered me out of my shock. I figured it out later, what he was doing. He needed to get me out of that insulated place as quickly as he could. I wasn't really going to take in any of what he was saying so long as I was in shock. So he leaned into me. 'Charley's dead. We can't undo that. It comes with the job. You've always known that. He's dead. I'm sorry. But now you've got to listen to me. Do you understand? You have to listen closely.' Over and over. He did a real number on me, Hitch."

"Sweet man."

"Charming."

"So what was his game?"

"Simple. He wanted to get into my brain and start to rearrange things. I swear, Hitch, he was like a hypnotist. And I was taking it in. I mean, I was empty. For Christ's sake, *I* wanted to be dead. I had just shot my husband. Alan instructed me not to say a word to anyone about what had happened. No one. Then he started talking about the man on the walkway. The one who Lou killed."

"Lou. Wait a minute. Is that Lottery Lou?"

Kate was surprised. "How'd you know that?"

I told her about dropping by the station and seeing this guy getting the homecoming queen routine.

"Kruk called him 'Lottery Lou.' "

"That's him. Lou Bowman. He was the detective on the stakeout. He's the one who shot the guy up on the walkway."

"For which you were given credit."

Kate grimaced at this. "Credit. Right." She sighed. "So anyway. This guy that Lou picked off, Alan kept telling me how much I hated that man. 'You hate him, Kate. You hate him, you hate his guts. He's responsible for this. You hate him . . . ' Like that. And then at some point I heard him saying, 'You killed him, you killed that man.' I said no, I killed Charley. But Alan was shaking his head. 'Listen. You killed that man, Kate. You shot him. That man killed Charley. It's better that way. He's scum. That's the way it happened. Listen to me. You tried to save Charley.' He said all of this over and over again. I just sat there. In shock, out of shock. I don't even know. Alan flipped open my head and poured it all in. I mean, he wasn't trying to actually *convince* me of all this. He couldn't do that. But he got the new version running in my head. That's what he was after. Alan is a powerful man. I respected the hell out of him. And he just stood there in that hospital office and he put me in his pocket. 'Keep this in the family,' he said."

Kate pulled a cigarette from her bag then tossed it onto the table. "Oh Jesus, Hitch, he ran a blah blah blah on me you wouldn't believe. He said that he had talked to Lou already, that Lou was on board, and that I just had to listen to what he was saying. 'This is for your own good, Kate,' he kept saying. On and on and on.

"Somehow he got me out of that hospital without anyone seeing me or talking to me. He brought me to his house. It was surreal. I woke up in one of the guest bedrooms to find that my husband was dead, gunned down in the line of duty. And I was the reluctant hero. *I* had killed the guy who supposedly shot Charley. Not Lou. Me. The story was out there. It was a done deal at that point. Alan played me perfectly. I swear it was as if he had watched me growing up and knew just which buttons to push. Hide the truth. Live the lie. Suck up the shame. That 'keep it in the family' garbage. That was the right thing to say to me. He put his finger on that big button and he pushed it and he pushed it and he didn't let up. I can't even tell you anything about the next several days, Hitch. Alan insisted that I stay with him and his wife until the funeral. I can barely remember any of it. I see that picture in the paper of me at the funeral getting that flag from Alan and I can't even remember it happening. I do remember burning every condolence card and letter and flower that I received. I remember that. As far as I was concerned they weren't condolences, they were accusations. They were the punishment that I wasn't even allowed to have. I had killed my husband and I wasn't even going to suffer for it. That was what Alan Stuart did to me."

Kate reached across the table and tapped on my glass with her fingernail. "I kind of lost my grip when all this happened." Her voice was just above a whisper. "Actually . . . I lost it big-time."

She picked up my hand and brought it up to her lips and held it there for several seconds, holding me with her eyes.

"I need to get out of here," Kate said abruptly. She stood up. She was halfway to the door before I even found my feet. I saw Sally out of the corner of my eye registering her disappointment. I guess it looked like a fight.

Outside, I asked Kate if she wanted to go home. "Alone, I mean. Or not." This was her call. I knew I was circling a wounded animal.

"I need to finish this," she said.

I knew just the place.

The idle factories across the harbor broke the night's horizon like silent blue mountains. Off to the southwest was Federal Hill, where just a few nights ago Kate and I had sealed our now very quaint-seeming date with a couple of kisses while overlooking the harbor. Now we sat without touching on the end of the pier. The inky darkness made it easier, I'm sure, for Kate to get the rest of her story out. She told it to the water below her feet. Or maybe she was directing herself to my black reflection. Either way, I listened.

Less than a week after the funeral of Charley Russell, Alan Stuart had summoned Kate into his office. He reminded her again what a brave thing she was doing. The department didn't need the ugliness of one of its own cops killing another, even if it was a terrible accident, etc., etc. Nor did Stuart himself need it, politically. He certainly didn't need a cop killing a cop under his watch. He reminded her—again—how a bad thing, a truly tragic event, had been spun into something positive. The good will was pouring in. The newspapers—and they were spread all over Stuart's desk—were suddenly the police department's new best pal. This was good, he reminded Kate. This was all very, very good.

There was, however, something that they needed to discuss. And this, he said, was something quite delicate. It certainly could not leave this room. Stuart surprised Kate then, by acknowledging the position he had put her in. He told her that he well understood how reluctant she must be to be receiving all of this attention and adulation for having avenged her husband when of course she was the one who had gunned him down. He acknowledged the irony and he apologized for the burden.

In other words, he was setting her up for more.

There was something he felt that she had to be told. It was something, he said, that Kate wouldn't particularly want to hear. He intimated that in a very, very small way it might take a fraction of the sting off of what had transpired—the real story—in that warehouse just a week before. Kate recalled thinking that this was an awfully ballsy claim. But by then she was already quite aware—and soon to become even more so—that Alan Stuart was one awfully ballsy bastard.

Charley was sour. This is what Stuart told her. A bad cop. Charley had turned. It is the biggest risk of undercover assignments, especially when large sums of money are floating around. Kate listened in silence as Alan Stuart sketched out the details. She couldn't sort through them. She saw Alan Stuart's mouth moving, and like an out-of-synch movie, she was hearing the words floating somewhere in the vicinity of his lips. *Illegal dumping. Secret deposits. Chemical waste* . . . Stuart was showing her some papers. The words in the air were saying "Charley" and "money"; they might as well have been saying "cheese" and "snowman." She just wasn't hearing.

Charley was a bad cop. This is what Alan Stuart was telling Kate and what he was telling her to leave behind when she left his office. He told her that the department had suspected it, had in fact been about to launch an internal investigation. They had been planning to pull Charley off of his assignment as soon as it was logistically feasible to do so. Ironically—tragically—they had been planning to pull him in in just a few more days. He would have been safe and alive and in very hot water.

Alan Stuart had then pulled up a chair and taken hold of Kate's hands. He made her look him in his eyes as he started twisting the knife. He told her that the department had reason to believe that Charley's cover had already been blown, that the people he was investigating and profiting from had been onto him. Stuart also believed that Charley knew that the internal investigation of his own actions had been instituted. He was tainted on both sides. No good place to turn.

This is when Stuart squeezed her hands. Squeezed them hard. And this is when his fingers—as he squeezed—crawled their way along her hands and up to her wrists, where they pushed gently, even as they remained gripped. It felt creepy. It felt intimate. It felt like she was being handcuffed.

"He said that Charley had cornered himself," Kate said. "That he had stepped on a bear trap and that it was snapping closed on him. He said the jaws were just about to get him when I shot him."

Kate stared down at the water. Finally, she threw her head back, tossing her hair out of her face, and nailed me with a hard look.

"He kissed me," she said. "The bastard."

As if on cue, a tugboat let off a long mournful blast. The bare trace of a smile curled Kate's lip. It was gone, however, by the time the sound stopped.

In the course of that single week she was recounting, Kate had detached from the world she once thought she understood. In those seven days, she had murdered her husband, borne the ill-guided sympathy of the people of the city of Baltimore, discovered that her husband was not who she had taken him to be, and begun an affair with her boss. She had returned the kiss.

"I had no sense of the ground," Kate said to me, swinging her feet out of tandem. "I had no sense of the meaning of conversations I was having. When nothing seems real, then nothing really matters. It didn't seem to matter, somehow, that my husband was suddenly gone from this earth and that I was going to bed with another man. The only real thought I had of Charley . . . two thoughts really. One was that had he lived maybe he would have aged and matured into someone as powerful and protecting as Alan Stuart. Maybe he would have made me insanely happy and secure. And the other thought was that I hated him. He had let me down. He had lied to me. He had lied to all of us. Then rather than face up to it like a man he had let me murder him.

"But the fact is, I was hating myself even more. Every time I let Alan Stuart into my bed over those next months I was hating myself. I was taking the punishment that I deserved. The price you pay for killing your husband and getting away with it, sexual doormat for your goddamn boss. And the better Alan made me feel in bed, the more I hated myself. That's how it works. It's pathetic, but that's how it works. You always hate the wrong person. Always. And the wrong person is usually yourself."

The affair went on for several months. Kate went back to work, but she was a robot. It wasn't right.

"I was no good as a cop. Not like that. On the nights when Alan wasn't using me . . . that's when my little relationship with booze started to get out of hand. It's a beautiful thing, isn't it. My relationship with my boss and my relationship with the bottle. But at least with the one you can stick it up on a high shelf where it's harder to reach. The other just walks through the door and takes you."

Kate leaned back on her arms and looked up at the sky. It was a cloudless night with about a dozen stars. Not much to look at, really.

"Alan finally suggested that I take a paid leave of absence. He had seen the brochures that Charley and I had collected for our postponed honeymoon. He suggested that I take a trip to Mexico. Sure. Mexico sounds okay. What's the difference? So I went to Mexico. I sat on the beach. I looked at the water. I looked at some Mayan ruins. I cursed at the moon every night. I was there for three weeks. I had a two-night stand with a waiter, for Christ's sake. This sweet Mexican boy. It was horrible. I had no idea who I was or what I was doing. Which was fine. All I wanted to do was forget. Forget everything. Then Alan came down, after the second week. He came down and he did his thing with me for several days and then before he left he told me that we had to end it. He was very firm and businesslike. He ordered me to sober up and to get back to work. He said that he would always be there for me but that we had to drop the relationship then and there. He was so smug. I made some smartass comment about how sweet it had been for him to spend three days screwing me before telling me we were over. He hit me for that one, and then he left."

Kate looked out over the water. Her gaze was in the direction of the Domino sugar sign. I suspected she wasn't even seeing it.

"It was the hit that sobered me up. Though I never want him to know that. *Never*. I refuse to owe him that. I swam and I sat in the sun and I walked along the beach for the rest of the week. I had my goddamned honeymoon alone. Then I flew back to Baltimore and started my new life. I was made detective. Lou had just inherited his little fortune and left the force, so there was an opening and Alan gave it to me. It was the most shameless promotion in the history of the department, but I grabbed it. I didn't care. Everyone assumed it was a sympathy move on Alan's part. I was sick of sympathy. And I knew better. It wasn't sympathy at all. I went into Alan's office when the word came down and asked him point-blank. 'Is this because you were screwing me for three months? Is this some sort of payoff for your taking advantage of me like that?' And listen to what he said, Hitch. I memorized it, word for word. I'll never forget it. He said, 'Do you know where you would be right now if it weren't for me? You'd be off the force and in a prison cell. Now you're a goddamn detective. I'll take my thank-you in the form of good solid work, *Detective*. Now get the hell out of my office and get the hell to work.' "

Kate looked over at me. "As you can see, he is a lovely man."

"He killed Guy Fellows, didn't he?"

She caught her breath. The tugboat sounded again.

"I think he did, Hitch. I really think he did."

Kate stayed with me that night. We didn't make love; she said she felt too much like a worn-out old rug.

"You're a very pretty old rug," I told her.

"Do I have to thank you for that?"

"No."

"Good."

Kate was happy to make the acquaintance of Alcatraz. The woman had a pulse, so Alcatraz was happy to meet her as well.

"He's friendly."

"He's a whore."

"He's beautiful."

"He is. And he's loyal. And he keeps the floor from floating off. And he's as dumb as a box of rocks. Watch this." I clapped my hands together. "Alcatraz! Sit! Lie down! Roll over! Speak! Give me your paw!" I turned to Kate. "See? The five basic instructions, and nothing."

"I think he's adorable."

"Oh, he's adorable all right. He's just not fulfilling my master-slave needs. He's more decorative than I'd hoped for when I got him. Maybe a big jade plant would have been better."

Alcatraz raised his big old square head and let off a chesty *woof!*

"What do you think he said," I asked.

"I think he said, 'Fuck you for the jade plant dig.' "

I sought out Alcatraz's big wet nose. "Is that what you said, big boy? Huh? Is the lady right?" He woofed again.

Kate was chuckling now. "That's a yes."

Kate and I got into bed and she slithered her way into my arms.

"What's it like to bury people for a living?" she asked after we had smooched for a few minutes.

"God, Kate, you'd better bone up on your pillow talk."

"I'm serious. How can it not get depressing? All those sad people. Who does the embalming?"

"My aunt and I trade off."

She shuddered. "Do you think you would have still been an undertaker if your parents hadn't been killed? If you hadn't gone off to live with your aunt and uncle?"

"I don't think so. I was sort of gunning for international spy when I was a kid. Though my mother said I was too good-looking to become a spy. She said all the other spies would be jealous."

"That's such a mother thing to say."

Kate nestled her head closer into my chest. After a few moments, she sighed. "God . . . I've got a lot of baggage."

I gave her forehead a kiss. "I've always felt that if a person doesn't have any baggage, it means they haven't really been anywhere. Stop beating yourself up."

We fell silent for a few minutes. I thought maybe she had fallen asleep in my arms. Then her lips moved against my chest.

"Alan Stuart nearly destroyed me."

"I know he did," I said softly. "But you toughed it out."

"I'm a tough girl," she said.

I shifted around and found a spot on her that wasn't so tough.

"No." Her voice was surprisingly frail. "Please."

I woke sometime in the middle of the night. A movement across the room caught my eyes. Kate was nicely silhouetted in the window, framed by the pale blue moonlight. I scooted up on my pillow.

"Are you all right?"

Kate didn't answer right away. When she did, I realized that she had been crying.

"I've never told anyone before . . . about what happened. I thought . . . I guess I thought I was going to feel better, getting it off my chest. But . . ."

She leaned sideways, resting her head against the window. She placed a hand on the glass, and after a few seconds, she tapped her fingers lightly.

"I'm ashamed of myself, Hitch."

"Shhhh. You're only human. Come on back to bed."

"No. I'm not talking about what I did with Alan. I'm ashamed how quickly I buried my husband."

"I don't follow."

I could see her turn in my direction, though I'm sure all she could see of me was darkness.

"I've never tried to find out what was going on with Charley's investigation. The reason he was in the warehouse that night. We had our agreement not to talk about what he was up to. But after I . . . when Alan called me in and told me that Charley had compromised himself, I just shoved it aside. On top of everything else it was just too much. I guess . . . in a way it made it a little easier. The idea of Charley as a crooked cop is . . . it makes him abstract. Like it wasn't really my Charley who I shot, but just a replica of him. The good Charley is still out there somewhere."

"So you think Stuart was lying?"

"No. I don't . . . I really don't know. The point is . . . I never checked. Alan fed me that story and I accepted it, because it *did* make it a little easier. Not until I repeated it to you tonight and I heard it out loud did it suddenly not feel right. I mean, maybe it's all true, I don't know. I've lost my perspective on everything. But what *isn't* right is the fact that I haven't checked up on it. What kind of wife is that?"

I didn't offer an answer. Kate's silhouette blurred in the window and vanished. Seconds later she was back under the sheets.

"I'm going to pull the file on Charley's investigation," she said. "I'm going to find out what my husband was up to before I killed him." She drew a sharp breath. "That's the least I can do."

In the morning I burned a set of warm-up waffles and fed them to Alcatraz, then cranked out
a bunch of perfect golden brown squares for
Kate and me and stacked them on a plate. My
coffeemaker sputtered and wheezed like a Model T, but finally trickled
its kick-a-poo into the pot. Kate made no mention of her decision to look
into her husband's last case. Nor did I. Instead I had a few questions that
I had refrained from asking her the night before. They concerned the
Guy Fellows murder.

"I'm curious about something. You've been assigned to the Guy Fellows
case, right?" I skidded a few waffles onto a plate and set it in front of her.

"That's right."

"But only after the sleek and beautiful Detective Kruk had gotten it
first."

"John Kruk is a solid detective," Kate said. A little defensively.

"I don't doubt that he is. I guess that's partly why I'm curious. Why
would Kruk be pulled off the case? Office politics is what both you and
he told me, but I still don't get it."

Kate had been indulging Alcatraz about the head and neck. She
stopped immediately.

"He told you? When did he tell you that? When did you talk to Kruk?"

I gave Kate a rundown of my run-in with the detective the previous
day. I told her about Kruk's warning to me that Kate and I shouldn't be

seeing each other. Kate was especially interested in the part where Kruk warned me that "things were going to get a little messy around here."

"Did he explain what he meant by that?" Kate asked.

"No. What do you make of it? Do you think he's onto Alan Stuart?"

Kate was pouring syrup onto her waffles. She seemed to be concentrating a lot harder than the simple task required. "I don't know. Kruk keeps his cards close to the vest."

"Does he know about the videotape?"

"God no, are you kidding? Hitch, I haven't shared that with anyone. Except you. Which I really shouldn't have done. I'm withholding evidence, you know. I could really get screwed for this." She set down the syrup. "Of course, if Alan turns out not to be involved in the Guy Fellows murder and I've turned the tape over anyway, I'm also screwed."

I got up from the kitchen table and fetched a dog biscuit from the biscuit jar and threw it at Alcatraz. He snorted and it disappeared. I leaned back against the counter.

"Can't you just ask Kruk what's the 'mess' he's referring to?" I asked. "He was your partner, after all. I've seen cop shows. Aren't you two supposed to be soul mates?"

Kate wrapped her hands around her coffee mug and stared down at it.

"Kruk was my senior partner. We didn't work together very long. His promotion to detective had already been approved, he was just waiting for the reassignment. Kruk was never thrilled about being partnered with a woman in the first place. He's always had trouble with the idea of a woman in a uniform." She looked up at me. "It's not what you think. He's not a chauvinist pig. He's . . . well, he's a chivalrous pig in fact. Partners always watch each other's backs. I mean, that's obvious. But Kruk's complaint was that his natural concern for his partner's safety doubled if the partner was a woman. You watch each other's backs, of course. But you can't obsess. You've got to trust that your partner can take care of himself. Or herself. Kruk just couldn't take that for granted with me. He tried, I give him that. But he really couldn't."

"You're saying the crusty little guy is a softy?"

Kate had found a chip in her mug and she was picking away at it with a fingernail.

"Kruk was devastated with what went down in that warehouse the night I shot Charley. He feels that he let up and that he never should have let me go into that warehouse. That I should have been the one to stay outside and tend to Connolly."

I returned to the table and sat down opposite her. "Second-guessing, Kate. It's a useless exercise. But look, what does this have to do with your not simply asking him what's this 'mess' he's talking about?"

Kate took a few seconds to form her answer. "Kruk and I aren't, uh, communicating very well these days. My promotion to detective . . . Like I said, it came pretty fast. No one ever said anything openly to me about my affair with Alan, but come on, these are detectives, for Christ's sake. You think they don't know? I'm afraid I'm tainted goods around the old precinct."

"Why were you put on the Fellows case?"

Kate smirked. "That's a good question."

"Stuart can't possibly want you to dig anything up. I mean, not if he's involved in the murder. Though of course you already have."

"The video."

"How did you get ahold of that nifty little memento, anyway?"

"From Carolyn's apartment. It's a copy."

"So do you think Stuart has the original?"

Kate shrugged. "He's sure as hell not going to tell me if he does. I have to guess that whoever killed Guy has got the tape. I mean, that only makes sense."

"And we're guessing that's Stuart. Or at least someone with Stuart's interests in mind."

"Joel Hutchinson?"

"I don't know. He certainly has the ability to, uh, overrespond. Anything's possible." The image of a blindfolded Alfred Smollett floated into view. "But wait. Here's the question. Does your boss know that you have that tape?"

Kate finally took a bite of her now-cold waffle. As she chewed it she was shaking her head no.

"No way. Remember? I never gave up Carolyn to him. That's what's got Alan ballistic. He *still* thinks that the partner is out there."

"So then . . . what kind of murder investigation is this? If Alan Stuart is somehow involved in Guy Fellows's murder, then who are you supposed to be looking for?"

"My original assignment for Alan . . . my 'favor,' if you remember, was to locate Guy Fellows's partner. To locate Insurance, as your college chum kept saying."

"Which you did."

"Which I did. I smoked out Carolyn pretty easily. But like I said, there was no way I was going to take that poor girl out of the jaws of Guy Fellows and stick her into the jaws of Alan. I know a victim when I see one. As it is, I lost her anyway. But at least I tried. I didn't throw her to the wolves."

Something was still not lining up for me.

"But they must have known. They must have figured it out. Like you said, they wouldn't dare go after Fellows if his 'Insurance' was still out there. But the moment Carolyn James kills herself . . . bye-bye, Guy. The Insurance plan had lapsed."

"Well that's the strange part, Hitch," Kate said. "Someone must have panicked. Because I never identified Carolyn to them as Guy's partner."

"Well then they figured it out for themselves. How hard could that be? They must have learned that Guy Fellows had made arrangements—cheap as they were—for somebody's funeral. That wouldn't have been impossible to discover. They must have figured Carolyn James for the cameraperson, been all pleased that she had so conveniently killed herself, and so then they went after Fellows. Case closed. Why do you say someone panicked? It sounds ruthless to me, but not panicky."

"I can't say, Hitch. Maybe you're right. Maybe they didn't panic at the time." She had stabbed another forkful of waffle. She brought the fork up next to her face, using it to emphasize her point. "But they're panicking now." She popped the waffle into her mouth and leaned back in her chair.

"Miss Zabriskie, do you have something you would like to share with our audience?"

"Alan is still being blackmailed," Kate said flatly. "Another package of pictures has showed up. No note. No demands for money. This was just a few days ago. Alan called me into his office. Joel Hutchinson was there. Alan wanted to know if I had any leads about Fellows's partner."

"Your lead is in the cold cold ground."

"I failed to mention that to him. Then he showed me a whole new batch of pictures he'd just gotten. He was furious. Alan does not like being toyed with. Not one bit."

"Who the hell could have sent the pictures?"

"The way Alan and Joel reconstructed it, there must have been some sort of argument over at Guy's place between Guy and his partner, probably over money or over what to do next with the photographs. They had some sort of argument, it got heated, and the partner grabbed the kitchen knife and ended the argument that way."

"That's insane. There *was* no partner by then. Carolyn James was already dead. They were making that all up. Why? Are they trying to throw you off the scent?"

"There's another option. It's possible that Joel Hutchinson and Alan don't really share everything. One of them could be trying to throw the other off the scent."

"You mean for example, Amanda Stuart killed Fellows, and hubby is pointing people in another direction?"

"Could be. Or as you keep wondering, maybe Joel got a little overzealous and now he wants to keep up the pretense of this murderous mystery partner."

"This is ridiculous," I said. "Someone is bluffing. This so-called new blackmail letter is pure bullshit."

"You're right. It is bullshit. No question about it. But I can tell you this, both of those guys want me to dig like crazy for this partner. That's why I was put onto the case and Kruk was pulled off. Nobody said this out loud to me of course. But if Alan is involved, he can't afford for Kruk to bring in a collar who's going to start shooting his mouth off. It's up to *me* to locate this partner of Guy's. And I'm guessing I'll be under orders to use all due force when I do."

"But the partner is already *dead*."

"Hitch . . . I know that. And you know that. But Alan doesn't. Don't you see? Within a week of Guy's murder Alan gets a fresh shipment of dirty pictures of his wife. And these were dropped off at the front desk. Not mailed. So it certainly wasn't Guy from the grave. You should have seen those two squirming. Alan is running scared. This would bury him."

"So either Stuart or Hutch is pulling a stunt," I said. "Or Fellows actually had another partner all along. Besides Carolyn James. Is that it?"

Kate was shaking her head no.

"Then who the hell dropped off the pictures?"

Kate pointed her fork at me.

"That bastard owes me."

She speared another forkful of cold waffle and put it in her mouth. Angrily. Triumphantly. Before I could even ask her, she was bobbing her head up and down.

That would be a yes.

CHAPTER 23

Because of the arrangement with the fireman's pole running down from Julia's studio
it's possible to literally "drop in" to the gallery, if you're already upstairs. I wasn't. I used
the door.

Chinese Sue was behind the register, reading a copy of *The Village
Voice*. She lowered the paper to just under her nose and said, "Not
here."

In the several years that Chinese Sue has been holding down the fort at
Julia's gallery, I have never once heard her utter a single polysyllabic
word. I used to try to bait her, ask her leading questions. But Chinese Sue
knows her game. I've long since given up.

"Any idea where she is?" I asked.

"No."

"Or what time you expect her back?"

"Don't know."

"Or how long she's been gone?"

"No."

I wandered around the gallery for a few minutes looking at Julia's stuff.
Julia once told me that she usually didn't know what she was painting
when she started a canvas, and about half the time she didn't know what
she had painted even when she was finished. These were the paintings to

which she gave titles chosen totally at random. *Mr. Green Eats His Bicycle* or *Tunisian Pancake, Part Two*. Julia knows her colors and she knows her shapes and strokes and I think some of her best works are these impenetrable ones with the ridiculous names. (There is a collector out there who is still scouring the city for *Tunisian Pancake, Part One*, which Julia neglected to inform him doesn't exist.) It is Julia's other paintings though, that seem to sell better. A lot of these are what you would call juxtapostional musings: a man with a hen for an ear; a waterfall cascading from the top of an office building; a family of cigars enjoying a day at the beach.

I asked Chinese Sue what she was reading. Again the paper lowered to her nose. "Shit," she said. Back up went the paper. Back out the door went Hitch.

Aunt Billie had asked me to help out with her wake that afternoon. It was one of those ugly situations, where the death—in this case of an elderly woman—forces the two feuding factions of a family to lay down their arms and try to get along under the same roof—ours—for an hour or so. You'd be surprised, we get this a lot. My task at these affairs is usually less the conventional one of facilitating grief than it is running interference. What I've learned is that you're likely to get your most volatile exchange somewhere in the vicinity of the coffin itself. That's to say, this is where your actual yelling—sometimes even hitting—is most likely to take place. The poor dead thing in the box just has to lie there and take it. Billie and I double up sometimes on these feud jobs, and we can run ourselves ragged, slicing every which way across the room in an attempt to insert ourselves between the antagonists.

Aunt Billie's testy clan gathering proved fairly manageable. No full-fledged fights broke out. We did have to put out a couple of brushfires, but all in all it was a low-key affair. We were even honored with a surprise visit from Edie Velvet. Edie did this occasionally, festoon her ninety-pound frame with ten pounds of costume jewelry and come onto the scene like Norma Desmond seeking her close-up. Sometimes this can be a little off-putting to the bereaved; Edie comes on a bit too gothic for some people's tastes. But on occasions like this one, where the level of melancholy was pretty damned low to start with, a visit from the bejeweled Miss Velvet wasn't going to bother anyone. Edie made her way up to the coffin and admired the corpse, shook a few hands, gathered a few confounded stares, then made her way back out of the room. She signed the guest book as she always does—*E. Velvet/E. Baltimore*—gathered her bags and returned to the streets.

"It was nice to see Edie again, wasn't it," Aunt Billie remarked during our postmortem up in her apartment. "She was looking well."

Billie and I were parked in front of the television set. My aunt was indulging in one of her dirty little secrets: soap operas. She's hooked. Murder. Rape. Incest. Abortion out the wazoo. Stampeding infidelities. Billie can't get enough of it. In an effort to disguise what she readily admits to as a tawdry indulgence, Billie will sometimes prepare a tea service on a silver tray for her afternoon's viewing, complete with little cakes or fussy overpriced pastries. She's like a duchess at a whorehouse, sitting there with her bone china, tittering away at the serial depravity unfolding in front of her.

Billie had just been bringing me up-to-date on one of the storylines ("Dimitri's temporary insanity is a ploy to win back his stepsister from his amnesiac half brother") when the program was interrupted by a news bulletin. Mimi Wigg's big head suddenly filled the screen. Her expression was deadly serious as she reported in a tortured monotone that Jeff Simons had just been taken to Johns Hopkins Hospital after having suffered a heart attack. The beloved newsman's condition, Mimi told us sonorously, was not known at this time, though there was a report—unconfirmed—that he had stopped breathing.

"We call that dead," Billie observed. "Poor Helen." Meaning Jeff Simons's mother. I noticed that the card table was set up, cribbage board ready and waiting.

On the screen, Mimi Wigg was gently and thoroughly chewing up the scenery—in this case, the set—as she asked the citizens of Baltimore to pray for Jeff Simons. Her own little hands were already clasped together, in case we had forgotten how it's done.

"We will . . . of course . . . keep you posted."

Mimi Wigg's image vanished and in its place Dimitri appeared again, still temporarily insane. He was on one knee, his arms raised beseechingly to a potted plant high up on a bookshelf. A rail-thin blonde was spying on him from the doorway.

"That's Gloria," Billie whispered conspiratorially, pouring herself a fresh cup of tea. "I believe she killed the mayor last year. Or had his child. I can never remember."

CHAPTER 24

Kate was standing at my front door wearing a thin blue dress and holding a large wooden bowl.

"Couscous," she said. I love it when she talks like that.

"Couscous to you, too," I responded. "In my country we say *Aloha*. Come in."

Kate pulled a manila folder from her bag and dropped it onto my coffee table before she set about dishing out the couscous. It sat there conspicuously as we ate. I complimented her on the food.

"Pretty fancy."

"It's grain," she said. After my second heaping helping, I finally asked Kate about the folder.

"Charley's?"

She nodded.

We set the dishes to the side.

"Do all investigations get one of those?" I asked her. "Is that how it works?"

She told me that they did. "They're all kept on file. You have to sign them out."

"How long was your husband working on this case?"

"Months. Four? Five? I think I told you, Charley didn't go undercover on it right away. He started off doing basic legwork. But too much overt snooping and asking questions can end up tipping off the very people you need to open up. You can kill an investigation if you show the wrong people that you're interested."

She was eyeing the folder. She was torn between knowing and not knowing . . . and not knowing which of the two was the better.

"I'm being silly, right?"

"No. You're being scared. And I don't blame you."

Kate tossed her head. "Okay. Let's get this done."

We moved to the couch. Kate took a deep breath and leaned forward to flip open the folder.

Apparently it all started when the wheels came off the cart. Though in this case the cart was a train, which in fact came off the track. But you see what I'm saying.

It happened in Indiana. The train was bound for Iowa, originating in Baltimore. According to the first report in the file there was nothing particularly notable about a train derailing. It happens with much more frequency than John Q. is aware of. Because most derailments are trains carrying stuff and not people, they don't usually make the news. This derailment was one of those. The train that was bound for Iowa hit some sort of a snag as it started over the Wabash River just outside Terre Haute and four of its boxcars left the track and tipped over. Three of the four cars were carrying inexpensive stereo equipment. Boom boxes that retail for around a hundred bucks. These were of little interest. The purchaser of the boom boxes would reject the shipment and they would be sold to a discount chain.

It was the fourth boxcar that drew more attention. This boxcar contained several hundred steel drums. The label on the drums read "silica gel." Silica gel is not a gel at all, but more like a powder. Or better yet, like sand. The most distinguishing feature of the stuff is that it draws moisture out of anything with which it comes in contact—providing that there is any moisture there in the first place. The most common brush that people have with silica gel is in the buying of electronic equipment. It's what is in those little packets that look like sugar packets. The packets are there to keep ambient moisture out of the box. Apparently the stuff is also good for drying flowers.

As many as three dozen of the drums on the fourth derailed boxcar broke open when they tumbled onto the tracks. What spilled out of the drums and began marching toward the river, however, was not sandlike silica gel. What spilled out was dirt. Or more precisely, mud. Dark and slimy, very moist and apparently quite terribly aromatic.

The logical first step was to contact either the sender or the receiver to inform them of the derailment and to determine what to do with the hundred steel drums marked silica gel, at least three dozen of which contained this slime-choked dirt. It was at this point that the discovery was made that the drums did not contain any information concerning the source of the so-called silica gel and only listed its intended recipient as a warehouse in the railyard outside Des Moines. No individual or company was listed on the labels. That's a problem. And the problem was seeping into the Wabash River. After some testing was performed it was determined that the dirt seeping out of these barrels was, in fact, toxic.

And that's a crime.

Kate looked up from the file. "Here comes Charley."

The point of origin being Baltimore, the Baltimore Police Department was notified. Detective Charles Russell took the call. It became his case. Russell filed his reports. Along with whatever hard facts that the detective was gathering, the reports also included his own thoughts and speculations, such as they were. Acting on one such speculation, Russell took a trip out to Des Moines where he was escorted to the railyard warehouse that had been the ill-fated barrels' intended destination. What he found were not one hundred, not two hundred, but over *four hundred* steel drums bearing the exact same label as the bogus silica gel that was currently poisoning the bottom feeders of the Wabash River. Charley didn't even have to pop the lid on the barrels to determine that they likewise contained slimy dirt. Some hundred or so of the barrels were stacked in the fenced-in area outside the warehouse, where the forces of nature had done a number on a lot of them, swelling, rusting and rupturing them. The stuff was oozing out. In Detective Russell's own simple words: "You could smell it in the air."

Charley Russell inspected the books, the manifests, the schedules, etc. There was practically no paperwork on the mysterious shipments of drums from Baltimore. The origin of the barrels went unnamed. Likewise, the order to off-load the barrels into the Des Moines railyard bore no indication of ownership. If the barrels had any subsequent destination other than the railroad's own warehouse and fenced-in yard, Charley Russell could find no hint of it. This, then, was when Detective Russell began to formulate the plan to conduct an undercover investigation.

Kate got up and stretched her legs and paced back and forth as she read over her husband's rationale for going undercover. I suppose in a way she was hoping to determine that his decision had been the only conceivable one to have made. For it was this decision, after all, that would result in his being in the warehouse that evening, stepping out from behind a stack of steel drums.

Kate read:

"Have determined ownership of receiving warehouse to be B&O. Railroad officials in Des Moines know little about warehouse. According to records, unused for over a year. Truth? Origin of shipment unknown. Baltimore. Point: boxcars don't load themselves. Don't hook up to trains by themselves. Postponing interviews with B&O in Baltimore pending internal investigation. Contacting teamsters for immediate 'employment,' B&O railyard, Sparrows Point."

She lowered the report.

"He didn't want to confront anyone at the railroad. All they would have to do is lie and begin covering their asses. The trail would have grown cold before he ever got on it."

"Assuming that it was railroad people doing it," I pointed out.

"Oh it was definitely railroad people. Charley was right on the money there. Somebody had to load those drums. And somebody had to look the other way."

We went back to the reports. Charley Russell had continued to file his reports religiously, once a week. Through whatever connection it is that the police have with the teamsters, Russell found immediate employment in the railyard, helping to load train cars. He kept his eyes and ears open and after a while began letting it be known to the right people that he was interested in any "moonlight shifts" they might know about. At first this merely landed him offers to work double shifts. He did so—complaining to Kate that all of his overtime salary was being funneled into a city escrow account to eventually be returned to his employer. But he hung in there, advertising his desire to earn extra cash and his willingness to bend a few rules—if necessary—to do it. Eventually he was approached by a fellow named Earl DeLorenzo. I recognized the name from Kate's newspaper clippings.

"The man on the walkway."

Kate confirmed. "DeLorenzo. That's the man I supposedly shot and killed. He's the one Alan identified as Charley's killer."

DeLorenzo offered Charley another moonlighting job. This one, however, was off the books. It was pretty simple, really. DeLorenzo led Charley to a warehouse in Sparrows Point. It was empty. Charley was told to return two nights later, at midnight. When Charley did as he was instructed, a flatbed truck was parked in the loading dock. The truck held close to a hundred steel drums. Charley and Earl DeLorenzo and the driver of the truck unloaded the barrels into the warehouse. They used hand trucks. No forklifts. No cranes. According to his report, Charley attempted to ask a few casual-sounding questions about the drums and what was in them and where they had come from, but DeLorenzo made it clear that he was being paid to work, not to ask questions. Two nights later Charley was summoned to the warehouse again, where he and DeLorenzo and the driver slapped labels on the drums. Silica gel. The three men then loaded the barrels—again by hand—onto a boxcar that was parked on the loading dock track. When all of the barrels were securely loaded onto the boxcar, Earl DeLorenzo handed each of the men ten one-hundred-dollar bills, reminded them that none of this had ever happened and wished them a good morning.

Kate sat back on the couch. For nearly a minute she said nothing. She was staring at the floor. Though in fact, she was staring into the past. She was looking at a thousand dollars in cash being handed over to her husband. No doubt she was looking very intently into his eyes, trying to read what might have been in them.

Finally she spoke. "Is that enough?" she asked.

"What do you mean?"

"I mean is that enough? Is a thousand dollars enough money for work like that? For two nights of moonlighting. Something clearly illegal? Is a thousand dollars enough money?"

I was confused. "What are you asking?"

"I'm asking if Charley is lying in the report. I'm asking if Earl DeLorenzo didn't hand him twice that much. Or maybe three times that much. Charley did make that comment to me more than once, the one about all of his salary and his overtime going into the escrow account. If Alan was telling me the truth, that Charley went bad on this assignment, it's right here, Hitch. This is where it would have happened. Earl DeLorenzo hands Charley, I don't know, maybe three thousand dollars? Five thousand dollars? Charley writes it up as a thousand, hands that much in and pockets the rest. Who loses, right? He's busting his tail and he's pulling down his detective's salary, which is not exactly a cash crop, believe me. Some dirty money comes into your hands. What do you do? That's what I'm asking. Is a thousand dollars enough? Does this sound legit to you?"

"Kate, don't do this to—"

"Don't try to soothe me!" she snapped, cutting me off. "This is why we're doing this, damn it. This is why we're here." She took a deep breath. "I got this damn file out so I could decide one way or the other if my husband was a criminal. That's it. If it turns out to be true, so be it. I can't be hurt any more than I already am. I just have to learn this. So please. Don't patronize me, Hitch. Help me, okay?"

I nodded. "Okay."

"So what's your guess? Is a thousand dollars enough? Does it sound like enough or does it sound low?"

"You're right," I said. "It's a guess. And my guess is, it sounds okay. It's a good round figure. A thousand clean. Tax free. It sounds legit."

"You're sure you're not Mr. Nice Guying me here?"

"You're asking me to tell you something that I can't possibly know."

"It could have been two thousand. That's a round number too. A thousand a night, Hitch. Isn't that a round number too?"

"Kate . . ." I didn't know what to say. With the man who gave the money dead and the man who took the money dead, how could she ever know the truth on this one? And she knew this was the case as well; I could see it in her eyes. She picked up the report and then let it drop again onto the table.

"This doesn't tell me shit. Goddamn it, Hitch. This stuff isn't telling me shit. How am I supposed to know if my husband pocketed a couple thousand dollars or not? He's sure as hell not going to include that in his report. 'Oh, and by the way, I skimmed a few grand off the top. Hope you don't mind.' How the hell am I supposed to figure this out?"

It was not really a question that she expected me to answer, so I didn't even try. Instead I said, "Let's go over the rest of it. Maybe something will pop up."

"I pop up," she said grimly. "With a gun."

Kate flicked her hair off her shoulder and leaned forward one last time to finish going over her husband's final days. "I hate this." She shot me a warning look. "I'm having a drink after this. I'm just telling you now."

"Fair enough."

"No," she corrected me. "*More* than fair enough."

She turned to the last report.

After the loading of the boxcar, Charley had informed the authorities in Des Moines to be on the lookout for its arrival. As with the previous shipment, the minimal paperwork had been mysteriously slotted into place, an untraceable invoice marking the shipment of barrels to be unloaded at the warehouse outside Des Moines.

Charley had ventured to ask Earl DeLorenzo two important questions that he prayed the man would answer. DeLorenzo answered them both. The first question was: Will there be a chance of running this same job again? The answer that he received was yes. When, Charley wanted to know. DeLorenzo could not be specific, but he estimated sometime in about a month.

Russell laid out his deductions and his hypotheses thus far. Somewhere out there, in or near Baltimore, a considerable amount of earth was being excavated. That earth was saturated with chemical waste, toxic sludge. It was garbage dirt, and for one reason or another, somebody was terribly interested in removing this tainted dirt and shipping it the hell out of Baltimore. And they were terribly interested in doing it quietly. Charley Russell's next course of action was to locate the origin of the toxic dirt. Whoever owned the property from which it was being dug up and loaded into steel drums . . . that was the person—or people—to whom Detective Charley Russell would next be paying a visit. That was the key. Who owned this shit?

That was the end of the file. If the word "abrupt" springs immediately to mind, feel free to indulge it. It *was* abrupt. One minute Kate and I were sifting through the story of Charley's investigation of the toxic dirt, seemingly one step away from discovering along with him the source of the stuff . . . and then suddenly, no more reports. Of course we both knew why.

Pow.

Kate and I fell silent. There was—literally—nothing to say. The ending of the file reports was abrupt and it was final. I wanted to reach out to Kate, but I didn't dare.

Suddenly Kate opened the folder and began flipping furiously through the reports.

"Something's wrong." She grabbed a handful of the reports and began comparing them. "Something's not right here."

"What is it?"

"Look," she said breathlessly. "Look at this. Look at the dates. We noted this earlier. Charley was incredibly methodical about this. Every week. Religiously. Every week he filed a summary report. Some of these are interim reports. But no matter what, he always filed a summary report every single week. Same day of the week. Wednesday."

I looked at the reports and basically followed along with what she was saying. "So?"

"So this," she said excitedly. "So I . . . so Charley was killed on a Friday. I think you can imagine that I'll never forget the date. Friday, November eighteenth. But look at this last report. Look at the date." She poked at the date with her finger. "This is dated November ninth. Wednesday."

"Yes? All of his summary reports are dated Wednesday."

"Exactly. So then where is November sixteenth? Wednesday the sixteenth? It's not in here. It is the only Wednesday that shows no report. That's not my Charley. That's not our Detective Russell. You take one look at this folder and you can tell that. Three entire months of reports filed every single Wednesday, and then . . ." She held her hands out, palms to the ceiling.

"Hitch. Charley filed a report on November sixteenth. I would bet my life on it. And two days later, he was back in that warehouse. He filed a report, Hitch. He had to. And according to the sequence of events we've got here, I'm also willing to bet my life that I know what was in that report."

"The location."

"The location. The source of that goddamned dirty dirt that someone was so all-fired interested in getting rid of. He found it. Charley located the source of that stuff. He put it in his report. In this folder. And that report is missing. Someone took it."

"But who?" And since I was asking primary questions, I added, "And why?"

Kate was gathering up all of the reports and stuffing them back into the folder. Her eyes were on fire.

"Somebody got scared," she said. "Somebody got very scared. I'm going to find out who it is. When I return this file tomorrow I'll see who was the last person to sign it out. I'm going to find out who stole that report. Maybe they think they're safe now. But I'm going to make them scared all over again."

She then did a beautiful thing. She drop-kicked the file folder. A perfect kick. It flew into the air, the pages flying all the hell over the place.

"I'm going to find out who it is."

Kate stayed over. She was as supple as an oyster as she slid between me and my sheets.

I was awakened in the middle of the night by someone licking my face. It wasn't Kate; it was Alcatraz. I opened my eyes. My dog's happy yap took up the entire screen. I was just about to mutter "What is it, boy?" when I heard the front door click. As Alcatraz flipped his head around to look at the door, one of his ears whipped me in the face. Some dogs tell you when people are entering your place. My dog tells me when they're leaving.

I scrambled out of bed and over to the front door and pulled it open. I heard the click of the downstairs door. Kate was already out of the building. I ran down the stairs, purposely pigeon-toed to keep from tumbling and breaking my stupid neck. Alcatraz was right behind me. By the time I dashed out to the sidewalk, it was empty. She could have gone left or she could have gone right, popped around either corner. The pale moon cast little light on the matter.

A light in the house next to mine flipped on and I saw a face appear at the window. Alcatraz let out a big chesty *woof.* I looked down at myself. I was incandescent. And totally naked. Alcatraz barked again. A second face appeared at the window. Pale moon or not, I was apparently a sight to behold. Well, what did my neighbors know? Maybe I *always* take my junkyard hound out go for a naked late night walk around the block.

I squared my shoulders and did a smart about-face.

"Heel!"

To my astonishment, Alcatraz slotted obediently into place.

Shoulders squared, head erect, eyes fixed on the front door . . . man and dog returned to their home.

Jeff Simons was in serious but stable condition. As rumored, he had suffered a heart attack. The story on the airwaves was that the beloved newsman had been washing his car in the driveway when he keeled over. His heart condition had been diagnosed several months earlier but had been kept from the general public. Simons was under doctor's instructions not to indulge in strenuous activity. It's a fair crapshoot as to whether or not washing one's car should be considered strenuous activity. I suppose one could do it nice and slowly, making an entire day of it.

But it's a fatuous debate anyway. Helen Simons told Billie the real truth. The veteran newsman's heart had seized up while he was driving home a point to his young protégée out of Cleveland, Mimi Wigg. As it happened, Simons had been driving home that point in Mimi Wigg's bed at the time. She was the one who called 911. The car-washing scenario had been quickly fluffed together by station management and rushed out onto the airwaves. Check the tape of Ms. Wigg's special bulletin and you'll note the missing earring and the uncharacteristically not-perfect hair, not to mention the misbuttoned blouse. Neither Simons nor Mimi Wigg were married, so on that count, the libidinous activity of two single adults ain't nobody's business but their own. But it would look bad. To those critical of the fast-rising Mimi Wigg, it might even look calculating. Or if Simons were to die . . . criminal.

It was Sunday, and I had an afternoon rehearsal to attend. I tried reaching Kate several times by phone and several times I failed. I headed off to the theater.

Since granting me my pith helmet and funny mustache and Michael Goldfarb and Libby Maslin their mother and son yarmulkes, Gil was now swamped with special requests from other members of the cast. The guy playing Howie Newsome, *Our Town's* milkman, had brought his pit bull to rehearsal and wanted to incorporate it into the show. The waitress portraying Lady in the Box was anxious to juggle fruit downstage during scene changes. The guy Gil had picked to play Emily's father—a pompous locksmith from Lutherville—was lobbying for a silent part for his twelve-year-old daughter, a bob-haired girl of about two-hundred pounds. "Why can't my character have a second daughter? Just set her at the kitchen table and give her something to eat. She doesn't have to have any lines." I was fearful that Gil would point out that poor creature was larger than the table itself. But Gil's razor had been dulled by the onslaught of suggestions and demands. He said nothing.

The part of Mrs. Gibbs was being essayed by Frances Lamm, formerly of Long Island, New York, and formerly a meat eater. Ms. Lamm had suddenly developed a powerful problem with the section of the play where she is tossing seed to the chickens. She told Gil that maybe this would be a good time to advocate the growing of vegetables for our nutritional needs as opposed to the slaughter of innocent chickens. "The script says chickens," Gil responded wearily to Lady Lamm's advocacy. "Well you're the director, for goodness' sake," she shot back. "Is Mr. Wilder going to shoot you if you turn his chickens into vine-ripened tomatoes?"

Ms. Lamm pressed. The chickens were scratched. She got her tomatoes.

As I said, I stood as apart from the swells of this sea of insanity as one can hope to stand on the Gypsy Players' tiny stage. Julia was still absent from the scene and nobody seemed to know where she had run off to. The obnoxious locksmith shoved a straw hat onto the head of his beloved daughter and walked her over to Gil.

"Emily," the locksmith snarled.

Gil cried, "No!"

"Why not!"

For a moment Gil looked like he was about to disintegrate. Suddenly he shot to his feet and made a gesture as if tossing a shawl from his shoulders—or better yet, a cape . . . or perhaps his last fragment of sanity . . .

"Because *I'm* playing the role of Emily!"

The sound of pins dropping all over the little theater was deafening. Jaws dropped along with them. Even the obnoxious locksmith was momentarily muted. His fat little daughter was grinning from ear to there. Who knew theater was so fun? Gil certainly hadn't planned it this way, but with this single outrageous shot across the bow he had just regained his directorial control over the production. The old fire reignited in his eyes as his head swiveled around the room, singeing everyone ever so lightly as his gaze slanted by. The first to speak up was Michael Goldfarb. Yarmulke in hand, like a supplicant, he took a tentative step in Gil's direction.

"Y-you're Emily?"

The locksmith finally found his voice. "You're going to play my *daughter*?" Gil nodded. "But . . . but you're a *man*!"

"Hasn't anyone here heard of alternative casting," Gil snapped. It was his "concept" voice. He had found it. "It's standard in New York. I think we *rubes* might be able to stretch just a little, don't you?"

He wasn't bluffing. I could see this quite clearly from my perch behind the lectern. Gil Vance was voyaging.

"But you're a *man*!" the locksmith groaned again.

"That's right," Gil said. He grabbed hold of the two-hundred-pound girl and flipped the straw hat off her head. "And the milkman is now a woman." He pointed to the guy with the pit bull. "You're not the milkman anymore. I don't care what you do, but you're not the milkman. She is. Will there be anything else?"

The question was intended for the entire troupe. No one spoke. After one more triumphant glare at his cast, Gil clapped his hands. Over his head. Flamenco-style.

"Okay. Let's get started."

People moved quickly and silently to their places. Libby Maslin was near tears. Betty, the prop mistress, was already rummaging for wigs, muttering under her breath.

I didn't wait for a cue. I rapped my lectern harshly with my pointer and began the show. "The name of the town is Grover's Corners, New Hampshire, just across the Massachusetts line: latitude forty-two degrees forty minutes . . ."

There was still no word from Kate when I got back. And she still wasn't answering either of her phones, work or home. I had a wake scheduled, so at least I had something to occupy my time while I waited to hear from her. The deceased was a fiftyish man named Harvey Sprinkle. I know that's a funny name. It's even funnier in light of the fact that Mr. Sprinkle had apparently taken the name to heart over the course of his life, taking three wives from whom he begat a total of nine children. As if this weren't enough—and apparently it hadn't been—the old goat had accompanied each of his marriages with an extramarital affair, spawning exactly one child per mistress, for a total of three Sprinkle bastards. Grand total, a dozen Sprinkle kids, three wives and three mistresses. A grand old party. Apparently the prolific Mr. Sprinkle had kept in active contact with all of these various factions for they all most certainly got word of the man's untimely demise (heart attack, no real surprise) and they all showed up for the viewing. We certainly had to pull open the curtain for this one; it was a two-parlor affair with Sprinkles and near-Sprinkles and former-Sprinkles from wall to wall.

When the crowd finally began to disperse I was able to duck into my office. My phone machine was blinking furiously. The first message was from the coffin salesman in Nebraska who had been after me to try out a few of his new models. I hit the fast-forward. The next message was from Kate. It was all of three syllables long.

"*Hitch. It's Kruk.*"

Kruk?

I rewound the tape and listened to the message a second time. Maybe she had said "crook," though that would have made no sense.

But the second time around, she still said *Kruk*.

And that made no sense either. I phoned her at both numbers but she still wasn't answering. *Kruk?* I just couldn't make sense of it.

No sooner had I hung up the phone than it rang. I snatched it up.

"Hello!"

"*Bonjour mon chou. Comment ça va?*"

It was Julia.

"Jules! Where the hell have you been!"

"*Ici et là.*"

"English please."

"Here and there," Julia said. "Mainly there."

"I see."

"Aren't you going to ask me where is there?"

"Julia, I'm really not in the mood for your games."

She clucked her tongue at me. "*Mon Dieu.* Are we in a *pissoir* mood?"

"Okay. Where?"

"Do you remember our honeymoon?"

"Vaguely," I said. "I wore gray, you wore nothing."

"Well that's where I've been."

"You've been to Paris? What in the world were you doing in Paris?"

Her tone went coy. "Well if you'd come out and play I'll tell you all about it."

"Jules . . ."

"Oh all right. Be a mudstick. I was hoping you'd say, 'Julia, darling, how fantastic that you're back. Let's go get drunk and you can tell me all about your amorous adventure.' "

"I'm waiting for a phone call," I said. I felt sort of foolish saying it to her. "It's important," I added.

Just then there was a rapping at my office window. I looked up. Through the blinds I could see a person standing outside tapping on the glass.

Julia was saying on the phone, "You look so handsome in that suit."

I went over to the window and pulled up the blinds. It was Julia. She was wearing a cranberry beret and holding a tiny telephone to her ear. She gave me a little wave.

"Just one little drink?"

"What happened to your hair?"

Julia and I were in the Admiral Fell Inn. Julia likes their martinis.

"You like?"

"You look like Louise Brooks."

"A truly wonderful man would have said, 'I *love* your hair!' "

"Aren't you going to miss fiddling with your braids and all that?"

"I've already caught myself grabbing at phantom locks. But I'm getting used to it."

"You got it cut in Paris?"

"Yes. Three hundred dollars. Isn't that obscene?"

It was a pageboy cut. Bangs and pointy V-shaped sideburns.

"What would that have cost in Baltimore?"

"I wouldn't have it done in Baltimore. It's a souvenir of my trip."

"I understand those Eiffel Tower thermometers come in at a little under the three-hundred-dollar mark."

"Watch out, Hitchcock. You're beginning to remind me why we divorced."

"Julia," I said. "I *love* your new haircut. It makes your breasts look even bigger."

Julia turned to our waiter, who had just come over with our drinks. "This man is trying to seduce me," she said, batting her eyelashes outlandishly. "And he's *very* good at it."

Julia and I drank martinis and got caught up. She asked me about *Our Town*. "Gil left a number of bizarre messages on my phone," she said, popping an olive into her mouth.

"Bizarre pretty much sums it up. He's taken your part away from you."

"I know. I'm so crushed I could dance. Do I gather from his giggles that *he* is going to play Emily?"

"It's a concept, Julia. You understand."

She laughed. "I say go for it. Gil will bring something new to the role."

"Julia. Gil is bringing a penis."

She told me about Paris. I had already guessed who had financed the spur-of-the-moment jaunt. Peter Morgan.

"It was one of those impulsive things," Julia said, rolling the martini olive around in her mouth. "Peter and I were having dinner at Marconis. He had been telling me how renowned the place is for its sweetbreads. Well, they were out. Okay. But Peter got all huffy about it."

"Huffy over a restaurant's running out of calves' glands?"

"I know. I should have seen it right there. But I didn't. One thing led to another and before I could cry 'Insane!' I was sitting up in the lounge of a Paris-bound seven-forty-seven sipping champagne and getting a foot massage from my millionaire boyfriend."

I know about these foot massages of hers. "You can spare me the carnal details," I said.

"You're no fun." She smiled at the waiter as he brought over a fresh pair of drinks. "I have to say though, Hitch, I had more fun in Paris on our honeymoon than I did this time. I'm not a snob or anything, but too much money really does take the edge off. We started off at the Ritz, which when you get down to it is boring. I finally convinced Peter that we should go to Les Marais, but I could tell he didn't like it there."

"Too bohemian?"

"But it's not bohemian. I don't know what his problem was. We had a mouse in the house—in our room—and he got all uppity about it. Please, it's a mouse. I was leaning out the window looking up the block at Place des Voges. Peter was taking a bath and he was bitching about it. Too small or not enough hot water, I can't remember. Okay, so it wasn't the Ritz." She laughed. "Suddenly this mouse appeared on the windowsill right next to me. His little nose was going. I swear, Hitch, he was looking up the block too. Like he was curious to see what I was looking at. It was very cute. You know these French mice. And then suddenly Peter comes charging out of the bathroom and flips his towel at it like a whip. He knocked the poor thing right off the windowsill and down to the street."

She took a sip of her martini. "Beginning of the end."

Julia went on in this fashion. She's a very elaborate storyteller. I followed her down the side streets and cul-de-sacs of her various tales.

"He's not my prince," she sighed at last. "He's more of a king, which I don't need. It was fun while it lasted. It's the old thing about traveling with people. That's when you learn what you need to learn. Peter's bossy and he's self-centered. And you know, Hitch, we can't have two of those in the family."

I laughed. Julia frowned. "Answer me this though, will you? Nobody ever dumps *me*. It's always me dumping them. Why do I always have to do all the work?"

"You're too beautiful and sexy for any man to dump. We'd all rather suffer along."

"That's sweet." She reached for a nonexistent braid. "Hell. We never even got the damned sweetbreads that supposedly kicked off this little romp in the first place."

Julia moved on to the breaking-it-off portion. She told me that after one too many snide remarks, she finally read Peter Morgan the riot act in front of a group of sidewalk artists whom she was trying to talk with. "I did it in French, so that they could hear it too. Peter stormed off and went back to the Ritz."

"Did he make you walk home?"

"I had my return ticket. I ordered champagne for the entire plane. Charged it to Peter."

"Good girl."

She batted those lashes again. *"La vie da."*

After we left the restaurant I steered Julia back to her place. There was an enormous man in the gallery, literally four feet wide. He was standing in front of a large painting of a sandwich. Julia beelined for the counter where Chinese Sue handed her a Polaroid camera. Julia snapped off a shot. When the guy turned around at the sound of the camera's *wrrrr*, Julia was already aiming the camera at me. She lowered it, a big fake pout on her face.

"You never say 'cheese' anymore."

CHAPTER 26

I considered heading straight over to Kate's after dropping Julia off, but then I remembered that by now Alcatraz would be debating which of the many corners of my apartment he should pee in and so I hurried home and let him outside to lay down his love trail. Back inside, I picked up the phone and dialed Kate's number. Her machine answered. *Hello, you've reached the home of Kate Zabriskie. I can't come to the phone right now—* My doorbell rang. I took the phone with me to the door—*so please leave a message and a number and I'll get back to you.* I opened the door just as the beep sounded. Kate was standing in front of me. I muttered into the phone.

"I'll talk to you later."

Kate stepped past me into the apartment. I was too slow in closing the door; the dark cloud that was trailing her wafted in as well. I followed her into my living room where she had already dropped onto my couch and was pulling the sleeves of her loose sweater up past her elbows.

"You are pouring me a drink and I am telling you a story," she said.

"Kruk?"

She let out a sharp laugh. Almost a bark.

"Yeah. Kruk. Good old goddamn John Kruk."

I went to my liquor cabinet. Which is also my Cheerios and peanut butter cabinet. I fetched a bottle of Jack and a pair of glasses. Kate patted her hand on the couch next to her.

"Here. Sit."

Before I could get there, Alcatraz had hopped up onto the couch.

"How do you do that?"

Kate didn't answer. She was scratching Alcatraz under the chin. With her other hand she pointed at my easy chair. "Over there. Sit."

I did. I poured out a pair of drinks and took mine over to my chair. Two could play this game.

"Speak."

John Kruk was just outside the entrance of the Sparrows Point warehouse last November 18 when he heard the short volley of gunfire come from inside. Kruk and his partner, Officer Kate Zabriskie, had responded to an emergency radio call—*officer down*—and hightailed it over to the Sparrows Point address given out by the dispatcher. They found Detective Tom Connolly just outside the warehouse trying to staunch the blood flow from his right thigh. Kruk had been the first to reach him. He stopped to help as Kate Zabriskie charged into the warehouse.

A well-trained cop, especially a well-trained cop with good instincts, can follow a trail of silence as readily as a trail of sounds. Officer Zabriskie got her whiskers going and she moved steadily and cautiously through the unlit warehouse—gun drawn—down a hallway, through a pair of swinging doors, into a room full of concession machines, out through the swinging doors at the other side, past a glassed-in office and a loading dock and around a corner to a large room about the size of an airplane hangar. Metal shelving ran some sixty feet up to the ceiling.

This was where Kate found Detective Lou Bowman, who was standing stock-still against a large crate, his service revolver poised by his ear. Bowman was tense. His partner had been hit. There were two men out there in the dark warehouse with guns, feeling cornered. Bowman never smiled much anyway, according to Kate. Especially at women cops. If he at all considered that Kate Zabriskie represented the arrival of the cavalry, he didn't show it.

There are two versions of what happened next. Far and away the more popular (and highly fictitious) version is that Detective Charley Russell, present in the warehouse as part of an ongoing undercover investigation, stepped out from behind a stack of boxes, in clear view of Zabriskie and Bowman. He stepped into view and then—in police lingo—a spark and a bark came from somewhere up in the black tangle of the warehouse walkways. Russell fell. As Kate Zabriskie spun in the direction of the shooter, a second shot was fired. This one grazed her left shoulder. Kate fired. The gunman, Earl DeLorenzo, fell. He was dead. Kate had allowed her husband's killer to enjoy all of three additional seconds of life before putting him down. It was later determined, in this version, that Charley Russell's cover had somehow been compromised and that is why DeLorenzo had taken him out. The End.

Version Two of the events in the warehouse lines up precisely alongside Version One, right up to the point where Detective Russell has stepped out from behind the boxes. As with the previous version of the story there is also a spark and bark. But this one comes from the service revolver of Officer Katherine Zabriskie, responding instinctively to a man in a cap raising a hand with a gun. A second shot rings through the warehouse, grazing Kate Zabriskie's left shoulder. And then two quick shots as veteran Lou Bowman fires up at the figure on the walkway. One shot misses Earl DeLorenzo. The other takes him out.

Fact and fiction. They slammed together, blended, bonded, snarled together and then came roaring out of that warehouse like a tidal wave. Certainly Detective Zabriskie got knocked over by the tidal wave. And certainly when it had receded, she found herself on a shore that she only partially recognized. A widow. A hero. A liar. In another month or so Kate Zabriskie would find herself literally on another shore, a real one, a Mexican beach. She would watch the water coming in and going out over and over and over. Her husband would seem like a man who had never really existed, not in the real world. He would seem like an idea that Kate had planted in her own head, an idea that she could use for her own pleasure as well as for the exorcising of her own shame; she would have an additional means of feeling wholly miserable about herself as well. She would not always require the shifting memory of a dead husband. And the tides brought in a handsome brutal older man who wrapped her in his arms and punished her just fine, thank you. In Version Two of the story, Kate Zabriskie's murder of her own husband did not go unpunished. Not really. Not in the least.

John Kruk played a minor role in both versions of the story. In both, he helped apply a tourniquet to Detective Connolly's wounded leg. In both, he heard the gunfire and he ran inside and found two bodies down and dead, and one body slightly wounded. In either version you choose, Kate Zabriskie is already bent over the still body of her husband, sobbing into his chest, her tears mixing with his blood.

The very next morning, Kruk was summoned, along with Lou Bowman and Detective Tom Connolly—on crutches—into Commissioner Stuart's office for a frank discussion, a frank rearrangement of the facts, a frank reassigning of the truth. Stuart was grim and he was firm. Nothing good will come out of this event, the men were told, if it is exposed to the light in its current form. Officer Zabriskie—who has lost enough already—loses. The department loses. In a way, Stuart calmly told them, the city of Baltimore loses as well. Allowing the unfortunate truth of what happened in that warehouse to be spun into rabid headlines and infect the bloodstream of the television media would be in the best interests of neither serving nor protecting.

Kruk and the others were then presented with a few alternative facts. These facts squared with Version One. These facts *created* Version One. The coroner was due in Stuart's office in about an hour. He would be informed by Alan Stuart himself as to the caliber of the bullet that had killed Detective Russell. Conveniently, the caliber would match that of the pistol pried out of the hand of Earl DeLorenzo. As for DeLorenzo, he had been felled by a police bullet. No need to play fast and loose there. That bullet, Kruk and the others were instructed, had come from the service revolver of Officer Zabriskie, not from Lou Bowman's. A slight adjustment, that's all. Then Stuart gave his warning. Any intimations, under *any* circumstances—and this included watercoolers, local bars and the privacy of their own bedrooms—any intimations that something other than the scenario just laid out took place, Alan Stuart calmly guaranteed, would result in swift and most unhappy reprisals. "Let's stay on the same page. Let's serve and protect, not expose and destroy. Can we all live with that?" Nobody had said that they couldn't. Stuart had then dismissed them, all except for Lou Bowman, whom he said he needed to talk with privately for a few minutes. Kruk and the others assumed that the boss felt the need to go one-on-one with the veteran detective. Bowman was, after all, about to lose a notch on his belt. His quick and appropriate response under fire was about to go unmentioned and unrewarded. Certainly Stuart owed him a little quality time.

Kruk didn't like it. He didn't like it one bit. He told no one that he didn't like it, least of all Kate, to whom he spoke only briefly at her husband's funeral. He didn't like what he saw in Kate's eyes at the funeral. Alan Stuart's everybody-wins scenario certainly was not taking Kate Zabriskie into account. She looked horrible. She looked haunted. There was no winning there.

"Kruk is a good detective," Kate said, finishing off her drink and indicating that she wanted another. "A good detective's mind works like a natural sieve. Images and evidence just pour into it day and night. You don't even will it to happen; it just happens. That's how you eventually solve your cases. You sift and sift and sift and you keep your eye out for the nugget. It's always there. Somewhere. You just have to load enough information into the sieve and then learn to keep alert. Old Johnny boy kept alert on this one."

The image of Kate Zabriskie hunched over her husband, sobbing as his life literally bled from him, was one that apparently wouldn't sift through Kruk's sieve. It wouldn't drain away. Granted, it is a chilling and bitter image. But Kruk was playing the scene over and over again for a reason he couldn't identify. It wasn't even something he was choosing to think about. The image simply kept landing in his brain and rattling about in the sieve. And what finally came to Kruk was simple. There was too much damn blood. The puddles of blood around Charley Russell's body had grown swiftly. Kate's tears, as voluminous as they were, stood no chance of competing with all that blood. *All that blood.*

"I met with Kruk this afternoon," Kate said. "At the cafe at the museum."

Kruk told Kate how he had followed Alan Stuart's directives to the letter. He had spoken with no one about the events of that night in Sparrows Point, except to mouth the version that—as Stuart would have it—was best for everyone. But he had been unable to shake the image of her and her dying husband out of his head. The blood. Kruk then made a decision that was not easy for him to make. He decided to arrange a bump-in with the coroner and to fall into an innocent chat with him. Kruk's chat with the coroner violated the directive Alan Stuart had placed on the Russell case, but he managed to do so in a manner that never once left the coroner suspicious. And John Kruk came away with confirmation of what he had come to suspect.

Two bullets had entered Charley Russell's body. Not one. Two.

Kate paused to allow me a moment to take this in. She also paused because—I think—this was the first time that she had spoken this fact aloud.

"Two bullets?" I said.

She nodded and held up two fingers, waggling them in the air.

"Uno. Dos."

Two bullets had ripped though Charley Russell. And Kate knew full well that she had only fired once.

"If another shot was fired it was fired at the exact same time. I never even heard it. Or maybe I did. I just don't know. I've gone over that scene in my head a thousand times. It just gets more and more surreal each time."

Kruk told Kate that he had guessed a second bullet was involved even before the coroner confirmed it. And it didn't take a veteran of fifteen years to run through the elimination process and come up with the only two possible persons who could have fired that other shot. Lou Bowman or the walkway gunman, Earl DeLorenzo.

Kate told me that—to put it mildly—she could barely believe what she was hearing. This entire fiction that had been draining her for nearly six months now . . . it was partially true all along. Alan Stuart's fiction of Earl DeLorenzo shooting Charley . . . it wasn't a fiction after all. The truth and the lie had collided and now they really were the same thing. Yes. A cruel joke. A punch line right to the gut.

"Kruk must have seen it on my face," Kate said. "I can't imagine what I must have looked like when he told me this, but he suddenly did a very un-Kruk-like thing. He reached across the table and touched me on the arm. 'Hold on, Kate,' he said to me. 'You're not lined up here.' It turns out that the coroner told him that there were indeed two bullets in

Charley, and that it was odd that I had only remembered firing one shot at my husband."

"But you did fire one shot."

"I know I did. And Kruk does too. After his talk with the coroner he checked the ballistics report on my service revolver. And on Lou Bowman's."

"Bowman's?"

"Bowman didn't miss his first shot at DeLorenzo up on the walkway," Kate said grimly. "He got him with a single shot. Bowman's a top marksman. He can take dead aim better than any detective on the force. And . . . he would be able to squeeze off a shot in incredibly close approximation with someone else shooting."

"What are you saying?"

"The other bullet that the coroner found in Charley . . . Well, *both* bullets is a better way of putting it. Neither of them was the same caliber as DeLorenzo's gun. They were both the same caliber as mine. As my service revolver. It was a cop bullet."

"But I—"

"It came from Bowman's gun," Kate said flatly. "Lou Bowman shot my husband."

Kate came off the couch like a snake. Her feet and her legs glided out from beneath her and took a liquid course to the floor, the rest of her body effortlessly lifting as she went. Without so much as a glance in my direction she finished off her drink in a single hard gulp, then stepped into the kitchen. Two seconds later I heard a crash. I leaped out of my chair.

Kate was standing on the white tiles of my kitchen floor looking like she had no clue where she was. The glass was in shattered pieces all over the floor. Kate's chest was heaving. Tears welled up as the blood rushed into her pale face, bruising it crimson.

The shriek was a horrible sound. The curses that followed were more manageable. She threw herself against my chest and wailed.

Eventually I guided her back into the living room and to the couch and we sat there while she cried and cried and cried her hazel eyes out. At some point I realized that a large sliver of glass was protruding from the arch of her foot. I plucked it out. She didn't even notice. My phone rang and I let the machine pick up. It was Julia and she gave her message in the form of a limerick. Kate cried on. Tears like those are manufactured way in advance—way way back in some cases—and are bottled up and put aside for later. Kate had a large stash. And I think she was deciding— or it was being decided for her—to finally empty the reserve. It was time. Just clean it all out.

It was maybe an hour later when Kate's well had dried up. She gave me a look that rivaled the best of Alcatraz's saddest faces.

"Let's get you to bed, cheesecake," I said gently. "This day has been long enough."

She did as she was told. I got her out of her clothes and into my bed and she was asleep within five minutes. Asleep even before I had turned off all the lights and joined her. There was no doubt in my mind that it was a very very deep sleep.

CHAPTER 27

They say the devil is in the details.

I made omelets. Clean and scrape some mushrooms, sauté them in a pan along with some diced onions and red pepper pieces, scatter a little salt and pepper . . . now scoot that off to the side, pour your already whipped-up eggs (the secret ingredient here: dill weed) into the pan. Nudge the mushrooms, onions and pepper pieces onto a third of the egg pancake, sprinkle some pregrated curls of yellow and white cheese over the concoction, cover for one and a half minutes, then use a pair of spatulas to roll the whole thing up into a flat tube, cover again for another thirty seconds, then come in from opposite sides with the two spatulas to lift the whole creation from the pan onto the plate, make like you're dropping a parsley sprig on top, sing out like an idiot pretending to be an Italian chef as you take the plate to the table and set the plate in front of the woman who is once again wearing one of your button-up shirts and is again looking terrifically sexy as a result, her puffy eyes notwithstanding. Tell her that she looks good enough to eat, but that we'll start with the eggs.

Devil anyone?

We got through most of our breakfast without alluding to the previous evening's revelation. I made coffee, poured juice, opened a new jar of ginger marmalade and forked open a couple of English muffins. Kate left the last several bites of her omelet untouched. Alcatraz raised his paw to let her know that he'd be happy to finish it off. Our domestic charade had run its course.

"I think you have a question," Kate said, then took her coffee cup into the other room. I followed.

Kate was sitting on the floor, up against the wall, her head about level with the jade plant on the windowsill of my bay window. She was picking at one fingernail with another. Her coffee cup was on the floor, between her legs. I slid onto the couch. Kate addressed her coffee cup.

"You want to know if Lou Bowman shot Charley by mistake too, like I did. You want to know if two trained cops can make the same fatal mistake at the same time. You want to know if it was utter coincidence that Lou Bowman took a few steps backwards so that he was essentially behind me when he fired at Charley and that he fired almost precisely when I did. That's what you want to know, isn't it."

"Yes," I said.

"The answer is no."

Kate picked up her coffee mug. She was finally looking a little refreshed. That's good. She had her detective's face back on, even if she was half naked in a man's shirt sitting on the floor with her lovely legs splayed out.

"Lou Bowman shot my husband on purpose. He knew it was Charley. He shot to kill. He murdered my husband."

"Why did he do it?" I asked.

Kate set the mug back down. "Why don't we go find out?"

CHAPTER 28

"Don't say anything."

"What do you mean don't say anything? Look at this, it's pathetic. It's an insult."

"Here, take mine. I don't want it anyway."

"That's not the point. The point is this is ridiculous. When did they start doing this?"

"What's the difference? I'm sure you'll complain about the taste anyway. Why don't you look at it this way, they're giving you half as much to complain about."

I looked at the half sandwich in my hand. In a way, Kate was right. Thin white bread, a layer of pink meat spread and a large flake of lettuce. Why the hell would I want two halves of such a sandwich? I wasn't likely to eat the half that I had been handed as I boarded the plane.

"I'll bet the people in first class didn't get half a sandwich."

"There is no first class," Kate observed. "This is a bargain airline." She indicated the slender white triangle in my hand. "That's a bargain lunch."

I picked up the miniature cellophane bag of peanuts that accompanied the half sandwich. "These things are usually half full to begin with. Do you suppose there's even anything in it?"

"Hitch, you didn't come here to eat."

"But I didn't come here to be insulted either. Somewhere on this plane is the other half of my sandwich. I'm sharing a sandwich and I don't even know who I'm sharing it with."

"Why don't you just pretend it's me?" Kate suggested.

"What will they do next? Come on over the intercom and tell us they're only taking us halfway to our destination? Or maybe that the fuel tanks are only half full? Or one of the two engines is out?"

Kate sighed. "Or that there is no co-pilot?"

"Yes! Exactly." I shook the white sandwich wedge in the air. "This could be just the beginning. Maybe the flight attendants dropped out of flight attendant school halfway through and this stupid airline got them on the cheap."

The seat belt light came on (no accompanying *ding*, I noticed). The plane was backing away from the terminal.

"Do they even give you both parts of the damned seat belt?" I asked, squirming in my seat to locate the strap part and the buckle part. "Look! It's only the buckle part." I held up two buckle parts. "Two of them! It's only buckles."

"Hitch, that's your belt and the one for the seat next to you. Come on, quit it."

A stewardess appeared and reached dangerously close to my lap as she freed the strap portion of the belt from under my tushy.

"Buckle up," she said cheerfully. She moved on down the aisle. That's when Kate finally saw that I was sweating like crazy.

"Hitch," she said in a tone choked with honest-to-God endearment. "You're afraid of flying, aren't you?"

I sucked on my lower lip and tugged my seat belt as tight as I could get it. I gave the answer that all of us in the brotherhood give.

"No. I'm afraid of crashing."

In a way I was right. About going only halfway. Kate and I got as far as Boston on our bargain airline and then we had to pick up a rental car to continue our excursion.

"Have you ever seen Boston?" Kate asked as I steered out of the airport. The two signs ahead read "Boston Left Lane" and "Points North Right Lane."

"No," I said.

"Too bad. Go right."

The people who built the roadways in the Boston area way back when devised a little dilemma they dubbed "the roundabout." Disguised as an efficient means of allowing drivers to head off in any direction they chose from a central point, the roundabout is actually a nasty little joke whereby the uninitiated (Hitchcock Sewell, for one) find themselves in an anxious cluster of automobiles that are orbiting the central point, cut off from any chance of escape by an ever-steady flow of other automobiles entering the circle. Twice I got caught in one of these. The first time I grew old and died; the second time I traveled a few helpless loops and then decided to risk all by steering with my horn and my gas pedal, which is what everybody else seemed to be doing.

Kate held a map partially unfolded on her lap and tracked our progress with her finger. Once we had cleared Boston and its numerous outskirts, and after our several spins with anarchy in the roundabouts, the traffic thinned out, the roadside crap thinned out and we settled down to a two-lane highway bordered by pines, heading north. The sky opened up in front of us like a large blue and white widow's peak. Deer-crossing signs appeared, the distance between exits began to increase and the air rushing through my driver's-side window was developing a bit of a bite, despite its being May, May, the lusty month of May. Maybe I should have packed a sweater.

It was as a result of Kate's confab with John Kruk about the missing report that Kate and I were hightailing it to the upper right corner of America.

Yes, John Kruk had signed out Charley Russell's investigation file. But if Kruk could be believed—and Kate assured me that Kruk was, if nothing else, a bundle of frankness—he had not been the person who removed that final report from the file. The report had already been removed by the time Kruk got to it. During our hideous plane trip Kate recounted for me her colleague's explanation.

According to Kruk, even before his intentional run-in with the coroner several weeks after Russell's death, he had observed what he told Kate was some piss-poor, care-less, do-nothing detective work from one Lottery Lou Bowman. After the death of Charley Russell and the subsequent cover-up of its particulars, Bowman had been assigned the mislabeled silica gel case. The idea of Bowman's resuming Detective Russell's undercover operation was obviously out of the question. Not even taking into account Lou Bowman's age and his girth—neither of which would have slotted him unnoticed into the world of tough young men who load and unload train cars—the entire on-site portion of the investigation was a compromised shambles. So Bowman took up the investigation as a desk jockey, and as far as John Kruk could observe, the veteran detective gave the affair maybe an hour or so a day, if even that. True, no good detective enjoys being partnered with a phone and a desk. But sometimes that's a part of the job.

Still, before too long the word was seeping out that the investigation had no legs. Rumors of Charley Russell's having been on the take seeped out as well—though from exactly where they seeped out was its own little mystery—and the unspoken scuttlebutt on the drums of mislabeled silica gel was that the entire affair was becoming a nonevent, an unsexy investigation of a largely victimless crime. Bowman was clearly feeling no heat about getting to the bottom of the matter. Kate told me that there are always cases that degenerate this way, ending up in the "Who Cares" department. And that's where Lou Bowman's investigation had come to reside by the time Bowman's aunt conveniently died and left him with enough of an inheritance that he could quit the force. Apparently the unsolved crime was not going to plague the man's conscience in his early retirement.

Kruk thought the whole thing stank. Fron the beginning, Kruk had found himself replaying the events of that November night in the warehouse, never quite liking what he saw. And so after his talk with the coroner, when not only was his hunch about the two bullets confirmed but the additional nugget was unearthed that one of the bullets very likely came from the gun of Lou Bowman, Kruk began to better understand the stink. As Kruk observed Lou Bowman's lackadaisical attitude toward the continuation of the late Detective Russell's investigation he found himself forming the opinion that Lottery Lou Bowman was working to hide something. Something even beyond his role in the shooting of Charley Russell.

And then, Lottery Lou's ship bearing his dead aunt came in. The detective turned in his resignation and he was gone.

Kruk opened up his own investigation. He began to dig. And before he had even shoveled out more than a bucket's worth of dirt, he got his first piece of the puzzle. Bowman's story proved to be such a pathetically shallow hole that Kruk truly marveled at the man's ballsiness in even trotting out such a charade. There was no rich aunt. There was no rich anybody. The Bowman clan were solidly working class, with not a bon vivant in the crowd. Lou Bowman stood to inherit the debts that his ailing mother had inherited from Bowman's deceased father. That was it. Ten more years on the force and Bowman's full pension would have arrived and with it he could have chipped way at that obligation.

It was at this point that Kruk had pulled the folder on Charley Russell's investigation of the mislabeled silica gel drum barrels. Kruk read through the exact same reports that Kate and I had pored over. Like us, he noticed that Charley Russell had been on the cusp of discovering the source of all those barrels of toxic dirt. And like us, Kruk suspected that Charley's final report had been pulled from the file. Kruk knew full well who the last person in possession of that file folder was. Lou Bowman. If a missing report existed, Lou Bowman had it.

All of which brings us back to a small four-door rental car zipping along a relatively quiet two-lane highway in the upper right corner of these United States. Kate and I were headed for Maine. Kate wanted that report. And then she wanted Lou Bowman's ass in a sling. I wanted to help her, because I had sort of grown to like the lady. Helping to nail the guy who shot your lover's now-dead husband is one of those little things that you can do to earn a special place in her heart. It most definitely qualifies as a smooth move.

Kruk had contacted a Boston-based private investigator friend of his and out of his own pocket hired the guy to take a few weeks' vacation up in Maine—"America's Vacationland" I was now noting on the license plates around me—where he could visit the lighthouses if he wished, or contemplate the cold Atlantic's incessantly dramatic relationship with Maine's rocky coastline, so long as he kept his private eye on the comings and goings of one Lou Bowman, new homeowner, new 4x4 Jeep owner, new boat owner and happy new early retiree. The PI tailed Bowman and made a detailed report of his every activity: his food shopping, his nights at the local bar, his numerous fishing excursions, his rapid progress into the bed of a mean-looking woman named Molly who worked at the local

NAPA Auto Parts store . . . Kate had the report with her. It was a fairly unremarkable report on the face of it; a retired cop enjoying his recreation and his leisure and his recreation and his leisure, day in, day out, day in . . . like the tides. The PI returned to Boston at the end of his two weeks and that would have seemed to have been the end of it. But a month later, in March, Kruk sent him back. Having gone over the PI's report and accustomed himself to the general cadence of Lou Bowman's activities, Kruk wanted the PI to gather another two-week sample, for comparison. Kruk was looking for an anomaly, or a pattern, or . . . he didn't know what exactly he was looking for. But he hoped to recognize it when he saw it. That's how it's done. Sift the shit. And apparently Kruk found what he wanted. Or at least he found a part of it.

What he found was a visit to the NAPA Auto Parts store that included more than a simple nuzzle with mean-looking Molly. During this particular visit, Lou Bowman picked up a small package that had been delivered by Federal Express. Kruk might not have placed any particular significance on the event except for the fact that upon collecting the package, Lou Bowman had proceeded directly to his local bank. When he got home he did no work on the Jeep, which was probably under warranty anyway. So why was this package delivered to a car parts shop? And why take it directly to the bank? Even from all the way up in Maine . . . the big fish continued to stink.

As Kate and I crossed the Maine border, Kate gave me a bit of a rundown on Lou Bowman. Specifically, she wanted me to know a little something about the man's attitude toward killing other people, since at least one of her plans would involve my entering into a tête-à-tête with the guy and I should know what it was I was getting into.

Lou Bowman had lots of paper and cloth attesting to his skills with both rifles and pistols. He was a firing range regular, an NRA member and a man who wore a red-and-black checked jacket in the winters with a plastic license tag pinned to the back fingering him as a certified killer of helpless animals. Over the course of his police career, Bowman was also responsible for the abrupt deaths of three members of the criminal class. Two had been gunned down during the commission of their crime. The third had apparently met his death for looking the wrong way at Detective Bowman while bringing a cellular phone—what Bowman claimed looked like a pistol—to his mouth. Though why the guy would want to whisper something to his pistol before taking aim at a police detective was apparently an issue that never found resolution.

There are some police officers who have to work through a bit of a funk after an in-the-line-of-duty killing of another human being. A real live (real dead) flesh-and-bone person is a whole different thing from a tin target with a paper heart. But apparently Lou Bowman had not been one of those cops. Killing people didn't gum up his day. He slept well at night. Kate wanted me to know this about Lou Bowman.

The little town—or village—where Lou Bowman had chosen for his retirement was a picturesque place on the coast, called Heayhauge. I've no idea how to pronounce it either. A few of the locals pronounced it for me while I was there, but to be honest I'd have had a rough time understanding their pronunciation of the name "Bob." The closest translation I can come up with is "Hee-Haw." That's it. Hee-Haw, Maine.

Heayhauge was born and raised as a fishing village. A break in the coastline allows the sea to spill into a large natural harbor, shaped like a teardrop; around its bulbous side the commercial portion of the village clusters. This is where the fishing boats are docked. The wharves are extra wide to allow for the off-loading of the fish and lobsters that the fisherfolk pull out of the sea. Wooden crates are stacked and scattered everywhere. Dogs too (scattered, not stacked). I would have thought that it was cats that would migrate to the fish wharf—they do in Baltimore. But up here in Maine it's dog country. Maybe Alcatraz could include Heayhauge, Maine, in his retirement plans. That is of course if he ever gets around to doing anything worth retiring from.

As the fishing industry became more centralized, or as the near-shore pockets of fish and lobsters became increasingly picked over, fishing villages like Heayhauge began to diversify. Diversify or die. Well past its heyday as a "bustling" commercial fishing community, the shrinking fishing fleet of Heayhauge now shares its harbor with several outfits that take on paying customers for a day of recreational fishing and with something like two dozen slips that harbor the various sailboats and yachts of the town's more well-to-do residents and visitors. There is a harborfront hotel just to the west of the docks. They have a restaurant patio on the water as well as a fleet of a half-dozen paddleboats so that the hotel residents can get in the way of the larger craft. As with practically any drop of water these days, there are also Jet Skis buzzing all about like very loud oversized gnats. Basically it's a devil's deal, pretty common among picturesque places that are no longer able to support themselves solely by means of the single industry that spawned their existence in the first place. Like the rest of us, they call on their good looks if they possibly can. Shops and cafés that would have been laughable to the town's original old salts had cropped up along the piers and along the village's narrow main street: places that sold paper lamp shades and jewelry that no local could afford (nor figure out a local occasion worth wearing it for), varieties of soap, enough scented candles to illuminate an entire Wiccan hoedown, country club clothes, overpriced coffee from Seattle, the whole thing. The place is still a "bustling" village. It's just that the bustle now has less to do with the clinking of pulley chains on the docks as it does the clinking of tourists' change being dropped into cash register drawers.

Kate and I took all of this in from inside our rental car, which we had pulled over at the townside of the metal drawbridge that reaches out over the natural break in the coastline. We were afforded a nice view of both the mighty Atlantic on our right, and the town harbor and docks to our left and behind us. Kruk's private investigator from Boston had noted this particular spot in his report; we weren't onto anything new here.

The reason that we remained in the rental car was simple. Kate could not risk being spotted by Lou Bowman. To ensure against this, prior to pulling into town Kate had wrapped a scarf around her hair and donned a pair of black cat's-eye sunglasses. To my eye she looked as incognito as an Italian movie star attempting to look incognito.

"I'm Polish," she reminded me when I made the comparison.

"But in that getup you look Italian. You look like Gina Lollobrigida."

"Then it's a good getup."

We sat in the rental car for about a half hour, getting our feel for the village of Heayhauge. As I said, the inlet harbor here is bulbous, like a teardrop. Along the far shore, opposite the village and the main dock, maybe a quarter of a mile from where we were parked, the land rises steeply. I guess I shouldn't even say "land." I should say "rock." It's a small cliffside basically, tufted here and there with scraggly outcroppings of hard grass and scruffy pine. Along the top of the rocks Kate and I counted seven houses. There were good-sized places, two and three stories, and each with either a large glass front or a wooden deck—or in some cases both—which no doubt afforded a spectacular view of both the Heayhauge harbor and the mighty Atlantic out beyond. A long steep set of wooden stairs led down from each of the houses to the water below. Half of the houses appeared to enjoy a little private beach down there on the water's edge. All of them enjoyed either a motorboat or a sailboat.

Kate was scanning the far horizon with a small but powerful pair of binoculars.

"There!" she said, pointing with her free hand. She handed over the binoculars and guided me in the right direction. The far shore bobbed about in a large circle. For a brief moment the binoculars found a skinny girl in a bathing suit up on one of the wooden decks, shaving her legs. Kate set a finger on the binoculars and lowered them to the water's level.

There it was. Just as reported by Kruk's Boston PI. Proof that at least Lou Bowman had something akin to a sense of humor, twisted as it was. Bowman's thirty-two-foot pleasure boat sat bobbing in the water, moored to his private dock. The name of the boat was printed in bold red block letters. LIFE SENTENCE.

I lowered the binoculars. Kate had removed her Gina Lollobrigida sunglasses. She was tapping the stems against her teeth.

"Is that a son of a bitch bastard prick or what?" she said. I think the lady pretty much summed it up.

We took a room in the waterfront hotel. We were fortunate to have arrived in advance of the season, when both the rates and the occupancy level of the place would skyrocket. Our request for a room facing the harbor was granted. Kate's anxiety level had increased the moment she got out of the car. There seemed little chance that Lou Bowman would be hanging around the hotel lobby, but Kate remained anxious anyway. I'm sure her fidgety energy fed the imagination of the pimply desk clerk. This lady couldn't *wait* to get up to her room. Hoo-wee! I signed us in as Mr. and Mrs. Frank Sinatra, winked and paid the guy in cash.

"You get a free hour with a paddleboat, Mr."—he consulted the book—

"Mr. Sinatra." He turned red, then chuckled softly. "You and *Mrs. Sinatra* can take advantage of the paddleboat anytime before sundown."

Kate and I were sitting out on the small balcony when we got our first glimpse of Lou Bowman. He was making his way down the long steep stairway from his house to the dock below. Kate saw him first and she picked up the binoculars from the little glass table there and took a look.

"Bastard sighted. Port bow." She handed me the binoculars.

There he was. Tony Bennett's evil twin. Sunbaked skin. Blue polo shirt. Khakis. The kind of guy you wouldn't notice on the street, unless he was pulling a gun and aiming it at you. Then you might notice.

I watched as our prey reached the bottom of the steep steps and began making preparations to take his boat out.

"He's taking the boat out," I said. I lowered the binoculars and looked at my lovely detective friend. "Should we go now?"

Kate shook her head. "Not inside. Not yet. It's too risky. We don't know how long he'll be out. We haven't even driven by the house. We want to cut down on the unknowns first. There might be a dog."

"You're good with dogs."

"I'm good with dogs whose owners like me."

"I never said I liked you."

Kate gestured. "Give me those."

While she snooped on Lou Bowman, I snooped a moment on her. It's just so damned peculiar how it is that a person suddenly shows up in your life out of nowhere and in what really amounts to practically no time at all you are sitting with them on a motel balcony in Maine, making plans to break into a nouveau-riche man's house across the water. Kate had piled her hair up and made it stay there in that mysterious way that women do. She was all neck and legs and arms slender and taut. Her cool empress's profile was continuing to look inexplicably sexy as she peered into the binoculars, her lips slightly parted. Her toes were partially curled around the iron railing of the small balcony. I wished I had a camera. I was sitting there in boxers and an Orioles T-shirt.

"Put your clothes on," Kate said suddenly, as if misreading my mind.

"Take yours off."

Kate gave me a tsk-tsk look. "I think all this fresh air is getting to you, Mr. Sewell."

"That's Frankie boy to you," I said. "And it is. I love this air." I tilted my head in the direction of the room. "I like the air in there even better. Wink Wink."

"We didn't come all this way just to lie around in bed," Kate said, getting up from her chair.

"Who's talking about lying around?"

"Hitch," she snapped. "This isn't a damn vacation." She slid open the screen and went into the room. A few seconds later, my shirt came flying out.

Like hell.

We took the main road that runs through the town and loops up to the rocky overlook that Lou Bowman shared with his neighbors. These weren't spectacular houses actually, not in the sense of being outrageously opulent and show-offy. These places were spectacular first and foremost for the view afforded from their rocky perches. Their location location location was wow wow wow. As Kate and I drove slowly along the road, we caught glimpses of the view, the long, slowly curving coastline with its tumbles of rocks and boulders, sea spray bursting on them at regular intervals like exploding white fireworks. And of course beyond all that, the gunmetal blue ocean and the huge half-bowl of sky.

Once we had located Lou Bowman's house and pulled to the end of his driveway, Kate and I were treated to an additional view, that of the teardrop inlet below, the picture-postcard town and the tiny armada of sailboats and windsurfers. Sails of many colors tilted this way and that into the wind, or at least into the hope of wind. The day was unusually still.

"He's got himself a nice view," I remarked.

"And he bought it with my husband's blood."

Well. Okay. That was it for the sightseeing tour. Maybe Kate was right, I was getting too much clean air all at once. We weren't here for nice views and fun and frolics. Kate had a real weight on her and I was to try to help lift it off.

We cased the joint. It turned out there was no dog, and that was good. I did spot a box turtle at the base of the back steps leading up to the kitchen, but I didn't consider it much of a threat. Kate went up onto the wooden deck in back and determined that none of the neighbors could see through the trees that sheltered the property. She put her sexy nose to the glass door. She was looking—among other things—to see if there was an alarm system. As best she could tell there wasn't.

"What do you see?" I asked, joining her on the deck.

"I see the usual sloppy bachelor's pad."

We went around to the far side of the house. Kate pointed out a row of three narrow windows on the ground level, behind some unkempt shrubbery.

"What do you think?"

"I think they could use some trimming."

"The windows, wise guy. Do you think I can fit through one of those windows?"

"It would be tight."

"But I could do it."

"Why these windows?" I asked her. "There are a lot of big windows in this place. Is slithering a requirement of stealth?"

"I'm guessing all of the windows are locked," was Kate's answer. "But if I have to break one of these, it's very possible Bowman won't even notice it for a couple of days."

"Why do you care if he notices?"

"I don't want him to see right away that someone has broken into his place. This isn't the movies, Hitch. I'm not going to break in, go to the guy's study, find what I'm looking for in fifteen minutes and pop right back out. I mean, I might. But I might not. I might have to come back a second time."

"So how do we do this? You shimmy in through the basement window and then come let me in?"

"You're not coming in with me."

"I'm not? You mean I really did just come along for the ride?"

"No. The first thing you're going to do is to come up with an accent. You've got to get the Baltimore out of your voice."

Accents I can do. The question is, why?

"Why?" I asked.

Kate said, "I don't want Bowman guessing that you're from Baltimore."

"When exactly is it that you don't want him guessing this?"

"When I'm inside his house and you're wherever he is, heading him off at the pass if it comes to that."

"I see," I said. Although I didn't. Not exactly. "You want me to run interference?"

"Only if you have to. I don't want Bowman coming home when I'm going through his things. You've got to see to it that he stays away. We'll set a certain time. I'll feel completely free up until a preset time and then I'll go. Your job is going to be to keep him away until that time."

This was news to me. "Have you thought about how I'll do this?"

Kate grinned at me. One of those grins that make you gulp.

"I hope you brought along your fake mustache. You're going undercover, big boy."

CHAPTER 29

If somebody were to tell you about a local bar way the hell up in Maine called The Moose Run Inn, you'd likely figure it to be located somewhere in the general vicinity of a river or a creek or some such waterway sporting the name Moose Run. Wouldn't you? I would.

Or would you expect to encounter a woodsy sort of place with the full-grown body of a moose (all but the head) protruding from the outside wall while the rest of the moose (the head) looms from the interior wall just above an old Green Hornet pinball machine? These are funny folk up here in Maine, I'm telling you; I don't think it's happenstance that we've stashed them all off in a corner of the country.

I was having a fairly successful dalliance with the Green Hornet pin-ball machine at The Moose Run Inn. This was despite the sizable distraction of the gigantic moose head on the wall, directly above the machine. Whoever did the taxidermy on this thing had given it one blue glass eye and one brown one. Somewhere along the line other cutups had affixed a red rubber nose to the beast's snout, stuck a plaid hunter's cap on at a jaunty angle between the two enormous antlers, dangled an unlit cig-arette from the poor thing's mouth and, to complete the offense, fash-ioned a necklace from empty shotgun shells and draped it around the moose's stout neck. If it were in the nature of the dead animal to rue, this moose most surely would have rued the day that he ran into this place.

I was slamming and banging the old Green Hornet pinball machine pretty well, getting a ten-second rendition of "The Flight of the Bumblebee" every time I landed the ball in the Green Hornet's nest in the center of the table. For my first undercover gig I wore jeans by Lee, a simple yet elegant plain white T-shirt offset by a rather bold flannel statement (checked, unbuttoned and untucked) and a forest green baseball cap with "Skoal" embossed on the front. Shit yeah.

After going over John Kruk's Boston PI's reports on the daily activities of former Baltimore Police Detective Lou Bowman, Kate and I had determined that the guy was anything but a creature of habit. His days took an infuriatingly random shape. Some days he slept late. Some days he didn't. Some days he took his boat out into the open sea and went fishing. Some days he sat on his deck with a six pack of Bud and a bag of cigars. Bowman might spend an entire afternoon down on his dock fooling around with his boat or he might knock about all day in his 4x4. He was retired. He could flop around any damn way he chose. The same pretty much held true for his evenings.

What the PI *had* seen, however, was a weekly visit to The Moose Run Inn every Monday night accompanied by mean-looking Molly from the NAPA Auto Parts store. Mondays were apparently mean-looking Molly's night to let her hair down, such as it was. Molly's idea of a good time in Heayhauge was a night of flavored vodka at The Moose Run Inn, followed sometimes by a roll in the hay with former Baltimore Police Detective Lou Bowman, sometimes at his place, sometimes at hers.

It was due to this "sometimes" nature of things that I found myself that Monday night in a love embrace with the Green Hornet pinball machine under the forlorn blue and brown gaze of the mightily maligned moose up there on (in) the wall.

Kate and I had kept our eye on Lou Bowman from our hotel room patio. Somewhere around seven-thirty or so, Bowman had climbed into his 4x4 and backed out of the driveway. Kate and I killed about twenty minutes then got into our rented car and cruised by The Moose Run Inn. We spotted Bowman's 4x4 in the gravel parking lot and gave each other a grim thumbs-up. I drove back to Bowman's place and dropped Kate off at the driveway. She had vanished even before I could say good luck.

If God was on our side, Kate would break into Bowman's place and be led directly to the missing report that she was convinced Bowman still had in his possession. It would be sitting out on the kitchen table under a golden celestial spotlight. However, if God was asleep at the wheel—or maybe just not paying too much attention to things that go on in Maine—then Kate would need several hours in which to sift and search. That's where I came in. We had chosen eleven o'clock as the absolute latest that Kate would stay before having to get her fanny out of that guy's house. My job was to see to it that Lou Bowman didn't leave the bar until eleven o'clock. If it came down to simply having to tackle him—which I hoped it wouldn't—then that's what I'd have to do. Kate said that in the event she got out before the deadline, she would phone the bar and have the bartender call out a fictitious name. That would be my cue that I wouldn't have to tackle Lou Bowman or trip him or otherwise keep him distracted from leaving. I suggested the name Harvey Sprinkle, the name of the prolific seed-sewer I had recently buried.

"Isn't that sort of a silly name?" Kate asked.

I reminded her, "I don't have to answer to it. I just have to hear it."

But standing there playing the Green Hornet pinball machine, I wished we had chosen a more conventional name. The bartender didn't look like the type who would hesitate to hang up on anyone he thought might be attempting a crank call. He certainly didn't look like the type who would necessarily hold the phone to his chest and call out, "Hey! Is there a Harvey Sprinkle here?"

Especially since there were just four people in the place so far. Lou Bowman, mean-looking Molly, a bleached-blonde barfly and myself. Things were most definitely *not* hopping at The Moose Run Inn.

It was the bleached blonde that had me worried. Possibly a pretty young thing at one point in her history, she was now somewhere in the northern neighborhood of her forties and had clearly moved on to the hard-maintenance portion of her life. Her cheeks were an unnatural pink, her eyelids an unnatural blue, her eyebrows an unnatural brown and her puckery lips an unnatural red; the full-palette attempt to conjure up what youth and Nature had once provided for free. Her bottle-blonde hair, anchored by pitch-black roots, fell in large unkempt waves down to around her shoulders. She was wearing a tight leather miniskirt meant for an eighteen-year-old, and a simple white blouse meant for a ten-year-old.

A cigarette was smoking itself in one hand and a glass was in the other. The woman's eyes scanned the dark bar like an exhausted lighthouse beam.

When I had walked into The Moose Run Inn I had made accidental eye contact with the woman—the only person in the place who had bothered to look up—and been swept by those lighthouse beams. Before I could turn away she had launched a challenging smile and teeter-tottered her half-empty/half-full glass at me in an unabashedly provocative manner. My peripheral vision caught sight of Lou Bowman and mean-looking Molly sitting at a table near the bar arguing. They didn't register my entrance. I spotted the pinball machine beneath the moose head and stepped immediately over to it, praying that God would drop a few quarters into my pocket. He did (or He had) and so there I was, my back to the bar, slamming the hell out of the machine while trying to regain my bearings. I could feel the woman's overpainted eyes drilling holes willy-nilly into my back.

Quarters are finite. And people are only human. I missed an easy flipper shot on the fifth and final ball of yet another game. I knew, even as I reached into my pocket, that the quarters were now gone. A couple of Abes and Toms played off my fingers but that was it. I nodded gravely at the bar's namesake and turned slowly around. The blonde was still looking right at me. She gave me a great big drunken smile and waved an unlit cigarette in front of her face, like an unsteady metronome. Her voice traveled on gin vapors across the uncrowded room.

"You gotta light?"

Lou Bowman chuckled as I stepped past his table on the way to the bar. Mean-looking Molly slapped his hand.

"You look like someone? Who do you look like?"

It was possibly the seventh time that Carol had put that question to me. The first few times I made the mistake of believing that she had an answer on the tip of her tongue. But she didn't. I learned quickly enough that this was Carol's way of telling me who she looked like. Or who she thought she looked like.

"You know that lady on *M*A*S*H* who likes to kiss everybody?"

"Hot Lips."

"Yeah. Her. I look like her."

Okay. Fair enough.

"Remember Jayne Mansfield? She was in that cowboy movie? You know her?"

"The one who got her head chopped off in a car crash?"

"Yeah," Carol said. "Her. Before the crash. I look like her too. How about another drink?"

Carol was slamming gin. I was sticking to beer and she was calling me a sissy for it. I told her that the last time I touched hard liquor I killed five people. She laughed. She thought that was a riot.

"I kill people every day," Carol told me. "But they don't know it."

She aimed a finger pistol at Lou Bowman and fired. She was right. He didn't even notice.

At some point she asked me about my accent, which I was still in the process of perfecting.

"Where are you from?"

I took a bite off my beer. "Idaho."

"Everybody from Idaho sound like you?"

"What do I sound like?"

"You sound like a *sissy*."

A number of other people had finally drifted into the bar. I noticed that a few of them—mainly the men—glanced over at us with an undeniable expression of relief. The Moose Run regular had new blood. Carol was body-languaging the hell out of me. She wanted me to see her legs and she wanted them to accidentally brush mine every few minutes. I had taken the stool on her right, so that I could look past her and keep an eye on Lou Bowman. Bowman and his friend appeared to be in a heated argument about something. I couldn't make out what.

"Whatta you do for a living, Bob?"

I had given her an easy name to remember.

"Why don't you guess?"

Behind Carol, Lou Bowman suddenly slammed his fist down on the table. "Get over it!" I heard him snarling.

"Traveling shoe salesman," Carol was saying.

"Excuse me?"

"I said traveling shoe salesman. That's what you do."

I'm pretty sure the word "shoe" got in there by accident, but I wasn't going to quibble.

"Well, you're a smart lady. That's exactly what I do."

Carol grinned and hiccuped at the same time. Behind her, mean-looking Molly was snapping at Bowman, who very blithely held up his middle finger at her.

"Ask me what I do," Carol slurred at me. The fingers of her right hand were toying again with the buttons of my shirt. I had already pulled Carol's fingers away from my buttons about a dozen times already, but now it seemed as if she was using them to steady herself. Her swaying had picked up considerably in the last five minutes or so.

I obliged. "Carol, what do you do?"

She gave me a catbird-seat smile and pitched forward as if to whisper her answer. I grabbed her shoulders to keep her from falling off the stool. What she gave was a stage whisper at best; loud enough even for the dead moose across the room to hear.

"I *fuck* traveling shoe salesmen."

Things happened fast just then. Whatever it was that Molly and Bowman had been arguing about reached its peak. Mean-looking Molly didn't throw her glass at Lou Bowman. But she did flip its contents into his face. Immediately he reached across the small table and slapped her—not once, but twice—and then bolted up from his chair. I stood up too. Rather, I slid off my barstool, the result being that Carol continued to pitch forward. She fell unceremoniously off her stool and onto the floor, landing with an audible thud. I knelt down and yanked the woman up into a sitting position on the floor, her back up against the bar. Her eyelids were half open and her lips were attempting to form a word—I'm guessing it was "sissy." She was breathing. That's all I had to determine.

I looked up and saw that Bowman was making his way out of the bar. He was halfway to the door. Molly was right behind him. I looked at my watch. It was only nine-thirty. Shit.

"Nice meeting you, Carol," I muttered hastily, then started for the door.

"Hey!" The bartender jerked a thumb at my and Carol's drink glasses. "Is Rockefeller comin' by to pick this one up?"

I pulled out a fistful of bills from my pocket and tossed two twenties onto the bar. I bounded for the door.

"Hey, it isn't *that* much," the bartender said.

"Use the change to call her a cab."

The bartender laughed. "She don't need a cab. She lives upstairs."

I had reached the door. I stopped, my hand on the doorknob, and turned around. "She what?"

The bartender waved his hand in the air. "She owns this place. That's my boss." He leaned far over the bar so that he could see the nearly comatose Carol sitting on the floor. "How ya doin', boss?"

I hurried outside. Lou Bowman was standing next to his 4x4, snarling at mean-looking Molly, who was snarling right back. Really, they made a lovely couple.

"You're a bastard!"

"Get over it."

"No, *you* get over it!"

"I am over it!"

"What's that mean?"

"What's it fucking sound like?"

"You're a bastard!" she said again.

I could see it was a pretty limited discourse. Bowman yanked open the door to his power vehicle.

"Go back inside," he instructed his friend.

"Go fuck yourself!"

That's when he hit her. He took a step away from his Jeep and belted her. It was sort of an amateur karate chop to the side of the head. But hard.

"Hey!" I ran over to the two of them. Neither seemed especially pleased to see me. I turned to Molly. "Are you okay?"

"Who the fuck asked you," Bowman snarled. His lips curled as he checked me out. I took a step closer. Around the knees, I was telling myself. Tackle him around the knees.

"Keep your hands off her," I said.

"Mind your own fucking business." Bowman pointed a finger at his lady friend. "I'll call you."

"Don't bother," Molly called after him as he climbed into his Jeep.

"Don't fucking bother." Bowman slammed the door and turned over the engine.

"Wait!" I took a step—literally—in front of the vehicle. I held my hands up. "Hold on."

"Get the hell out of my way!" Bowman bellowed, gunning the engine.

Molly concurred. "You'd better move, man. He'll run you over. He's a prick!"

The prick hit the gas. I leaped out of the way. Bowman fishtailed on the gravel as he roared out of the parking lot. I took a large stone on my shin.

"Bastard," mean-looking Molly sputtered, not for the first time. She scowled at the settling gravel dust, then looked over at me. "Thanks."

I didn't have time for conversation. I limped over to my rental car and got in. As I turned the key, the passenger door suddenly opened and in dropped none other than the proprietress of The Moose Run Inn, fresh off the floor of her bar.

"What are you doing here?" I cried. "Get out!"

Carol was murmuring. "Needair. Lessgo."

I didn't have time to talk with her. And I didn't think it would be polite to open the door and shove her out onto the gravel.

"Christ." I put the car into drive and did my own little fishtail past mean-looking Molly, who was looking less mean at this point and more confounded.

"Where's the fire?" Carol mumbled as I hit the main road and slammed down on the accelerator. And then she passed out.

Bowman's 4x4 appeared on the horizon. He was definitely headed in the direction of his house. I got the rental car going sixty on the narrow thirty-miles-an-hour road. I was closing the gap, even as I was desperately putting together a plan to keep Bowman from reaching his home and discovering his former colleague rifling through all of his stuff. Given the mood that he was presently in, it was especially doubtful that his response would be calm and reasoned. And the thought that this ex-cop probably still kept a pistol handy didn't sweeten the image any.

As I caught up I formalized my plan. I didn't much care for the plan but I went about launching it. Pushing the pedal to the floor I swerved to the left and began to pass the Jeep. Bowman was traveling pretty fast himself, but I had the jump on him. I was passing him easily, when he noticed me and began to speed up. At the same time, a red pickup truck appeared on the road in front of me, coming my way . . . coming directly my way. If I was going to pass Bowman I had to angle in right now and shoot the shrinking gap. My plan—and I now realized it was a stupid plan—was to get in front of Bowman's Jeep and hit my brakes, forcing him to run into the rear of my car. Assuming no serious loss of life, I figured I could tie him up for a while on the side of the road with bickering. Stupid plan, yes? And with this pickup truck coming, I now had about one point zero seconds to implement it.

That was when God appeared. No burning bush, no barefoot carpenter . . . He appeared in the guise of Carol the bar-owning floozy. Carol's head lolled sideways on the headrest and her eyes came open (one more than the other). The pickup truck was almost on me. I could hear its horn blaring.

Carol hissed, "Is your name Sprinkle?"

I pumped the brakes and slid in behind Bowman's Jeep . . . just as the pickup truck flashed by. I got a snapshot view of the shrieking driver.

"What did you say?" I yelled as the rental car continued to slow down.

"Got a call at the bar," she muttered. "Sprinkle somebody. Somebody looking for Sprinkle. Is that you?"

My foot was off the pedal.

"Yes!" I cried. My voice filled with an excitement that Carol could not possibly comprehend. "I'm Sprinkle!" We rolled to a halt.

Carol looked at me cross-eyed. "You know . . . you look like someone."

"Who's your friend?"

"That's Carol. Get in."

Kate got into the backseat. I had cruised past Bowman's place and caught up to her as she was walking back down the road into the village. She pulled the door closed.

"Is she dead?"

I put the car in gear and continued down toward the village. "She's passed out. It's a long story."

"Christ, Hitch," Kate said, "I only left you two hours ago. How long can it be?"

"She owns the bar. She needed some air. Don't worry about her. Tell me. How'd you do? Did you find it?"

Kate sat back in her seat. "It's a long story." Uh-oh, I thought. She's pissed. But when I caught a glimpse of her in the rearview mirror she was wearing a Cheshire grin.

"I didn't find it," she said to my reflection. "But I think I found something else. In fact I'm sure of it."

"Do tell."

"I think maybe we should drop off your buddy first. What's her name again?"

"Carol."

Kate poked her head between the two seats to peruse the situation.

Carol was sprawled in the front seat like a sodden rag doll.

"Wow."

Carol stirred just then. Her heavy eyelids lifted. She didn't seem particularly surprised to see a new face. I'm guessing a woman like Carol becomes pretty accustomed to surprises after a while.

"I'm Carol," she said.

"Hello, Carol. I'm Kate."

Carol shifted her beams over to me. An approximate grin grew on her face. "Bob fucking Sprinkle." She asked Kate, "Do you know him?"

Kate's voice was filled with mirth. "Oh, Bob's a dear friend of mine."

Carol declared solemnly, "He's killed five people."

Kate hit me playfully on the shoulder. "Bob, you never told me it was five."

"I was going to surprise you."

"Where are we going?" Carol seemed to be aware for the first time that she was in a car and that it was moving. She floated out a hand and set it tentatively on the dashboard. Yes, it's real.

"Well that's a question. Where would you like to go, Carol? Would you like to go back to the Moose?"

"Aw ffffuck the Moose."

Kate sat back in her seat. "That sounds like a no to me."

Carol cranked her window down and tilted to the right, letting the air hit her in the face. She closed her eyes and for a moment I thought she had passed out again. But then she said, "I think you're going to be sick." She didn't have it quite right, but I knew what she meant to say. I pulled over immediately and Carol reached her head farther out the window and took care of business. We were on the approach into town, on the hillside loop overlooking the harbor. The little village gave Kate and me something nice to look at while the woman in the passenger seat retched like a sailor.

"I found bank records," Kate suddenly announced. "Every month, on the sixteenth, Bowman deposits five thousand dollars into his account. Every month."

"This tells you something?" I asked.

"You're damn right it does. There's no dead aunt, just like Kruk said, but somehow this guy has got a big house and a boat and that Jeep, and he's pulling in five thousand a month from somewhere. Somebody has got Bowman on a monthly allowance. Why?"

I echoed her. "Why?"

From the passenger seat, Carol gave a grunt as she continued her purge.

"It's a payoff, I'm positive," Kate said. "Bowman had no reason to kill Charley. No personal reason, I mean. This whole thing, the house with the view, all of it . . . Bowman's so-called dead aunt was just somebody paying him off to kill Charley. That's what's been going on. It was a hit, and I just happened to get in the way. Bowman's pulling down a free five thousand a month, on top of whatever else he got in order to get set up in this place. For killing Charley. If I could have found that report we could have figured out who owned that land and who wanted so badly to shut Charley's mouth about it."

"But you didn't find the report."

"No. But I found the bank records. Whoever owned that property is sending Bowman money every month. Now if your date here would stop throwing up so we could get back to the hotel we can check the PI's report and find out what date Bowman got his FedEx package. Bowman's deposits are like clockwork. The sixteenth of every month. My bet is that he gets the FedEx package the same day. And do you know why I *know* we're going to nail this bastard? Because today is the fifteenth," Kate said triumphantly. "We're here just in time to watch Bowman pick up his hush money. God is on our side."

Kate's declaration was met with a rousing punctuation from our front-seat guest. It was a finale. Carol brought her attention back into the car. I detected a certain new steadiness as she leveled me with her lamps.

"Bob," she said hoarsely. "I need coffee."

Carol's last name was Shipley, of the Heayhauge Shipleys no less. Carol's mother had been mayor of Heayhauge way back when, before the tourists started arriving. Her father had owned The Moose Run Inn. And now—in the interest of symmetry perhaps—Carol's brother, Roger, was mayor and it was Carol who owned the Moose.

"Politics wasn't in my blood," Carol told Kate and me as she took in a coffee facial. She gave off a hard laugh. "You know those T-shirts? 'All I got was this lousy T-shirt?' That's me. My mother ran this town and all I got was that lousy bar."

We were sipping java at the hotel's restaurant, out on the deck. The night was cloudless. From where we were sitting we could see Lou Bowman's house up on the cliffs. The lights were on. The monster was home. Kate kept glancing up there.

"My brother hates my guts," Carol went on. "I hate his too. He's turning this town into a sissy town." I expected her to aim that barb in my direction, but Carol had apparently forgotten her taunting me with that adjective just a few hours ago. "This was a nice little town when my mother ran it. No outsiders."

"And now you've got to put up with people like us?" Kate said.

Carol didn't seem to hear her. "You think I'm a hard case, don't you? You both do. Well I am. I'm pissed off every day and I don't even know why that is."

Kate asked, "Have you ever thought of leaving? Maybe you'd be happier somewhere else."

Carol shook her bleached-blonde head. "Everyone knows me here. They don't all like me, but they know me."

"Is that such a good thing?"

Carol chewed on this for a moment. "Maybe it's not such a good thing anymore," she agreed. "I'm probably getting stale here, aren't I?"

Kate flashed me a look. *Don't answer*, was what it said.

"Were you ever married, Carol?" Kate asked. "I know it's none of my business, but—"

"Don't worry about that. Yeah, I've been married. Hell, I'm the local Elizabeth Taylor. I been married three times. Four, actually, but one of them doesn't count."

"Why's that?" I asked.

"You don't want to know," Carol said darkly. And convincingly.

Now that I was no longer in her sights, Carol was showing no further interest in hearing anything about me. Or Kate either. Carol herself was clearly her most fascinating topic of conversation and as she continued to sober up and replace gin cells with caffeine cells, Carol rambled on about her life in Heayhauge, Maine. The general theme I had already heard back at the Moose. Men are shits. To this theme she added that women younger and prettier than herself were a bit of an irritation as well. Even so, she was completely civil to Kate, who was both. And Kate was being very encouraging to Miss Shipley, providing all the verbal cues necessary to keep the woman talking . . . not that they were really necessary. It was female bonding, right before my eyes. Or so I thought.

Carol admitted at one point that she was rotten with figures and that despite owning a popular local watering hole she was heavily in debt. In addition, twice in the past year alone she had been forced to close the Moose, for ten-day stretches each time, as a penalty for selling alcohol to minors.

"Teenagers with motorcycles," she said, shrugging. "I see a tattoo, I serve it a drink. Call me old-fashioned."

Carol blamed her brother the mayor for her problems. Carol was convinced that he was the one who had directed the local sheriff to send in the motorcycle teenagers just so that he could bust his sister.

"He wants my ass in a sling, what can I tell you?"

Conclusion: Carol was a lousy businesswoman and she couldn't conduct a lucid personal life.

"I don't even own a car," she said. "The bank took it this past winter. Do you have any idea how cold it gets up here in the winter? You sure as hell don't want to walk everywhere. I'm goddamn forty-six years old and I'm fucking hitchhiking everywhere. Excuse my language, Bob."

"Swear on, sailor," I said. Carol turned to Kate.

"He's cute."

Kate didn't confirm. Her mind—I could see—had gone elsewhere. And I knew roughly where that was. After a few more minutes of Carol's fascinating autobiography, Kate suddenly piped up.

"Carol. Listen. How would you like to make some money? Real fast?"

Carol eyed her suspiciously. "I'm not doing anything kinky."

"No, it's nothing like that. Honest. It's a little complicated to explain . . . but how would you like to make five thousand dollars?"

"I could find a place in my budget for that kind of money."

"There's only one hitch I can think of," Kate said. "You'd have to take a little vacation. Right away. For your own safety."

"So this is illegal? Or just dangerous?"

"It's not really illegal," Kate said. "It's . . . well, it's a gray area. But yes, it might be dangerous. I just think you'd be safer disappearing for a few weeks. Could you do that?"

Carol snorted a laugh. "Half the time I'm gone anyway." In a frightful flashback to the Moose-bound barfly, Carol leaned over and put her face right up to mine. "Maybe I'll go to *Tim-buck-too!*"

I turned to Kate. "What do you have in mind here?"

"I think Carol deserves a break," Kate said flatly. "I think she needs some money and I think she could use some time away from this place." She turned back to Dame Shipley. "Will you help us out?"

"Hey, lady. For five thousand dollars?" She pointed at me. "I'll dance on that guy's face."

Kate's plan was deceptively intricate. Its first requirement was that Carol stay over with us in the hotel. This part was not so much intricate as it was eyebrow-raising. I've described Carol to you already, so I'm not intending to be mean—only accurate—when I say that she had "hotel room" written all over her. And now that she was being squired upstairs by the ubiquitous Mr. and Mrs. Frank Sinatra . . . well, desk clerks do have their imaginations to keep them company, don't they.

I insisted on taking the cot and letting the two ladies crash in the double bed. I lent one of my shirts to Carol, a painful lending to an old romantic like myself. They giggled together like a couple of schoolgirls after lights out.

The next part of Kate's plan required Carol's leading us early the next morning to the local drugstore, which had a Federal Express kiosk off in the rear. We grabbed one of each of the several different-sized mailing envelopes. We also picked up a pen, a package of pink tissue paper gift wrapping and a hard plastic beach bag, a wide-mouth number with a shoulder strap and an illustration of Disney's *The Little Mermaid* embossed on the side. Our next stop was the local Tru Value store, where I picked up a box cutter. The folksy man behind the counter warned me not to cut myself with that thing. "They're sharp, you know?"

Well, yes. That's why they're called cutters.

We also picked up a new cap for me to wear. This one read "Roadkill" over the top of a cartoon image of a hitchhiking hippie frozen in fear in oncoming headlights.

Now came the intricate part. Carol directed us to the road that would take us to the NAPA Auto Parts store. We dropped her off just around the corner from the store, armed with the pen and the FedEx envelopes inside the Little Mermaid bag, then we continued on past the yellow NAPA sign and parked in the parking lot next door, which serviced a pizza joint, a Laundromat and a video store. There we waited. A little over an hour later we watched the Federal Express van pull up. The guy in his shorts and blue FedEx shirt hopped out of the van carrying a mailing envelope and entered the shop.

"Clockwork," Kate said. She had Kruk's PI's report out on her lap. "We're rolling, Bob."

I was a little worried about a few things. I had been worried that the little dustup I had witnessed the night before between Bowman and mean-looking Molly might interfere with the monthly FedEx arrangement that the two apparently had. But Carol had assured us that the two fought like that all the time. My second concern had involved the part of Kate's plan yet to be implemented. Its success would hinge on Lou Bowman's pulling over to pick up a hitchhiker from the side of the road.

"What if he just drives on by?" I had asked. We were all in the hotel room at this point. I had asked my question from the cot, in the dark, as the sorority sisters giggled.

"He'll stop," Carol said.

"But how can you be sure?"

The tone of voice she used in her answer squelched all further conversation on the matter. And all giggling as well.

"He has before."

Bastard.

It was maybe another hour after the FedEx drop-off that Lou Bowman's 4x4 pulled into the NAPA parking lot. Bowman got out and went into the shop. He was as mean looking as the day before. Maybe that's what Molly saw in him. Kate, who had already gotten behind the wheel of the rental car, lowered her Gina Lollobrigida sunglasses onto her nose.

"Here we go."

She turned on the engine, pulled out of the parking lot and drifted slowly across to the NAPA lot, pulling up directly behind Lou Bowman's big Jeep. The vehicle was between us and the shop. I opened my door and hopped out. Remaining in a squat, I dug into the rubber of the Jeep's right rear tire with my new box cutter. They're sharp, you know? It took a bit of frantic hacking before the blade finally made the first puncture, at which point I ripped as quickly as I could at the side of the tire.

"Get in!" Kate snapped suddenly. I crab-walked back into the car and pulled the door closed, keeping my head down below the window level as Kate pulled smoothly out into the road.

"Okay," she said, eyeing the rearview mirror. "You can come up now."

I slide up in the seat and tossed the box cutter out the window.

"Why'd you do that?" Kate sounded annoyed.

"That's how it's done," I assured her. Being a detective already of course, Kate was not terribly impressed with my theatrics. I could tell.

We rounded the corner and Kate rapped twice on the horn. The sister of the mayor of Heayhauge stepped out from the shade of an old oak tree. I won't swear to it, but I believe she had hiked her leather mini even further up on her hips. It was a bright blonde, a big bust and a whole lotta leg that stepped to the side of the road and stuck out its thumb. I reached out the window with a thumbs-up of my own, but missed her by about a foot. Kate slowed down. She was still eyeing the rearview mirror.

"Okay . . . down!"

I turned around and got a glimpse of Carol's hitchhiking pose: legs spread, arm way up in the air, head thrown back. She was right. I'd been silly to worry that Bowman might not pick her up. The most conservative TV evangelist in the business would have picked her up. I saw the 4x4 round the corner and then slow to a stop.

"Get down!" Kate hissed again. I did. We didn't want to risk Bowman's recognizing me from the bar. As far as recognizing the car, we simply had to gamble on its nondescriptness. Most rental cars don't look like anything anyway. Ours certainly didn't. White. Four doors. Antilock brakes. No tape player. Ubiquitous. The road was narrow along this route, and winding. There was no decent place to pass. Kate maintained the speed limit, and no more. The idea was to keep Bowman from zooming off to the bank. He'd have to chug along at the legal thirty-five, like the rest of us.

Except that unlike the rest of us, his right rear tire had been hacked away by an undertaker from Baltimore with a brand-new sharp box cutter.

"Yes!" Kate cried suddenly.

"He's stopping?"

She was triumphant. "He's stopping."

Kate drove on past Lou Bowman's bank and parked across the street in front of a coffee shop. We figured it would take Bowman at least a half hour to change his tire, so Kate and I went into the coffee shop. It was a new coffee shop, not an old one. No photographs of Cher or Steve and Edie on the wall. I ordered a cup of coffee and the bubbly high school girl behind the counter rattled off a litany of optional caffeine formats that I might want to consider.

"Just coffee," I said. Gently but firmly. "Mud in a mug. That'll be fine."

The deceptively intricate plan was now in its final phase. While Bowman was jerking around behind his Jeep with the jack and the spare tire, Carol's job was to locate among her FedEx envelopes the one that was the same size as the envelope that Bowman had fetched from the NAPA Auto Parts store. She was to slide the shipping label out of Bowman's package and copy all of the information down on the label from her own package. Kate had emphasized *all*. "Don't overlook code numbers or routing numbers. Copy it *all* down." Carol was to then stuff the appropriate amount of tissue paper into her own envelope to match the thickness and feel of Bowman's, slide the original mailing label into the plastic sleeve of the tissue-packed envelope, drop Bowman's package into her Little Mermaid bag and start making her holiday plans.

"Bowman's into something crooked, isn't he?" Carol had asked after receiving Kate's instructions.

Kate said, "He killed my husband."

"Oh, honey, that's way crooked. Do I kick him in the balls for you after I take the loot?"

Of course not. The idea was to get her away from Bowman as quickly as possible. After some debate though, we had rejected the idea that Carol leave Bowman behind and start walking—or hitchhiking—into town while he was busy changing his tire. He might suddenly check on the envelope, discover the switch and race after Carol on foot, at which point he would likely be too incensed to give her the opportunity to plant her foot in his soft and tenders.

"Knee him, actually," Carol had corrected herself. "You've got to let them get close first."

Kate and I took a table and kept our eyes glued to the window. We had a clear view of the bank across the street. As soon as Bowman pulled up and went inside, we had to move fast.

"Are you enjoying detective work?" Kate asked as we sat there hunched like vultures over our coffee cups.

"Honestly? It feels vaguely criminal."

"That's very perceptive, Hitch. When you're playing games with the bad guys sometimes you've got to adopt some of their rules."

"I guess that's why some cops go bad, eh?" I regretted it the moment I said it. Kate frowned.

"I'm sorry," I stammered. "I didn't mean—"

It was too late. Kate's eyes glazed over as she stared a hole into her coffee cup.

"I don't believe Charley went bad," she said softly. "Alan concocted all that. He saw the chance to knock my stool out from under me even more and he took it. And he made sure he was there to catch me himself."

She stared blindly out the window. "I'm weak, Hitch. I'm probably the weakest person you've ever met."

"That's the most ridiculous thing I've ever heard. You couldn't be more wrong. Kate, you are one of the *strongest* people I have ever met." I added, "And one of the prettiest."

"Then you don't know me." She took a sip of her coffee then looked at me over its rim. "Do you really think I'm pretty, Hitch?"

"Kate, that is such a woman question."

"It is such an insecure woman question. Hitch . . . You have no idea what it was like growing up the way I did. I know, I know, I'm not the only one and I know plenty of others had it much worse, but *I don't care*. My father . . . that bastard put the spook into me, Hitch. I grew up wanting a good man to replace the bad man but doubting that a good man would have me. It's an old story, I know. I was more familiar with the bad men so that's where I'd go, blah, blah, blah. I knew that world and I knew my place in it. Meeting Charley was . . . he was a better man than any of the others I had met. We had a decent thing going. And then, wham. Not to be. Back to the bad men. Back to the Alans. Back to the Guy Fellowses. Back to the game I knew best."

Kate's eyes had welled up with tears. She was angrily refusing to let them flow. She had finished her coffee and was balling the cardboard cup up in her fist. Christ. How had we gotten to this conversation? She was staring out the window again. But I don't think she was seeing anything out there.

"So what about me?" I asked. "I'm not such a bad guy, am I? And we seem to be doing okay."

Kate broke from the window and looked over at me. She was looking extraordinarily sad.

"You're a good guy, Hitch." She managed a small laugh. "I'm not so sure about this job of yours, but basically you're a good guy."

"See? You're not as doomed as you say you are."

She made a single line of her lips and gave me that sad frank look. "We don't count. We're too new."

"Jesus, Kate, your glass is sure as hell half empty, isn't it. How about a little faith here."

"Hitch, as far as I'm concerned, I don't even have a fucking glass."

I was going to challenge her on that, but suddenly we became aware that the sunlight had disappeared. And there was no passing cloud. A large white and green bus had pulled up directly in front of our window. Apparently this was where they loaded and unloaded passengers for the trip in and out of Heayhauge. There were only a handful of passengers getting off the bus. The driver—who looked like Boris Yeltsin—lumbered down off the bus and yanked open one of the luggage doors on the side of the bus. The new arrivals de-bused and gathered their suitcases and duffel bags. Mr. Yeltsin slammed the luggage door closed, shared a quick word with a young woman with a clipboard, then climbed back into the bus. Several passengers boarded the bus, and Yeltsin pulled the door closed. Even inside the coffee shop Kate and I could hear the loud *hssss*, followed by the grunt, as the bus pulled away, popping a little balloon of gray smoke from its exhaust pipe.

A woman was running in the direction of the coffee shop, from directly across the street. She was arm-pumping like crazy so as to maximize speed on her high heels. Her face was wide open in a silent shriek. Bowman's 4x4 was parked in front of the bank. It was Carol.

"Holy shit! Let's go!"

Kate and I bolted from the coffee shop. The high school girl trailed a "Thankyoucomeagainhaveagreatday" behind us as we ran out onto the sidewalk. Carol was breathless.

"I got it!" she shrieked, waving a FedEx envelope in the air. She addressed me. "He's pissed about his tire."

"Good," Kate said. "Let's go."

We piled in to the rental car. I drove. I weaved our way past the town harbor.

"Do you need to pack anything?" Kate asked, turning around in her seat. "It would have to be fast."

I glanced up at the rearview mirror. Carol had yanked open the FedEx envelope and was peering down into it. I checked the road, then the mirror again. A big smile met me there.

"Children . . . I'm packed!"

CHAPTER 31

It would have been nice if the return address on the FedEx label had given us the exact name and street address of the sender. Hell, actual directions how to get to the place and which bed to look under in case the guy was hiding would have been nice too.

Kate had warned me not to expect too much.

"The package isn't even being sent directly to Bowman. His name certainly won't be on it. And if Bowman has taken that kind of precaution, you can bet the sender has too."

The return address section of the label gave only a post office box and a zip code. The return zip code on Bowman's package was 21030.

"That's Hunt Valley, out in Baltimore County," said Kate.

I was directing the rental car through one of those damnable roundabouts. I had already passed the exit for Boston twice; it was coming up again.

"The industrial park?"

"Yep. You know that all used to be cow country out there. And now . . . it's like someone dropped an atomic bomb in the middle of a cow field and voilà, a thousand acres of office buildings."

I made the exit. "Pasture," I said.

"What?"

"Cow pasture. You said field."

"Whatever."

"It's pasture."

From the back seat, Carol snapped, "Get off it, Bob. What are you, a fucking farmer?"

I glanced the rearview mirror. "Actually, I'm an undertaker."

Kate added, "And I'm a detective."

Carol exploded into laughter. "And I'm a college professor, ha-ha. And I don't even know how to play this game!"

She sat back in her seat to count her money . . . again. Maybe she thought that it multiplied with multiple countings. I saw in the mirror that she moved her lips as she counted. The peculiar thing was, it *had* multiplied. Not since the first time Carol counted it, but from what Kate and I had expected. Based on the bank statements that Kate had located while snooping around Bowman's place, we had expected the FedEx envelope to contain five thousand dollars. But when Carol announced her tally after the first counting, it had been eight thousand. Kate and I had no way to account for the uptick.

In a way, we had all wanted to stick around to see Lou Bowman bursting out of the bank in all his distress and fury. I could just picture him ripping up that FedEx envelope and its pink tissue paper.

"He'll kick the first dog he sees," I predicted.

"He'll punch the first person who looks at him sideways," Kate said.

Carol's guess was more solemn. "He'll take it out on the Moose."

This last prediction had prompted us to pull over so that Carol could phone her bartender to warn him in advance of the possibility of a rough customer on the way. Carol announced as she climbed back into the car, "I told Mike to juice up the cattle prod, just in case."

"You keep a *cattle prod* behind the bar?" I was astounded. "Is that legal?"

"Hey, Bob, I run a place where people crowd into a dark room to get drunk. If I gotta prod them once in a while to keep them in line, go ahead, sue me."

After a few minutes of almost silence (I say "almost" because I could hear the crinkling of hundred dollar bills being counted in the back seat . . . again) Carol had upgraded her statement.

"Excuse me . . . I *used* to run a place."

Kate turned in her seat. "You're not going back?"

Carol waved a handful of money in the air. "Not in this lifetime, honey."

Carol came with us to Baltimore. She had never been on a plane before. Maybe that's why she didn't understand that she was supposed to get sweaty palms, like I did, and find it a little hard to breathe in that skinny tin can. Like I did. Instead, she acted like she enjoyed it. I gave her my half sandwich to go with hers. She brought the two halves together and managed to make it look suggestive.

"I'm a bad girl aren't I, Bob," she asked, giggling.

A storm delayed our landing. Oh goody. Kate explained to Carol that we just circled around until the storm cleared.

"And if we run out of gas?"

Kate aimed her answer at my green face. "Probably a nosedive, don't you think? Bob?"

We landed. Carol walked off the plane talking about maybe becoming a stewardess. Brimming with all sorts of plans for her new life, she was holding on to that FedEx envelope like it was her only child.

Down at the end of a jut of land along the east side of the Fells Point harbor is a large brick building that used to be a warehouse. It has been converted into pricey condominiums and a high-toned hotel. The rooms are spacious, splashed with sunlight and nicely appointed with prints of clipper ships and framed nautical charts and the like. Personally, for that kind of money I'm not sure I'd care to look out over a harbor that is three-quarters industrial . . . but hey, I wasn't buying. Carol was. This was where we installed her. Kate had offered to let Carol stay at her place, but the former proprietess of The Moose Run Inn in Heayhauge, Maine, intended to splurge a little.

"I want a place where I can pick up the phone and have some cute boy run up to my room with one of those carts like you see in the movies."

"You like those carts, do you, Carol?" I teased.

We got Carol installed in her new temporary digs and then she and Kate went out to shop for some new clothes. I wasn't sure if I'd be able to handle Carol in anything other than her leather mini, but it looked like I'd have to try.

The sun was calling it a day by the time I left the girls to their foraging and made my way to the funeral home. I had only been gone a couple of days, but as you can maybe imagine, people keep dying. Aunt Billie was glad to see me.

"Sad news, Hitchcock," Billie announced. "Jeffrey Simons passed on. I just got off the phone with Helen. She wants us to handle the arrangements."

"That'll be a media event," I observed. "A two-parlor number."

"Oh it certainly will be. We're going to have a full house."

While Billie made the arrangements for Jeff Simons's body to be delivered I rushed home to shower and change. I flipped on the TV in time to catch Mimi Wigg already settling in at the solo anchor desk.

"An institution left the building today," she intoned. I switched off the set.

Back at work our phone machine was already clogged with messages from callers trying to get the details of the newsman's funeral. I even had a tearful message from Tony Marino — offering to play his bagpipes at Jeff Simons's funeral, for free. *Listen*, said Tony's voice and a bleating dirge came out of my machine's tiny speaker. It took me a moment to pick up on it. It was the news theme for Jeff Simons's station, slowed down, flattened out.

I had about a half dozen other messages. Several were from Hutch. His first message asked that I call him as soon as I could. The others carried the same request but with considerably more urgency. *Where the fuck are you?* I also had a message from Gil Vance, chiding me about missing the last rehearsal and reminding me that there was a run-through of the final act this evening. Apparently I had not yet impressed upon Gil the fact that, as I would be reading my lines directly from the script, I really wasn't required at all of his rehearsals. Of course it's true that as swiftly as Gil was thrashing his conceptual machete through new territory, I might want to keep up on the latest twist, otherwise I might well show up on opening night to find the whole damn thing set in Beirut.

The final message was from Julia.

"Hitchenstein. I need your opinion on something. Peter has asked me to marry him. The millions, the mansion, the cars, the whole thing. Can we picture this? What do you think? I'd love your feedback, sugarcube. Call me. Lord knows you've got my number. As nobody else has."

I phoned her immediately. She answered on the fourth ring.

"It's me," I said.

"Oh . . . Hitch. Look . . . listen, I can't talk right now."

"But I got your message."

"Not now, Hitch."

"Julia, I think—"

"*Hitch.*"

"Oh. He's there?"

"He's in the bathroom."

"Am I interrupting something?"

"Is it any of your business?"

"I thought you guys ended it in Paris."

"I thought so too. But he came crawling on his knees and called himself a shit and told me that I was completely right and he was completely wrong. I love it when a man talks that way."

"Oh come on, Jules, he's only saying that to get back into your bed."

"Well I guess it worked." She must have suddenly muzzled the phone. I could hear her garbled voice, and then she came back on, dripping with insincerity. "It sounds like a lovely magazine, darling. But who has time to read these days. Thank you anyway."

Click.

I went ahead and caught up on some of the less sexy parts of my job. I finally called the earnest coffin sales rep in Omaha, hoping to just leave a message. But he was still in. I told him to send me the information on his latest models. "I already did," he said, sounding disappointed. And so he had. I was looking at the info as we spoke.

"It must have gotten lost in the mail," I said. "Send it again." I then proceeded to explain what I *wasn't* interested in, taking my cues from the specs and prices on the papers in front of me. I could practically hear the air going out of him all the way out there in Omaha.

"Good talking with you, Chet," I said.

I heard his voice, tiny and tinny, as I was hanging up. "It's Curt."

Click.

I called Hutch's number. An answering service routed me to his pager number and a few minutes later my phone rang. The connection was lousy. He was on a cell phone.

"Man, where have you been? I've been trying to reach you."

"Sorry. My cell phone is in the garage for repairs."

Hutch wasn't in any mood for jokes. "Can you meet me? I need to talk to you."

"And what we're doing now, what's this? Hand signals?"

"Face-to-face."

"You sound serious, Hutch."

"I am. I'm also incredibly squeezed for time."

Just then a huge crunching noise sounded through the phone.

"Hutch, where the hell are you?"

"Curtis Bay. There's a big . . . you'll get a kick out of this, Hitch. It's a pyrolysis plant. You know what that is? It turns waste products into energy. Shit mulching, basically. It's a prototype. Senator Stillman stepped on all sorts of toes and kicked all sorts of asses in the legislature to ram this thing through for the state. Tons of federal bucks. Anyway, there's a big ribbon cutting tomorrow. Photo op for Alan. I'm just going over the layout. But look, can we meet? I mean, immediately?"

He gave me a time and a place. I wrote them down on the back of an envelope and hung up. Eight o'clock in front of Baltimore's Washington Monument. It was hardly something I needed to write down. Especially since it was already seven-thirty.

Hutch had failed to specify what "in front of" means when you're dealing with a lighthouse-shaped structure. I came up from the south. I located Hutch on the west. The road surface on the circle around the monument is made up of crushed glass mixed in with the asphalt. "Glassphalt" they call it. When light hits it a certain way it sparkles.

Hutch guided me across the sparkling street to a small park. As we walked, I jerked my thumb over my shoulder, indicating the monument behind us.

"Until about five years ago my mother's voice was the one on tape in the little historical display area there," I said.

"What happened five years ago?"

"They renovated the whole thing and got someone else to rerecord the tape."

"That's stupid. Did history change or something?"

"Hutch, you see it like I do."

We took a seat on a bench in the little park. There was a small statue in front of us. A boar devouring a wolf. The statue was called *Courage*. Frankly, I think *Ravage* would have made more sense. Hutch wasn't paying attention to the statue.

"Hitch, we need to talk."

"That's what you said on the phone. What's up? This feels vaguely cloak-and-dagger. Why didn't we just meet at a restaurant? Or a bar? Or is your candidate's war chest getting low already?"

"My candidate has deep pockets, that's not a problem. I just wanted to talk to you somewhere . . . It's safer here."

"Safer? Hutch, what's up? This *is* cloak-and-dagger."

"You're in trouble, my friend," Hutch said plainly. His arms were crossed and he was tilted back on the park bench, his legs straight out. Like a plank. He was staring into the middle distance. "Deep shit," he added.

"What kind of trouble?"

"Alan."

"Your Alan?"

"Alan thinks you had something to do with the murder of Guy Fellows."

Well there was a piece of work. Alan Stuart thought *I* was involved? I had the same damn feelings about him. I started to say as much to Hutch, but he hadn't finished.

"How well do you know Kate Zabriskie?" He adjusted his question. "How well do you *think* you know her?"

"I'm not sure a person can actually answer a question that's put like that."

"Did you know that Alan and Kate Zabriskie are lovers?"

Hutch reeled in his nowhere stare and looked over at me. It was clear that he felt he was delivering a bombshell.

"*Were* lovers," I corrected him. "She told me all about it."

"She told you everything?"

I shrugged. "That's a judgment call too, I guess. But she told me plenty. The good, the bad and the ugly. And your boss wasn't exactly among the good. She told me about Mexico."

"Mexico."

"How Stuart traveled a thousand miles to sleep with her a few more times, dump her and rough her up a bit for good measure."

"And you believe her. Hitch, you barely know her."

"I go by gut."

Hutch frowned. "She's working the Guy Fellows case."

I told him that this wasn't exactly a news flash.

"Has it ever crossed your mind that this involvement between the two of you might be a part of her investigation," Hutch asked.

I laughed. Hutch didn't appreciate it, but I couldn't help myself.

"Oh come on, Hutch. You need to get out more. Kate is going to get *involved* with me because I'm a suspect in a murder? What the hell kind of story is that?"

Even as the words left my lips, my heart skipped a couple of beats. Kate *had* gotten involved with someone—Fellows—as part of a criminal investigation. Just who was maybe being naive here? Hutch was pulling something out of his bag. I added, "And besides, why would I kill Guy Fellows in the first place? To drum up business?"

"You were seen arguing with Fellows at the cemetery, when was that . . . two weeks ago? Something like that?"

"I went through all this with Detective Kruk."

"I know you did. And right after that he was pulled off the case and Kate was put on."

"Office politics," I muttered. "What does any of this have to do with me?"

"Hey, don't kill the messenger, okay? I know you better than Alan does. I don't think you're a murderer, Hitch, any more than I am."

Small comfort there. Hutch tossed a large brown envelope onto my lap.

"Guy Fellows was blackmailing Alan. He had a partner working with him. I figured it was that woman that you buried. Alan and I both figured that."

"Carolyn James."

"Her. But then the next thing we know someone sticks a knife in Guy Fellows and then a few days later . . . this."

He indicated the envelope, which I picked up. I knew what I'd be finding inside.

"What's this?" I asked.

"It's the reason Alan Stuart isn't your biggest fan."

"He thinks I sent these to him?"

Hutch's eyes narrowed and I immediately recognized my mistake.

"Sent what to him, Hitch? You haven't even looked in the envelope."

I was able to recover quickly. "You said Fellows was blackmailing Stuart. So . . . let me guess." I pulled a pair of eight by ten glossies from the envelope. "Well. Dirty pictures of Grace Kelly. Go figure."

"Not everything is a joke, Hitch."

I slid the pictures back into the envelope and handed it back to him. "I know that. But the future governor of Maryland thinks that an unassuming undertaker from Fells Point is a murderer and a blackmailer . . . There's either a joke in there somewhere or a punch line."

Hutch put the envelope back into his bag. About ten feet away, a one-legged man was hobbling in our direction. He was using a single crutch for balance. His pants were undone and he was barefoot. A filthy white towel was duct-taped to the top of the crutch, for padding. Hutch stood up from the bench.

"I've got to be going. Fund-raising dinner."

"Gee, and I wasn't invited?"

"A thousand dollars a plate."

"Gee, and I just remembered I'm busy?"

The one-legged man had reached us. He shook a paper coffee cup at Hutch; the few coins in the cup made a sad echo. Hutch dug into his pocket and pulled out a twenty-dollar bill, which he tucked into the man's cup. He looked over at me. "I'm not heartless."

The beggar continued on his way. "Hitch, I really don't know what's going on here. I'm thinking you're just in the wrong place at the wrong time. And that's all. I've tried to convince Alan of that, but Alan's not exactly in a reasonable mood about any of this. *Somebody* out there has got him by the balls. The man is seeing red. I just want to warn you, as a friend, to keep an eye out."

It was occurring to me that sometimes there's an awfully thin line between a warning and a threat. I hated myself for feeling it, but I couldn't shake the sense that my political-operative buddy was traveling deftly along that line.

I stood up. "Have a good dinner, Hutch. Make sure you clean your plate."

I phoned Kate and left her a message to meet me at the Oyster. I didn't mention my meeting with Hutch. Not on the phone. I wanted to see her reaction to the news that her follow-up blackmailing efforts were apparently yielding high dividends. I also wanted to hear from her just what she was planning to do next. I hadn't yet decided for certain how many of Hutch's suspicions I would share with her. I was certain that his speculation about Kate and Stuart still being involved was ill-founded. As was his suggestion that Kate was playing me like a fiddle.

I had another ticket on my car. I'm sleeping with a cop, for Christ's sake. Shouldn't I be able to have these taken care of? I stuffed it into the glove compartment to keep the others company.

I swung by Carol's new temporary digs to see how she was settling in. She met me at the door in a straw hat, a pair of white bell-bottoms and a low-cut blue-and-white striped T-shirt with three-quarter sleeves. In other words, she was dressed like a Venetian gondolier.

"Do you like my toes?" she asked.

She was barefoot. Her toenails were painted like confetti.

"How much do people charge for that?" I asked.

She guffawed. "Eight thousand bucks. I'm broke!"

We headed over to the Oyster. Kate was waiting for us. Carol looked around the dark bar. A shiver went through her.

"Jesus Christ, I'm homesick. Goddamn it." She fetched a drink from the bar and drifted over to the dartboard. Bookstore Bob and Al the video guy were there. Arguing as usual. I watched as Carol took a dart from each of them, then turned to the target and took aim.

Kate had come up with a name. Epoch Ltd.

"I went out to the Hunt Valley post office this afternoon and flashed my badge around. I had to do some quick double-talking to explain why a city detective was out there in the country nosing. But eventually I got what I wanted. The P.O. box on Bowman's FedEx package belongs to something called Epoch Ltd. That's who has been sending him the money."

"Who the hell is Epoch Ltd.," I asked. "Or what?"

"I don't know. The post office didn't have an address on file. Or they couldn't find one. They didn't even have a phone number. I tried information, but they didn't have a listing."

I thought about this for a minute. "Well, whatever Epoch Ltd. is, it must be located in Hunt Valley, right? It's in one of those buildings."

Kate agreed. "Sure, but do you have any idea how many office buildings there are out there? And how many different businesses are in each one?"

"You don't think we could just go from building to building checking the floor directory in each of them?"

Kate shook her head. "There are hundreds of buildings."

"So? We split up. We'll make some sort of map and we'll each take a section each day. Maybe we can get Carol to help out."

"We don't have that kind of time."

"Why not?"

"Bowman," Kate said. "Bowman is not going to just sit up there in Maine with his pink tissue paper, you know. We set the clock running when we snitched his money. Bowman's going to know full well that Carol didn't just *happen* to peek into his FedEx package or just *happen* to have a bunch of pink tissue paper with her. He'll know that he didn't just *happen* to get a flat tire right after he *happened* to pick up Carol hitchhiking."

"You're saying he doesn't believe in happenstance?"

"Not that kind. Don't forget, Hitch, this guy was a detective for fifteen years. He is trained to be suspicious, especially of coincidence."

"I love coincidence."

"Which is why you'd make a lousy detective. Hitch, the point is this. Bowman already knows that someone is onto him. He knows that someone plotted to lift that envelope from him. And he's going to know that it wasn't Carol acting all by herself. I mean . . . look."

Over at the dartboard, Carol was giving the tip of one of the darts a good-luck kiss. She had the full attention of Bob and Al, who had momentarily ceased their bickering.

Kate continued. "Bowman was a good detective. He's going to remember you hitting on Carol at the bar—"

"I wasn't hitting—"

"And he's going to definitely remember your hijinks with the car, when you tried to cut him off. He'll remember all that. He'll put it together. Then he'll nose around the local hotels for anything odd looking. Detectives do that sort of preliminary in their sleep. And I hate to say it, but Mr. and Mrs. Frank Sinatra registering at that hotel qualifies as odd looking. I shouldn't have let you do that. I wasn't thinking."

"Oh come on, Kate. The guy can't possibly track us down."

"Did you put the car's license plate number on the registration form when you checked in?"

"Well yes, but—"

"And didn't you use your credit card to rent the car at the airport in Boston?"

"That doesn't necessarily mean—"

"Are you beginning to get my drift?"

"Sure. But—"

"Hitch, we don't have the time to go traipsing from building to building in Hunt Valley looking for Epoch Ltd. in a haystack. Lou Bowman killed my husband. And he knows we're onto him. That makes him a desperate animal, Hitch. If you think—"

A scream split the air. It was Carol. For a fraction of a second I thought she must have gotten a bull's-eye. But it wasn't that kind of a scream. It was, in fact, the kind of scream you let out when a burly guy you've just flamboozled out of eight thousand dollars up in Maine suddenly throws open the door of the bar in Baltimore where you are innocently tossing darts.

Kate had just enough time to mutter "Shit" before she dove under the table.

Lottery Lou was back in town.

CHAPTER 32

I think I've already described the general layout of the Screaming Oyster Saloon. Only two
features in particular are relevant in order to
understand what took place in the thirty sec-
onds following Lou Bowman's entrance. The first feature is that black
door down at the end of the bar, the door that leads directly out to the harbor. The second is the weathered old dinghy that hangs from chains
attached to the ceiling, chock-full with years and years of empties.

I didn't mention one other feature. At the time, it seemed totally
inconsequential. The bar phone. Over at the far end of the bar. Near the
black door. I mention it now for the following reason. At approximately
the same moment that Carol spotted Lou Bowman standing there in the
door and let out her very impressive scream, the bar's telephone rang.
Sally answered it. It was for me.

"Hitchcock!" Sally called out. Kate had just that instant disappeared
beneath the table. Powered purely by reflex, I stood up when Sally called
out my name and started for the bar. And that's what caught Bowman's
attention. That's what stopped him in his initial lurching in Carol's direction and caused him to redirect his lurching . . . toward me.

"Son of a *bitch*!"

He meant me.

Being closer to that end of the bar to start with and having longer legs anyway, I reached the phone in about five strides. Bowman had the whole length of the bar to travel. He never made it.

The hero of the moment was Edie Velvet. I hadn't even noticed her sitting there, which of course is what happens when a person becomes a regular fixture in a bar; they come to look as innocuous as . . . well, as a fixture. Lou Bowman had blood in his eyes. Edie was just emptying the last of her beer into her glass as the Pamplona bull charged past her, I reached the bar and on some inexplicable form of autopilot, calmly took the phone from Sally . . .

She tossed the empty up into the weathered old dinghy hanging from chains over the bar.

"Hello?"

"Hitchcock?" It was Aunt Billie.

"Yes."

"Hitchcock. A man was just here looking for you. I mentioned that he might try the Oyster. But now—"

I never heard the rest of it. What Sally had been crabbing would happen for so many years that we had all long ago ceased even hearing her . . . happened. And it happened quickly. I remember seeing a pair of tiny explosions of plaster dust up where the chains holding the dinghy were attached to the ceiling. And then it was all noise.

CRASH!

The dinghy came down partway onto the bar and partway onto Edie and partway onto Lou Bowman, who had just passed Edie's barstool. The old boat exploded into splinters on contact as hundred and hundreds of bottles and cans—and a few other interesting items—*burst* into the air, over a dozen years of shrapnel launching out in all directions. I took a bottle to the head and one to the mouth. Sally's arms windmilled madly as she staved off the barrage of cans flying at her. Frank got clunked right between the eyes, dropping where he stood. Others in the bar avoided the direct attack, but many got caught in the push of others who were leaping back from the explosion. Something akin to a wave gently mowed them all down. I saw Carol go under.

Edie Velvet and Lou Bowman had caught the brunt of it. The two of them lay half buried on the floor beneath chunks of wood and the hundreds and hundreds of empties. I'll allow you only about three seconds to picture the tableau, for that's about how long it took before Lou Bowman stirred. His nose was bleeding and a gash had opened up over his left eye. His mouth was bloody too; he was literally tasting blood. And I could see that he wanted more. He wanted mine.

I acted without thought. Years of witnessing Sally's swift mobilizations probably helped.

"Sally!" I barked. "The door!" And Sally knew exactly what I meant.

Even as I waded into the cans and bottles that half buried Bowman and Edie, Sally had flipped up the hinged end of the bar counter and yanked open the black door. Lap lap lap went the harbor.

I grabbed hold of Bowman's collar with one hand and his belt with the other. Bowman's attempt to stand—slipping and sliding on the debris—simply propelled him toward the door. I helped him along. The two of us shot forward, me like the guy who is pushing the bobsled up at the start of the track, he like the sled. And thus it was that within thirty seconds of Lou Bowman's entering the Screaming Oyster Saloon, I literally ran the bastard right back out.

Alas, there was no time to savor the moment.

"Kate! Carol! Let's go!"

Kate had already popped up from beneath the table. Carol was extricating herself from the human tide.

"Move!"

As I picked my way through the bottles and wood and cans I paused to look down at Edie. She hadn't yet moved.

"Go!" Sally yelled. I turned and saw her plant a chubby shoe on Lou Bowman's forehead and push him back into the water.

Kate and Carol and I raced out of the bar. Taking great gulps of air, I managed to gasp, "Follow me!"

They did. We moved swiftly across the square and over to Julia's gallery. It was closed. I checked the windows overhead. Dark.

"Damn!" And then I remembered. Rehearsal. "Come on!"

In another minute we were all safely inside the Gypsy Playhouse.

"Well, well, well, we were beginning to wonder," Gil's voice sounded from somewhere in the theater.

The stage was lit. About a dozen amateur actors were seated in folding chairs on the left-hand side of the stage, hands on their knees, staring

stonily forward. I've seen this look before, or at least the look that the ama-
teurs were attempting. They were playing dead. Gil had stupidly
arranged the chairs in pairs, with an aisle space between the pairs. It
looked like the seating on a bus. Occupying Emily's seat up front, which
in this ridiculous arrangement made it look like the bus driver's seat, was
none other than Chinese Sue. Sue wasn't playing dead; she was playing
bored. For that matter, she probably wasn't playing. On the right side of
the stage stood the remainder of the cast, the living, holding on to their
open black umbrellas. The locksmith from Lutherville was standing in
for me at the lectern. He was wearing my pith helmet.

"Well, we all thought that you had forgotten about us, Mr. Sewell," Gil
said. "So glad you could join us." I could see him now, he was seated in
the middle of the house. He was shading his eyes with his hand. A clear
affectation; looking in our direction, there was no light that could possibly be in his eyes.

"Who have you got there with you?"

"Two more bodies," I said.

Gil was delighted. "Oh good. Living or dead?"

I looked down at both Kate and Carol. In perfect unison, they both
shrugged.

Despite all the excitement, Carol drifted off to sleep during the rehearsal.
Gil had placed her in one of the dead seats so it didn't make a whole lot
of difference. From my place at the lectern I saw her eyes flutter and her
chin begin to dip. I made eye contact with Kate, who was doing a superb
job as one of the mourners; she looked deeply troubled, dark and beautiful beneath her umbrella.

Gil approached me afterward to commend me on our two new cast
members.

"Where did you find them, Hitchcock?'

I told him, in all seriousness, "Between a rock and a dead place."

I phoned a cab company from the lobby. Hats borrowed from
wardrobe pulled low, Kate, Carol and I scurried into the cab and directed
the driver to take us to Carol's new temporary digs. For the time being this
was our official safe house.

Carol rallied only for the length of the short taxi ride back to her place, then passed out anew on her king-size . . . queen-size . . . her royal family–size bed. Kate saw to her disrobing and called me in to help tuck the gal under the sheets.

Kate and I had some thinking to do. We did it out in the living room. As Kate had predicted—almost to the second—Lou Bowman had clearly flexed his investigatorial muscles upon the discovery of pink tissue paper where crispy greenbacks should have been. Even though Kate had walked me though the process by which the police veteran had come up with my name and address, I was still mightily impressed.

"He must have gotten an A in detective school."

"Routine stuff," Kate assured me.

The implication of Bowman's colorful return to Baltimore was clear. Unfortunately. It was more sobering than the coffee I'd been gulping down over at the Oyster.

"He wants to kill me."

If I was hoping that Kate would pooh-pooh my conclusion I was doubly disappointed.

"Right now I would guess that killing you is Lou's single purpose in life."

I gave her a grimace. "Feel free to throw in a gray area there if you'd like."

"I'm sorry I dragged you into all this. I shouldn't have let it happen."

"You didn't drag me. I insisted. Remember?"

"Still, I should have said no."

"I'm just so damned irresistible, what can I tell you?"

"You're in deep shit, dear, that's what you are."

It seemed I had recently been told this exact same thing. The smile wiped right off my face.

Kate was trying to piece everything together. She was pacing the carpeted floor. Barefoot, as if charging her batteries from the static electricity off the rayon plush. I remained seated, uncomfortably perched on the edge of a leather Eames knockoff.

"Now the good part, if Lou can stay rational, is that he'll want to know how the hell it was that you caught on to those FedEx deliveries. I'm sure he didn't talk it up around old Heayhauge."

"His lady friend knew," I reminded her.

Kate shook her head. "No. She knew he got the packages. That doesn't mean she knew what was in them. And I'm sure she didn't know why. But that doesn't really matter. The question for Lou is, who the hell are you? Carol he knows, and I'm sure he figures she's basically in the dark about all this. You used her to get hold of the money and that's about as far as she goes. But you . . . Once Bowman got ahold of your name and saw that you were from Baltimore, you can bet the alarm bells went off. That's why he got down here so damn fast. He knows that you know something. But what he doesn't know is how much you *do* know."

"You mean how much I don't know."

"Same thing. But see, our advantage right now is that Bowman can't be sure how much of the truth you've learned. Right now he has to assume . . . or he has to worry, that you know everything. He has to assume that you've got the whole story. Whatever that is. That means that you know what's going on with Epoch Ltd. and that they've been paying him off for killing Charley."

"But I don't know any of that. And you don't either. You're just guessing at all of this."

"Hey, *I* got an A in detective school, all right? I know I'm right. Epoch Ltd., whatever the hell that is, set this guy up nice and comfy up there in picture-postcard Maine and they've been keeping his pockets filled on a monthly basis ever since. Why? Bowman did a job for them. It's as simple as that."

"So why not just give him a huge one-time payoff? Why dribble it out every month like that?"

"I thought about that," Kate said. She stopped at the sliding glass door and looked out onto the night. "I've got a couple of guesses."

"Throw one at me."

"One guess is that this is the way it's done, for insurance reasons."

"Insurance? You don't mean insurance insurance?"

Kate was still looking out the sliding glass door. Her reflection was looking back at me.

"No. I mean to ensure that Bowman remains quiet. Suppose he gets one big payoff and he basically blows it all. He'd come asking for more and they'd have to give it to him. But this way it's actually very smart.

They throw him a big bone up front, a nice chunk of change, but not really enough to set him up for life. Then they dribble out the five grand a month. It's the hand that feeds him. He's not going to bite it."

"And your second guess?"

"Not as interesting. But maybe true. A great big payoff shows. It's on the books somewhere. Whoever this Epoch Ltd. is, they probably couldn't risk that kind of unaccounted-for expense. But five thousand is chump change. Petty cash."

"So you think we're looking at a fairly substantial company. Deep pockets."

"Do you want to hear my third guess?"

"Does the pope poop on the bear?"

Kate turned back around. "Lou Bowman is on a retainer."

"A retainer?"

"Yep. Let's keep aware of what we do know. Lou Bowman gunned down a fellow officer and then got paid off and sent away. This is known in my profession as . . . are you taking notes? A hired killer."

"Thank you, Professor."

"You're welcome. Now we should stop thinking of Bowman at this point as a bad cop or a crooked cop or any sort of cop at all. That's just obscuring things. Lou Bowman is a hired killer. That's what he left town as. A hired killer. You pay him enough, he will kill for you."

"So you don't think this was a one-time thing?"

"I have no idea whether it was or it wasn't, Hitch. All I'm saying is that we ought to keep this in mind. The man killed for money. He is getting money every month. I think they've got him in a position where he's their heavy if they need one. In fact, now that I think about it, it's actually kind of funny."

"Joke please."

"Think about it. He can blow the whistle on them, they can blow the whistle on him. It's like two guys yelling 'Freeze!' They're each pointing a pistol at the other."

"A Mexican standoff."

"Exactly. My guess though is that this Epoch Ltd. has definitely got the upper hand. Whoever they are, they could probably hang Bowman out to dry if it really came to that. He fired the gun. And they've clearly gone to some lengths to hide their involvement. My guess is that this is a pretty damned uneasy alliance. Bowman is being paid to keep his mouth shut as well as to be available in case they need him again. That's what I mean by his being on a retainer. Look, Hitch, we've focused on Lou Bowman's shooting Charley. We have nothing that tells us he hasn't done this sort of thing before. I told you already how trigger-happy the guy is."

"So we're back to where we started," I said.

"Where we started?"

I fell back in my chair. Suddenly I didn't like detective work anymore. I just wanted the pretty girl and to be a hero, not all of this. I just wanted to go back to burying people who had died because it was their time to die.

"Lou Bowman doesn't leave town until I'm dead." I gave a hollow laugh. "I guess I'd better tell Billie to clear some space."

Kate didn't respond immediately. She came over and knelt down next to my chair. Her eyes went wide and searching. I locked onto them and we played a sort of visual patty-cake with each other. Smoke began to rise. Kate's plump lips parted.

And then, well . . .

At the end of it, breathless, I opened my eyes and gazed out the sliding glass doors. The nighttime harbor looked beautiful; the sailboats with their mast lights, the pink glow from the Harbor Place promenade. Even the inky blackness of the water itself was impressive; it looked like an elaborate shard that had dropped from the night sky. The sizzling red glow of the neon Domino sugar sign set the water quietly on fire. It was all insanely beautiful.

But when Kate finally stirred, when she slid her leg down off of mine and backed away from me, placing her hand on my chest . . . when she whispered in the dark, "Oh, Hitch. Be careful," my perfect moment dislodged. What light there was coming into the room glistened off Kate's moist skin and literally rolled down her cheeks along with her tears.

She whispered it again, her voice deliciously husky. "Be careful." Then she got to her feet and walked across the floor—an absolute vision—and disappeared into the bathroom.

I felt like a man who had just been served his last meal.

Kate and I discussed the situation the next morning over breakfast.

"Can't we just have him arrested? Hell, can't *you* arrest him?"

"On what grounds?"

"How about murder? And strong suspicion of intent to murder some more."

"Where's my evidence?"

"For murder? There's the coroner's reports. Two bullets. Two police bullets. How about that?"

"Who is to say they didn't both come from my gun? Bowman and I used the same caliber gun."

"But it didn't. You only fired once."

"Hitch, I left my pistol behind when I followed Charley to the hospital. Bowman told me to. It was evidence at a crime scene. He could have easily taken it outside and fired off another shot. The ballistics report shows two shots fired. And I can't account for that. The point is, I can't pin Charley's death on Bowman. I've got nothing to arrest him on. This is even presuming that he'd let me get close enough."

"You think he'd kill you?"

"How can I open your eyes here?" Kate was frustrated. You could see it in the lousy way she was buttering her toast. "Bowman is desperate. His whole little bubble has been exploded. The man has got nothing to lose right now. His arrangement with Epoch Ltd. has been found out. You've tapped him for five thousand . . . no, eight thousand dollars. What next? You either want more money or you're planning to blow the whistle on him."

"Yes! Blow! Let's blow the whistle. Let's tell all and then duck out of the way."

"We don't know all yet. That's the problem, Hitch. We have to track down this Epoch Ltd. And I think I figured out a way. It's very simple, really. It hardly takes detective school to figure it it."

Right. I knew her "simple."

"Tax records," she said. "Epoch Ltd. has got to file a corporate tax statement of some kind."

"If they're legit, I suppose. But what if they're not legit, Kate? I mean, all we know about them is that they have apparently been mailing a hired killer a big bag of money every month. How legit are they going to be?"

"The question is, how smart? If there even *is* such an entity as Epoch Ltd., they'd be fools not to file a tax statement. Face it, Hitch, you and I are just a couple of irritating pests compared to the Internal Revenue Service. If whoever they are want to steer clear of trouble, they'll keep their noses clean with the IRS. You can count on it."

"So what are you going to do?"

"A little research. There's bound to be somebody around the station who has got an in with someone at IRS. Or a favor to be returned. I ought to be able to dig deep enough to find something out." She gave me her best false smile. "Don't forget, Hitch. I'm a trained professional. Meanwhile, my suggestion to you is that you keep your big ugly head out of sight."

Sweet girl.

"What about you? Bowman knows that there was a Mrs. Sinatra. He'd have gotten a description. Hunchbacked. Shriveled. Wart on the end of the nose. Don't you think he's tagged you as my partner, partner?"

"I'm sure he has," Kate said. "But I don't think he'll be so quick to go after me."

"You're being inconsistent. If he's in danger from me, he's in danger from you."

Kate set her toast down. "I'll be fine. It's you I'm worried about." She reached across the table at that point and took hold of my hands. Her sleeve dipped into the yolk of her unfinished eggs, but she didn't care. Whatta gal. Her eyes were pleading.

"Hitch. Just do me a favor, please? Stick around. See what you can do about not getting yourself killed by this guy. I think I'd miss you."

"That's almost the sweetest thing anyone has ever said to me."

Her grip tightened. "I mean it."

We met over the middle of the table for a slobbery morning-after kiss. Which was how Carol found us as she shuffled in from the bedroom.

"Bob, you're getting egg all over your hands."

Edie was dead. Sally fetched a plastic Christmas wreath from her attic and draped it with a black cloth and hung it on the front door of the bar. Naturally, Billie and I were to handle the arrangements. And this was going to present something of a logistical problem. Jeff Simons's body had been sent over from Hopkins already and we were busily clearing the decks for the crush of well-wishers who were already beginning to come by to pay their last respects to the TV newsman. Where in the world were we going to put Edie? Jeff Simons had seemed like a nice fellow on TV and all that, and I knew firsthand that his mother was a kindly old sweetheart, but I was damned if I was going to sit back and let Edie's final hours on earth be shunted aside like an afterthought as the result of a celebrity funeral. The old gal certainly deserved better.

I looked to Edie. The coroner's report found that the lethal blows to the head had come from "multiple smooth hard objects." Which is coroner's lingo for beer bottles. She had suffered a number of cuts to her face but nothing so terribly disfiguring that she couldn't be put on display for all of her chums and well-wishers.

Not that I wish the untimely death of anyone, but I have to admit that there was a part of me that was glad to have something to occupy my energies. Preparations for the funerals of both Edie and Jeff Simons allowed me to be distracted for a while from the sobering fact that an angry ex-cop out there apparently desired a very brief and definitive meeting with me.

"More flowers," Billie announced, pulling open the door.

"Hi, Mrs. Sewell. I gotcha more flowers here."

This was Fred, the flower delivery guy. We've known Fred for ages. We call him Fred Flowers. I have no idea what his real last name is. Billie had to go on voice recognition alone; all she could see was a pair of skinny legs in green pants and a pair of skinny arms hugging a flower arrangement fit for a winner at Pimlico.

"Anywhere, Fred. Thank you."

The legged flower arrangement tottered off into Parlor One. Fred emerged a moment later.

I was taking all this in from my office. My door was open: a) because I'm the welcoming sort; and b) I thought it would be a smart idea to know as quickly as possible if Lou Bowman were to pay a visit. I have to admit, the sight of Fred crossing the lobby completely obscured by the bouquet of flowers gave my stomach a turn. What if Lou Bowman thought of that? What if a mountain of lilies came crabwalking in through the front door and then suddenly pulled a gun and started shooting at me? There were several levels on which the image disturbed me.

I stepped over to see how things were shaping up. Billie and I had already pulled open the plastic curtain. The two-rooms-as-one was choked with flowers. Somewhere in town was a smart operator who was turning a quick buck peddling terra-cotta vases—about one foot square—that were fashioned in the shape of a television set. Somehow this fellow had gotten the word out fast—these guys always manage to do this—for we must have already had close to two dozen of the things, some holding flowers, some holding flowering plants. They all included a photograph of Jeff Simons taped onto the front. His publicity photo. Before the face-lift. Maybe ten years before. That cowlick looked like a little question mark.

I had asked Fred if he knew where the terra-cotta TVs were coming from. He told me he didn't.

Billie joined me. "Looks like a funeral." Billie loves that joke.

"What are we going to do about Edie?" I lamented. Edie was currently down in the basement, along with Jeff Simons.

"We just have to hold off for another day, dear. There's really nothing to be done."

She was right, of course. One look at our flower-choked parlor and the growing collection of terra-cotta TV vases confirmed it. It just hit a mean bone in me, that's all.

"Edie deserves better than to just sit in the basement waiting her turn."

Billie left my side and wandered in among the flowers. I knew what she was thinking. I was thinking it too. My parents' funeral. That had been a two-parlor event. That one had emptied most of the local florists. *That* one had brought out the bigwigs.

Billie put her face to a bunch of lilies and took a good sniff. She turned back to me.

"I have an idea. See what you think."

We brought Jeff Simons up from the basement just before noon and got him all situated. His mother had come over to help. She did a little motherly fiddling with her son's tie and she brushed some invisible specks off of his blue blazer. Mrs. Simons went to adjust Jeff's trademark cowlick, but drew her hand back sharply the instant she touched it. Consulting the publicity shot, Billie had hairsprayed the cowlick to within an inch of its . . . well, it was as hard as granite. But it looked good.

Despite the outpouring of flowers and terra-cotta TVs, we weren't actually expecting a crush for the afternoon wake. This would be mainly family as well as close friends and colleagues. A sizable flow of people to be sure, but not the makings of a riot. That would come for the funeral itself, which the station planned to cover live. They were apparently pushing it heavily on air. What the hell. On air was where the guy had lived and where everyone knew him. A TV funeral was fitting. Stupid, but fitting. The real crowds would turn out for the funeral. Cameras draw people like flies. And we know what draws flies.

Billie assured me that she could handle the lion's share of the Simons wake. She freed me up to make the arrangements for Edie, which I set to immediately.

Tony Marino was very helpful. He went around to the liquor stores in the area and collected several dozen boxes. I picked up some heavy-duty plastic trash bags and a pair of scrub brushes. Sally met us at the front door of the Oyster. Her eyes were soft and puffy. I could see that she was taking this hard. Like I said, Edie was a fixture at the Oyster. Now the fixture had been ripped out.

Sally let Tony and me in and we went to work, tossing bottles into the boxes and loading up the trash bags with all of those cans. We also came across some interesting artifacts that had found their way into the dinghy lo these many years. We found a wallet belonging to one Ashton Trice III. It contained his driver's license, an admission ticket to the Museum of Pornography in Indianapolis and a photograph of a handsome young feller with a waggish sneer on his face, holding up a bowling ball into which had been stuck a long red candle. Birthday, apparently. Sally tucked the photo into the bar mirror. Among the debris we also found several caps and hats, a fireman's helmet that no one could account for, a leopard-print brassiere, a pair of crutches, an AM transistor radio, a "Nixon's the One" campaign button (up on the mirror, next to young Mr. Trice), a *Look* magazine heralding the comeback of the suburbs, some decorative screw-on knobs from the beer taps, a spiked dog collar (which I suggested Sally slip around the neck of her sexy old husband) and a paperback copy of *War and Peace*, ripped perfectly in half.

Tony and I hauled the bottles and cans out front, where the street gremlins would whisk them away for the recycling nickel. We gathered up most of the splintered wood and tossed it out the black door into the harbor. Fitting end for a dinghy. I was checking my phone machine every half hour or so. I was anxious to hear from Kate. So far, no calls.

A large piece of the dinghy had remained intact. The bow and about a six-foot-long section of the starboard wall. Tony and I propped this section of the dinghy up against the far wall of the bar, the pointed bow aiming up at the ceiling, then went and fetched Edie. I had put the old gal into one of our coffins with a lid that can be removed altogether. We loaded the coffin into our hearse and drove it over to the Screaming Oyster, carefully set the box into the propped-up remnant of the dinghy and removed the lid. Edie looked beautiful.

It had been Billie's idea. And it was a brilliant idea. Edie was an Oyster regular. She lived here; she died here. Sally got the word out that Edie was going to be remembered here. Edie's wake was to be held that evening at the Screaming Oyster Saloon. Drinks on the house. The squeamish need not attend.

CHAPTER 34

The terra-cotta TV count had crested the forty mark by the time I got back from the Oyster. Billie had learned that they were going—without flowers, mind you—for a cool twenty-five bucks. I'll do the math for you: whoever was hustling these things had just hit a thousand bucks. Even as I did the math, it ticked up to a thousand and twenty-five as a tearful young woman appeared with another contribution to the shrine. Between sobs she explained to Billie—who had not asked—that she grew up with Jeff Simons. Of course she had never actually met the man in the flesh. But in the twentieth century a person can now officially "grow up with" a complete stranger, love them, hate them, grow cold and indifferent to them, reconcile with them, laugh and cry with them and even attend their funeral . . . and never once meet them. Kind of creepy, isn't it.

Billie reported not having seen a stocky man barging through the front door wielding a clutch of lilies and a blazing pistol. In truth I hadn't filled Billie in on the possible threat to my life and limb. I don't see the point in being an alarmist, unless you happen to enjoy calling attention to yourself. There wasn't anything my dear aunt could do to protect me, so why put her in a tizzy? I tried Kate's number at the police station a few times but all I got was the message that Detective Zabriskie was out of the office. I like that. They call the police station an office.

Fred arrived with another load of flowers. That's when I noticed a police car parked across the street. I rewound the tape in my head and realized that the car had been there when I came back from making my preparations at the Oyster. As Fred took the flowers inside I crossed the street and tapped on the passenger-side window. I crouched down to peek into the car. A skinny young guy with his police cap pushed back on his head was sitting behind the wheel scratching the silvery stuff off an Instant-Win lottery ticket. Several dozen losing tickets were strewn about on the seat next to him. He looked familiar to me.

"Hi," I said.

"Hello."

"Having any luck?"

The policeman finished scratching his card. He blew at the silver dust and squinted at the little box.

"I won another ticket." He indicated the dead soldiers on the seat next to him. "That's what half of those are." He picked up another card off of a stack on his dashboard and leaned over and handed it to me. "Here. See if you get lucky."

I scratched at the silver dust with my fingernail. "Let me ask you something. Are you parked here for a reason? I mean, besides trying to win the big one? Are you keeping an eye on this funeral home?"

"I keep an eye on everything, sir. That's my job."

I had to wonder if sitting in his patrol car scratching Instant-Win tickets fell under the guise of "doing his job," but I let it pass.

"You know what I'm asking."

"Yes sir, I'm keeping an eye on it."

"Did Detective Zabriskie send you here?"

"Zabriskie? Uh, no sir. I was sent here by Detective Kruk."

"Kruk?"

"Yes sir."

Now I remembered where I had seen this guy before. At the Baltimore Country Club. He was the one who drove Kruk out there the day they found Guy Fellows hugging the knife.

"Did Detective Kruk tell you specifically what you were to keep an eye out for?" I was tempted to say *who*, but I held back.

"Anything suspicious," came the answer.

"That's all he said?"

"That's all he needed to say, sir."

Sharp cookie this kid. "I don't mean to tell you how to do your job or anything. But all sorts of people have been going in and out of that place all day. Bringing flowers and whatnot. I just . . . I guess I was wondering, what *would* you consider suspicious?"

"I'd consider it suspicious if a person coming this way stopped when they spotted my patrol car and turned around and went the other way," he said. "I'd consider that suspicious."

"Would you go after them?"

"I'd take note."

I had been scratching the card without looking. I blew away some of the silver dust. Jackpot! Five million dollars! I exaggerate. I won a free soft drink. I tossed the card onto the car seat.

"Gee," said the policeman. "This must be your lucky day."

Can't say I was feeling so lucky. "Do you know a guy named Lou Bowman?" I asked.

"Lou Bowman? Sure. I mean, we weren't tight, but sure, I know who he is. I talked to him sometimes. You know, before his aunt died and left him all that dough."

Yes. His aunt. Aunt Epoch.

"So if, say, you saw Lou Bowman coming down the street here, would you find that suspicious?"

"Suspicious?"

"Would you take note?"

"Well, I guess I would. Lou's up in Maine. He's got a huge place right on the beach. And a big sailboat."

Well, it's a decent-sized place and it overlooks a harbor and the sailboat is a motorboat . . . but why quibble.

"So you'd be surprised to see him here. Would you get out of the car and say hi to him?"

"If I saw Lou Bowman on the street? Sure, I'd say hi." He chuckled. "I'd ask him to put his blessing on the rest of these stupid lottery tickets. Hey. You never know."

"Thank you, Officer. I'll let you get back to your job."

I was just pulling my head back from the window when suddenly the officer started.

"Hey!" He was pointing down the block. "Look!" I looked. But I didn't see anything unusual.

The young policeman frowned, and then he shrugged.

"Wow. Power of suggestion, I guess," he said. "For just a second there I thought I did see Lou Bowman. Some guy came around the corner down there. You didn't see him? He turned around and went back."

"He ducked back after he saw your car? Does that qualify as suspicious?"

"Sure." He looked over at me. "I've taken note."

I went back to the funeral home. You tell me, should I have felt safer now?

I met Fred on his way out. "Those TVs are getting creepy," he said to me.

I agreed. Everything was.

By late afternoon I was getting worried. No word from Kate. I had left several messages on her machine at her home by now as well as the several at the station.

I called Julia. She answered on the fourth ring. She said that she had heard from her mother about the wake this evening for Edie and that she would see me there.

"Can't you talk now?" I asked.

"I'm busy now, Hitch."

There was something in her tone. "Is he there again?"

"Yes."

"Are you screwing again?"

"That's right, dear."

"As we speak?"

"Practically."

"Am I almost part of a phone sex ménage à trois?"

"You would be if you were invited," Julia said sweetly.

Click.

I was restless. I called Hutch. He wasn't in. I asked to be put through to his voicemail. I left the following message:

"Hi, Hutch, Hitch here. I've been thinking about it and I've decided that I'm pissed off at you for your so-called friendly warning and for these innuendos about Kate. I've grown very fond of her and I think that you should wake up. The guy you're trying to help put in the governor's mansion is a bastard who takes advantage of people and who fools around behind his wife, who also happens to be a tramp. All this can be proven and you know it. Your insinuations about Kate have no basis in fact, and you know that, too. She's not the one trying to play me like a fiddle. You are. You're keeping company with sleaze, Hutch, and if you don't watch out it's going to start wearing off on you. If it already hasn't. Oh, and I know why you're so certain that I had nothing whatsoever to do with the murder of Guy Fellows. It's because you *do* know who is involved. You know all too well, don't you? As if you were practically there yourself. You've picked a fine line of business, my friend. I hope you're enjoying yourself. Hi to the wife."

It's amazing what a forum somebody's voicemail can be. It was a hell of a speech. I doubt I could have pulled it all together like that in person. So what if it was a sucker punch? Hutch deserved it. Enough already.

As I sat there congratulating myself over my armchair heroics, the phone rang and I nearly jumped out of my armchair. I figured it was Hutch, calling me back to tell me how quickly I could go to hell.

It was Kate.

"Kate! Where are you?"

"I'm at a pay phone."

"Come over."

"I can't. I've got to run down a few things. There's someone I have to go see."

"Run them down over here. Or tell me where you are. I'll come over and we can run them down together."

"I can't. I'll call you as soon as I can. But listen. I've got some information about Epoch Ltd. A picture is definitely developing, Hitch. It's quite a picture."

"Tell."

"I need to do a little more digging. I'll call you. I promise."

"Come on, Kate, give me something. Who's in this picture? What did you find out about this Epoch thing? Christ. Give me something to chew on."

"Okay, Hitch. Here's something you can chew on. Chew on Grace Kelly."

"Amanda Stuart?"

"That's right. Member in good standing of the board of directors of Epoch Ltd."

"But—"

"Hitch, I've really got to go."

"No! Kate, I—"

Goddamn click.

I had to tuck that little piece of information in my pocket for later. I showered and shaved. I put on a pair of slightly wrinkled slacks, a denim shirt and a tie, and a sport coat that Aunt Billie once described as "seedy tweedy." I popped next door and filled a plastic trash bag with flowers from the Jeff Simons collection. The march of the terra-cotta TVs had finally trickled out.

"This place looks like a nightmare," Billie commented as I stuffed my trash bag with flowers. She was right. Depending on how you looked at it, the flowers sprouting from the terra-cotta TVs looked either like antennas for the TVs or like they were simply sprouting right out of the dead newsman's head.

I finished filling my bag with flowers, got Billie's reassurance that she could handle things on her own for a while, kissed her on the top of the head, shouldered my bag and headed off to the harbor. I noticed as I left that my police guard was gone. I guess Kruk couldn't push through overtime for the guy. I kept close to the buildings as I picked up my pace.

I held up my trash bag. Sally planted a big wet kiss on my cheek.

"Flowers! Oh, Hitchcock, perfect!" She took the bag from me and emptied it right there on the floor. "Edie would have loved it."

To no one's great surprise, Sally proved herself a great hostess for a wake. Word of the demise of both Edie and the dinghy had spread quickly, as had word that drinks were on the house. The place filled up in no time. Sally kept the drinks flowing. Some of the Oyster regulars had taken stabs at sprucing themselves up for the occasion. Al the video guy and Bookstore Bill were there, each sporting ties. Bow for Bill; string for Al. They stood over by Edie—on opposite sides of the coffin—arguing. Generally speaking, shirttails were tucked in and lipstick made a strong showing and an authentic sense of bonhomie worked its way around the room. A woman came into the bar about an hour after I had arrived. She was dressed completely in black, all the way to the veil, which covered her face. Appropriate though it was, the outfit stood in stark contrast to the more loosey-goosey garb of Edie's bereaved revelers. The woman came directly over to me and snarled.

"I bought this special. You said this was a wake. This looks pretty damn casual to me."

It was Carol.

"You look great," I said.

Carol raised the veil so that I could see her face. "Call me the Black Widow." She winked, then lowered the veil again and slid onto a stool with the liquid ease of a person who had been doing this over half her life.

Sally had sent word to the Cat's Eye Pub over on Thames Street that she was holding an old-fashioned wake; she had managed to pry loose from the place a young fiddler and a leathery-skinned cuss who played a mean pennywhistle. The pennywhistler wore a black eye patch. If you watched closely, you could see when he would switch it every so often from one eye to the other. Sally herself got the dancing started. She hiked up her big skirt and began a sort of square dance and clogging combination that threatened to topple the guest of honor. At one point in the middle of the dancing, Frank stepped slowly from behind the bar and went over to Edie. He solemnly raised a glass to her. I won't swear to it, but unless the man happened to have gotten a piece of dust in his eye at that exact moment, I believe the little glisten I saw there was an actual tear.

In the midst of all of this dancing and carrying on, Julia arrived. She stood at the door and looked over the crowd. She was dressed in a white jumpsuit with a lime green scarf and she was drop-dead gorgeous as usual. Lots of stuff on the eyes. Lots of lipstick. She caught my eye across the room and blew me a Marilyn Monroe–style kiss. And then Peter Morgan stepped though the door behind her.

He took in the entire scene with a single glance. No question about it, the son of a son of a millionaire was slumming. Guys like Peter Morgan don't frequent places like the Screaming Oyster. Morgan was dressed in a linen suit and five-thousand-dollar loafers and he looked great.

Julia and her millionaire headed over to the bar. I watched as Julia spoke to her father, who bobbed his head a few times then reached out across the bar and shook hands with Morgan. Morgan gave him one of those two-handed clasps. I felt the *grrrrrr* rising up in me. I hate those handshakes. The millionaire signaled Frank for a bottle of champagne.

I had been in a conversation with Tony Marino, who had been telling me about deep-sea fishing off the Orkney Islands in Scotland's North Sea. Of course Tony had never been deep-sea fishing off the Orkney Islands in Scotland's North Sea. He was just recycling a monologue he had once heard in a bar in Inverness. And Tony is no Jack London. I couldn't really feel the spray. I wasn't straining to haul in the nets. I wasn't bone cold and longing for home. When Tony saw Julia over at the far end of the bar glancing in our direction, he shut down his North Sea documentary. "Go to her," he keened softly to me. Poor man. He really does hold the franchise on lost love.

I stepped down the bar and greeted the lovebirds.

"Evening, folks. Can I show you to your table?"

"Good evening, Hitch," said Julia. "I believe you've met Peter."

His hand was already out. "Peter Morgan," he announced.

"Frank Sinatra," I said.

We shook. One handed. Good. Julia was eyeing me carefully.

"You're dead, you know," Morgan said, gracing my tomfoolery.

"I know. One minute I'm a boozing misogynist from Hoboken, and the next . . ." I snapped my fingers. "I'm crooning with angels."

Morgan chuckled. "I actually met the man once. Down in Bermuda. If you can believe this, he was out in the driveway washing his own car. Mercedes 280 L."

"Gosh, Frank sure was a man of the people, wasn't he?"

Julia's radar caught that one immediately. She moved in to cut me off.

"Peter's not a man of the people, Hitch. He's a millionaire. Despite the burden of his riches though, he's a good person."

"I never said a thing," I said.

"You're a local dog on home turf, my sweet. And I do believe you've been drinking. I stand ready to kick your tailbone if I have to."

Peter Morgan was taking in this ping-pong match with an amused expression. With altogether too much charm, he said to Julia, while looking at me, "I'll kick him if I have to, dear."

"I'm bigger than you are," I reminded him. Smiling.

"You boys are so cute." Julia turned to Morgan. "Peter, I'm going to tell Hitchcock our news."

"By all means."

Julia turned to me. A rare blush came over her cheeks. "Hitch, Peter and I are getting married." Her eyes sparkled mischievously. "I'm going to be rich."

Morgan had worked the cork out of the bottle.

"Will you join us in a toast?" He signaled to Frank. "Another glass?" I believe he might even have snapped his fingers. Watch out, I thought. That ain't no hired help there; that's your future papa-in-law. As Morgan reached for the glass I was able to catch Julia's eye. I rolled mine. She launched a blazing comet with hers. It was a "be nice" comet. It crashed and burned just past my shoulder.

Morgan handed me a glass of bubbly and we three lifted our glasses. If Morgan said "To us," I wasn't sure what I'd do. Luckily he didn't. He proved smoother than that.

"To Julia Finney. God's gift to a few very fortunate men."

Wow. I could maybe quibble about his definition of "few," but for conciseness, compliment and fake humility it was a gem of a little toast. Julia blushed again as we clinked glasses and sipped. I knew she was annoyed that she was blushing in front of me. It was a rare moment of fluster for Lady J.

We sipped. We took the tickle of the bursting bubbles. It's a funny thing about champagne. Not everyone knows this, but champagne's origins are as a flop, a dud, a failed harvest of the white grapes of the Champagne region and an instantly acknowledged inferior step-cousin of the esteemed French wine family. The original champagne was a bona fide disappointment—all that snap and sizzle—and had been gladly turned over to the undiscerning palates of the peasant class. Chalk it up to the great masters of spin that the soda pop of wines would come to be elevated to the ranks of the Rolls-Royce.

Julia and Peter Morgan were downright goo-goo eyed. Quite a turnaround. Just a week ago these two lovebirds had choked on their tunes in gay Paree. I was dying to know how he had won her back. I started my inquiry so subtly as to be almost completely oblique.

"Did you know that champagne was originally considered an embarrassing flop and was relegated as swill for the lower classes?"

"It was a failed harvest," Morgan said.

"I'm the one who told you that," Julia reminded me.

Okay then, time to throw off the cloak of subtlety.

"How did you win her back, Peter?" I asked. "Julia told me your behavior in Paris repulsed her beyond imagination."

"He exaggerates," Julia said.

Morgan answered me frankly. "I had a lot on my mind during that trip. I behaved like an ass."

"Do you always behave like an ass when you have a lot on your mind?" I asked.

Julia said, "Hitch, *you're* sounding like the ass right now."

"I'm only trying to look out for the future welfare of my past wife." I turned to Morgan. "You understand."

Julia chuckled. "Hitch, I'm surprised to see you pissing on trees this way. I must say, I'm flattered."

Morgan spoke up. "Julia is just the sort of person I need to remind me not to act like an ass." He tapped his glass of effervescent peasant swill against hers. "She helps me keep my perspective."

"Funny, I had always found her to have just the opposite effect." Since I was in interview mode I turned to the lady herself and put the question to her. "And you, what do you hope to get out of this union?"

"All of his money, his great big estate. And his gold-plated weenie."

I hung my head. "Alas, I could offer her only tin."

I could see that Peter Morgan was only pretending to be fully amused by all of this. It is an undeniable truth that people get fidgety when their fiancées and their exes banter openly about sex. The three of us moved the conversation around a little bit. Julia wanted to know what happened to the dinghy. I gave them the abbreviated version. I left out the part about a murderous ex-police detective having been seconds away from inflicting serious personal harm on my person as a result of my helping to burst the bubble by which he was being funneled five thousand dollars a month—now, eight thousand—from an organization that included on its board of directors a woman who just happened to be the twin sister of the only man in the room who could truthfully call himself a millionaire. It would have been such a mouthful. Instead I simply told them about Edie's bottle toss and how the whole thing came crashing down on her. Morgan wanted to know if Frank and Sally were going to be liable.

"Edie was a friend," Julia explained to the rich man. "Friends don't sue friends."

"Especially when they're dead," I added.

Julia ran her finger around Morgan's champagne glass. "If you don't mind my saying, you're too litigious, Peter. That's one of the things I'm planning to change about you."

Morgan chuckled. "Women always want to change something about their men."

"Julia never wanted to change anything about me," I bragged. "I was perfect."

"Then why did you two divorce?"

I deferred to Julia. "You tell him."

"I was more perfect," she said.

A certain nausea was beginning to set in. It wasn't jealousy. It's just that the three of us were becoming altogether too smug. Too chummy. I grabbed hold of the wheel of our conversation and yanked it abruptly in a new direction.

"Your sister is married to Alan Stuart, isn't she?" I said.

Morgan looked momentarily perplexed. But he recovered quickly. "That's right."

"Twin sister, right?"

"Right again."

"Which of you came out first?"

"Amanda did. By five and a half minutes."

"Five and a half minutes. What were you doing all that time?"

Morgan smirked. "Packing."

That was a good one. Though I'm sure he had used it before.

"You don't look that much alike," I observed.

"Brother-sister twins don't necessarily. We're not identical. Different eggs."

Julia groaned. "I hate reproductive conversations."

I asked, "How long have your sister and Stuart been married?"

"Oh, I don't know. Let me think. Eleven? Maybe ten years?"

"She married young."

"I guess. I think she was twenty. Is twenty young?"

Julia answered that one. "It's getting younger every year."

"And they've never had kids?"

"Amanda and Alan? No they haven't. Amanda can't have children.

She's got something screwed up and the doctors told her just to forget about it."

"Did Stuart know about that condition when he married her?"

Julia was looking at me like I was nuts. "Don't answer, Peter," she said.

Morgan ignored her. "I don't think he knew," he said flatly. He wasn't bothering now to disguise his growing displeasure of either the topic or his sister's selfish lack of candor. I couldn't be sure.

"That wasn't very nice of her," I said.

"If you know Amanda, you get used to that."

"I don't know Amanda." Though I've seen her freckle-free bum.

"She's the evil twin," Morgan said. He laughed, though it was a flat and unconvincing laugh. Julia was flashing me eye signals like crazy now, but I purposely kept away from them. And she knew I was doing it.

I pressed. "I saw your sister a week or so ago, out at the Baltimore Country Club." Then I embellished. "She was playing tennis."

Julia pounced. "What were you doing out there?"

"I was out there to see a guy named Rudy. He's the head grounds-keeper. There was some talk about him taking on some work at Green-wood Cemetery. It was a business meeting. I saw your sister on the courts. She was being coached by the tennis pro at the club. I watched him help-ing her on her backhand."

"Amanda's got a good backhand," Morgan noted dryly.

"Then I guess the guy did a good job with her."

"Amanda has always had a good backhand. We had a tennis court growing up. Amanda has always been very competitive."

"Plus she gets to show off her nice legs."

Julia cut in. "Yeah, yeah, and they're insured by Lloyd's of London. Look, boys, believe it or not, I can't keep up with all this testosterone. Why don't you two swing your clubs at each other a little longer while I go over and talk to my mom."

As she left she caught me with one more of her eye signals. *Cool it.* I believe that was the message.

It was just the two of us now. Man to man.

"Am I detecting an inordinate interest in my sister?" Morgan asked as soon as Julia was out of earshot.

"Just making conversation."

"She *is* married, remember."

"Of course. To the future governor of Maryland no less."

Morgan rapped his knuckles on the bar.

Interesting. "What's that for," I asked. "Don't you think your brother-in-law is a shoo-in? Isn't he going to bury Spencer Davis?"

"I thought that was your job. Burying people."

"Isn't he?"

"So far, yeah. That's what the polls say. But you know politics. It ain't over till it's over."

"Yogi Berra for president."

"Whatever." Morgan was doing little at this point to disguise his weariness of me. I downed my champagne and held the glass out for a refill. Morgan topped it off for me.

"So, you think Commissioner Stuart might have a weakness?" I asked.

"I didn't say that."

"But something could turn up that tosses the election to Davis?"

"Well in theory, yes. That's possible."

"But in fact? Is there something factual out there that could trip him up?"

"I haven't the slightest idea," Morgan said. "Why are you asking me?"

"Well, you're his brother-in-law. You're a big contributor to his campaign. I figure all of that makes you an insider. I also happen to be a friend of your brother-in-law's campaign guru. The last time I talked to him he seemed to be a little worried too. I guess I'm wondering if he's worried about the same stuff you're worried about."

"Who said I was worried?"

"You knocked wood."

"Well you can never be too sure, can you?"

"I don't know. Can you?"

He snapped. "What the hell is this about!"

Bingo. I pulled the rope. My man went up in the net.

"Did you know that the man your sister was taking tennis lessons from was murdered?"

"Of course I know that. It's terrible."

"Did you know him?"

"I'm active at the club. I knew who he was."

"Is it strange that your sister was taking tennis lessons? I mean, when she already had such a killer backhand?" Killer. That just slipped out.

"How about answering *my* question first?" Morgan said angrily.

"I'm sorry. Could you repeat it?"

"What the hell is this all about?"

"I'm just making conversation," I said.

"Well it's not a very interesting one."

"Really? I'm sorry. It is to me. A good-looking woman taking tennis lessons that she doesn't need from a good-looking guy who is found murdered? The good-looking woman is married to a powerful man who is running for governor, seemingly unstoppable except when you talk to his campaign manager and his millionaire backer, who also happens to be his brother-in-law? I mean I know it's nothing. But like I said, I'm a political junkie. It just all sounds so nice and sexy I can't help it."

"Maybe you should try to help it. You're talking about real people here. Not characters in a novel."

I set my glass on the bar. "Do you have any thoughts about who killed Guy Fellows?"

"No, I don't. Maybe my sister did it. With her killer backhand."

"It was a knife."

The millionaire sighed. "Christ. Whatever."

"Do you think she's capable?" I asked. I hadn't even brought it up. "I mean, we're just talking here. Couple of guys, chewing the cud. That's all."

Morgan set his glass down on the bar next to mine. "Look, I think Amanda is capable of anything she puts her mind to. But let me tell you a little something about my sister. She didn't kill Guy Fellows. Especially if it was a crime of passion. My sister has no passion. That's her ugly little secret, though if you know her, it's really no secret. Amanda is the original ice queen. You're insinuating that she was sleeping with Fellows. Maybe she was. You're not going to shock me if that's the case. But I can guarantee you that if she was it meant absolutely nothing to her. She'd have no motive to kill him. The lady just doesn't care."

"When did she sign you up as her publicity person?"

Morgan sighed again. "You forced it out of me, old man. I'm just defending her."

"Interesting defense. 'Too cold to kill.' "

"Take it or leave it. The truth is, I don't really care."

He picked up the bottle and refilled his glass. "Listen, I'm going to go schmooze my future mother-in-law. It's been . . . well, we've certainly talked, haven't we?"

"Like a couple of old biddies," I agreed. He started to leave. "Oh. One more question. If you don't mind."

He stopped. He didn't look particularly enthusiastic.

I asked, "Do you know anything about a company called Epoch Ltd.?"

Morgan did. I could absolutely see that he did. Come on, his *sister* was on the board, for Christ's sake. Kate had given me that much to chew on.

But he lied. He shook his head slowly, as if he were really thinking it through.

"No. Can't say I do. Now excuse me." And he went over to charm the great big pants off of Sally.

But he had lied.

Just then the door flew open and in stepped Tony Marino—I hadn't seen him slip away—in full Scottish regalia. The kilt, the furry belt, the Beefeater hat. He entered piping. The acoustics in the bar were astounding. "Amazing Grace" filled every available molecule of air in what I firmly believe was Tony Marino's most impassioned and heartfelt rendition ever. He marched solemnly, in abbreviated goose-step, across the room toward Edie, chin high, squeezing his bag, choking his pipes. He was blubbering like a baby. It was the most noble spectacle I have ever seen.

CHAPTER 36

My head was ringing.

No. It was the phone.

Correction.

What my head was doing was pounding. The sound of distant tom-toms joined in with the mix as I fumbled for the phone on the table next to my bed. I found it, brought it near and made a noise into it, something between a groan and a grunt.

It was Kate. She was angry. She snapped, "You didn't return my call."

The pounding of the tom-toms increased. Not so distant at all. They were inside my head. I found my voice, enough to croak, "In my country we say hello."

"Fine. Hello. Didn't you get my message?"

My phone machine was blinking accusingly.

"I didn't play my messages, Kate. I'm sorry. I . . . I don't remember getting into bed. I must have passed out."

I looked down at myself to see that I was still wearing my dress shirt and tie (loosely knotted, thank God), a pair of boxers and on my feet a pair of bright orange thermal socks that normally hibernate over the warm months in the rear of my sock drawer. I have no idea how they found their way out of the drawer and onto my feet.

"Too much fun at the wake, huh?" Kate asked snidely.

A scene from the night before was burning into focus. Thames Street.

Late in the evening. A procession. Edie's coffin being carried aloft. The remnant of the dinghy being tossed into the harbor. I shot up in bed.

"Shit!"

This got the attention of Alcatraz, who lifted his head from the floor and let out a bark.

"What? What happened? Are you okay?" There was genuine alarm in Kate's voice.

My memory was coming back to me in patches. Fortunately the next patch included Edie's coffin being safely delivered back to the funeral home.

"I'm fine. I just thought for a minute . . . never mind." The tom-toms were drumming even harder now. They definitely wanted out. Alcatraz barked again—he definitely wanted out too—and so I missed the beginning of what Kate was saying.

". . . has really hit the fan. I don't want you to worry about me."

"What'd you say? Kate, I'm sorry. I've got—"

"I don't have time to go into it now. Listen, Hitch, I'm sorry about . . . about everything. I told you I didn't want to drag you into all of this. I'm sorry."

I scooted up in bed. "Wait. What are you talking about, Kate? Hold on for a minute. I'm awake now. Look . . . you've got to tell me, what's going on? I'm sorry I didn't get your message. What did you find out yesterday? What's all this about Amanda Stuart and Epoch? I ran into Peter Morgan last night and he pretended he had never heard of Epoch. He was lying."

There was a pause.

"You ran into Peter Morgan?"

"Yes. Julia brought him along to the wake."

Kate said nothing. For a moment I thought she had hung up.

"Are you still there? Kate? I—"

"I'm still here. Hitch . . . I want you to be careful, okay? Please. Don't worry about me. Just do me a favor. Walk away. Turn around and just walk away. No matter what happens."

"What are you talking about? What's going to happen?"

"Nothing. Don't worry."

"Kate, you've got to tell me what you're talking about."

When she spoke, there was a waver in her voice. "I'm tired, Hitch. I'm just really . . . I'm tired."

"Kate. Are you crying?"

This time when I heard nothing it was because she *did* hang up.

I immediately dialed her home number, but all I got was her machine. Maybe she was sitting there listening, I don't know. I didn't leave a message. I swung my legs over the side of the bed. What a miserable time to feel miserable. I had no idea what Kate was talking about. When *what* happens? Why was she telling me to walk away? Walk away from what? From her? I had nothing but questions. And nothing but pounding tom-toms for answers.

I padded across the floor on my orange feet. Alcatraz didn't budge; I had to step over him. I found some aspirin in the bathroom and chewed them raw. No diluting. Then I shrugged out of my clothes and heaved my carcass into the shower and stood there until the hot water ran out. It was painful, but it worked. I emerged from the shower considerably more alive than when I had gone in. Now, if I could stick my head into a bucket of coffee I would be a brand-new Hitch.

I put on my charcoal suit, white shirt and burgundy tie. I sure as hell wasn't in the mood for a funeral, but there was nothing to be done about it. I clicked a leash onto Alcatraz's collar and the two of us headed over to the funeral home. Alcatraz took care of his ablutions on the way. He bounded upstairs to Billie's apartment, trotted over to the lambskin rug she keeps for him in the corner of her living room, dropped onto the rug, yawned and settled in for the morning.

Sam had already pulled the hearse up around the side. The rear door was open and ready to swallow. Sam was leaning against the car aiming his face up at the sun as I came back outside.

"Good morning, Sam. Ready to rumble?"

"Let's rock and roll."

"Come on then."

Billie was having tea with Mrs. Simons inside.

"I'm so sorry about Edie," Mrs. Simons said to me as Sam and I entered. I glanced over at the two coffins on the far side of the room. Apparently we had parked Edie here last night after the wake.

"Would you boys care for some tea?" Billie asked.

"I don't think so, Billie. We'd better get moving."

Mrs. Simons let out a sigh. "It's going to be a zoo at the cemetery, isn't it?"

I shot her with a finger pistol. You got that, girl.

Billie helped Mrs. Simons select the flowers she wanted placed on top of the coffin, as well as which ones were to be taken out to the grave site for decoration. I went on ahead and took the batches of flowers out to the cemetery. I had instructed the folks at Greenwood to put up the largest canopy they had, and I didn't think that two dozen folding chairs were too many for the occasion. After arranging the flowers by the grave, I saw that I still had a little time before I had to be back at the funeral home. I plotted a course due north and in five minutes was standing in front of a headstone that read "Sewell." I knelt down and plucked a few weeds from around the main stone as well as the three smaller stones identifying my parents and my never-born little sister.

My parents made me very happy when they were alive. And although my little sister never got the chance to charm me, I have always assumed that she would have been the most fantastic sibling. I know I had been looking forward to her arrival. I remember that my father and I had joked that we would use the new baby as a football, for a few months at least, until it grew too big. My mother's response had been that certain persons—in particular, a certain Sewell and son—can never get too big to be used as soccer balls either and that if we dared to try out the great American sport on her brand-new child, she would gladly try out the great Italian one on the two of us. "I'll kick-a your high-nees" was sort of how she put it. Of course she never got the chance.

I patted the stone and stood back up. "Incoming," I announced to the family Sewell. "Film at eleven. I love you. Gotta go."

As I headed back to my car though, I was no longer thinking about my absent family. I was thinking about Kate. I was worried. I wondered if maybe I had been underestimating the kinds of pressures she was under. Even if Kate were to discover that it was really Bowman's bullet that had been the one to kill her husband—and that was still a big "if"—she had nonetheless also shot him herself. She had known that shock and had lived with that agony for six months now. And in that time she had been pressured first into an affair with her boss, then into sleeping with a known hustler. Somebody had killed the hustler. Possibly Stuart. And now, all the recent revelations about Lou Bowman and this Epoch Ltd. situation . . . Kate was settling a lot of scores. She was under the kinds of pressures that I could only muse about. And they all seemed to be coming to a head. No wonder Kate was so brittle on the phone. And so fragile. I wished to hell I knew where she was or how to get ahold of her.

Don't worry. Could two words ever be more useless?

As I got into my car I thought about something else that Kate had said to me on the phone. *Just walk away.* I started the car, then just sat there, my hands gripping the steering wheel. Kate was cutting me loose. In the past twenty-four hours our contact had suddenly whittled down to a pair of fairly abrupt phone calls. She was steering clear of me for a reason. Was all this happening too fast for her? Too much too fast, that sort of thing? I could all too easily envision Kate as one of those people who have a difficult time relaxing into a good thing. It spooks them; they start thinking that they don't deserve this or that it's all going to go away soon so why not blow it up in advance and get it over with. Certainly Kate's history suggested the "I don't deserve it" frame of mind.

It also suggested the hero mentality. The one who will give herself up to the brutal blows in order to keep others safe. I steered my Chevy Nothing through the gates of Greenwood Cemetery and headed east on North Avenue, which ought to be impossible. I stopped at a red light. Maybe I was being paranoid. Maybe *I* was the one suffering the misguided hero complex. Maybe *I* was the one beginning to show signs of relationship freakout. I'm sure I could turn Dr. Freud's magic magnifying glass on old Hitchcock Sewell and write an entire book about it. It's easy to swim in clear water; it's a whole different thing to navigate a swamp.

I turned right onto Broadway. I tried to tell myself to relax. Kate and I would hook back up before I knew it and I would dump all these silly fears into the Dumpster of silly fears. It didn't work. Something *was* terribly wrong. I could feel it.

I drove past Johns Hopkins Hospital on my left, where my parents and

sister were pronounced dead and where I was born. Downtown was a
mile over to my right. In front of and behind me . . . the rest of the world.

Sometimes you have to take stock of where you are.

Everything back at the funeral home was set. The guests had already
started to arrive. Billie took the front hallway; I stood just inside the parlor
doors, pressing the flesh and handing out the programs. We had arranged
the chairs in as wide a crescent curve as the rooms would handle, with a
large aisle running down the middle. We left enough room in the back
for the minicam crew that the station had sent out to cover the event. The
advance crew the day before had hung a few of their lights, mainly up
front where the coffin sat, and these had already been turned on. They
were as bright as hell.

I was to discover later that in addition to the neglected message from
Kate on my home machine, I had received a few messages at work that I
had failed to retrieve as well. And so I was taken completely by surprise by
the arrival of the entourages of the two main contenders for the governorship of Maryland. They arrived within five minutes of each other.

Spencer Davis arrived first. I had just fetched a handful of programs
and was pressing one into someone's hand when the hand made a fancy
move and took hold of mine with a firm grip.

"How do you do? Spencer Davis."

There he was. The candidate. He had toned down his million-dollar
smile in deference to the occasion, but he was a dashing young liberal
nonetheless. He was about my height and even with his hair neatly
combed down, you could still tell that it was something of a boyish cut. It
made him look ever so slightly mischievous, despite his present gravity.

"Hitchcock Sewell."

"May I introduce my wife?"

Well sure, why not. He presented a pleasant-looking woman, a trifle
shy I thought, but fighting it gamely. There was a darkness around her
eyes that brought to mind—unfortunately—the look of a raccoon. Her
hair was cropped at the shoulders, black with a full spiderwebbing of pre-
mature gray. It was not difficult for me to imagine Mrs. Davis in her college years: baggy overalls, no bra, no shoes, handing out fliers protesting

God knows what, smoking a lot of pot, painting flowers on her boyfriend's cheek, yanking open the sliding door of a VW van and piling in. In other words, a mildly rebellious youth, a lot more active spunk than I saw now in the woman whose hamster hand was already slipping from my grip.

A person could make a million bucks if they could read someone's future just by shaking someone's hand. They once made a movie about that. Reading their past that way is more of a parlor trick.

The candidate and his wife found a spot near the front. Davis's advance man—a cheerless Joe named Bill—came rushing into the room (not exactly in advance, you'll notice) and told me that he had called and left several urgent messages on my machine alerting me to the fact that the candidate would be attending the funeral.

"What was the urgent part?" I wanted to know. I indicated Mr. and Mrs. Davis down front, reading their programs. "He seems to be doing just fine."

"I . . . well . . . the cameras . . . I—"

"I see," I said. "So everything's fine then?"

Bill couldn't really say.

Aunt Billie and I had placed Reserved signs on about a dozen of the chairs closest to the front. Mrs. Simons of course would take one. Jeff was an only child, as well as a bachelor. The family factor wouldn't play a big role here today.

"Who are those seats reserved for?" Bill wanted to know. Actually, he was demanding to know.

"Weather, sports, news and entertainment," I answered. "And consumer affairs. Maybe even that gal who pulls the lottery numbers."

Bill looked confused. "What?"

"Colleagues," I explained. "Could you please move along? You're blocking the door."

Bill moved along. Evidently he wasn't happy with the arrangements. His man was not being hit by the TV lights.

Some of those colleagues of the late newscaster were now arriving. TV people. I detected a trace of discomfort among a few of them. These are people who are used to smiling when they're out in public; it's usually tacked on with superglue. But this was a funeral. They had to put on their bad-story faces. Multiple murders. Killer tornadoes. The Orioles' miserable loss to the Pirates in '83 when they were up by three . . . *by three* . . . and couldn't close it. I directed the troubled faces to the reserved chairs. Mimi Wigg was among the mourners, of course. Her skin looked . . . well, frankly, she looked like a corpse. Dull and shiny at the same time. I handed her a program and aimed her toward the front.

The next thing I knew I was face-to-face with a stunning blonde. The last time I had seen her she hadn't exactly been dressed for a funeral.

Alan Stuart loomed behind his wife like a mighty Colorado Rockie. Snowcap and all.

"Mr. Sewell, isn't it? My campaign manager has been telling me about you." He placed a large hand on the woman's shoulder. "I don't believe you've met my wife?" I took the hand that was offered. No parlor tricks this time. No need. Millionaire's daughter. Spoiled and cold. How hard is that?

"How do you do, Mrs. Stuart?"

"Hello, Mr. Sewell," she replied. "It's a pleasure to meet you."

Was it just my lion's pride or had I detected a little flash of light in her cool blue eyes? Was this lady flirting with me with her husband standing right behind her? Alan Stuart offered a sort of private smile over the top of his wife's head, almost as if to say, "I know what she just did. She always does it. Just ignore it."

I did.

"Did you know Mr. Simons well?" I asked. A little patter of the trade. I realized that my palms were sweaty.

Amanda Stuart answered. "Yes. He was a supporter of Alan. Impartial on the air of course. Jeffrey had tact."

"I saw your brother last night," I said, quickly changing the subject.

An eyebrow. "Oh?"

"Yes. He's been seeing my ex-wife. Who I still see. Though not the same way, of course."

A crack formed on the ice as the lady Stuart frowned.

"Mr. Sewell is just kidding around, Amanda," Alan Stuart interjected. He reached out and gave me a burly handshake. "Perhaps we could talk after the funeral."

It wasn't really a suggestion. It was a politely issued order. We *will* talk. Stuart pointed down the aisle. "Are those seats reserved?"

"Yes, they are."

"Good. Thank you." Alan Stuart grazed me with a flesh wound. His wife sank one deep, right between the eyes. And off they went. Lovely couple.

I watched Bill the advance man take gas as Alan and Amanda Stuart slipped into two of the reserved seats, right next to the popular sports guy. The minicam was picking it all up. Bill made his way over to me.

"What's that all about! I demand that Spencer be seated in the VIP section!"

"There is no VIP section," I answered him. "Those seats are for family and close friends."

"Alan Stuart was no friend of Jeff Simons's. They hated each other's guts!"

"I didn't seat him there. He just took it."

"Arrogant bastard!" Bill stormed off. I wondered if he meant me.

The room filled. As Billie had predicted we had an overflow crowd. A lot of people were clearly fans, not friends or family. A number of them were clutching photographs of the late Jeff Simons. A little late for autographs. I escorted Mrs. Simons to her seat. Just as I was about to steer her into the aisle, she suddenly stopped and performed one of those religious curtsies. I almost ran over her.

I caught Alan Stuart's eye as I turned to head back up the aisle. It was a stern and displeased eye. I remembered what Hutch had said to me out in the park by the Washington Monument. Whether or not Stuart was still seeing Kate—and I was positive that he wasn't—he was still an unreasonably possessive man. It was my connection to Kate at the very least that was earning me this pissiness. I guess it wasn't enough that he had this beautiful filthy-rich trophy wife sitting next to him. Of course if Hutch was to be believed, the man also suspected that I was attempting to blackmail him and to destroy his career, not to mention getting away with murder. I changed my direction and stepped over to where Spencer Davis and his perfect no-bullshit wife were sitting quietly, holding hands no less.

"Mr. Davis, would you and your wife like to move to, uh, more prominent seats? I didn't intend for you to be shunted off into the corner like this."

Davis glanced over to the . . . okay, to the VIP section. Alan Stuart was glaring at us. Good.

"That's okay, Mr. Sewell. I think Beth would find those lights a little uncomfortable anyway. We're fine here."

Impulsively I reached out and shook the man's hand. He responded with a hearty pat on my arm.

"Thank you though."

I had to fight to keep the swagger out of my step as I headed back up the aisle. Take that! I've got Kate Zabriskie *and* I'm getting all chummy with your opponent. I shouldered my testosterone and returned to the back of the room.

Hutch was there. He was yakking with the minicam crew and he didn't take note of my presence until the priest took his place up behind the coffin, took the nod from me and started into his spiel. Hutch made his way over to me then and leaned in close. It was all whispers now.

"I got your phone message," Hutch hissed. "You are so far out of line."

"The truth hurts?"

"You're in way over your head on this one."

"What's this? Two platitudes for the price of one?"

"Alan will bury you, Hitch. You did not choose your enemies wisely."

"You know what I've learned, Hutch? You don't choose your enemies. They simply show up."

Hutch glared at me. "We'll talk."

He moved off to resume has flack duties. Both Hutch *and* Alan Stuart. What were they planning to do, take me out back and work me over? Maybe I could get them to wait until Lou Bowman showed back up. That way everyone could pile on at once.

I turned my attention back to the priest, who was explaining to a roomful of adults that Jeff Simons would henceforth be lying down with lambs and lions. Heaven as a petting zoo. I don't know who comes up with this stuff.

There were several eulogies on the docket. The main event of course was Mimi Wigg. If I expected the diminutive newslady to regale us with details of Jeff Simons's final earthly ecstasies, I was to be disappointed. Instead, the large talking head of Mimi Wigg regaled us with cute behind-the-scenes stories about her fallen colleague. The minicam was recording it all. I realized that the cadaver makeup I had noticed on Mimi Wigg when she arrived was in fact her on-air makeup.

Mimi Wigg had chosen to offer her eulogy in the happy news style that had served her and Jeff Simons so well in their on-air time together. To my astonishment, right in the middle of her happy memories of Jeff, the tiny newswoman improvised. She knelt down and picked up one of the terra-cotta TVs—one with black-eyed Susans sticking out of it—and set the damn thing on top of the coffin. Suddenly it was Jeff and Mimi again, for one last time. The minicam drank it up: a priceless two-shot, tawdry and unquestionably in bad taste . . . and great TV.

My tepid admiration of the itsy-bitsy big-headed newswoman's chutzpah was abruptly interrupted by the loud chirping of a cricket, which I only recognized as a cellular phone when I saw Hutch snatch the plastic thingy off the holster on his belt. It was a short call and clearly one that troubled him. Storm clouds gathered with astonishing speed. Hutch spat a few words, then disconnected. Immediately he dialed another number and then he looked off toward the front of the room. I followed his gaze. Alan Stuart gave a little start then reached into his jacket and pulled something out and looked down at it. From where I was stationed I couldn't see what it was, but it must have been a beeper, for he turned partway around in his chair and found Hutch. Stuart turned and whispered something to his wife, then stood up and made his way to the aisle. Mimi Wigg lost her place for just a second, but seasoned professional that she was, she managed to turn the interruption into a dramatic pause. She surveyed the crowd with a sugary smile. "Jeff so loved doing zoo stories. He was *wonderful* with animals . . . so great . . ."

Alan Stuart hurried up the aisle. Hutch was already into another conversation on his little phone; I heard another chirping and saw one of the news guys down in front taking a call. What should I have done, collected all cellular phones at the door? Mimi Wigg skipped another beat, then her voice raised in strain as she pressed on. I think the woman now realized that she was missing something. She wanted to wrap it up. Bye, Jeff, nice knowing you. Gotta go.

Alan Stuart reached Hutch and signaled him to cut off his call. He gave his campaign manager exactly one second and then he snatched the phone out of his hand and snapped it closed. Hutch leaned in and spoke in a low tone to his boss. His boss did not respond in kind.

"*Shit!*"

Heads turned. But Stuart didn't care. The crowd in the entrance hall had pressed forward to get a look at Mimi Wigg. Stuart and Hutch were already at the door, trying to work a wedge into the packed crowd and get the hell out. I stepped over.

"What's going on?"

"Fucking Lou Bowman," Hutch snarled.

Lou Bowman? My blood turned to ice.

"What about him?"

Alan Stuart lost it. He reached into the crowd and started shoving citizens aside. The voters pulled back. Hutch followed. He barked over his shoulder at me as he and Stuart plunged forward.

"He's been shot!"

CHAPTER 37

Lou Bowman was in critical condition at Union Memorial Hospital. His room was under police guard.

So why didn't I feel safe?

As far as news stories go it might not have been an especially big one, if not for the identity of the suspected shooter.

Kate Zabriskie.

I had my obligations. This was too big a funeral to palm off on Aunt Billie. We were expecting an even larger crowd at the cemetery and there was simply no way I could duck out on it.

We wrapped up the festivities in Parlors One and Two. Jeff Simons's colleagues from the station—plus an uncle who looked like he might possibly be my next customer—shouldered the coffin and carried it outside to the waiting hearse. Sam was itching to meet Mimi Wigg but, unfortunately for him, the little newslady went left when the coffin went right. Doubtless she was being called back to the station to deal with the shooting of former police detective Louis Bowman. I had grabbed hold of the news guy whose phone had gone off inside. He was the one who told me that Detective Zabriskie was being sought in connection with the shooting.

Outside, Spencer Davis and his wife came over to me.

"What's going on?"

"Someone was shot," I said.

"Who?"

"A guy named Lou Bowman. He was—"

"I know who he is," Davis said, cutting me off. He looked terribly troubled. "Do they have a suspect?"

I didn't want to say who. "Not in custody," I said.

Then Davis hit me with a two-by-four. His quiet, peace-loving wife didn't even flinch.

"Is it Kate Zabriskie?"

Well hush my puppies and send me off to bed . . . how the hell did he come up with *that* name.

Davis heard my unspoken question. Probably got it from my slack-jawed face.

"I met with Detective Zabriskie last night," Davis explained. "I'm up to speed on this thing."

"You met with Kate?"

"Last night. She phoned my office at the end of the day and said that it was urgent that she see me right away. Among other things, she had, uh, something she thought I should take a look at."

At that precise moment Amanda Stuart stepped right past without so much as a glance in our direction and got into a black town car.

Spencer Davis gave me a look, then checked his watch. "Look, Mr. Sewell, I wonder if I could ask a big favor of you. I'm going to have to get back to the office and start dealing with this. I feel terrible about leaving right in the middle of a funeral."

I was going to note that Alan Stuart had expressed no essential grief about pulling out early, but I let it pass.

"Could you see that Beth gets to the cemetery?" He turned to his wife. "You'll be my representative?"

She nodded.

"Wonderful. Thank you." Davis kissed his wife on the cheek then turned and gave me another shoulder grip. This was apparently one of his things.

"Thank you, Mr. Sewell. Ms. Zabriskie told me how you've been helping her. I appreciate it. I want you to know that my office will do everything we can to help her in all this. But the first thing is to get her safely in. Do you have any idea where she might have gone? Any place that none of the rest of us would have thought of?"

I didn't right offhand. Or maybe I did, but my brain was going a little spastic at the moment.

"No, I don't."

"If you think of something, call me directly. Beth can give you my personal number. Don't worry about anything, Mr. Sewell. We'll sort this all out."

He pounded my shoulder again then gave a head flick to advance-man Bill. The two ducked into a waiting car. Bill shot me a hostile look just before he closed the door. I made a mental note to remove the Hate Me sign that must have been taped on my jacket.

The coffin was loaded. Sam shut the rear door.

"All set, boss."

I held out my arm for Beth Davis to take.

"Shall we?"

I was a bit distracted at the cemetery. As predicted, the turnout was impressive. Neighboring graves were indeed being trampled. The news of the shooting of former police detective Lou Bowman had robbed the guest list of some of its heavy hitters. But Jeff Simons's fans did themselves proud. I went ahead and seated Beth Davis under the canopy, just behind Mrs. Simons. Amanda Stuart was nowhere to be seen. Apparently she didn't feel the need to make a graveside appearance as her husband's representative. I introduced Beth to Mrs. Simons. The younger woman's consolations to the older woman were touching.

"Would you like me to drop you somewhere?" I asked Beth Davis when the service was over.

She checked her watch. "I normally volunteer at the soup kitchen in Cherry Hill," she said. "But it's kind of late." She added, "Though I guess they can always use a hand in cleaning up."

"You volunteer at a soup kitchen?"

"Tuesdays and Thursdays."

"You're kidding."

"There are a lot of elderly in the area. On fixed incomes. Why?"

"Oh. Nothing." I would have driven the dedicated citizen to the ends of the earth, but she insisted that the corner of Calvert and Lombard would be fine.

"You're going to take the bus, aren't you?"

"Yes."

How many times am I allowed to vote?

Arriving back at the office I leaped for the phone, which was ringing as I came through the door.

"Mr. Sewell, this is Detective Kruk."

"Detective Kruk. Hello."

"Are you all right? You sound like you're out of breath."

"I am," I said. "Both. I'm . . . What's up, Detective? What's going on?" I slid around my desk and dropped into my chair. "What can I do for you?"

"You can tell me where to find Detective Zabriskie." It wasn't really posed as a request.

"Unfortunately, I can't. I wish I could."

"You are aware of what has taken place."

"I've heard that Lou Bowman was shot," I said.

"That's right."

"How is he?"

"He is still in surgery. He was hit, it appears, five times."

Five times?

"If you know where Detective Zabriskie can be located, Mr. Sewell, you have a legal obligation to tell me. Besides that, it's best for her anyway. I hope you're planning to cooperate."

"Don't bully me, Detective. I've told you I don't know where she is. I wish I did."

"I wish you did too."

"Can you tell me what happened?"

"That's being investigated."

"Well, then tell me why you suspect Kate is involved in this."

Of course I knew the answer to that already. And my guess was that Kruk knew I knew. His answer suprised me.

"We have an eyewitness."

"You do?"

"She claims to know you. Would you like to speak with her? She's in the next room. Hold on."

The phone went silent. Twenty seconds later, who should come on the line but my very own ex-wife.

"Hitch? Hey, fellow, your girlfriend's pretty mean with that pistol of hers, I must say."

"Julia, what the hell is this all about? Kruk said something about an eyewitness. Did you—"

"Long story, Hitch. The police don't want me telling it to anyone else just yet."

"Screw the police! What happened? How did you see it? Where did it happen? Is she all right?" I could have gone on like that all afternoon.

"The detective here will hang up on me if I start telling. He's eyeing me right now." She lowered her voice. "Some hair on that guy, huh?"

"Look, Jules, can you get the hell out of there and call me on a pay phone? Or come over. I've got to know what's going on."

"I'm with Peter."

"Was he there too?" Damn. Here I'd been burying a dead newsman and all the action was taking place somewhere else.

"We're at Peter's house. It happened here." I heard the phone being muffled and Kruk's and Julia's voices garbled in the background. What I could make out was Julia's voice. "*Who the fuck cares?*" She came back on the line.

"I've got to go, Hitch. I think your girlfriend is in big trouble." Then to Kruk she said, "That's not a fucking state secret, is it?" Once more then to me. "I've got to go. The anti-Kojak is all pissed off."

Kruk's voice suddenly sounded. "I'm coming out to talk with you," he said. "Don't move." He hung up.

Don't move. Where was I going to go? I shoved the papers on my desk to the side and bongoed softly against the desktop as I tried to sort out what was taking place. Kate had shot and critically wounded Lou Bowman out at Peter Morgan's estate. How? Who had confronted whom? Had Lou Bowman tracked down Kate and tried to kill her? Or had Kate gone after the man who had accepted money to shoot her husband? I was hoping against hope that it was the former, that Kate had acted in self-defense in shooting Lou Bowman. But a shiver traveled through my body as I involuntarily pictured Kate out there somewhere, a classic double grip on her pistol, the gun bucking in her hands as she fires off one . . . two . . . three . . . four . . . good Lord, *five* shots. Even as I tried to dispel the image from my mind, I knew the truth. The shooting of Lou Bowman was not going to turn out to have been an act of self-defense. If it was, why wouldn't Kate have immediately turned herself in? Why was she still out there? And why so many bullets? No. It was time for Lou Bowman to pay for his crime. I could see it in the image that I had conjured up. And I knew it in my heart. Kate was settling scores. It was payback time.

And Julia had witnessed it. How? Did the shooting take place inside Morgan's mansion? Did Julia happen to look out the window and witness the grisly scene unfolding on the front lawn? And what were Kate and Bowman doing out at the Morgan estate in the first place?

That last question was one that I could answer. Sort of. Epoch Ltd. I recalled the frozen look on Peter Morgan's face the night before when I had brought up the name Epoch Ltd., on whose board of directors sat his slutty highbrow sister. He had lied about having never heard of Epoch Ltd. Why?

I phoned information and asked the computer voice for the number for Epoch Ltd. A human voice came on to tell me that there were no listings for Epoch Ltd.

"There is an Epoch Books," I was told. "And an Epoch Consulting Group."

I asked for the number for that second one, as well as the address. It was a downtown address, not Hunt Valley. But I called the number anyway. The very sweet voice that answered the phone responded very sweetly to my inquiry. "We're a headhunter firm."

Oh. "Do you happen to have an office out in Hunt Valley?" I asked.

"No sir. But we do do a lot of placements there."

"Would you by any chance keep a post office box there?" This was stupid. I was wasting time. Kate doubtless covered this angle right out of the gate.

"No sir. Not that I know of."

"Does the name Amanda Stuart mean anything to you?"

"No sir."

I hung up and looked helplessly around my office walls. Which one should I climb first? I couldn't just sit here. I had to think. Epoch Ltd. Okay. Whatever other business this corporation allegedly conducted, one of their monthly activities was to pay off Lou Bowman for shooting and killing a fellow cop. Amanda Stuart was on the board of Epoch. Amanda Stuart was Peter Morgan's sister. Bowman had been shot by Kate at Peter Morgan's estate. I had to assume that Morgan knew Bowman. I thought about Bowman's cushy digs up there in Heayhauge. And his boat. His shiny new Jeep. That's an awful lot of down payments. Epoch Ltd. clearly had deep pockets. And I was beginning to suspect just who it was who might have been filling them.

I reached for the phone to call information again. I doubted that Peter Morgan's home phone number was listed, but it was worth a try. I needed to get ahold of Julia. I wanted her out of there.

The phone rang the instant I touched it. I snatched it up.

"Is this Bob?"

"No, I'm sorry," I said. "You've got a wrong . . . Carol?"

"Hello, Bob. How's it hanging?"

I've never really known what the answer to that question is supposed to be.

"As well as can be expected," I answered cautiously.

"Maybe you want to come over and see me, Bob," Carol said.

Maybe I wanted to do naked cartwheels down the streets of Baltimore in a lightning storm. But not today.

"I don't think so, Carol."

She was insistent. "Well maybe you want to think again. Maybe it's the one and only thing you want to do right now. Maybe it's even important. *Maybe* I've got someone here who wants to see you."

Maybe I was beginning to get her message. Kate.

"Maybe I'll be right there," I said.

"Maybe that's a good idea."

Click.

No maybe. She definitely hung up.

I flew like the wind. Down two blocks and out to the far end of the pier.

"Carol Shipley," I said breathlessly to the guy at the front desk. "She's expecting me."

The desk clerk pushed a button on his intercom. "Name?"

I took a beat. "Bob."

The guy dipped down to address the intercom.

"There's a Bob here, Ms. Shipley."

Carol's voice crackled over the tiny speaker. "Send him up."

I was already at the stairwell. Too hyped-up for the elevator. I took the stairs like Groucho Marx, down low and long-striding, two and three at a time. Very efficient.

Carol met me at the door, looking grim.

"She's been shot and she's being a pain in the ass."

She stepped clear to avoid being flattened as I charged into the apartment.

Kate was seated on the couch. She looked up as I lurched to a halt. Almost everything about her looked darker than usual: her hair, her eyes, even her lips. I realized that this was because her skin was as white as an eggshell.

"Hello, Hitch."

That's when I noticed that she was gripping her left biceps, near the shoulder. She was wearing a rose-colored T-shirt and jeans. Beneath her grip was a fistful of pink gauze inexpertly held there with adhesive tape.

I moved over to the couch and sat down next to her, gingerly, as if she were a porcelain piece on a shaky shelf. She was losing her fight to keep the fear out of her eyes. We held a short staring contest. She spoke first, in a hoarse whisper.

"Is he dead?"

I shook my head slowly. "He's in surgery. I spoke to Kruk."

"Kruk."

"He called me. He's looking for you."

"Did you tell him where I was?" Her voice was so incredibly small.

"I didn't know where you were. Carol called after I'd already spoken to him."

Kate closed her eyes and leaned back against the couch. She stayed that way for nearly twenty seconds or so. I almost thought she had drifted off to sleep, but then her eyes opened and she looked over at me again.

"He shot first," she said in that hoarse whisper.

"That's okay. We can talk about it later. We have to get you to a doctor."

She shook her head. "I'll be fine."

I pointed at the pink gauze. "That's blood, Kate. We human beings need to keep that stuff inside our bodies."

"I'll be fine," she repeated.

Carol was standing over by the doorway to the kitchen. "See what I mean? Pain in the ass."

This got a little smile out of Kate. Out in the harbor, a tugboat let off a loud *BLAUUUUUU*. It was fairly distant, but it gave Kate a start anyway. She jerked and then she winced.

"Let me see that," I said.

"Hitch, you're no doctor. Why do you want to see it? It's a bullet wound. It hurts like hell. It's not going to kill me."

"Fine," I said, slapping my hands down on my thighs. "No problem. So, what do you gals say? Want to go out and grab some lunch?"

"Don't be angry," Kate whispered.

"Then don't be so stubborn. You can't just sit here with a bullet in your arm."

"I don't have a bullet in my arm. It went straight through."

She forced me to say it. "Whatever."

We were all three silent for a moment. I broke the moment by reaching out and getting Kate's hair our of her face for her. I tucked it behind her ear. Or tried to. Half of it slipped right out again. Kate's large hazel eyes were watching me closely.

"You need bigger ears, darling," I said.

And suddenly Kate's face was against my chest and she was sobbing. Good for her. I stroked her back. "It's okay," I told her. "You just go right ahead. It'll be all right."

Carol stepped discreetly out of the room and left the two of us alone. We remained folded into each other that way. Kate muttered "I'm sorry" several million times. I didn't try to stop her. It was time to empty out. At one point I noticed Kate's silver-blue pistol sitting on a magazine on the edge of the coffee table. The magazine cover was a photograph of a celebrity actress and her six- or seven-year-old daughter. The gun was pointed at the daughter. Not a pretty sight.

Kate's sobbings finally subsided and she pulled back from my chest. We were eye to eye, nose to nose. Kate sniffed back her tears after another minute and located a crooked smile.

"Wow, huh?"

I kissed each of her damp eyes. "Okay, good-time girl," I said. "Is it time to tell Mr. Sewell a story?"

Kate nodded. "How about a drink?" When she saw me hesitate, she added, "Pretty goddamn please? My arm is killing me. It'll help."

I called out to Carol. She popped her head around the corner. She'd been listening.

"I'll call downstairs."

"Bourbon," Kate said.

Her cry had done her good. While we waited for a bottle of bourbon to arrive on a cart, Kate began. She started with her perusal of the tax records for Epoch Ltd. She said that besides Amanda Stuart's, there were two other names listed for the board of directors. She also said that the corporation had not been a particularly active one. As best as Kate could make out, Epoch Ltd. had come together several years ago to conduct a single pair of transactions. They bought a plot of land and then they sold it. Not terribly exciting. What was interesting, though, was how well they did on their investment. Between the time that the Epoch Ltd. board of directors agreed to purchase their piece of property and a year later, when they unloaded it, the silly little sum of ten million dollars had poured into their collective pockets.

Carol and I both echoed the sum.

"Ten million dollars?"

"That's right," Kate said. "Three people. A ten-million-dollar pie."

"Who were the other two?" I asked.

"Names I doubt you've heard. Mitchell Tucker and Joe Pappas."

She was right. The names meant nothing to me. "Who are they?"

"Mitchell Tucker. Lawyer. Low profile, except for the fact that he happens to be the son-in-law of Harlan Stillman."

"Senator Stillman?"

"Yes. Married to the old gentleman's daughter. The quick and easy way to keep the Stillman name out of the picture but very much in the game."

"And Joe Pappas?"

"Also a lawyer. A graduate of the University of Virginia law school. Have you ever been down to Charlottesville? It's a beautiful campus they've got there. Thomas Jefferson founded the university. They still have about a dozen or so of his old slave quarters on the campus, these little shacks which they've converted into housing for upperclassmen. It's considered prestigious housing."

"And the award for irony goes to . . ."

"Guess who Joe Pappas shared his slave quarters with when he was a student there?"

"Surprise me."

"Alan Stuart."

"Our Alan Stuart?"

Kate nodded her head. "Joe Pappas is scheduled to announce for lieutenant governor in another week." She winced. "Where the hell is that whiskey?"

As if on cue, a knock sounded at the door. Carol answered it. In came a bellhop. Carol only let him partway in, took the bottle and handed him a tip, then shooed him back out the door. She brought the bottle in to where Kate and I were sitting and set it on the coffee table, next to Kate's pistol.

"I'll get some glasses," Carol said. As she was on her way into the kitchen, another knock sounded at the door.

"What is it now?" Carol muttered, pulling the door open.

I guess we all expected to see the room service guy standing there. So I guess we were all surprised when, instead, Detective John Kruk stepped into the apartment. He barely acknowledged Carol as he stepped right under her nose and into the front room.

"Hello, John," Kate said.

He nodded once, tersely, then began to read her her rights. Beside me it felt as though Kate were melting. Though when I glanced at her she was sitting fully erect, completely attentive to Kruk's recitation of her Miranda rights. When Kruk had concluded and asked Kate if she understood her rights as he had just explained then to her, she lifted her chin.

"What am I charged with, John? Assault with a deadly weapon?"

"Not anymore," Kruk said. "I got the call on my way here. You're under arrest for murder. Bowman's dead."

Kate rose from the couch. I rose with her. It was as if we were being pulled up by the same string. The only difference was, Kate had another string pulling at her as well. It started pulling the moment Kruk said the word "dead." It pulled at the sides of her mouth; and it was pulling her face into an unmistakable smile of unmistakable satisfaction.

Kruk saw it too, plain as day. He cocked an eyebrow.

"Charley," Kate said simply.

Kruk nodded. He uncocked his eyebrow and he took Kate Zabriskie into custody.

The following morning, Police Commissioner Alan Stuart released a statement through his campaign manager, Joel Hutchinson. For "personal and professional reasons," Hutch read— his hands literally shaking as he clutched the prepared statement— Commissioner Stuart was dropping out of the race for governor. Hutch answered the barrage of questions in a manner most uncharacteristic of him. "No comment." His single ad-lib was an innocuous mumbling about quote family considerations unquote.

Two days after Stuart's departure from the race, readers of the Baltimore Sunpapers were able to pursue their own "considerations" of Alan Stuart's family, specifically of Mrs. Alan Stuart, whose grainy image appeared in a photograph above the fold, smoking a cigarette in bed, her arms crossed over her breasts, the blurry head of someone evidently not her husband resting on her vivacious thigh. There was some confusion caused by the two photographs that accompanied the story on the inner pages. These were stock shots of former police detectives Charley Russell and Lou Bowman, both deceased. If you didn't read the whole story, you could get the impression that one or the other of the two faces belonged to the blurry image of the man who was using Amanda Stuart's thigh for a pillow on the front page. The rookie cop photograph of Kate cropped up later, and finally one of Guy Fellows, looking like an advertisement for

Rakish Good Looks Unlimited. No wonder the general public was confused. Everything was going into the blender at once.

My personal favorite was a photograph snapped of Amanda Stuart getting out of a car, failing to remain incognito behind a pair of sunglasses. In the photograph she is lashing out at the photographer. Her lips are curled like a junkyard dog's and her perfect hair is . . . well, far from perfect. I liked the picture best both because it is such a nonglamorous shot of the woman and because I liked to imagine Alan Stuart having to confront that sort of anger on — I hope — a daily basis. The Stuarts were finally being forced out of their golden limousine. And the mud outside the door was knee-deep.

And getting deeper.

Peter Morgan stepped into it too. And down he went. Four days after Kate's arrest for the killing of Lou Bowman, Julia phoned me to tell me that she had broken it off for good with Peter Morgan.

"I don't like how the other half lives," she told me. I reminded her that the Peter Morgans and Amanda Stuarts of the world are not really the other half. They're the other one-trillionth.

"Whatever. Their shit still stinks."

Nearly three years ago, Peter Morgan had arranged for the sale of a worthless tract of railroad land to a corporation called Epoch Ltd. The railroad had picked up the land — the site of a long-defunct chrome-plating factory — decades earlier, with plans of expanding its railyard. The expansion plans had died on the vine. Presumably the railroad board could have had no idea back then that Senator Harlan Stillman would be lobbying so hard in the next two years to win the federal contract to build their gleaming new prototype pyrolysis plant (their shit-recycling plant) right here in Charm City or that the government would be seeking an appropriate piece of industrial property on which to build it. Well, maybe the railroad board hadn't known this, but it now seemed abundantly clear that Peter Morgan had certainly caught a whiff of the plan. So too his brother-in-law, Alan Stuart. The property was unloaded to Epoch Ltd. for a pittance. Of course one of the reasons for the low asking price was that the property was still littered with hundreds of drums of chemical waste from its old chrome-plating days, many of them leaking and seeping their toxic sludge into the ground. And so Epoch Ltd. had picked it all up for a song. Peter Morgan quietly arranged for one of the railroad's storage warehouses to be made available to store the drums of waste. The bogus silica gel labels were slapped on the drums, loaded on a boxcar and shipped off to the Midwest. Lo and behold, when the government came looking for a place to build their pyrolysis plant, where do you suppose Senator Stillman directed their attention? To land owned by a corporation controlled in part by his own son-in-law and by the wife of the man Senator Stillman hoped to see in the statehouse in a few years?

Do goddamn tell.

Maybe you can see why all of this got to be a little confusing to the average Sunpapers reader. What does a bunch of barrels of chemical sludge and a waste-recycling plant have to do with naked pictures of the embattled police commissioner's wife? At first blush, nothing. But for those who stayed with the story the tale finally fell into place.

Alan Stuart and his political buddy, Senator Stillman, dreamed up the scheme. A nifty skim. Pulling in Peter Morgan to broker the land deals and installing Stuart's own wife on the board of the newly formed Epoch Ltd., Stuart was able to direct several million dollars of pure profit into his pocket. So was Senator Stillman, via his son-in-law. Ditto Joe Pappas.

However, on an otherwise unnotable day when a train derailment dumped several dozen mislabeled drums from a boxcar way out in Indiana, events were set in motion that would threaten exposure of all of this increasingly ill-gotten gain. Events that, if uncovered, would surely snuff out several political careers on the verge of their budding as well as one in full and venerable flower. The political lives of Stuart, Stillman and Pappas would be, quite simply, obliterated. This was the power that Detective Charley Russell held as he made his way closer and closer to learning the source of the sludge barrels. And the poor guy probably didn't even live long enough to realize it. It was the power that would get him killed. Alan Stuart saw to that. The sweetheart deal for Lottery Lou Bowman was fifty thousand dollars for the hit and a lifetime allowance of five big ones a month, cash, delivered by Federal Express, right to the NAPA Auto Parts store of his choice. The fact that on that fateful night in Sparrows Point Kate Zabriskie pulled her service revolver and fired at her own husband just as Lou Bowman himself was taking aim simply made the evil deal sweeter. For all but Kate, of course.

Question: Why was it that when Carol opened up the Federal Express envelope in Bowman's 4x4 in Heayhauge it contained eight thousand dollars instead of the usual five thousand dollars?

Answer: The rising price of murder. Kate explained this part to me the day she was released on bail. Kate told me that she and Spencer Davis pieced it together the night they met at his office and she turned over the videotape of Amanda Stuart and Guy Fellows. The five-thousand-dollars-a-month bonus that Lou Bowman received in untraceable fifty-dollar bills had indeed been more than a simple ongoing payoff to keep Lou Bowman quiet about the Charley Russell murder. It had also served, as Kate had surmised earlier, as a retainer. Bowman had killed for cash. Perhaps he had even done so prior to Charley Russell. He was certified scum; he could be bought. Or at least rented.

And according to Kate, that's what Alan Stuart had done. Soon after the naked pictures of Mrs. Stuart showed up in the mail, Alan Stuart had called Lottery Lou Bowman down from his Heayhauge home and aimed him in the direction of Guy Fellows. It was no secret that Lou Bowman had been in town that week. Even I saw him. Kate and Spencer Davis speculated that Stuart must have sweetened the pot as an enticement to kill Fellows. An additional three thousand a month is an additional thirty-six thousand a year, not too terribly far from the paltry sort of salary level at which a police detective can hope to top out. Kate and Davis further speculated that after killing Fellows, Bowman had located the videotape that Fellows kept at his place but that he had not turned it over to Stuart. Bowman had kept it for himself. Insurance.

That very night of their meeting, District Attorney Davis had pulled the necessary strings to arrange for a search of Lou Bowman's house on the harbor cliffs. Kate had him tell the Heayhauge police to take an especially close look at any Disney classic videos they might find. Sure enough, right there among the handful of tapes in Bowman's small video collection, the Heayhauge police had located a copy of *Fantasia*, or, at least, a tape in a *Fantasia* cover. But there weren't no Mickey on the tape. No sorcerer's apprentice sweeping up floods. The tape featured Amanda Stuart and the late Guy Fellows. They were doing quite a number of things, but sweeping up floods wasn't one of them. The tape was the clincher.

A confession would have been nice. But of course Kate had fired five bullets into the guy out at the Morgan estate. Bowman had never regained consciousness.

Justice delayed . . . but justice swift.

Ultimately, it was Julia who won Kate her freedom. As the sole eyewitness to the encounter between Kate and Bowman, the re-creation of events pretty much hinged on her account. And her account squared with what Kate had told me up in Carol's place. Bowman fired first. Not only did he fire first, he hit Kate in the arm. His bullet ripped right through her biceps.

Kate's return volley ripped right through Bowman's cheek, his right lung, his left-side kidney, his throat and his heart. Fancy shootin', girl-friend.

Julia was questioned as to whether in her opinion Bowman had been subdued by any particular one of those bullets. The question was intended to suss out whether Detective Zabriskie had shown excessive force in her self-defense shooting of Lou Bowman. Julia told me that she had laughed at the question, unable to restrain herself.

"Was he *subdued* by any particular bullet? Please. I told them that each bullet seemed to subdue the guy a little bit more than the previous one. I mean . . . *come on!*"

Was it excessive force? Otherwise known as overkill? You bet your ass it was.

Kate walked. The district attorney's office—Spencer Davis's office—gathered the information and issued a statement that Detective Katherine Zabriskie acted in self-defense in the shooting of Lou Bowman. The report went on to recommend a thirty-day paid leave of absence for Detective Zabriskie. Kate went them one better. She handed in her resignation.

She also broke it off with me. She wouldn't explain her reasoning except to say that she needed to get away from everything and everyone. I protested.

"Don't push away the people who care about you. Push away the jerks and the ones who want to use you."

We were at the Oyster. Kate had been cleared earlier that day.

"I need time to think," Kate said.

"Then think! Think all you want, Kate. Please. I'm not going to stop you from thinking. Why don't you take a thirty-day leave of absence from me? From everybody. Go out to the desert somewhere, where it's just you and sand and nothing else for hundreds of miles around. Take sixty days. Take as long as you need, Kate. *Then* start making decisions. Don't start slamming doors now."

Personally, I thought it was pretty good advice. But when I finished, Kate got up from the table, leaned down and kissed me gently on the lips. Then she walked out the front door of the Screaming Oyster . . . letting it slam behind her.

Spencer Davis barely had time to conduct his gubernatorial campaign. Then again, his only serious contender was out of the race. In fact, his only serious contender was placed under arrest within a week of Jeff Simons's funeral and formally charged with accessory to murder in the cases of Charley Russell and Guy Fellows. Peter Morgan was charged as well in connection with the Russell case. He was charged with conspiracy to commit murder and with obstruction of justice. In fact, obstruction of justice charges were being handed out like pancakes in a church basement. The case against Morgan and the fine people of Epoch Ltd. was the one that promised to become the most tangled. Senator Stillman would be sucked into the investigation for his lobbying efforts on the part of Epoch Ltd.'s dirty patch of land, as would Alan Stuart for his role in the whole boondoggle. A fine mess, no two ways about it. The kind of mess that makes me glad that I simply bury people, not prosecute them in a court of law. By comparison, my job's a cinch.

Alan Stuart was denying everything. There was no direct evidence linking him to the murders of Guy Fellows or Charley Russell, nor was there direct evidence of his involvement in the payoffs to Lou Bowman. He protested in the media that he was being persecuted because his wife had turned out to be a tramp. That good old "tramp defense." A surefire winner. Everybody loves that one.

Amanda Stuart kept the house. Released on bail, Alan Stuart moved into an apartment in Bolton Hill. A clever reporter for the Sunpapers pointed out that the ground-level windows of Stuart's new digs had barred windows. Spencer Davis picked up on the observation and was quoted more than once saying that Stuart would be well served to get used to the bars as soon as possible. God, how the winner in us loves to gloat. I don't know how Beth Davis slept at night; it looked to me like that husband of hers had lost all ability to shut off that hundred-watt smile. He was ear-to-ear practically every time I saw him on the news.

Hutch was also investigated but was cleared of any suspicion. He hadn't known a single thing about the land deal. And, of course, he hadn't knifed Guy Fellows. I picked up the phone about a half-dozen times to call him, but each time I put the phone back down before I finished dialing. A leave of absence from that friendship seemed appropriate.

The beat went on. Other people died. I put on my dark suit and my somber face and I helped their loved ones bid them adieu. Sometimes I'm asked if it doesn't get to me after a while, dealing with the dead so much. I don't know. I've always felt that it's a good job. I meet a lot of people, many of whom are insanely grateful for what I'm doing for them. I get to observe a little waltz of human behavior, sometimes a minuet, occasionally even a slam dance, after which I'm handed a fat check for my troubles. Also, I get outside a lot. In between deaths, I'm a free bird. And if I'm ever in the mood for finger food and conversation, a daytime cocktail party is mine to attend practically any day of the week.

But I know what it really is that people are asking me. It's all the death. All that living in the Land of Farewell. I don't know what I can say to that. Maybe for balance alone, a guy like me should marry a pediatrician. Or better yet, a midwife. The mortician and the midwife. Sounds like a bad

TV show, doesn't it? My midwife would run off at all hours of the day and night bringing new life into the world while I spend my days lowering lids on caskets.

A show like that wouldn't last a season. Or maybe it would. But I sure wouldn't watch it.

Besides, I didn't want a midwife. I wanted a traumatized former police detective with dark hair and nice long legs. Call me crazy. Go ahead.

CHAPTER 40

Julia said that she needed the distraction. Don't tell anyone, but I happen to feel that what she needed was to climb back on her pedestal and dangle her legs over the side. She wanted to deflower Michael Goldfarb. As carefree an exterior as Julia presents to the world, she's not without her ability to be hurt. The entire Peter Morgan fiasco had left her a little hurt, a little angry and a little embarrassed. She was knocked off her stride. There were several avenues of response that Julia could choose to travel. Popping a virgin seemed the easiest. And the most fun.

Gil Vance was thrilled to have Julia rejoin the cast of *Our Town*. Chinese Sue had not been working out as Emily. Her Kabuki approach to the role of the loquacious teenager had given the other actors just too little to work off of. Faced with an Emily so sullen as to be bordering on the hostile, the other actors had reached the point where they basically ignored the character and were attempting to restitch their scenes with improvised chatter to one another or, at times, directly to the audience. A week before opening, several members of the Gypsy Players board sat in on a dress rehearsal. By the end of the run-through, two of them were sitting onstage as dead people in the final scene, one had tendered her resignation from the board effective immediately and one was backstage flirting with the costume mistress. And so the show went on.

This rehearsal had proved to be Chinese Sue's farewell appearance. At the conclusion of the run-through she had approached Gil to suggest a last-minute alteration in the script. She told him that instead of dying of natural causes, as Thornton Wilder had penned it, she felt that Emily should kill herself. She argued that decisive action was more in keeping with the character. And she made her arguments in single syllables. The look the director gave to Sue in response indicated that perhaps Gil would consider going so far as to have the entire population of Grover's Corners simply stone the sullen girl to death. But Gil held his temper. "It's a little late for suicide," he said. Then he added, "But I'll think about it." And I'm sure he did.

No matter. Julia had a talk with Sue at the gallery the next day and the Emily switch was made. Professionally speaking, Gil was thrilled to have Julia back in the show. On a personal level, he soon enough saw that he would be no match for my ex-wife as concerned Michael Goldfarb. When Julia showed up that evening for the rehearsal Michael Goldfarb was more the puppy than ever. Julia would have no trouble whatsoever clicking her leash onto him. Sit. Speak. Beg. Lie down . . . He would heed his mistress's voice.

When we spoke about *my* fiasco, Julia was as tender as could be.

"I'm sorry about Kate, Hitch. The whole thing is a goddamn mess, isn't it?"

I had to agree with her.

"She might come back around," Julia said hopefully. "She's seen more than her share of bad men. She knows you're a good one. Give her time."

I asked Julia to explain more specifically what had happened out at Peter Morgan's.

"What did Kate tell you?"

"Very little. She said that she went there to confront Morgan about his role in the contract killing of her husband. Once she saw Morgan's sister's name listed as a board member of Epoch, she went straight to Morgan's place. She said that Bowman was standing at the front door when she arrived and that when she got out of her car he shot at her. She shot back."

Julia added simply, "That's how it happened."

"And you were at the front door?"

"I was passing by it on my way to the den when Bowman knocked. I opened the door just as Kate was getting out of her car."

"Did you hear Kate say anything to him before he shot her?"

Julia picked up my Teddy Roosevelt glasses from the lectern. Her eyes locked on mine, she parted her lips and very methodically huffed on each of the lenses, then tugged out a corner of my shirttail and wiped them clean. She handed the glasses back to me.

"You want to know?" she said finally.

"That's why I'm asking."

"Yes. She did say something. She yelled out, I believe it was, 'Hey! You bastard!' "

"I see."

We fell silent. Onstage a piece of scenery fell over. The church, I believe.

Julia finally asked, "Any other questions?"

"Just two."

I looked up at the black ceiling. It was easier for me to reconstruct the scene there.

"Was Kate's gun already drawn when she yelled out at him?" I asked.

"It was out and it was aimed right at him."

"I see."

"What was your other question?"

I put the glasses on. They weren't plain glass but were in fact a very weak prescription. I could see perfectly, everything just looked very flat. Even Julia's scrumptious body looked as if I could have slipped it under my arm like a cardboard cut-out and walked it out of the building.

"My other question was, did you tell that part to the police? That Kate was out of her car, aiming her pistol at the guy before she said 'boo'? That she provoked him. That *he* was shooting in self-defense? Did you tell the police all that?"

Julia drew in her lower lip for consultation. "I seem to recall that I missed that part."

"Remind me to buy you a drink sometime," I said.

"You don't have to thank me, Hitch. I didn't like the way that guy looked at me anyway when I opened the door."

"Yeah, well. I don't think that's why Kate shot him."

Julia's eyebrows rose. "Hitch, have you ever seen Kate handle a pistol?"

I told her that I hadn't. She rolled her eyes.

"Wow."

I didn't hear at all from Kate for the next week. I left several messages on her answering machine and once I even drove by her place at night but saw no lights on in the windows. Possibly Kate had taken my suggestion and skedaddled out of town for a while. Her name and photograph were in the papers and on the news again. Anywhere but Baltimore would seem like a smart place for her to be.

Gil's final instructions to the *Our Town* cast on opening night were as follows:

"I want to thank each and every one of you for the enthusiasm that you've all shown in exploring the depths of this wonderful play. And now I want you all to knock it off. Hitchcock is your Stage Manager. He is your pilot. He is your god. Hitch, I'm putting it all on you. The moment you think any of your fellow cast members are getting out of line—or especially *inventing* a new line—step in. Just start talking. Does everyone understand that? No unscripted soliloquies tonight. This is not the Improvisational Playhouse, it is the Gypsy Playhouse. You are Gypsy Players. Now go out there and act like it!"

And because Gil is snippy, and lonely, and only human after all, he turned on Michael Goldfarb, who was staring down at his delicate fingers. "That goes for you too!"

I was barely listening. I was preoccupied. Among the several opening-night cards and flowers that I had received had been a tissue-thin Western Union telegram. It had been sent from Las Vegas.

Hitch—I'm still thinking. I wish I would stop already. I miss you. Break a leg, if you must. Love—Kate.

I took the telegram with me onstage and stuck it on the lectern next to my script. Several times during the evening I missed my cue due to my split attention. There really wasn't much deconstruction I could perform with Kate's message, but I went ahead and tried anyway. The only truly ambiguous portion of the telegram was its point of origin. Las Vegas. The test tubes of my imagination sputtered and smoked in trying to figure out what the hell Kate would be doing in Las Vegas. As far as the message itself, it was cautious but hopeful; I couldn't squeeze any more than that out of it.

As I said, I missed a few of my cues on account of my three hundred glances at the telegram. I also failed to perform the Higher Authority task that Gil had assigned to me. I interrupted on occasion, but, generally speaking, I stood by—looking like an idiot in my pith helmet, wire rims and whip mustache—as the cast of *Our Town* frolicked like an untrained modern dance troupe through the ashes of Thornton Wilder's Grover's Corners.

Julia especially enjoyed herself, having waited until this evening to acknowledge the very existence of Michael Goldfarb. And not just acknowledge it. Suddenly he was bread and bad-girl Julia was white-hot butter. Others seemed to follow Julia's lead, albeit less effectively, and by the end of the evening it almost seemed as if a pheromone gas attack had been launched on the sleepy burg. It was one hopped-up bunch of citizens up there onstage, that's for sure. At one point I lowered my wire-rim specs to the tip of my nose and took in the full spectacle being wrought. *Our Town* meets *Peyton Place*. Gil Vance had himself a peach of a concept, whether he wanted it or not. Personally, I thought it worked pretty well.

Goldfarb and Julia showed up about an hour into the cast party. I call him "Goldfarb" now instead of "Michael" for the simple reason that whatever it was that transpired between the two between the final curtain and their entrance at Julia's gallery—where the cast party was being thrown—had forever altered the somber young boy. He sauntered into that gallery like a big-balled bull fresh from his Pasture of Dreams. As for Julia, her face was lit up like Times Square on New Year's Eve. She and I passed a few quick words, in code. Starting with me.

"Pedestal?"

"Brute."

"Happy?"

"Yippee!"

A tipsy Libby Maslin made a pass at me at one point. It fell short. I wouldn't have caught it anyway. I noticed as I was slipping away early from the soiree that Libby was wiping some wine off the shirt of one of the Gypsy board members, who was already backed up against the wall.

I headed down to the pier that runs alongside the Screaming Oyster. I went out to the end and looked out over the inky water. The R had gone out of the neon Domino sugar sign across the harbor, giving it a somewhat funky new look: DOMINO SUGA. Other than that, it was the same old harbor that I knew like the back of my heart.

But there was something about the big neon sign being even so slightly altered that seemed to match my feelings. I was feeling restless. I was feeling out of sorts, or rather, out of synch, as if something was just not right. It was the feeling of the other shoe not having yet dropped, even though you are staring at two shoes that have already come crashing down to earth and are sitting right there side by side. There they are. They've dropped. So what's the problem?

The problem began to come to me. I had thought as I stood there gazing out over the black water that I was clearing my mind, that I wasn't really thinking of anything in particular. And maybe that's so. Or at least on the conscious level that was so. But down deeper, that second shoe that had dropped must have begun to come into clearer focus. And as it did, the source of my restlessness began to come into focus with it. It was the wrong goddamn shoe. It didn't match the first one. The *real* other shoe hadn't dropped at all.

And then it did. Nearly beaned me.

Kate had told me that immediately upon hearing of Carolyn James's suicide she had entered the woman's apartment and located Carolyn's copy of the nefarious videotape featuring Amanda Stuart. The assumption was that whoever it was who killed Guy Fellows a few days later— Lou Bowman—had taken Fellows's copy of the tape, perhaps as a future bargaining chip, perhaps simply to while away the hours counting the number of freckles on Amanda Stuart's bare bum. It made perfect sense to me that someone like Bowman would think to pocket the notorious tape after killing Guy Fellows. Forget even the boredom of those lonely Heayhauge nights when mean-looking Molly was being especially pissy. Consider the flexibility that would be Bowman's to enjoy by having possession of the tape. Especially since once Alan Stuart had announced for governor, the value of the tape had certainly gone up. Was it possible that the extra three thousand dollars a month that was being stuffed into Bowman's FedEx package had in fact been the result of *Bowman's* blackmailing Alan Stuart? Essentially picking up where Guy Fellows was forced—at serrated knife point—to leave off?

No. That made no sense. It was already determined that Bowman's extra bonus was his payment for killing Guy Fellows in the first place. That being the case, of what practical value was the videotape? For *that* matter, wouldn't one of Alan Stuart's instructions to Bowman have been to locate the tape after killing Guy Fellows and to deliver it to him? Of course it would. That would also explain why Bowman used a knife instead of a gun to kill Fellows. He would need time to search for the video, time he would not have had were the neighbors to have reported hearing a gunshot coming from Guy Fellows's apartment.

I must have been standing out on the end of the pier longer than I realized. Or was so lost in thought that I simply hadn't noticed a fog coming in over the harbor. As I came out of my own haze, I saw that the Domino Suga sign was surrounded by a silver and pink mist. I felt the dampness on my own skin as the mist tumbleweeded right over me. Halos formed around the streetlights. The more distant lights and buildings disappeared altogether. Those in the middle distance lost some of their edges. The night sky was gone, replaced by a low cloud cover, as black and gray as a nun with a dirty habit, so to speak. A distant rumbling of thunder sounded . . . and then another, not so distant. Within a minute, I was standing in the pouring rain.

And down came the shoe.

Kate Zabriskie had killed Guy Fellows. Not Lou Bowman. Lou Bowman would have brought along his own knife, not relied on finding a knife in Fellows's kitchen. I'm no detective, but murder by kitchen knife does not denote—at least in this instance—premeditated murder. Certainly not a contract killing. It denotes crime of passion. Or self-defense. Or both.

Kate's killing of Lou Bowman, especially as outlined for me by Julia, had been both. She had provoked Bowman into firing first. Kate's *first* shot then, might well qualify as self-defense. But shots two, three, four, five? Ripping through Bowman's lung, kidney, throat and, finally, his heart? I'll let you judge that for yourself.

It wasn't my speculation about the kitchen knife, however, that led me to my conclusion. It was that mismatched shoe that had dropped. But I should stop talking about shoes, and talk instead about videotapes. Kate's videotape, lifted from Carolyn James's apartment, was disguised as a *Pinocchio* video. The tape in Bowman's house was a Disney match. *Fantasia*.

But neither Guy Fellows nor Carolyn James had hidden the tape in Carolyn's apartment in a *Pinocchio* box or with a *Pinocchio* label. The night that Kate showed the tape to me she had taken credit for the simple yet effective disguise. It had been her extra measure of security, a way of hiding the evidence in plain sight.

As the night sky unloaded on me, I saw how simply it had all taken place. I couldn't piece together the scenario of the actual killing, of course, but the rest of it came into an all-too-clear focus. Knowing the lengths to which Kate had considered going to get Carolyn James out of the abusive clutches of Guy Fellows—the harebrained scheme to arrange a fake funeral for her—I can well imagine that Carolyn's suicide had not exactly set well with Kate. Maybe Fellows mouthed off about the suicide and Kate's temper snapped. Or maybe it was Fellows whose temper had snapped. It's possible that he had learned that Kate was sleeping with him on the direct orders of Alan Stuart, and had then gone after her.

Or might Kate have simply seen red? Had Kate maybe seen in Guy Fellows all of the brutes who had taken their pieces of her over the years? Her father? Alan Stuart? Others? Was the act of sticking a knife into Guy Fellows a belated act of heroism? Did she place herself between the evil man and the helpless little girl? And to even out the odds, had she brought with her a knife?

If, if, if . . . Maybe, maybe, maybe . . .

"Didn't your mother ever tell you to come in out of the rain?"

For a moment I thought that this was just one more of the too many voices in my head screaming *what if maybe*. But it wasn't. I turned around to see a figure with an umbrella walking toward me along the pier. It was Kate. She stopped about four feet away from me. Her face was half hidden by the umbrella.

"I thought you were in Las Vegas."

"No. I only flew out of Las Vegas. I sent your telegram from there this morning before I flew back. I took your advice, Hitch. I went to the desert. I went to Death Valley. Zabriskie Point."

"How ever were you able to withstand all the symbolism?"

"You're angry."

"That's right. You're not sharing your umbrella."

She tipped the umbrella away from her and gave it a little toss. It landed upside down in the water.

"You killed Guy Fellows," I said.

Kate looked back up at me. Her expression was terribly frank.

"Yes. I did."

"Was it self-defense?"

"You say that like you don't believe it."

"You haven't said it yet."

"It was." When I didn't say anything, she added, "He was going to kill me."

"You mean like Bowman was going to kill you?"

Kate took a deep breath. She wiped some of the rain out of her eyes.

"Carolyn left Guy a suicide note. She left me one too. She was such a lonely girl. I . . . She wrote to me what I already knew. She told me that Guy had involved her in a blackmailing scheme and that she was scared to death. Literally, as it turned out. She wrote that she didn't know why it was that she couldn't just walk away from Guy and from the whole mess. But she couldn't. He beat her. He abused her. But she couldn't walk away. I understand that. If I . . . Carolyn's note to Guy said pretty much the same thing. It said that this—she meant her suicide—this was the only way she could come up with to get away. And she mentioned me in her note. She said I knew everything that she and Guy had been up to."

"Why in the world would she do that?"

Kate shrugged. "Stupid, right? I guess it was the best she could do to get the last lick in. Some little measure of control. Who knows?"

"So he wasn't happy with you."

Kate shook her head. "Very much unhappy."

"What happened?"

"He called me up and said that he had to see me right away. He made it sound like he was all torn up about Carolyn's having killed herself. He had just gotten back from the funeral. I went. I wasn't two steps into his apartment and he slugged me. I was afraid he had broken my nose. He was furious. He had the note Carolyn had written to him and he shook it in my face. 'Why'd she tell you this? What the hell is going on!' He didn't give me a chance to read it. He slapped me and then he grabbed me by the hair and yanked me out of the kitchen."

"Sweet guy."

"Hitch . . . he was seeing red. It was 'bitch this' and 'goddamn bitch that.' . . . I was scared to death."

"Where did he take you?"

"Right where his body was discovered. In the living room. As I was stumbling out of the kitchen I saw a bunch of knives that Guy kept in a ceramic jar on the counter. I just grabbed blindly and got ahold of one. He didn't see me do it. I didn't even know what I had. I just grabbed at any handle I could. It might have turned out to be a little paring knife."

"But it wasn't."

Kate had a large purse hanging from her left shoulder. Her right hand disappeared into it. When it came right back out, it was holding a long narrow knife. Black handle. Serrated teeth.

"No," she said. "It wasn't a paring knife."

We stood there a moment, the rain coming down all around us. It was splattering into the water like . . . well frankly, like bullets. Out of the corner of my eye I noticed that Kate's umbrella had tipped sideways and was taking on water. In another few seconds it disappeared below the surface.

I looked down at the knife in Kate's hand. The blade was shining and dripping with raindrops.

"He dragged me over to the couch," Kate went on. "He grabbed at the front of my dress. I knew what he was planning to do. I can't in all honesty swear, Hitch, that I knew he was going to kill me afterwards. Maybe not. I don't know what a jury would think. But that didn't matter. He wasn't going one step further with me. No way. I swung the knife and hacked it against his hand as he ripped my dress. And I didn't stop there. I lost it. Call it a shark after blood, I don't care. He wasn't going to touch me anymore. I was sick of it. I was . . . I have no idea how many times I stabbed him. He lost his strength pretty quickly and I just kept stabbing until he finally slumped down to the floor. I . . . I didn't check to see if he was dead. I fetched the note that Carolyn had written and I located the videotape. It was taped under one of his dresser drawers."

"Not very original."

"What can I say?"

"So Carolyn didn't have a tape."

Kate shook her head. "No. There never really was the insurance that Alan was so worried about."

"So what did you do next?"

"I ran. There were only two pieces of physical evidence that could link me directly. This." She cradled the knife in her palm. "And the other was my own blood, from when Guy hit me. My nose had bled. Some of it got onto his shirt. Forensics took a sample."

She looked into my eyes and acknowledged my unasked question.

"As they say . . . it's gone missing."

"Gone missing." I had to shake my head at that one. "But that." I indicated the knife. "Why didn't that disappear?"

Kate turned the knife over in her hand. "I can't really say. I guess I just have a guilty conscience, despite everything. I'm trained to let the system be the final arbiter. I guess . . . I don't know. Maybe I was reserving the option of turning myself in."

"So where did Bowman fit in?"

"Bowman? A fluke. Simple as that. My guess is that he came to town that week in order to shake down Alan for some extra cash. The extra three thousand. I think that Alan's announcement for governor might have gotten Bowman thinking about the cash value of silence."

My speculations had run somewhat similar to this.

"So when we went up to Maine . . . ?"

Kate said, "I made a copy of the tape. I stuck it in the *Fantasia* box. That was a mistake, but I didn't realize it until later. I planted that tape in Bowman's house when you and I were up there, when I broke in that night. Since Bowman had been in Baltimore the same week that . . . that Guy was killed, I was hedging my bets. Once Kruk told me that Bowman had taken a shot at Charley, planting the tape on him seemed . . . well, like good insurance."

Kate allowed herself a hard laugh. "When it came out that Alan was behind Bowman's shooting Charley . . . Hitch, I almost believed in God again. I had both of them in my sights. Alan and Bowman."

"Did you kill Bowman to keep him from telling his side? Was that it? Did you kill him to keep him from proving that he didn't kill Fellows?"

"I killed Bowman in self-defense."

"Fine. Besides that."

"He killed my husband."

"Fine. Besides that."

"Jesus Christ, Hitch! Besides *what*? Guy Fellows hounds Carolyn James to her death . . . to her *death*, Hitch. And then he attacks me. Meanwhile Bowman has killed my husband and then he goes after *you*. And now *I'm* supposed to justify what I did? I'm sick of it. I'm sick of the whole damn thing."

"And Alan Stuart is the source of it all."

"And the bastard is under arrest."

"A good day's work?"

"You'd better damn well believe it."

She stepped toward me. As she did, the sky lit up like a flashbulb. Kate's skin looked bloodless blue. Her eyes were black and unreadable. The lightning flickered again and a glint came off the knife. The hand holding it was raising as she took another step forward. Her mouth formed the words *I'm sorry* . . . but the actual words were obliterated by a ripping snarl of thunder.

She handed me the knife.

We stood there for some time saying nothing. The rain started coming down more heavily. It was impossible for me to tell if there were tears mixing with the rain on Kate's cheeks. She was searching my face, look-ing, I suppose, for an indication of what I was thinking, of what I was going to do. Would I take her by the elbow and lead her off the pier? Drive her downtown and hand her—and the knife—over to John Kruk? Good Citizen Hitch?

Or what if the knife were to slip from my fingers—oops—and spiral slowly to the bottom of the harbor? So easy. One little toss—and time, silt and silence—assigns the entire sad affair to history.

I looked over at Kate. Her eyes were empty. Alone. She was already serving her sentence. Even if she were to go scot free for the killing of Guy Fellows and Lou Bowman, she would always have a haunted heart. So then what did it really matter? Why not just toss the knife aside and take the woman into my arms? Maybe I could give her what she seemed to have been looking for ever since she leaped over her father and into the arms of her savior cop. Maybe I could make the noble effort to be Kate's big hero.

Except that "noble effort" in the face of certain failure is not really noble at all. It is just plain stupid.

Something which I'm not.

Kate was still standing at the end of the pier, head bowed, as I made my way down Thames Street toward The Dead End Saloon and a welcome whiskey. And a plate of steaming mussels. Maybe two whiskeys. Why the hell not? I had no one to bury tomorrow. And I sure as hell had something to bury tonight.

I made my way down the street. Collar up. Rain dancing all around me. Low thunder and the throbbing of live music coming from the squatty bars . . .

The knife was back in Kate's hand.

I wished her luck.

About the Author

In addition to serving as a story analyst for such companies as American Playhouse, ABC and Hallmark Entertainment, Tim Cockey has promoted professional opera productions, helped run a farmer's market and edited books about how to get other people to give you money. He now lives in New York City. This is his first novel.